Lure of Oblivion

Also by Suzanne Wright

From Rags

The Dark in You Series

Burn

Blaze

Ashes

The Deep in Your Veins Series

Here Be Sexist Vampires

The Bite That Binds

Taste of Torment

Consumed

Fractured

The Phoenix Pack Series

Feral Sins

Wicked Cravings

Carnal Secrets

Dark Instincts

Savage Urges

Fierce Obsessions

The Mercury Pack Series

Spiral of Need

Force of Temptation

SUZANNE WRIGHT

THE MERCURY PACK SERIES

This is a work of fiction. Names, characters, organizations, places, events, and incidents are either products of the author's imagination or are used fictitiously.

Published by Montlake Romance, Seattle

www.apub.com

ISBN-13: 9781542049726
ISBN-10: 1542049725

Cover design by Katie Anderson

Printed in the United States of America

For you. Yes, you.
I almost said "Ed Sheeran"—I'm in a weird mood.

CHAPTER ONE

Gwen Miller slammed her foot on the deck, bringing the swing to a halt. They were here again. She could hear their footsteps rustling the high grass as they muttered complaints about the scents of marsh gas, salty water, and humid air.

She sighed and rubbed her temple. God, she was too tired for this shit.

Making as little noise as possible, she rose from the wooden swing and padded down the boardwalk that ran over the marsh, protecting her feet from the muddy soil and water pools. She stuck to the thickening shadows as she crept closer to her home. And there they were. All three males were nineteen, but she couldn't help thinking of them as boys, even though they were built like linebackers and had proved they were capable of seriously sick shit.

Apparently, they weren't getting the message that they needed to keep their asses away from her damn house. That was unfortunate.

She slipped her hand into her pocket and threaded her fingers through the knuckle stun gun in her pocket, but she didn't switch it on. Not yet.

As one of the boys raised a bat to the windscreen of her truck—*motherfucker*—she made a tsk sound. All three swerved to face her, eyes wide. Going by the state of their pupils, they'd all been drinking. And going by the cans of spray paint at their feet, they'd come prepared to make a fucking mess of her truck and maybe even her home, which doubled as a B&B.

The buzz and drone of the insects stopped, and the cool breeze paused—as if nature itself was waiting to see how this would play out.

"Evening, boys," Gwen drawled. "So, you're back. Not getting bored of this at all?"

The ringleader and pain in her ass, Brandt, gave her a mocking smile and put his hand over his heart. "You don't like my company? I'm offended." His expression sobered as he went on. "You know what to do if you want me out of your life."

Yeah, she did.

"You can make this stop so easily, Gwen. You just have to do a little thing for me first. Change your statement. Hell, even *she* had the sense to alter hers."

"She" being the female shifter he'd beaten months ago with a metal pole while his friends had watched, urging him on. Gwen had found them in the trees near the border of her family's land, and she'd shot at them several times to chase them off. She'd then taken the drugged and shaken shifter, Andie, to her home, where Gwen had called the sheriff.

That call had proved to be a waste of time.

The sheriff hadn't arrested the boys—he'd brought them in for questioning. That had lasted mere minutes before all three were released. He was tight with Brandt's socially influential father, Ezra Moore. Neither of them thought of Andie as a person with rights. The police hadn't taken photographs of her injuries or done a drug test that would have proved her drink had been spiked. They'd pretty much swept the incident under the rug, like it was nothing.

That didn't mean Brandt would get away with it, though. Andie had reported the attack to the shifter council, which was originally formed to appease humans who didn't like that shifters solved problems mostly through violence. While the council's rulings often prevented wars between packs, it also punished humans who committed crimes against shifters if human law enforcement didn't take care of it themselves. As such, Brandt would have to stand before the council—something, not surprisingly, he didn't want to do.

The boys had harassed Gwen for weeks, trying to force her to alter her statement. They'd also done the same to Andie, who was scared out of her damn mind and eventually folded under their intimidation tactics. Gwen couldn't really blame her. Andie wasn't part of a pride, so she had no protection from her kind. Gwen, well, she didn't back down for anyone.

The shifter council didn't care that Andie had backed off. Once an incident was reported, the council always investigated it.

"You need to get off my land," Gwen warned the boys.

"I go *where* I want, *when* I want," said Brandt, dark eyes drilling into hers. His attitude was quite typical of the Moore family. The rich bastards lived in fancy homes, drove fancy cars, and had more money than sense. That would have been fine, except that they were also extremely arrogant and considered themselves superior to just about everyone.

Brandt stepped out of the shadows, and the moonlight illuminated his face—that was when she saw the bruised jaw, swollen eye, and split lip.

Gwen couldn't help but smile. "My, my, my, don't you look pretty." Seemed like Ezra had lashed out at his son—most likely for bringing this kind of attention to the family. It wasn't uncommon.

Brandt's face hardened. "You'll look just as *pretty* soon enough." He twirled his bat—a move that was meant to intimidate her. A move that also didn't work.

"Does your mommy know you're out of bed?"

He stilled, and his two friends let out low whistles.

"That mouth of yours is gonna get you in trouble one day, honey," said Mack, chewing on gum.

The third boy, Rowan, nodded with a smirk that he appeared to wear permanently. "Maybe we should find a way to keep that mouth busy." He leered. "Yeah, I think you should suck my dick."

"You'll need to get one first," she said drily.

Brandt laughed, not at all bothered by the "traitor" look that his friend sent him. To these idiots, this was one big game.

Gwen cocked her head, glaring at Brandt. "You're not at all sorry for what you did, are you?"

He shrugged, snorting. "She's a shifter—why should I be sorry? They're abominations. But you . . . you're human, so why would you care what happens to her?"

"She's a person, just like you and me."

"She's *nothing* like us," he snarled. "She's a goddamn animal."

"Funny . . . the only one I saw behaving like an animal that night was *you*. You drugged her and then beat her with a pole while she was weak and unable to defend herself. You think that makes you a big, brave guy? It doesn't. You don't have that thing"—she clicked her fingers a few times—"a soul."

His eyes flared. "I'd be careful if I were you, sweetheart. You don't have your shotgun with you this time."

She gave them each a dismissive look. "I don't need a shotgun to deal with three little boys." The knuckle stun gun she discreetly pulled out of her pocket would do nicely.

Brandt licked his teeth. "Little, huh? Maybe I should show you just how big I really am." He grinned. There wasn't just heat in his gaze, there was something else—something ugly and twisted. "Yeah, you'd like that, wouldn't you, babe?" He advanced on her, mouth curled. "Why don't you spread those legs for me? I think you'd enjoy it."

"No, I wouldn't." She yanked the bat out of his grip and slammed it into his bruised jaw so hard she was surprised she didn't hear his teeth rattle. At the same time, she switched on the stun gun and hit him in the solar plexus just long enough to send him dropping to his knees, dazed and shaking.

Rowan and Mack stared down at him, eyes wide. She braced herself for them to come at her, but shock seemed to have immobilized them.

Snapping out of his daze, Brandt stumbled to his feet. "You fucking *bitch*." He idiotically took an aggressive step toward her, but then froze at the cock of a shotgun that came from somewhere behind her.

Mack and Rowan swallowed nervously—probably because they had a good idea who was holding that shotgun. The person in question wouldn't hesitate to shoot a trespasser. Hell, he wouldn't hesitate to shoot anyone.

"Brandt, we should go," said Mack, a tremor in his voice. "I'll back you all the way on this, but I ain't getting shot or Tased for you."

Licking his lips, Brandt took a step back.

"That was smart of you, freezing like that," Gwen told him. "Because I gotta say, the idea of Donnie blowing your brains out fills me with a morbid kind of joy. I don't like to deny myself joy. Life's too short for that." She flicked a look at his crotch. "But I guess you're used to things being short."

Brandt's eyes blazed with indignation. "My father will—"

"I don't care. You wield his name like it's a sword, thinking it will protect you. No matter what you do, I'm standing by my original statement. In light of that, I suggest you stop wasting both of our time, run along home, and never come back. Ah, I can see your bruised ego's struggling with that, but coming back here would be a serious error on your part.

"Now, personally, I think it's *far* past time that you boys left. I advise you to back up slowly. If you run, you'll trigger Donnie's hunting instincts, and he'll start firing like he's facing an invading army. That would suck. Not so much for me, but definitely for you."

Mack and Rowan did as she advised, but Brandt stood firm as he glowered at her, fists clenched, clearly at war with himself.

"You need to fight that ego, Brandt. If you want to live, that is. I'd be thoroughly glad to hear that you don't want to live."

He took a deep breath and *finally* backed away. Casting looks at her over their shoulders, the three boys jogged away and disappeared into the trees.

She knew that wasn't the end of it. The Moores never backed down. But then, neither did Gwen.

Balancing the bat on her shoulder, she turned to the large three-story house and climbed up the stone steps and onto the wraparound porch. The wooden boards creaked as a tall figure stepped out of the shadows, dressed in camo gear and holding a shotgun, looking like he'd just walked right out of a war zone.

"You handled that well," said Donnie, her foster uncle. He was ex-military and the ultimate conspiracy theorist. He was also a little unstable and often disappeared in the woods for days at a time, "on patrol." Donnie felt more at ease outside, surrounded by nature.

The locals thought of him as an eccentric, and he let them believe that because it meant they underestimated him. The truth was that Donnie was extremely intelligent and a strategic mastermind.

"You didn't think to shoot at their feet to scare them off?"

He rolled his eyes. "I had my gun trained on them the whole time; you were never in any real danger. You don't need my help anyway."

That was because he'd trained her to defend herself. He'd also trained her to use many of the weapons he'd stashed—some of which she was pretty sure Uncle Sam would want back, especially the rocket launchers. When she'd asked why he had all the weapons, he'd simply said, "Just in case."

Pulling a leaf out of his fuzzy salt-and-pepper hair, Donnie looked in the direction in which the boys had disappeared. "The Moores are scared. They thought you'd back down by now, and they're starting to panic because they have no idea what it will take to make you do it."

Nothing would make her back down.

"What I want to know is how they're managing to electronically mess with you. Draining your bank account, maxing out your credit cards, and canceling your cell phone contract—that takes skill." He shook his head, lips thinning, and began to pace . . . and she sensed one of his rants coming.

"You know, this kind of thing happens too easily because we have the Internet," he insisted, words coming fast and sharp. "Now it's so simple to invade people's privacy using spam, viruses, and Trojan horses. I'm telling you, the Net is evil. It has no ethical guidelines. Think of all the child pornography, cyberbullying, and websites that actually promote suicide—"

"Donnie."

"—and encourage depressed teens to make *suicide pacts*. Not that the CIA, FBI, or any other organization cares. Oh, no. They're too busy spying on us using—"

"Donnie."

His expression cleared, becoming one of total calm. "Hmm?"

She sighed. "You coming inside?"

He lifted his gun. "I want to check the little pricks have left first."

"All right. Be careful." Pulling open the front door, she winced at the squeak of the hinges. She would have oiled them, but most of the guests came to experience what it was like to stay in an allegedly haunted house. They seemed to like hearing creaks, thuds, squeaks, and other weird noises.

Was the place haunted? Well, plenty of people believed so. Gwen wasn't gonna lie, there was *something* in the house. A few *somethings*, actually. It was rumored that they were the spirits of a man and his two teenage daughters who'd died in a fire long ago. She'd never gotten the feeling that there was anything malevolent about them. They just seemed nosy and bored.

She was also betting they enjoyed spooking the guests, because many claimed to have "felt a presence," heard someone pacing on the third floor, or seen shadows moving around. Some guests had been so freaked out, they'd actually packed up and left earlier than planned.

Not all were believers, though. Some had complained that it wasn't as haunted as they'd hoped—one even whined that it didn't *smell* haunted. If by that he'd meant it didn't smell dusty and moldy, he was right. The place smelled like fragrant oils, wood polish, and lavender air freshener. She was happy for it to stay that way.

Humming to himself, her foster brother came striding down the hall with a mug of hot chocolate topped with whipped cream. Marlon cocked his head, nose wrinkling. "What's with the bat?"

She headed up the stairs as she replied, "It's Brandt's. He, Rowan, and Mack were going to vandalize my truck. I wasn't down with that."

"They came *again*?" Marlon followed her, listening as she gave him a quick rundown of what had happened. "They'll be back. Brandt's too used to his father buying his way out of trouble to care if he takes it too far."

"Yep," agreed Gwen, reaching the second floor. "It's probably why Brandt doesn't have any sense of right and wrong." She walked straight to her room and went inside, leaned the bat against the wall, and—passing her cluttered dresser, overfull laundry basket, and half-open closet—sank onto her unmade bed.

Gwen rolled her shoulders, sighing. Noticing the angry flush on Marlon's dark skin, she decided to change the subject. "I like the shirt." He always looked like he'd just come back from a photo shoot. He was also as camp as Christmas, much like his boyfriend. "In fact, I like the whole outfit. It's not fair that you can so effortlessly look cool and stylish."

He smiled, pleased. "It's all about accessorizing and color coordination. I'm good at it, for someone who's color-blind."

She sighed. "You are *not* color-blind." But he insisted on claiming to be simply to annoy her for his own amusement.

"How would you know?"

Looking away, she waved a hand. "Forget it."

"Yes, forget it, because we're not finished with Brandt. Are you going to call Colt and tell him what happened?" he asked.

"What's the point? He's firmly lodged up Ezra Moore's rectum. He won't help. Besides, a nightly visit from the sheriff wouldn't exactly look good on the B&B's reviews. And, you know, it's not such a bad thing that Brandt's acting like an ass."

Marlon's brows snapped together. "How do you figure that?"

"Each time the little bastard does something dumb or hostile, I have more tales to share with the shifter council that prove he's dangerous and not worth shit."

In the beginning, Brandt had done stupid crap like throw eggs at her truck, make prank calls, and toilet-paper the yard. The pranks had gotten worse, but she still hadn't reacted. Then he'd stepped it up by putting ads in the paper for BDSM parties, subscribing her to kinky magazines, and posting bogus awful reviews on the B&B's website.

When that hadn't worked, the cyber shit had started. She doubted Brandt could have done that, so she was guessing his father had hired someone to do it. Ezra was just as bad as Brandt when it came to bullying people to get what he wanted.

Marlon sipped his hot chocolate and then licked some whipped cream from his lip. "I still don't like any of it. You know, I think part of the sheriff's problem with you is that you rejected his son."

"That was two years ago. Randy's married to some woman in Idaho now. Besides, he wasn't exactly heartbroken—he was using me to get to Julie." Something many guys had tried over the years. Her foster sister was beyond beautiful, both inside and out; she was tall and shapely, with gorgeous thick dark hair. Gwen was not tall or shapely or beautiful. She didn't think of herself as ugly, but she wasn't pretty either—kind of average, really.

She didn't envy her sister, though. Didn't envy that all people saw when they looked at Julie was her looks, didn't envy that Julie was ogled and heckled wherever she went, didn't envy that she was often surrounded by shallow people who wanted to use her as arm candy. Now that Julie was engaged, the attention had eased somewhat.

"Nah, I think Randy actually liked you, but it doesn't matter. He's not what you need. What you need is someone who isn't put off by your 'Don't get too close' vibe. Hey, don't give me that innocent look. You don't try to get to know people, and you don't let them know you. What you don't seem to realize is that your aloofness comes across as a challenge."

"Yeah? I don't see a bunch of guys taking up any such challenge."

"Oh, they try. You just don't notice."

"I *like* being on my own."

"But you're not happy. Julie and I want better for you. We want you to find contentment. Peace."

"I am content. And I'm all about peace."

He lifted a brow. "Peace? Really? You just bludgeoned someone with their own bat."

"'Bludgeoned' is a strong word."

"And that's not conducive to living a peaceful life."

"And yet, I feel *great* after clocking Brandt right on the jaw."

He chuckled. "You would."

"And if he's dumb enough to come back, I'll be able to do it again." Positively cheered by that idea, she smiled. Marlon just laughed.

"What about a bookstore?"

"No."

"A coffeehouse?"

"No."

"A diner?"

"Fuck, Shay, you've got your motel—be happy with that."

As his Alphas continued to argue, Zander Devlin exchanged an amused look with his fellow enforcer, Bracken, and slung their duffels in the trunk of the SUV. The other members of the pack who'd come to wave them off looked just as amused by the Alphas' byplay.

Zander wasn't sure whether Shaya genuinely wanted to open more businesses or whether she just kept making suggestions to annoy her mate for fun. If it was the first, Zander suspected that she'd eventually get her way. Nick hated disappointing his mate . . . which was why the pack now officially owned two businesses.

The motel was still a work in progress and not yet open, but their other business had been open for a while. It was a club managed by their only nonwolf pack mate, Harley, who was mated to one of Zander's closest friends, Jesse. She also regularly performed at the club, playing her electric violin alongside DJs and other artists.

"Enough," Nick growled at Shaya, slashing a hand in the air. He turned to Zander. "Don't think I didn't notice that you purposely brought up her other business ideas so that she'd change the subject."

Zander shrugged, unapologetic. He also tensed when Shaya's eyes slid to his, once again filled with compassion. "I'm fine." He closed the trunk and walked to the driver's door. "Me and Bracken can manage on our own for a few days."

"I know that," she assured him, clipping her red curls behind her ear. "But it would be okay if you weren't fine, you know. Your uncle just died."

"I told you, we weren't close."

"But he was still your uncle. Are you sure you wouldn't rather take someone other than Bracken to the reading of the will? I mean, he's not exactly the comforting type."

The wolf in question frowned, affronted. "Hey."

Shaya shrugged at him. "Well, you're not."

Zander didn't need or want comfort. He'd cared for his uncle, but he wasn't broken up about his death. He didn't seem to feel grief the way others did anyway. He hadn't cried when his parents died either. Hadn't been deep in grief. Hadn't felt much other than a faint regret for what could have been if they hadn't cast him off long ago. If that made him cold, there wasn't much he could do about it.

"I didn't think people did that anymore," said Jesse, scraping a hand over his dark stubble.

"What?" asked Zander.

"Gathered in an office while an attorney read the will. I thought they just sent out copies of the will to the relevant people, like the beneficiaries."

"That's what I thought. The attorney said that it was Dale's wish for it to be done this way."

"You sure you don't want me to come along?" Jesse asked for the tenth time, brow creased.

"Since when have I ever needed anyone to hold my fucking hand?" Zander said without heat.

Dark eyes softening with amusement, Jesse snorted. "Fine, fuck you. I just don't like the idea of you in the same room as Rory, even though I know you can deal with the motherfucker easily."

Rory had never been a true brother to Zander. In his twin's mind, they were in competition. It was a warped sibling rivalry that Zander had never wanted any part in, but Rory hadn't cared.

The only people in the Mercury Pack who'd ever met Rory were Jesse and Bracken, because they'd once all belonged to another pack. As such, the two wolves knew every sneaky move Rory had made and just how toxic and twisted the guy was.

Their mother, Pearl, had come down hard on Rory for the sibling rivalry . . . right up until he was seven and caught an infection in the hospital after—very begrudgingly—donating a kidney to Zander. The infection had almost killed Rory, and their mother had felt guilty for pushing him to go through with the operation. Rory had played on that guilt, and he'd hated Zander for "stealing his kidney" ever since.

After that, Pearl let Rory get away with pretty much everything. Maybe that was why he was so arrogant, egotistical, and self-indulgent. Or maybe her lack of discipline just made those traits more defined. Whatever the case, Rory had been a nightmare to live with.

He became even worse when Pearl got pregnant with their sister. Rory didn't like sharing *anything*, particularly Pearl's attention. Striving to ensure Rory didn't feel "left out," she'd emotionally neglected Shelby. Zander suspected that had fed Rory's bloated sense of self-importance.

Jesse played with Harley's dark hair as he spoke to Zander. "Do you think Dale will have left you much in his will? He was unmated and had no direct descendants, but Rory somehow managed to manipulate your parents into making him their sole heir—not that there was much money left when they died, since Rory had bled them dry over the years. But he might have found a way to do the same to your uncle."

Zander shrugged. "Maybe. I haven't spoken much to Dale over the years, so I don't know if he was in constant contact with Rory or not." He'd find out soon enough.

Eli, the Head Enforcer, folded his arms over his broad chest. "What's Rory like? You said he was fucked up, but how, exactly?"

It was Jesse who answered. "I'd like to dismiss him as a dumb asshole, but Rory's smart. *Too* smart. That's why he does so well as a computer analyst. He's not nerdy, though. He dresses like a CEO, comes across as slick and charming."

Rory was also one of those guys who waxed his chest, back, and eyebrows—Zander would rather walk through fire than do girlie shit like that to himself.

"When he was a juvenile, our pack was wary of him," Jesse went on. "He wasn't quite so smooth back then, and it was easy to sense that something wasn't right with him."

"Even though he's smart, he's immature," Bracken added. "He's not happy unless he has a rival who he can ridicule and compete with—winning is more important to him than anything else. If someone upsets him in some way, he never lets it go; he carries it with him like a rucksack on his back."

"He's a spiteful piece of shit too," clipped Jesse. "If Zander wouldn't give him something, he'd shift into his wolf form and piss on it. Remember when you were kids and you had those pet mice, rats, gerbils, and ferrets, Z?"

Zander nodded. He'd gone through a phase where he'd wanted to be a vet, so his father had indulgently bought him lots of small pets to care for as "practice."

"When Zander refused to give him his new *Star Wars* figures, Rory went down to the basement where Z's pets were kept," Jesse continued. "He let out the mice, rats, and gerbils. Then he let out the ferrets and watched while they killed the smaller rodents."

Shaya's mouth fell open. "That's cruel." She turned to Zander. "What did your parents do?"

"Nothing," Zander replied. "Rory said he hadn't let them out, that I'd done it and was trying to pin it on him. Pearl sided with him, and Jerold went along with it. Our father was submissive, and she was very dominant. She used that strength against him until he eventually learned not to question her."

Nick's green eyes blazed. "That kind of abuse should be rare, but it isn't."

"No, it isn't," agreed Zander. "And neither is a parent favoring one child over the others—it's just life." He'd long ago accepted it.

"Blood isn't thicker than water, no matter what anyone says," said Harley. The margay cat shifter would know that well, taking her own dysfunctional family situation into account. "Still, I'd have thought you being identical twins would make a difference. I've heard they're usually pretty close and feel each other's pain and stuff."

"We don't have any kind of mystical connection." It wasn't hard for them to be apart, Rory wasn't his ideal companion, they were not best friends, and they didn't have a psychic link that told them what each other was thinking and feeling. "We do understand each other well, though—that's why he knows how to get under my skin."

"The only way Zander and Rory are alike is that they can both read people easily," said Jesse. "Rory will size you up, find every hot button you have, and sense how best to manipulate you. If manipulating you doesn't work, he'll push those hot buttons as hard as he can. And he knows all Zander's hot buttons. *That's* why I don't like them being in the same room."

Ally, the Beta female and Seer, twisted her mouth as she looked at Zander. "Hell, no wonder you're predominately calm. I'll bet you spent your life having to keep a lid on your emotions so you didn't give him the reactions he wanted. You're never too happy, never too sad, never too anything . . . which I have to say is a little weird."

Well, she'd know, thought Zander. Part of the Seer package was that she was also an empath. "He was harsher with our sister, Shelby, than me."

Jesse cocked his head. "Will Shelby be there for the reading of the will?"

"She said she would," replied Zander, "but I doubt it. She doesn't go out much anymore."

She'd been through a lot over the years, more than anyone should have to endure. He'd worried when she'd adopted Luke, her friend's orphaned seven-year-old son, concerned it would be too much for her, but it had seemed to heal her. When Luke was later kidnapped by human anti-shifter extremists and hunted within a game reserve, she'd fallen apart.

Zander hadn't known Luke long, but he'd considered him his nephew. It hurt to imagine what the kid had gone through. Hurt to know that Luke would have expected them to come for him, would have believed they'd save him. But they hadn't found him, and they couldn't even pray his death had been quick and painless. It would have been far from it.

Bracken's uncle and Jesse's sister had also been snatched by the same extremists. With the help of the Mercury wolves, Zander, Bracken, and Jesse had hunted down the people who ran the game reserve—both motherfuckers had suffered long and hard before dying, just as Luke likely suffered when he was set free in the wild, hunted like an animal, and then killed.

"Having heard about Rory," began Ally, "I really think me and Derren should go with you."

Bracken snorted. "You just want to see if the B&B is really haunted."

Derren blinked. "Haunted?"

"I looked at reviews from guests," said Ally. "There were a lot of them, and they were all good. It gets a lot of tourists and ghost hunters, since the locals claim it's haunted." At Derren's scoff, she said, "You all believe in the soul, right? And you believe it vacates our body when we die. Is it such a stretch, then, to think that maybe some souls might stick around a little while?"

For Zander, yeah, it was a stretch. He just wasn't a believer in all that stuff. Turning to Bracken, he said, "Ready to go?" The enforcer nodded, so Zander opened the driver's door and said, "See you all in a few days." As the pack called out quick goodbyes, he and Bracken hopped into the SUV.

In honesty, Zander wasn't looking forward to spending the weekend around humans. He had nothing against them per se, but humans often fell into three camps when it came to shifters. They either feared shifters, were disgusted by them, or found them so fascinating that they gave them the kind of appraisal they'd give an ancient artifact. He supposed whether humans were prejudiced against shifters or not, they were often unable to see them as "people."

Jesse leaned slightly into the open window. "You sure you don't want additional company? It wouldn't hurt the pack for me to come with you. Everything's been quiet and peaceful for a while now. We've had no trouble at all."

An odd note in the enforcer's voice made Zander's mouth curve. "You're bored out of your mind, aren't you?"

"It's wrong, isn't it?" said Jesse, rueful. "But I'm a person of action. There's been no action."

"You're too whipped to cope without your mate for a few days."

Bracken chuckled. "He's right, Jesse, so stop with the growling."

"I could bring Harley along," Jesse offered.

Zander shook his head. "She has the club to run and performances scheduled. And really, Jesse, do you want her exposed to Rory? Because I don't."

Jesse sighed. "No." He pushed away from the SUV. "If you need any kind of backup, you call me."

Zander turned the key in the ignition. "Will do."

CHAPTER TWO

If you're so innocent, why didn't you call me or come to the station last night to report the incident?" challenged Colt.

Leaning back in her rocker with her legs propped up on the wooden rail of the porch, ankles crossed, Gwen lifted a brow. "And the point of that would have been . . . what, exactly? You wouldn't have done any, you know, *police* work."

The sheriff perched his hands on his narrow hips. He was a good-looking guy. Broad and rugged. He was also a high-and-mighty bully who needed a good bitch slap . . . and to have someone stick an oyster fork in his eye because, you know, it would just be fun to watch.

His nostrils flared. "Unless you want to find yourself in lockup, don't question my ability to do my job. Brandt claims that you attacked him with a bat, so that may well happen anyway."

"*Attacked* him? The bat barely clipped his jaw." Okay, that was an understatement, but whatever.

"Then how do you explain all his injuries?"

"He was already hurt when he got here. I only struck him with the bat once, and it wouldn't have happened if he hadn't brought it with him."

Colt's brow furrowed. "Brandt says the bat is yours."

"It has 'Brandt' scrawled on it." She pointed to the bat leaning against the wall. She'd grabbed it when she saw the sheriff's car pull up.

Colt picked it up and examined it. "Huh, so it does."

"You can tell the markings are old."

"There was mention of a knuckle stun gun too. You can hand that over."

Hell, no. "A knuckle stun gun?" Gwen let her eyes widen with interest. "They sell stuff like that now? Oh, I need to get me one of those."

He ground his teeth. "According to Brandt, you already have one. You don't want to mess with the Moores, Gwen. His father is calling for your blood—and he's calling for it *loudly*."

"Ezra does like the sound of his own voice," she mused.

Sighing, Colt adjusted his hat. "Brandt says he came here last night to apologize."

"With a bat and cans of spray paint? I think even his fancy attorney would have a problem making that sound innocent."

"If you didn't hurt him, who did?"

She snorted. "Don't insult my intelligence, Colt. You know it was Ezra. Besides, why would I hurt Brandt? He's giving me more ammunition to use against him when I go before the shifter council." She gave him an excited smile. "I'm counting down the days. Can't wait."

Colt's mouth set into a hard line. "I don't want this trouble happening in my town."

"You mean you don't want the shifter council looking too closely at how you neglected the evidence. Understandable. And not my problem."

"I neglected nothing. The cougar altered her statement; she said that she wasn't sure who beat her that night and that her attacker was a complete stranger. It's your word against the words of Brandt, Rowan, and Mack. They're from respectable families. Do you even know where you're from?" he sniped.

"Yeah, actually, I do." She remembered plenty about her life before she came to live with the Millers when she was eight. Remembered the smells of rust, mildew, beer, cigarette smoke, and garbage that tainted the muggy air of the run-down trailer. Remembered the screen doors slamming, her mother screeching, her stepfather bellowing, and the constant clanging of the broken air-conditioning unit. Remembered trying to drown out the sounds of their fighting by opening her window wide to let the meth-using neighbors' heavy-metal music filter through. Remembered huddling under a blanket to escape the rain dripping through the leaky roof, all the while wishing she was somewhere else. *Anywhere* else.

For some, going into foster care was a nightmare. For Gwen, it had been a blessing. "The shifter council won't care how *respectable* those families are. Ezra can't buy Brandt's way out of this." But she was sure he'd give it a shot.

Gwen looked to her left at the rumbling of a car engine. Moments later, an SUV parked in front of the B&B. This had to be Zander Devlin. He'd booked two rooms earlier that week, and she could still remember his voice; it was deep and throaty and sent a ghostly finger of need trailing down her spine.

Gwen lowered her legs. "Although nothing quite brightens my day like your presence, Sheriff, I have stuff to do, so . . ."

Tipping his hat slightly, he cursed. "Gwen, the Moores aren't going to let this go."

She gave him a hard look. "I hope you're not about to advise me to give them what they want, because I'd feel compelled to mention that to the council in the interest of full disclosure."

His eyes flared. "At least call me if Brandt comes back. I'd rather not have to arrest either you or Donnie for shooting him. Too much paperwork." At that, he turned and jogged down the steps to his car.

As Colt drove away, a male slid out of the passenger seat of the SUV. He was tall, dark, and incredibly masculine. Certainly pretty to look at. And a very nice distraction from Colt's bullshit.

Always the opportunist, Gwen took a moment to admire the stranger as he prowled to the trunk, grabbed two duffels, and then moved to the driver's side of the vehicle. That was when a second male slid out; he took a duffel from his friend as he scanned his surroundings.

Hard winter-gray eyes landed on her. No, they *locked* on her. She swallowed. The other male was hot, but this guy was a whole other level of hot. Like scorching, blistering hot.

He had a lean, toned build that screamed raw power and did plenty of interesting things to her insides. And, damn, that face . . . He had a perfectly sculpted mouth that she would bet curved into a wicked smile. The edge of stubble on his square jaw was a few shades darker than his short, choppy hair the color of a wheat field. A neat scar sliced through the lower part of his eyebrow, and it somehow suited him.

She didn't usually go for blonds. She'd always preferred males who were more like his friend—dark, broody, and clean shaven. But the blond definitely had her attention right then. *His* attention, on the other hand, quickly slid away from her. Not that that was a surprise or anything. She wasn't the kind of girl who would catch the eye of a guy like him.

Oozing dominance and a quiet, supreme confidence, he fluidly stalked toward the house with his friend close behind. Every step they took was predatory and self-assured. Shifters, she sensed.

Her heart began to beat a little faster. She'd always been intrigued by them and the dynamics of packs, prides, flocks, et cetera. She loved their animal grace, the way they seemed to glide rather than walk. And, *hello*, shifting into an animal had to be cool, right?

The trailer park where she'd lived as a kid had been close to a wolf-pack territory. So many times she'd heard them howling, caught glimpses of them running, and found herself wishing she was one of them—wishing she was surrounded by people who would care for and protect her.

Gwen was also fascinated by the whole true-mate thing. To have someone made specifically for you—someone who would never betray you, never hurt you, and would always cherish you—would be something special. She envied them that.

As they climbed the steps and reached the wraparound porch, she stood with a polite smile. "I'm guessing one of you is Mr. Devlin." Yeah, she played it cool. The blond might be all her fantasies rolled into one package, but he *really* didn't need to know that. Honestly, she wasn't brought to her knees by looks anyway. She'd grown up around perfection, so she was pretty much used to it. Her foster mother and foster siblings all had that "it" factor. Gwen didn't.

"That would be me," the blond rumbled, eyes once again locked on her.

A lesser female might have found that direct, penetrating stare unnerving. Okay, it did unnerve her just a little. Nonetheless, she walked toward the shifters, unable to help admiring the way Zander held himself. He stood tall and still, his solid shoulders back, his head held high and ever so slightly tilted in a gesture that seemed both cool and self-assured.

"I'm Gwen. I work here," she said, using that distantly polite voice she reserved for guests.

The dark wolf tipped his chin, eyes smiling. "Bracken."

Zander said nothing, just looked at her with a blank expression. Well, wasn't he a bag of delight.

"Good to meet you both," she said. "Your rooms are ready, so let's get you checked in."

Zander opened the front door and gestured for her to enter first. With a quick nod of thanks, she walked inside and straight over to the reception desk.

At that moment, her foster mother came out of the kitchen, wearing a wide smile. It would be easy to look at Yvonne's appearance and jump to the wrong conclusion—to think that the Botox injections, perfect hairstyle, slim figure, and inches of makeup on her dark skin meant she was vain and shallow. With Yvonne, it wasn't vanity; it was insecurity. Her second husband, now deceased, had trashed her confidence and left her with a false, distorted image of herself.

Gwen and Marlon had shielded her from the Brandt situation as best they could, not wanting her to see how bad things were. Yvonne wasn't stupid, though. She knew things were much worse than she'd been led to believe, but Yvonne was *the master* at burying her head in the sand.

"One of you must be Mr. Devlin," she said with a slight hint of a Caribbean accent.

Zander gave a curt nod.

"I'm Yvonne. I own the place." Patting her short, dark corkscrew curls, she studied them with a knowing glint in her eye. "You're shifters, right? I can always tell. Can I ask what kind?"

"Wolves," said Bracken.

"My Gwen *loves* wolves. I don't mean wolf shifters; I mean wolves—she's always been fascinated by them. Not that I'm saying she doesn't like wolf shifters, you understand. She's always liked shifters, always been interested in—"

"Is there a way to make you stop?" Gwen asked, staring at her in consternation. The males were going to think she was a shifter groupie or something.

"I was just explaining—" Yvonne cut off as the phone began to ring. "Excuse me," she told the wolves and then picked up the phone.

While Yvonne took the call, Gwen put the males through the check-in rigmarole. Finally, she unhooked the keys for rooms four and five and slid them across the desk . . . only to see that Zander was staring at her with an intense focus that almost made her squirm. Sadly, there was no sexual interest there, just curiosity and a hint of . . . suspicion. Huh. Whatever.

He stared at her, and she stared right back, drumming her nails on the reception desk. A strange tension gathered in the air, coiling and thickening with each second, but she'd be *damned* if she'd look away first and—

Her head whipped to the side as the living-room door slammed shut . . . the *empty* room. She looked back at Zander, whose eyes were now narrowed on the door.

Ending the call, Yvonne shrugged at the wolves. "The slamming of doors isn't an uncommon occurrence here."

Bracken took a key and said with a smile, "So we should expect ghostly activity."

"That all depends on whether the ghosts take an interest in you or not," Yvonne teased. "Most of the activity happens on the third floor, which is why we currently have a group of demonology students staying up there."

Zander's brow creased slightly. "You think you have demons here?"

"Oh heavens, no." Yvonne chuckled. "The ghosts are merely . . . mischievous."

Gwen nodded. "They've never hurt anyone."

Yvonne winced. "Well, there have been a *few* guests who said the spirits threw things at their heads, but I think they just made that up."

Gwen bit back a smile as Zander studied her and Yvonne, as if he couldn't decide whether they were being serious or not. "Follow me," said Gwen. "I'll show you where your rooms—" Hearing the back door of the house creak open, she looked down the hallway to see Donnie in the kitchen, still in camo gear and rooting through the cupboards.

After a moment, he turned and called out, "We have any Pop-Tarts?"

"Try the cupboard next to the pantry," Gwen advised. "Any particular reason why you have a headless water snake hanging around your neck?"

He blinked and looked down. "Forgot that was there." Pop-Tarts in hand, he then disappeared out the back door.

Turning back to the wolves, she ignored their puzzled expressions and gestured toward the wide, curved staircase. "I'll show you to your rooms."

Zander and his wolf were alike in many ways. Hard. Shrewd. Distrustful. They were also never rattled by anything. But there was something about Gwen Miller that made his wolf very cautious. The beast feared nothing, but strangely, he'd backed away from her. He now watched her carefully, still and quiet.

It wasn't that the wolf had taken an instant dislike to her. No, in fact, the beast particularly liked her voice—it was low and sultry, and there was something oddly soothing about it. The wolf also liked her scent. Zander could admit that it was potent, especially for a human. *Jasmine, orange blossoms, and wild berries.* But even while his wolf greedily inhaled it, the beast also stayed back.

Zander just didn't get it.

She was human, certainly no threat to him. And yet, his wolf had withdrawn from her, wary. It made Zander wonder what his wolf picked up about her that he himself was missing.

As a rule, Zander didn't "miss" things. He was good at reading and predicting people, but he couldn't quite grasp what troubled his wolf about the human. She didn't fall into any of the three categories that humans tended toward when it came to shifters. Nor was she setting off any of his inner alarms.

He studied her again. She was small. Slender. Very feminine. Had a sleek cinnamon-brown side-braid and long, blunt bangs. Nothing like the tall, curvy redheads he went for. She might have been called plain if it weren't for her eyes. They were exceptionally striking: a rich Prussian blue that seemed to stand out—maybe because the whites of her eyes were so clear.

No, Zander didn't understand his wolf's wariness at all.

Hooking his duffel over his shoulder, Zander followed her as she walked up the stairs . . . and found himself looking at a round, pert ass—it looked good in those skintight jeans.

Forcing his gaze up, he glanced around. He'd expected the proprietors to make the large house seem gloomy and play on the haunted rumor, but it was bright and airy. Paintings and mirrors hung on the white walls. The furnishings were antique and well cared for. The natural oak flooring was smooth and gave the place a rustic feel.

"It's a big house," he said. "You live here?"

She flicked him a brief glance over her shoulder. "Yep."

"Isn't it hard to share your home with strangers?" Zander would hate it. He was private and territorial.

She shrugged. "I'm used to it."

It didn't really answer his question, but Zander let it slide. In truth, he didn't like inane chatter or talking for the mere sake of it, but he was trying to feel her out and understand what his wolf sensed that he didn't. He wasn't a *friendly* person, but he knew how to project a nonthreatening image so that he seemed approachable and relatable. "Our wolves will want to be free to explore your land. Will that be a problem?"

"Of course not. Have at it." Reaching the first floor of guest bedrooms, she led them down a narrow hallway. Coming to a halt midway, she gestured at two rooms. "Here you go. Inside, you'll each find a Welcome Hamper and a pamphlet with breakfast hours, the Wi-Fi password, directions to local places, and important contact details. But if you need anything else, just call the reception desk. I leave for work at five, but there's always someone around. Hope you enjoy your stay."

As she began to walk away, Zander spoke. "You really think the house is haunted?" He hoped not, because he didn't want her to be crazy.

Her mouth curved a little. "I like it when skeptical people come here. It's always fun to watch them freak out." With that, she disappeared down the hall.

Bracken gave a low chuckle. "She's just fucking with us. The story is based on a family who lived here hundreds of years ago. A father and his two daughters were killed in a fire. The remains of the house were restored, and people say that all three ghosts now haunt the place."

Zander snorted. "Yeah. Right." Unlocking the door, he slipped inside and closed it behind him. Gwen's scent was present in the room. It was faint beneath the smells of clean linen, air deodorizer, and freshly made muffins, but it was no less potent.

He slung his duffel on the overstuffed armchair as he took in his surroundings. Much like the rest of the house, it wasn't gloomy. It was warm and restful. Bamboo shades, a fleecy throw on the armchair, a brick fireplace, a wall-mounted TV, a coffee machine, and a decadent-looking king-size bed with plump pillows and a soft comforter.

He quickly unpacked his things, slipping some clothes into the antique dresser and hanging others in the closet. After placing his toiletries in the adjoined bathroom, he made a cup of coffee and stepped out onto the balcony. There was a great view of the grassy plains, water pools, nearby creek, and the moss-covered trees that bordered much of the territory.

He settled into the deck chair, letting the peaceful air slide over him. All he could hear were birds trilling, insects droning, the burble of the creek, and the muffled conversation of other guests filtering through an open window. His wolf stretched within him, wanting the freedom to acquaint himself with the land.

There was the sound of a door creaking open, and then Bracken was leaning over the partition between their balconies, a half-eaten muffin in hand. "These are damn good. How's your room?"

"Better than some hotels I've stayed in."

Bracken nodded. "Same here." He bit into his muffin. "My wolf likes this place."

"How did your wolf react to Gwen?"

Bracken blinked. "He likes her well enough, I guess."

"He's not bothered by her?"

"No. Why?"

"My wolf backs away from her."

"Seriously?" Bracken blinked. "That's weird. Nothing about her raises my hackles, and she doesn't rub my wolf's fur the wrong way either. Then again, your wolf has always acted strange when a female shows an interest in you."

That was true. Zander's wolf might be attracted to a female, might like her scent or her confidence or any number of her qualities, but he never *wanted* her. In fact, he often became irritated by female attention, especially if it was sexual. There were very few females whose company he tolerated—thankfully, those included the females of his pack.

If Zander didn't know any better, he'd think the wolf had mommy issues or something. Still, one thing his wolf had never done was back away from a female. He'd growled. Snarled. Brooded. Turned his back on them. Hell, he'd even clawed at Zander if they annoyed him enough. But act wary and cautious? *Never* had he done that.

"Yeah, but she didn't show an interest in me." She'd acted cordial and professional. "I don't know what to make of it. My wolf's always been a fearless fucker. Nothing has ever thrown or shaken him. She unnerves him, and I'm not used to him being disturbed by anything."

Bracken chewed on that for a moment. "Is he fighting you on being around her?"

"No. That's the point. He's not engaging. He literally just backs away."

"That is odd. I wouldn't worry on it, Z. You have enough to think about, like the reading of the will tomorrow . . . and just how hard we'll have to work not to kick the living shit out of Rory." He shoved the last of his muffin into his mouth. "Let's go for a run. Your wolf might feel better afterward."

Zander was counting on it.

CHAPTER THREE

Later that day, acting on Yvonne's recommendation, Zander and Bracken headed to Half 'n' Half for dinner—a place owned by Yvonne's future son-in-law. The moment he strolled inside, Zander understood the name. The dimly lit place was half bar, half pool hall. Unlike the last pool hall he'd been to, it wasn't dingy or fogged by cigarette smoke. There was a slight smell of tobacco, but it was drowned out by the scents of beer, leather, oiled wood, and food grilling.

Rows of pool tables lined the left side of the wide space, where there were also plenty of stools and small round tables. On the right side was a long bar, a wall-mounted TV, cushioned booths, and wooden tables. Sports paraphernalia and framed photos lined the wood-paneled walls of the entire space.

The place was fairly crowded, but not enough for Zander to feel smothered. Most patrons were either sitting at tables watching the game airing on the TV or gathered around the pool tables.

There was a lot of cursing and trash talk, but it was all banter. Among the sounds of balls colliding and tumbling into pockets were the bleeping of the gaming machines, the sizzling of cooked food, and the music coming from the jukebox.

"Damn, I'm starving." Bracken patted Zander's arm with the back of his hand. "Hey, look, there's Gwen."

Zander tracked his gaze, not sure why a weird sort of anticipation began to slowly spread through him like warm syrup. His vision was blocked by a group of guys, but he could see her head, see her smiling that distant but courteous smile as she carefully took plates from the tray she was holding. Well, it would seem she worked for her brother-in-law as well as her mother. Or adopted mother. He knew from the females' scents that they weren't biologically related.

Spotting an empty booth nearby, Zander headed straight for it and slid onto the cushioned bench.

Bracken sat opposite him. "I can't help but notice that you found us a table in the area Gwen seems to be working."

Well, it would give Zander the opportunity to watch her, to see how she interacted with people, to work out what the hell was unsettling his wolf. The run hadn't helped ease the beast's tension at all.

Dressed in a lemon T-shirt and cutoff shorts, she weaved her way through the group, heading toward the door that he suspected led to the kitchen. Jesus, she had shapely, tanned legs that looked as smooth as butter. His cock twitched. He'd always been a sucker for legs. He could see himself hooking Gwen's over his shoulders as he—

Spotting him and Bracken, she blinked and then held up one finger. She went into the kitchen only to reappear moments later. "Hey," she greeted them with a smile, stopping at their table.

His wolf immediately withdrew. There was no submission or fear in the act, just a sort of primal wariness.

"Hey," said Bracken. "You do manly foods, right?"

Her mouth quirked. "Manly foods?"

"Red meat. Chili. Chicken wings. Stuff like that."

"Ah, yes, we do manly foods." She pulled a pen and pad out of her pocket. "Most go for the steak, fries, onion rings, and beer combo."

Bracken's smile widened. "That should hit the spot."

She raised a brow at Zander. "What about you?"

"The same," he said.

"And bring some nachos too," Bracken added.

"You got it." She scribbled down their order on a notepad.

"Yvonne said this place belongs to your sister's fiancé," Zander told her.

"That's right." Gwen turned to gesture at Chase . . . and saw that he was waving her over. She turned back to the wolves. "I'll send over another waitress with your beers and have her place your order so you're not waiting long."

As she walked away, Zander couldn't help but take another long look at those legs. Eyes seemed to follow them wherever she went, and he didn't think she even noticed.

He watched as she handed their order to another waitress and then crossed to a tall, well-built male in the corner. They stood close, not hesitating to enter each other's personal space. There was nothing sexual about it, but he found that he didn't like it.

Shamelessly, Zander used his shifter-enhanced hearing to listen to their conversation. It was pretty much impossible to catch more than a few words here and there, but what he *did* hear sure did send his curiosity spiking.

Gwen sighed at Chase. He stood there, a Marlboro cigarette balanced in his mouth, giving her his trademark glare that made most people—male and female—avert their eyes and back down. Given that Julie was nervous around guys, Gwen still had to marvel that the burly, tattooed male had somehow managed to earn her trust, let alone get her to accept his proposal.

Gwen liked that Julie had someone so tough. Her sister, delicate in many ways, needed that buffer from life. But Gwen didn't, and

Chase saw no need to acknowledge that. He shoved his nose into her business far too often and expected her to effectively report to him. As such, he was pissed that she hadn't immediately called him when Brandt paid her a visit.

"I should have heard it from *you*, Gwen, not through the fucking rumor mill."

"Give me a break, Chase. It only happened last night. I haven't even told Yvonne about it yet." A fan of sleeping pills, Yvonne had slept right through it. "Besides, I just gave you the full story—you can stop whining."

He took a pull of his cigarette and then tilted his head slightly when he exhaled so that the smoke didn't blow in her face. "Donnie should have shot the little bastard in the fucking head."

"He's not worth the jail time."

"No, he's not." Leaning back, he tapped his cigarette, sending fine gray ashes tumbling to the glass ashtray resting on the high-top table. "Maybe I should pay the Moores a visit."

"Don't. You'd be wasting your time. Right now, I'm the only thing that Brandt's concerned about. If you went there, he'd only twist the whole thing, and then Colt would arrest you—and he'd do it gladly, considering how much he seems to hate you." But then, Colt hated most people.

"I don't give a fuck about Colt," said Chase, his tone dismissive.

"Well, I give a fuck that he might arrest you, so please—for Julie—stay out of it."

He sighed. "Did you call Julie?"

She narrowed her eyes at how evasively he dodged her request. "Yes. I told her that I was fine, and I was being careful."

"So, basically, you lied. She's worried sick about you. She wants to see you, but I told her not to go to the B&B. If she was there when Brandt came, she'd have been terrified."

Yes, she would have been. Julie got thrown back to her childhood every time she heard a guy raise his voice. But . . . "She's stronger than you think, Chase. Still, I don't want her there either. Look, I know this situation is fucked up, but let it play out. Let Brandt dig his own grave; he's doing me a favor."

"Doing you a favor? Gwen, if he goes back to the B&B to confront you again, there's a good chance he'll take more of his friends with him."

"If that happens, I'll pull out the shotgun, the rifle, my hunting knife, and go get myself some human-skin rugs. I'll take Donnie. We'll make a night of it."

Taking yet another pull on his cigarette, Chase took a step forward and pinned her gaze with his. "No, you call *me*. Not *after* he's gone. You call me the second you see him. He's young, stupid, and arrogant . . . but he's also dangerous. You've seen for yourself what he's capable of; you saw what he did to that girl. I don't want that to be you."

No, neither did she. "If I see him, I'll call you," she promised . . . though she was crossing her fingers behind her back.

"Make sure you do." He stubbed his cigarette on the ashtray and left it there. "Now get back to work. At least when you're here, I can be sure you're all right."

She gave him a weak smile and patted his arm. "You're a big softie beneath that tough shell. Don't worry, I won't tell anyone. Your street cred's safe."

"Whatever," he grumbled, cheeks flushing slightly. "I'm holding you to the promise that you'll call me, Gwen."

Well, that was a shame, but it was unlikely that she'd keep it.

"Are you even listening to me?"

Watching Gwen disappear into the kitchen, Zander said, "No. I was busy listening to Gwen's conversation with her sister's fiancé." He hadn't been able to hear much, thanks to the shouting coming from the sports fanatics. "Seems like she witnessed some kind of crime, and someone's trying to bully her into not testifying against them."

"Really?" Bracken leaned back. "Shit."

Zander shifted in his seat, trying to relieve the discomfort caused by his half-hard cock pressing against his fly. It had begun rising to attention at the sight of her legs and was showing no sign of easing. Maybe if her voice wasn't like a fucking stroke to his senses, it would.

"Any idea what she witnessed?"

Zander shook his head. "I couldn't make out much of what was said."

A skimpy redhead appeared at their table, smiling widely. She slapped down two coasters and then set the beer bottles on top of them. "Anything else I can get you?" she asked, her smile suggestive.

Picking up his beer, Zander took a long swig, letting the cold liquid slide down his throat, hoping the shock of the cold would make his dick settle down.

"We're good," Bracken told the waitress. Once she was gone, he eyed Zander curiously. "It's not like you to turn away from a redhead."

"You say it like I'm a slut."

"No, that's Marcus—or it was, before he mated Roni. But you didn't even give the redhead an appreciative glance. I'm just saying, that's not like you."

"Is there a point to this conversation?"

"No."

"Then let's just end it." Zander put down his beer. He wasn't the only one to groan as the jukebox replayed the last song for the sixth time.

"Who keeps choosing that damn song?" one guy complained, holding a cue tight, as if imagining whacking the culprit over the head. That might have been why no one owned up to it.

The place was getting more and more crowded, but Zander's wolf seemed more curious about the people and his surroundings than bothered by how packed it was.

A door creaked open, and then Gwen was striding out of the kitchen with a tray of steaming food. And, yeah, Zander's eyes dropped to those legs that shouldn't be legal.

Moving straight to their table, she set down their plates and a platter of nachos with dips. "Here you go."

Just like that, his wolf mysteriously backed away again. Zander barely resisted the urge to grind his teeth. "Everything all right?"

She blinked. "Yeah, of course."

"Looked like you were having an argument with your sister's fiancé."

"Gwen, I got a challenge for you here!" someone called out.

Zander turned to see a guy in the pool-hall section standing near a high-topped table where glasses and bottles rested, gesturing for Gwen to come over.

Mouth curving, Gwen rolled her eyes. "Enjoy your meal." At that, she walked to the guy. A quiet fell over the pool hall, and people gathered to watch whatever was about to happen next.

"You got a challenge for me, Harry?"

"I don't care how good you are. There's no way you'll pot that." Harry pointed at the black ball on the pool table. "I've looked at it from every possible angle. It can't be done."

Gwen smiled. "It can always be done, Harry."

He put a wad of bills on the side of the pool table. "You pot that black, it's yours."

She shook her head sadly. "Why do you want to give your money away?"

Harry just grinned. "I'm telling you, this will break your perfect record."

Money changed hands, and Zander watched as Gwen circled the pool table like a predator, utterly focused on the two remaining balls on the table. Finally, she stopped and held out her hand. Harry passed her his cue, and she scraped the tip with a cube of blue chalk.

She stretched across the table and lined up the cue stick to the white ball. Damn if she didn't look good bent over like that. Zander wasn't the only one to take a moment to admire her ass.

Everyone seemed to hold their collective breath as, eyes narrowing, she aimed and took her shot. The white ball crashed into the side of the table, bounced over to the other side, hit the bottom of the table at a diagonal angle . . . and clipped the edge of the black ball, which then slowly rolled into a pocket.

Cheers went up and people clapped.

She grabbed the wad of bills and turned to Harry. "It almost feels like stealing."

With an affectionate smile, Harry waved a hand. "One day there'll be a shot you can't make."

"Sure, sure," she said, stuffing the bills in her back pocket.

"A master at pool, huh?" said Bracken. "My kind of girl. What are you glaring at me for? Just because your wolf doesn't like her doesn't mean that I can't."

Zander took another drink of his beer. "He doesn't dislike her; he's just wary of her."

"Isn't that pretty much the same thing?"

"No." He thumped his bottle down on the table. "Now let's fucking eat." He turned his attention to his meal, but he kept an eye on Gwen: observing her, studying her, assessing her . . . and, yeah, ogling her legs. His wolf watched her just as carefully, still cautious, and—for the life of him—Zander couldn't work out why.

"Zander."

He snapped awake at the whisper in his ear. There was no one there. Well, of course there was no one there. Blinking, he picked up his phone and swiped his thumb across the screen to check the time.

Seven thirty in the morning. He'd always been an early riser, so his body's clock had obviously woken him. Obviously. It happened often and—

The balcony door was open.

Suddenly alert, he slowly slid out of bed. There was no one in the room—he'd smell them if there were. Yet, he didn't *feel* alone. And he knew for sure that he'd locked the damn balcony door.

He silently padded onto the balcony, stepping into the humid air. There was no one.

Hearing muttering, he looked down to see an Aston Martin parked outside. Nice car. But something about the guy who was standing beside it, talking on his cell phone, raised Zander's hackles. Or maybe it was the draft that came from behind him and brushed over his nape. He already knew before he glanced over his shoulder that no one would be there.

He scrubbed a hand down his face, refusing to acknowledge any of the weird shit going on. His focus was on the shady-looking guy outside. A guy who was now walking toward the house, a determined expression on his face. He was probably a new guest arriving, but said guest was setting off Zander's inner alarms. Maybe he should go down there and find out why.

CHAPTER FOUR

Having finished their pancakes, Gwen and Marlon cleaned up their mess so they could prepare breakfast for the guests. The kitchen was pretty spacious, with oak cabinets, a large pantry, stainless-steel appliances, and the wooden island in the center.

As she swept the crumbs from the counter into her hand, careful not to drop any on the tiled floor, Yvonne walked in.

"Morning, darlings." Yvonne beamed. "Where's Donnie?"

"He came by a half hour ago," said Marlon. "I offered him breakfast, but he said he was still stuffed from the squirrel he snacked on last night. He went to his cabin."

"Well, of course he ate a squirrel as a late-night snack," said Yvonne drily. "Who doesn't?" She sighed. "I need to speak with him. I shouldn't be long."

"We'll be fine here," Gwen assured her.

Casting them a sunny smile, Yvonne disappeared out the back door.

Marlon shook his head. "Like we don't know when she's fake-smiling. She always gets like this around Asshole's birthday. I don't know why, because, as the nickname suggests, he's an Asshole."

"Yeah, but they were together for two years, and she's not good at being on her own. She goes to Donnie because she knows he'll verbally shred Asshole's character until she feels we're all better off without him—which we are."

"Why doesn't she like talking badly of him in front of us? She knows we despise him. It's not like she'd be poisoning our minds against him. He did that all on his own."

"I think she doesn't want us to see how much he hurt her; she doesn't want *that* to hurt *us* and—" Gwen cut herself off at the chime of the doorbell. "I'll get it." Hoping it wasn't Colt with more complaints from the Moores, she strode into the hall. But as she opened the door, it wasn't to find Colt on her doorstep. No, it was worse.

Gwen gripped the edge of the door, mouth tightening. It was hard not to snarl at the balding, impeccably neat male. His smile was wide and friendly, but it had a shady edge to it—the kind you saw on a slimy door-to-door salesman. At least Brandt didn't hide that he was a bastard. His father, however, lavished everyone with a false charm that grated on her nerves.

She noticed his chauffeur, Thad, leaning against the car, staring right at her. From what she could tell, the guy was also Ezra's right-hand man.

"Good morning," Ezra said brightly.

She arched a brow. "Is it?"

His smile faltered slightly. "Miss Miller, I've come in peace, I assure you."

"And yet, I'm not feeling assured, Mr. Moore."

"Please call me Ezra."

Yeah, that wasn't going to happen.

"I was hoping that you and I could talk."

"Is that not what we're doing?"

"In private, I mean." He glanced over her shoulder, hinting to come inside.

"This is private enough."

His eyes hardened a little. "Very well." Clearing his throat, he offered her a contrite smile. "I wanted to apologize for my son's behavior the other night. He confessed that the bat is his and that his injuries weren't caused by you—that you simply took the bat from him before he could smash the window of your truck. The incident shamed all three young men, and I know their families feel just as disappointed with their sons as I do with mine."

What a crock of shit. "While I appreciate your taking the time to come here, I don't want an apology. I want assurances that your son will stay away from me—that is all."

He gave a respectful nod. "Understandable." He slipped his hand into the inside pocket of his jacket and pulled out a check. "Allow me to offer this as compensation."

She blinked. "Compensation?"

"Ten thousand dollars."

"You're offering me ten grand . . . because your son acted like a dick?"

He seemed about to jump to Brandt's defense, but then his face molded into a remorseful expression that didn't reach his eyes. "Brandt is . . . troubled. I will admit that. But he would never raise his fist to a woman, let alone drug and beat one with a pole. He insists that you misread the situation you stumbled across, that he merely came upon the female shifter after she'd already been beaten by someone else."

Anger surged through Gwen. She somehow managed to bite back a curse. "You don't believe that. You want to believe it. But you don't. Look, I get that he's your son, and you don't want to see him punished by the shifter council, but you can't seriously think he doesn't *deserve* a punishment for what he did."

"He says he's innocent—"

"I know what I saw, I know what I heard, *and I know it was him.* I could hear him beating her—hear that pole hitting bone before I even laid eyes on them. You're insulting both my intelligence and your own by trying to insinuate differently."

"The shifter altered her statement."

"Because she's scared out of her mind."

"What do you care?" His upper lip curled. "She's a shifter. A *lone* shifter, which makes it worse."

"She didn't deserve what happened to her, and Brandt doesn't deserve to go unpunished for it."

"So high and mighty, aren't you?" he sneered. "Yet, you had no problem trying to shoot him, did you? Just like you had no problem hitting him with a bat or using a stun gun on him. He came home with a jaw so swollen he could barely talk."

"But he went home *conscious*. If he comes at me again, I can't guarantee he'll go home at all—not while Donnie's feeling trigger-happy. You understand that, don't you, Mr. Moore? You understand that if you want your son safe, you need to get him under control?"

"I came here in peace," he said once again.

"You came here to buy me off. It's not the first time you've waved money at people to solve Brandt's problems. If you weren't a father who's so quick to get out his checkbook to buy his son's way out of trouble, you might have a better shot of keeping him in line. He's used to Daddy saving his ass, so he doesn't see the need to behave himself. It wouldn't surprise me if he *likes* making you dance around and jump through hoops to get him out of trouble."

Cheeks reddening, he insisted, "Brandt didn't beat that shifter. Here's what you're going to do. You're going to keep that check and change your statement like a good little girl. Then, when you go before the council, you'll tell them you can't be sure who attacked her. If you don't, you'll find that the problems you've had so far were *nothing.*"

She leaned forward. "Bring it."

"You need to step away from her," rumbled a voice from behind her, loaded with menace. "And you need to do it now."

Shit. Gwen flicked Zander a strained smile over her shoulder. "Mr. Devlin, I'll be with you shortly."

But Zander's eyes were on Moore, and they were cold as ice. "You're still standing too close to her. I don't know why."

Moore lifted his chin. "Who the hell are you?"

"That's not important."

"This has *nothing* to do with you."

"I don't care. Gwen doesn't want you here, so leave."

Moore turned back to Gwen, mouth set into a flat line. "Make the right choice, Miss Miller."

"I already did. And I won't be changing it."

He gave a curt nod. "So be it." Then he was gone.

Only once he'd driven away did Gwen shut the door. Turning, she found that her brother and Bracken had joined Zander. "Marlon, could you help Mr. Devlin with whatever he needs—I'll be right back." Because she needed some fucking air.

As she made a beeline for the kitchen, she could hear Marlon trying to dissuade the shifters from following her. Shoving open the back door, she stepped out onto the deck and inhaled deeply. The cool air filled her lungs, soothing her.

Sitting on the deck, she let her head drop forward. She was just so fucking tired of all this shit. Not that she intended to back down. Hell, no. She just didn't want to be vilified for doing the right thing.

Hearing the door creak open, she glanced over her shoulder to see Zander staring right at her, hundreds of questions in his eyes. *Just fucking great.*

Zander hadn't heard all of Gwen's conversation with the human who'd just left, but he'd heard enough to grasp the gist of the situation. And he was fucking pissed. A female shifter had been assaulted, and neither the culprit nor his family gave a rat's ass. In their eyes, the victim was inferior to them and deserved no justice simply because she was a shifter. In addition, Gwen was the only person who was prepared to stand up for that shifter, even though it meant going against her own kind—people who were clearly harassing her.

His sister's face flashed in his mind. Shelby had been thirteen when she was hit by stray bullets in a drive-by shooting. Several humans witnessed the incident and had identified the human shooter, but by the time the trial came around, all of them had "forgotten" relevant details. Why? Because running up to the trial, the bastard had pretended to be the victim, insisted that shifters were simply out to get humans. He'd riled up other anti-shifter humans, and they'd all focused their hate on Shelby, who'd suddenly become the guilty party. The witnesses had also been slated, and they'd eventually folded under the pressure.

Shelby's testimony hadn't been enough, and the shooter had walked free. He'd later shot someone else, this time at point-blank range. The situation wasn't the same as Gwen's, but it was similar enough to bring back all the rage and contempt Zander had felt for the shooter and his prejudiced supporters.

Nowadays, many anti-shifter humans grouped together. The extremists were violent, radical, and seemed to know no boundaries. They were known to use car bombs, grenades, and other explosives to attack shifters, their territories, and even their businesses—uncaring that there could be human casualties. They'd gotten so bad that even other humans were turning against them. Risking their wrath wasn't advisable. Yet, Gwen was prepared to speak up for this female shifter who wouldn't even speak up for herself. He admired that. Respected it. Appreciated it.

"What was all that about?" Zander asked her.

"Sorry if your sleep was disturbed by the visitor," she said in that coolly polite and formal tone that, for some reason, offended him. "Marlon will prepare whatever you want for breakfast." She faced forward once again as Marlon listed various options.

Unwilling to be dismissed, Zander stepped off the deck and moved to block her view. “You didn’t answer my question.”

Gwen swallowed a tired sigh. “If you’re worried that you might get caught up in what’s happening, we’ll certainly understand that and give you a refund.” Personally, she thought that was a pretty reasonable offer, but he didn’t appear to like it.

“Tell me what’s happening.”

Gwen frowned. He really thought she’d share her personal business with him? Surely he’d heard enough to understand that this was a private and very serious matter, one she wasn’t about to share with a complete stranger just to satisfy his curiosity. “You’re a guest here.”

Not seeing what that had to do with anything, Zander pushed, “Tell me what’s going on.”

“Look, Mr. Devlin—”

“Zander. My name is Zander. Use it,” he clipped. He wasn’t sure why it bothered him that she didn’t, but he wasn’t sure of a lot of things when it came to Gwen Miller. His wolf had again backed away from her, and the situation was getting old, *fast*.

“You’re a guest here.”

“Yeah, you keep saying that. Not sure why you think it’s relevant.”

“This doesn’t involve you. Like I said, we can sort you out with a refund—”

“I don’t want a refund.” He squatted in front of her. “I want to know if I heard correctly, and you witnessed a shifter being physically assaulted.”

She inhaled sharply. “Good hearing.”

“You’re being *pressured* to change your statement?”

Marlon sat beside her. “*Pressured* is an understatement. They’ve tried pretty much everything to make her do what they want.”

Zander wondered just what “pretty much everything” entailed. “But you won’t give in?”

She blinked. “Why would I?”

"Some humans would prefer not to go against people like the asshole who was just here, especially when they're being targeted this way."

Bracken leaned against the porch rail. "How long is it before the matter goes before the shifter council?"

"A month," said Marlon.

"Where's the girl?" asked Bracken.

Gwen's eyes snapped to his. "Why?"

"We can offer her protection."

She tilted her head. "Why would you do that? From what I've heard, lone shifters aren't exactly liked or trusted."

"Our pack is closely allied with another, and one of the members helps run a shelter for lone shifters," Bracken explained. "She'd be safe there."

"She's already safe."

"You're hiding her," Zander guessed.

"Even though they bullied her into altering her statement, they kept terrorizing her; she needed somewhere to go."

Rising, Zander glanced around. "She's living on your land in her animal form, isn't she?"

"Not sure why you'd think that." With a sigh, Gwen stood. "Well, it's been great talking to you, but I have work to do."

And he and Bracken had somewhere they needed to be, thought Zander, but he was reluctant to leave her. As he watched her walk away, he didn't think he'd ever seen anyone who looked so lonely. There was an odd twinge in his chest.

"She'll be okay," said Marlon. "She's a lot tougher than she looks. Now, what can I make you guys for breakfast?" He again reeled off the menu. After Zander and Bracken placed their orders, Marlon retreated inside.

Still leaning against the rail, Bracken said, "Not many humans would do what she's doing for a shifter—hell, not many humans would do it for another human while being intimidated like that." There was a great deal of respect in his voice. "Listen, I know you don't like getting involved in other people's shit. I'm not a big fan of it either. But . . ."

"You want to stick around in case she needs help," Zander sensed.

Bracken pushed away from the rail. "I feel like we owe her. She's not doing this for us—I know that. But what was done to the female shifter was a serious crime. And by standing up for one of our kind, Gwen's placing herself in danger. We'd be bastards to just ignore that. I can't. It's not how I'm wired."

Zander scraped his hand over his jaw. "All this shit makes me think of what happened to Shelby."

"Me too. That bastard who shot her walked off into the sunset, free as a bird. Maybe we can make sure the same thing doesn't happen to the little fucker that Gwen's dealing with. I heard the way that human was talking to her just now. He's not going to let this go. He'll keep up the pressure. Gwen seems strong, but everyone has their limit. We could help, and I think we should."

"And you're bored," Zander pushed.

"And I'm bored," Bracken admitted. "But it's more than that. Like I said, I feel like we owe her. Shelby's like a sister to me. I hate what happened to her. If we walk away from Gwen and the shifter while they need help, we're no better than the people who let Shelby down."

Zander sighed, turning his gaze to the view of the marsh. "You're right." The "but" was clear in his tone.

"Why are you so reluctant to stay? Look, I'm not expecting you to sympathize with these females. I know empathy isn't really your thing. But I also know that you're a person who's rarely daunted by anything. So, what's holding you back? Is your wolf making it hard for you to be around Gwen?"

"No, he's not giving me a hard time. But I don't know if he'd help me protect her. It's possible that he'd even object to it. What use am I if, when she's in danger, he pulls back so hard that I'm distracted?"

Bracken frowned thoughtfully. "How did he react when you stepped in to warn away Moore just now?"

"He didn't react. Just stayed back. It's almost like he's hiding from her. What does that even mean?"

Bracken's mouth twitched. "It's driving you insane that you can't solve the mystery."

Damn right it was. "I don't like puzzles."

"In my opinion, the only way you'll figure it out is if you stick around awhile. But I'm not going to pressure you into staying. If you feel you need to go, go—I won't judge you for that."

Zander snorted derisively. "Like I'd leave you on your own." He, Bracken, and Jesse were like brothers; they'd stick together through anything. He sighed. "I'll stay. It's what Shelby would want me to do. And you're right. Walking away would make us like those people who let her down."

"And you want to solve the mystery of your wolf's reaction to Gwen. So do I. It's kind of interesting."

"Glad someone's enjoying the puzzle."

"No, you're not."

"No, I'm not." Zander tipped his chin toward the door. "Let's get breakfast. Then we can go hear Dale's will."

Zander flicked a look at the wall clock. Rory was late. Of course he was late. Everything had to revolve around him, so he was purposely making them wait for him. The bastard better fucking hurry, because the heavy scent of new paint was driving his senses crazy. Not even the strong smell of his coffee helped.

Bracken didn't seem bothered. He was busy watching the news on the wall-mounted TV. Although the volume was low, his shifter-enhanced hearing allowed Bracken to hear it perfectly, despite the continual ringing of the receptionist's phone and the noises coming from the children in the toy corner.

Zander had received a text message from Shelby informing him that she wouldn't be coming. He wasn't particularly surprised. He was also glad, because it meant she wouldn't have to deal with Rory.

With an inward sigh, Zander threw the newspaper he'd skimmed through back onto the coffee table. The young receptionist tried to catch his eye, but he didn't play the game. His mind was on other things. Like the reading of the will. Like how likely it was that Rory would be an ass. And like the question of whether Nick would sanction Zander's and Bracken's requests to stay in Oregon for a while.

He didn't doubt that his Alpha would sympathize with Gwen and the female shifter's situation, but Nick's priority was the pack's safety—especially since that pack included his mate and daughter. Also, Nick didn't like outsiders; he wouldn't put one before the needs of his pack, no matter the seriousness of the situation.

The front door swung open, and in walked a male with the same face that Zander saw every day in the mirror. Rory looked smart and immaculately neat with his slicked hair, black suit, shiny shoes, and briefcase. He also looked amused as his gaze found Zander, like Rory knew something that he didn't.

Rory introduced himself to the receptionist, who blushed as she assured him that she'd alert the attorney of his arrival. He then strode over to Zander, halting in front of him. "Hello, brother." It was a taunt, not a greeting.

Zander's wolf lunged for him, upper lip curled back. He'd happily rip the male to pieces and not give a shit about it. Zander held him back and didn't rise to Rory's taunt. Instead, he spoke in a toneless voice that gave Rory no emotion to work with or exploit. "Rory."

He cocked his head. "How're things?"

"Good."

Rory's eyes cut to Bracken, who was pointedly ignoring him—something he'd been doing since they were kids. Rory's mouth tightened at the clear dismissal, but he slid his gaze back to Zander and said, "I'm glad to hear it. Things are good on my end too. Work is good, life is good. I actually have plans to expand my business." He talked about his job, boasted of his new contracts, spoke of his "newest piece of fluff"—his words.

He was so caught up in chatting about himself that he didn't notice the bored look Bracken exchanged with Zander, despite the enforcer not being the least bit subtle about it.

The opening of a door was soon followed by footsteps shuffling down the hallway. Finally, a suited middle-aged male appeared. "Zander and Rory Devlin?"

"That's us," Rory confirmed with a smile as they walked toward him.

Zander took in the male's scent. *Fox shifter*. His wolf growled; he wasn't a fan of foxes.

"I'm Edward Simpson, your uncle's attorney." He shook each of their hands, his expression sympathetic. "I'm sorry for your loss."

Rory swallowed hard. "Thank you. We'll miss him."

Bracken snickered only loud enough to reach shifter ears, and Rory's face hardened as he tossed the enforcer a dark look that was completely ignored.

Rory turned to Zander. "I'm surprised Jesse's not here to console you too."

Zander didn't rise to the snarky remark, which only pissed the prick off.

Edward cleared his throat. "Please come with me." He led them down a hallway and into an office. With its white walls and gray carpet, the room was sterile. It was also obsessively tidy. Each item of stationery seemed to have its own place on the desk. The stacks of papers were perfectly aligned beneath the dolphin paperweight. The files and binders on the shelves were in alphabetical order.

There didn't appear to be even a speck of dust, and Zander got the feeling that the attorney would have an aneurysm if he found one. Maybe that was why the guy had a stress ball next to his coffee mug and why the astringent scent of hand sanitizer was so strong—fairly drowning out the other smells of paper, ink, and coffee.

Edward gestured at the padded plastic chairs opposite his desk. "Please sit." He then moved to the file cabinet, on which a framed photo of a woman and two children rested. Pulling out a slim folder, he closed the drawer.

Tension stretched the air taut; Zander and Rory remained so still that only the whirring of the fan and the shuffling of papers could be heard.

Sitting, Edward rolled his wheeled office chair closer to the desk and opened the folder. "I realize that reading the will aloud in an attorney's office isn't how things are usually done anymore. But your uncle was adamant that he wanted things handled this way. He attached a letter to his last will and testament, and he asked that I read it aloud first."

Rory leaned forward, but Zander didn't move.

"To my niece and nephews," began Edward, *"you may be wondering why you're now sitting in my attorney's office. Well, it is as simple as this—I knew that someone would be unhappy with the content of the will and most likely claim that the copy they received in the post was a fake. This way, you will all know that you each received the same copy."*

Rory tensed, smart enough to sense that was a jab at him.

"I have many regrets," Edward went on. *"Mainly that I sat around, waiting for my true mate to stumble into my path. It was a stupid move, considering shifters don't always recognize their mate at first glance, but I was so sure that I would know instantly. Maybe she did cross my path, maybe she didn't. In any case, I have spent my life relatively alone, and now I have died alone.*

"I encourage you all not to wait around as I did. Find your own path to happiness, and walk down that path whether it leads to your

true mate or not. Love and best wishes, Dale." Edward lowered the letter to the desk.

"Touching," Rory bit out.

"Yes," Edward agreed. "Your uncle didn't own any physical properties, but he received the same payment upon his death that all in his pack receive so that they may leave some for their families. Dale split it as follows . . ."

As the attorney read out the will, Zander briefly closed his eyes. He should have seen it coming.

"A dollar," said Rory, voice strangely calm. "He left me a dollar."

The attorney licked his lips. "Yes."

Rory jumped to his feet, hands curled. "Is this a fucking joke?"

Edward shifted in his seat. "He felt that you wouldn't need money, since you were your parents' sole heir."

"So, he did this to piss me off. He divided everything between Zander and Shelby *to piss me off*." Rory whirled on Zander. "Are you responsible for this? Did you convince him to change his will before he died?"

Utterly calm, Zander said, "You're judging me by your standards, Rory."

Expression sour, Rory pointed at himself. "I have *every right* to a portion of that money. I earned it."

Something about the way he said it made Zander realize . . . "You spent time with Dale near the end, didn't you? Helped him out? Did him favors?" Rory was manipulative and smooth, but Dale was far from dumb; he'd obviously known what Rory was doing.

"Oh, I helped him. Even wiped the old bastard's ass at one point. He owed me. *You* owe me. You'd probably be either dead or on dialysis if I hadn't given you that kidney."

With a bored sigh, Zander stood up. "Are we really back to that again?" Even his wolf was bored of that.

"Just give me half of what he left you. That's all I'm asking for."

"You really need it that badly?"

"I told you, I want to expand the business."

"So, it has nothing to do with your gambling debts? Not that paying them off will really help you. You'll just put yourself in more debt." Zander knew that Rory was a compulsive gambler with a bottomless greed that couldn't be satiated.

Rory's eyes narrowed to slits. "You owe me."

"Nobody owes you anything, Rory. But that's your problem—it's always been your problem: you think the world and everybody in it owes you. Fucking grow up."

A cunning glint entered Rory's gaze. "Maybe Shelby will go into business with me." It was a veiled threat—if Zander didn't yield, he'd turn his attention to Shelby.

"You'd have a hard time getting to her. She's part of a different pack now, and it just so happens that her Alpha hates you. He won't let you near her, and you know she doesn't leave her territory."

Face flushed, Rory stepped toward him. "If you won't give me what's mine, I'll take from you what's yours."

That was supposed to scare him? Zander inwardly snorted. "Don't be a prick all your life, Rory." With that, he strode out of the office and into the reception area. He almost felt bad leaving Edward alone with Rory, who was now shouting his intention to contest the will.

Bracken rose to his feet, brow cocked in question.

"I'll tell you in the SUV." Once inside, Zander switched on the engine and, as they drove back to the B&B, explained what had happened.

"A dollar?" Bracken echoed, amused. "Somehow, that's more insulting than leaving him nothing."

"I'll have to tell Shelby what happened and warn her that Rory might try to contact her."

"What do you think he was talking about when he said he'll take from you what's yours?"

"Don't know." But since Zander didn't own anything that particularly meant anything to him, he wasn't concerned about the threat. "It was probably just Rory chatting shit—he's been doing that since he learned to talk."

"Good point."

Later, when they were back on the balcony of his room at the B&B, once again surrounded by the sounds and smells of the marsh, Zander called Nick and put him on speakerphone so that Bracken could be part of the conversation.

As Zander told the Alpha how Dale had divided the money, Bracken shook his head in amusement—still tickled by the matter.

"How did Rory take it?" There was a smile in Nick's voice.

"Not well," said Zander. "Expect some trouble. Tell the others to look out for him—he could turn up at the club or the motel and act like an asshole. He won't do anything major like attack anyone, but he will fuck with you if he can."

"All right, we'll be on the lookout for him. What time will you be back tomorrow?"

Zander exchanged a look with Bracken before speaking. "There's a situation here at the B&B."

"What kind of situation?" asked Nick.

Zander explained, and the Alpha swore viciously. "Gwen looks worn out by it all," Zander added. "But she's still not folding."

"We plan on offering to stay and give her protection," announced Bracken.

There was a long pause before Nick spoke. "I don't like it, Bracken. We've had peace for months now. I don't want us to lose that."

"The pack as a whole won't be affected," said Zander. "We're not proposing taking her to our territory. We're talking about extending our stay at the B&B. If something happens while we're here, we can intervene."

"She doesn't need protection from shifters; she's up against her own kind, not ours," Nick pointed out.

"Yeah, and she's up against her own kind because she's helping one of ours," said Bracken. "It would be all kinds of wrong to walk away from that when our very presence could make them hesitate to harm her. If we went home and then later found out something had happened to her, I'd feel like a complete bastard."

Nick sighed. "They might not have any intention of harming her. They may just stick with trying to scare her."

"You're right," allowed Bracken. "If they don't try to harm her, great—it means we weren't needed. We'd just like to be here in case we are."

"Is there something else going on that I don't know about? You seem pretty insistent on helping her."

"Neither of us are involved with her, if that's what you're asking. She's not my or Zander's type. She has gorgeous eyes, though. I'm not really a guy who looks at eyes, but they're a seriously striking blue—if you saw them, you'd know what I mean. Great legs too."

Clenching his jaw because, yeah, he didn't like hearing Bracken talk about Gwen's eyes or legs, Zander said, "Gwen's situation is bad. The humans trying to intimidate her are rich and have the kind of social power that allow them to go unpunished by the local police and judge, so they're not likely to help her if these bastards step up their game. She needs protection. Maybe if she has it, the victim will feel safe enough to come forward again."

"I don't like to bring up bad memories, Nick," began Bracken, tone sensitive, "but think about what happened to Roni." Nick's sister had almost been gang-raped by humans long ago. One of the bastards had recorded the foiled attack, and that footage was later featured on a fucked-up website where prejudiced humans uploaded videos of crimes against shifters and actually *rated* them. "It's not the same as what's happening here, I know that. You saved Roni; you had evidence to prove their guilt. But let's say that Roni hadn't had any help that day; let's say that there was a witness who was being harassed into backing off. Wouldn't you like to think that someone would have stuck up for her?"

"Gwen's not your sister," the Alpha rightly pointed out.

Zander balled his hand up into a fist. "But my sister was shot, and you know how that turned out."

"So, in a sense, this is about Shelby." After a long moment of silence, Nick exhaled heavily. "I'll allow it, providing you agree to keep me updated."

"That we can do," said Bracken.

"For the record, I still don't like this. Nonetheless, I'll back you on it. But only to a point. If things get too bad up there, you both need to come home. That's not a negotiation."

Bracken nodded. "Agreed."

"Good. Remember to keep me updated." The line went dead.

Leaning back in his chair, Zander tapped his fingers on the table. "I thought he'd put up more of a fight."

Bracken pulled out his own phone. "Nick's a good guy. He's also practical enough to know that Shaya would guilt-trip him into letting us stay if he didn't consent."

Watching Bracken's thumbs flying over the screen of his cell, Zander said, "You're texting Shiloh again, aren't you?" The female margay shifter was Harley's cousin.

Without looking up or stopping texting, he said, "Presumably, you've noticed she spends most of her time on her phone." He lifted his shoulders. "How else am I going to seduce her? Technology is my way in."

"Why would you put so much effort into seducing someone who doesn't like you? It's not even personal—she doesn't like anyone."

Bracken's mouth quirked. "She's warming up to me, I can tell."

"How can you tell?"

"The majority of her responses are threats and offensive comments."

"And you find this positive?"

"You've met Shiloh. She takes aloof to a *whole* new level. Instead of ignoring me, she insults and threatens me—she's trying to push me away. I'm telling you, she's warming up to me."

"Whatever. I need to call Shelby." Zander dialed her number, but he didn't put the call on speakerphone this time.

"Hey," she answered softly.

"Hey. Thought you might want to know what went down at the attorney's office. It turns out that Rory was helping Dale, spending time with him, trying to win his favor. Apparently, Dale didn't deem that help as worth anything more than a dollar."

"Oh, God," Shelby muttered, amused.

"The rest will be split between you and me."

"I'm guessing Rory lost his mind."

"You guessed right, so it's probably good that you weren't here."

She took what sounded like a cleansing breath. "Enough about that. Tell me what's been going on in your life."

They talked for a while. He didn't mention the Gwen situation, knowing Shelby would likely see how it paralleled her own—he didn't want to drag up old memories for her. Once Zander had ended the call, Bracken spoke.

"Well, I guess we should go find Gwen and offer our protection. You know, I can't help wondering . . ."

"What?" prodded Zander.

"I know what drives *us* to want to help her with this complex situation. But what drives *her* to want to help the shifter? Because considering the pressure she's under and how unsafe she must feel, there has to be something big driving her."

He's probably right, Zander thought. And now he himself was wondering the same thing.

CHAPTER FIVE

When the doorbell chimed, Gwen's stomach rolled. And she hated that. She shouldn't be anxious in her own home. She shouldn't react so strongly to the simple matter of someone being at the freaking door.

Although she very much doubted it was Brandt, since he surely wasn't stupid enough to announce his presence, she nonetheless slipped her hand into her pocket and fished out her knuckle stun gun before opening the front door. Her shoulders relaxed when she saw a familiar female who was biting her lip.

Stepping inside, Julie wrapped her arms around Gwen. "I know you didn't want me coming here in case I got caught in any cross fire, but I had to see you. Chase won't like it, but you're my sister." She glanced around, almost as if she expected him to jump out any second. She didn't fear Chase, but she disliked disappointing him.

"Let me just shut the door." Gwen closed it, tucked her stun gun in the pocket of her jeans, and then led her sister into the spacious living room. "You didn't need to come here. I'm okay, Jules."

"Of course you are," she said with a smile as they both sat on the sofa. "I've never known you to be anything else." She lowered her voice as she added, "I'm ashamed to say that, in your position, I probably would have backed down and changed my statement."

"You're not weak, Jules." Fragile in some ways and a little dependent, but not weak.

Julie shook her head. "Well, I'm not strong. Not like you. We had similar childhoods, but you let it make you stronger."

Gwen's gut burned at just the mere mention of her childhood. Flashes of memory flickered through her mind, despite fighting them. Her stepfather beating her mother, Hanna, with the satellite dish. Her mother cowering in the corner as he whacked her over the head with their anemic Christmas tree. Her stepfather shoving her out of the trailer so hard that Gwen banged her head on the cement block, just so he could "nail" her mom in peace. Bleeding, head throbbing, Gwen had sat outside among the broken bikes, empty cans, wrecked furniture, old tires, and foul-smelling trash . . . and it hadn't even occurred to her to ask for help, because no one would have given it.

Gwen pushed the memories away. "We both left our personal hellholes long ago. None of it matters now."

"It'll always matter," she said softly. "That kind of thing stays with you. Our moms were abused, but we were victims in our own way. How many times did you clean your mom up? How many times did you pick up glass and food from the floor because your stepfather had thrown stuff around? How many times did you help your mother dress because she could barely move she was in so much pain? She wouldn't even let you get her help. *I* was too scared and embarrassed to share my family secret."

It hadn't been embarrassment that kept Gwen quiet. Her mother had firmly stated that she'd lie and cover for the bastard if Gwen told her teachers. The main reason Gwen had kept her mouth shut was that she'd known her stepfather would take it out on her mother. She'd kept quiet to protect Hanna, but it hadn't *felt* like she was protecting her. It had felt like she was ignoring Hanna's pain and need for help . . . just like the neighbors who never called the police, no matter how loud the yelling or screaming got. Not that Hanna was entirely innocent. No, she was just as volatile and mercurial as the bastard, but she never raised a hand to anyone.

"Like I said, none of it matters now."

"Of course it does," Julie insisted. "Witnessing domestic violence is a type of abuse all on its own. Watching our moms be hurt and terrorized was something that hurt and terrorized us. It's a frightening and distressing experience, and it impacts every part of a person's—"

"That's your therapist talking."

Julie clasped her hand. "Speaking of Aidan, he wants to see you. He wants to help you through this. It's going to be a trying time for you. A little support, a friendly ear, would be good for you."

Gwen gritted her teeth. "I don't want or need anything from him."

She'd attended therapy years ago after Julie stated that she wouldn't go unless Gwen did. Gwen had never liked it or the therapist. Never liked his probing gaze or his insistence that she "needed" his help to heal. It had creeped her out, but not nearly as much as when he admitted that he'd "developed feelings" for her. He'd seemed completely shocked that she didn't feel the same way, and he hadn't been at all happy that she told him to stay away from her.

Gwen had never told Julie because Aidan seemed to be truly helping her, and God knew that Julie needed that. "I'm glad you feel he helps you. Therapy is a good thing, I know that. But it's not for everyone."

Julie held up her hands. "Okay. I'm just the messenger."

"Yeah, I know. You sounded exactly like him." It almost made her shudder.

"He was very specific about what he wanted me to say."

"Who?" asked Marlon as he entered the room.

"Aidan," replied Julie.

Marlon's mouth flattened. "Is that so?"

Julie tilted her head. "Why don't you like him?"

Marlon sank onto the sofa opposite them. "I have my reasons." One of which was that Gwen had told him about Aidan's creepy and wildly unprofessional declaration of love. Her foster brother was the only person who knew.

Shrugging the matter off, Julie turned to Gwen. "Anyway, I came here because . . . It should be easy to do the right thing, but we all know it doesn't always work that way, and I wanted you to know that I'm behind you on this."

Gwen patted her hand. "Thanks, Jules."

Julie went to speak, but then two large figures entered the room, their footsteps eerily silent. Julie tensed under Zander and Bracken's scrutiny—she wasn't comfortable around men, particularly ones so powerfully built.

Placing a reassuring hand on Julie's arm, Gwen spoke, "Mr. Devlin—"

"Zander," he reminded her, his gaze intense as it fixed on Gwen.

"Right. Zander. Do you need something?"

"Yeah." But he didn't elaborate.

"Can it wait? I'm sort of busy right now." And Gwen would rather not talk to him if he would insist on revisiting their earlier topic of conversation.

Julie leaned into Gwen and asked quietly, "Is everything okay?"

"Yes," Gwen assured her. "Julie, this is Zander and Bracken. They're guests here. Zander, Bracken, this is my big sister, Julie."

Julie forced a shaky smile. "It's nice to meet you both."

"Likewise," said Bracken.

Zander just nodded before sliding his gaze back to Gwen, and that puzzled her. Julie was exceptionally beautiful, and guys ogled her all the time. Bracken's eyes held a flicker of appreciation, but Zander didn't seem at all affected. Maybe he was gay. Yep, that must be it. Ah, how disappointing for females everywhere.

Julie stood and straightened her sweater. "I should be going."

Gwen grabbed her hand. "You can't leave without seeing Yvonne."

"She's cleaning the rooms on the third floor," said Marlon, rising. "I'll come up with you."

As her foster siblings headed up the stairs, Gwen arched a brow at Zander. "What can I help you with?"

His head tilted. "Actually, this conversation is more about how we can help you."

She blinked, confused.

Bracken stuffed his hands in his pockets. "What breed of shifter is Andie?"

"She's a cougar."

"But not part of a pride?" asked Bracken.

"She was raised by humans. I don't know how that came about, didn't ask. I figured it was her business. People didn't realize she was a shifter until she was a teenager. She was always quiet and kept to herself." Maybe because she'd known she was different and thought people wouldn't accept her once they found out, thought Gwen.

Zander moved closer. "When did she change her story?"

"About a week ago. She wants me to do the same thing, or to at least lie to the council."

Zander's eyes studied her face, as if she were a puzzle he was trying to solve. "But you're going to tell the truth. Why?"

Gwen gave a nonchalant shrug. "Sometimes people need others to speak up for them." She knew that better than most.

"We want to help," said Bracken.

Recalling their mention of a shelter, she puffed out a breath. "I guess Andie might go with you. I'd have to ask."

Bracken shook his head. "No, we want to help *you*. We're also prepared to place her somewhere safe until this is over. She'll be welcome to remain at the shelter indefinitely, if that's what she wants."

Gwen looked from one male to the other. “I don’t see how you can help me.” Or why they would, for that matter. “I’m not fighting shifters.”

“No,” said Zander, “you’re up against people who are anti-shifter. That’s bad. These people aren’t rational when it comes to us, and they often think they’re a law unto themselves. You might be human, but you’ve allied with a shifter in this matter—to those people you’re dealing with, you’re now just as bad as us.”

“I know that, but I also know that it’s not your problem. There’s no reason for you to make it yours. And, as I said, I don’t see how you could help me.”

“It’s unlikely that they’ll try to physically harm you if me and Bracken are here. They hate our kind, sure, but they also fear us. Typically, fear is at the root of their hatred.”

Gwen pursed her lips. “So . . . when you say you want to help me, you just mean you’ll stick around in the hope that your presence here will be a deterrence?”

“No,” began Bracken, “we mean that if anyone turns up here to give you shit, we’ll take care of it.”

Suspicious by nature, she searched for what their angle might be here, but she came up with nothing. “Why would you do that?”

“The same reason you’re helping Andie,” said Zander. “It’s the right thing to do.”

Yeah? She wasn’t convinced. Plenty of people had known that saving her mother from her stepfather would be the right thing to do, but they still hadn’t done it. She’d learned that people preferred to look the other way. Shifters weren’t the exception.

“Here’s what I know about shifters,” she said. “You’re exclusive. Private. Insular. You avoid getting involved in other people’s business—even if those people are fellow shifters. Am I wrong?”

A muscle in Zander’s cheek ticked. “No.”

“Yet, you’re offering to help me when it could switch their attention onto you and, by extension, your pack. You’re offering to help a lone shifter even though she has no connection whatsoever to you. Nothing about this situation would benefit you or your pack in any way or make it worth any trouble that it could cause you. I can’t, for the life of me, figure out why you’d care to involve yourselves.”

“Like I said, it’s the right thing to do.”

She narrowed her eyes at the note of offense in Zander’s tone . . . like she should feel guilty for believing he was anything less than honorable. “Don’t think I’m buying that open, harmless, easygoing act. You’re good at it, I’ll give you that, but I know a merciless predator when I see one. Merciless predators don’t help people for nothing, especially when they’re suspicious of them—and you are suspicious of me for some reason, I can sense it.” She tilted her head. “But then, you don’t strike me as the kind of guy who trusts anyone.”

More than a little discomforted—yet also begrudgingly impressed—by that very accurate assessment, Zander said, “You don’t strike me as the trusting type either.”

“I’m not. Right now, my gut’s telling me that you’re not being totally honest with me.”

Sensing that only the truth would gain him her cooperation, Zander said, “We know someone who’s been through a similar experience. The culprit got away with it. If someone had stood up for them the way you’re standing up for Andie, the end result might have been very different.”

For a long moment, Gwen said nothing. She wondered if he partially blamed himself for his friend not getting justice. If so, there was no self-recrimination in his tone. “The hearing doesn’t take place for another month. That’s four weeks.”

“I know how long a month is,” said Zander drily.

“Then you know it’s a lot of time to stay away from your pack. Surely you don’t want to spend all that time here.”

"It's been a long time since we had a vacation," said Bracken.

Sighing, she flicked back her bangs. "I'd need to speak to my family about your offer. I won't make the decision for them."

"Then talk to them." Zander stepped aside as she walked out of the room, toward the stairs. "Gwen?"

She glanced at him over her shoulder, brow raised in question.

"Don't let your suspicious nature make you reject help. With the way things are, like it or not, you're going to need it."

Once she'd disappeared up the stairs, Bracken said, "She's more perceptive than I gave her credit for."

Zander nodded. She'd seen right through his act, but she hadn't called him on it until now. He'd underestimated her. He wouldn't make that mistake again.

"It surprised me that she didn't jump at the chance of having our protection," said Bracken. "Kind of makes me wonder if she was let down by another person who should have protected her. She relies on herself."

"It's possible." More likely *probable*, really. Zander sank onto the sofa, on the exact spot where Gwen had been sitting. She called Julie her sister, but his nose told him they weren't blood relatives. Also, Marlon wasn't biologically related to either of the females or Yvonne. That meant these people were either Gwen's foster family or adopted family. "We might as well wait here. Something tells me that Yvonne will be down here soon enough."

It was a good twenty minutes before Yvonne finally entered the room, alone. She looked from Zander to Bracken as she spoke. "My Gwen says you're offering to stay and help with the Brandt situation." And she sounded no more trusting than Gwen had. "Why?"

"What kind of people would we be if we didn't offer to help?" asked Bracken.

"Normal," said Yvonne.

"We don't know Andie," began Bracken, "but she's one of us—a shifter. She needs help, and the only person doing anything about that is Gwen. Your daughter could end up being the target of extremists, and believe me when I say they are not people whose attention you want."

Yvonne rubbed her arm. "We've seen the things they're capable of on CNN. I don't understand that type of prejudice and brutality. As Gwen says, it's all senseless. You think the Moores would contact the extremists and tell them what she's doing so they'll come after her?"

"Honestly, I doubt it," replied Bracken. "Even other anti-shifter humans avoid the extremists now—they're out of control. Plus, wherever the extremists are, The Movement soon follows." The Movement was a group of shifters that had formed to retaliate against the extremists. "No one wants to be stuck in the middle of their ongoing battle. Still, it's smart to envision the worst-case scenario so that you can be prepared for it."

"What is it you want from her in exchange for your help?"

"Her cooperation would be good." Bracken's mouth curved. "She fought us on accepting our help."

"My Gwen doesn't trust easy. And she likes to take care of herself. She's well liked around here by most people, so it's rare that anyone bothers her. Especially since she has a paranoid eccentric for an uncle. But the Moores don't care, and I doubt they'll care if she has the protection of two shifters—they regard your species as inferior."

"Yeah, we got that."

"My concern is that your presence here could rile the Moores enough to make this worse for her. Brandt won't back down; he's scared of going before the shifter council. If your support does aggravate the situation, are you going to then disappear and leave her to bear the weight? Or will you stick by her until the end? Because if you can't stick by her, you should stay out of the matter."

She's right, thought Zander. "We'll be here for as long as the situation requires us to be." And he meant it. Lack of empathy or not, he found himself *wanting* to help Gwen.

Leery of staying, his wolf released a low, disgruntled rumble—a tame response from his usually bold wolf who had no compunction about clawing the fuck out of Zander if he wasn't getting his own way.

Yvonne gave them a slow nod of respect. "Then we're in your debt."

Leaning against the doorjamb, Zander watched as Gwen cleaned the newly vacated room. It wasn't as spacious as his room, but it was just as warm and restful. He'd offered to help, but she'd politely declined his offer—and damn if that stiff politeness didn't still grate on him.

Once Yvonne had agreed to let him and Bracken stay, Zander had tracked down Gwen to ask her some questions while Bracken took a shower. Unfortunately, Gwen wasn't being very forthcoming. He got the sense that it was instinctual for her to keep her business private, and she was finding it difficult to push past that. He also got the sense that she liked keeping people at a distance.

"We can't help if we don't have the full picture, Gwen. Marlon said that the Moores have tried pretty much everything to make you back down. What exactly did he mean by that?"

Finishing stripping the linen from the duvet, she balled it up and dumped it in a basket. "At first, it was just dumb pranks. Egging my truck, toilet-papering the yard, and calling the house—sometimes no one would speak, other times a voice would threaten me to keep my mouth shut if I wanted an easy life. Once, he even snatched the clean laundry that was drying on the line and dumped it in the marsh. Another time, he left a dead skunk on the hood of my truck. He and his friends were watching from the other side of the lot, laughing. It was all juvenile shit." Tugging off a pillowcase, she added, "But then, it got worse."

"Worse how?"

She threw the pillowcase in the basket. "Someone emptied my bank account, canceled my cell phone contract, maxed out my credit cards—shit like that." Gwen thought it was lucky she hadn't kept much of her savings in the bank. Donnie taught them to hide their money, not to trust banks. If she hadn't followed his paranoid advice, she'd have lost it all. "Of course, I can't prove that the Moores had anything to do with it, but I know by the call I got from Brandt, passing on his sympathies to my situation, that his family was behind it."

Bastards. "He ever assault you?"

The dark note in Zander's tone made her look at him. "He came close to hitting me with a bat a few days ago when I stopped him from vandalizing my truck. Donnie scared him off."

Zander bit back a growl. Even his wolf didn't like that she'd almost been assaulted. "What did the Moores do to terrorize Andie?"

"Way worse stuff than they did to me. They threw bricks through her windows, spray-painted her house, slashed her tires, tried breaking into her home. Brandt and his friends always had alibis, but I doubt Colt would have acted even if they hadn't claimed to have them."

Zander watched her apply the fresh bed linen. She had very elegant hands. Pretty and smooth. Hands that would look so fucking good wrapped around his cock. Shoving that image out of his head, he asked, "I don't foresee the Moores backing down at any point. You?"

"No, they won't back down." And neither would Gwen. "I had a thought earlier. I was wondering if . . ."

"If?" he prompted.

Gwen shook her head, deciding it wasn't important. "Never mind."

"Tell me."

"No, really, forget it."

Zander walked toward her. "Tell me."

"It doesn't matter."

But it did, because one thing that made Zander crazy was people not finishing their sentences. "What were you going to say?"

"It doesn't matter," she repeated.

"Will you just fucking tell me." It wasn't a question, it was a demand.

"Not if you're going to fucking swear at me. A woman is entitled to her own private thoughts, you know. If you really want to stick your nose in something, grab a book." Done with the bedding, she lifted the basket of dirty linen. "I need to take this downstairs and then get to Half 'n' Half. My shift starts soon."

Zander rolled back his shoulders, shaking off his irritation. "Bracken and I will accompany you. We'll eat and play pool while we wait."

"None of the Moores will go there. Not only because Chase would throw them out, but because they wouldn't want to be seen in a place so *common*."

"They're getting desperate. Desperate people do stupid things."

Like turning up at my house drunk with a bat and cans of spray paint, she thought. "All right. I'll meet you downstairs in ten minutes. Be ready."

Ten minutes later, Zander stood near the front door with Bracken and Marlon as Gwen came jogging down the stairs. His cock instantly hardened at the sight of her smooth, bare legs. He gave her a severe frown, blocking her path to the door. "You need to put on some jeans." He didn't care how it sounded, didn't care that it would hint at just how attracted he was to her.

Her brows lifted. "Sorry?"

"You need to cover up those legs."

Gwen blinked, unsure if she should be offended or not. "Why, what's wrong with them?"

Forcing his jaw to unclench, Zander said, "You can't tell me you haven't noticed how much people stare at them."

Actually, she didn't recall people paying much attention to them. "They're just legs."

Marlon chuckled. "They're lethal. I've seen people bump into shit because they're so busy looking at your legs."

She shook her head. "Whatever."

Zander stepped into her personal space. "Let me ask you a question: Are your tips better when you wear shorts like those?" Her expression answered that question for him, and he watched realization dawn on her face, quickly followed by disbelief. "Cover them up."

Gwen looked at him, lost. "Why?"

"We just established why," he clipped. "People stare at your legs. I don't want them staring at your legs."

"Because . . . ?"

"I just don't."

Given that he was gay, Gwen had no idea what his issue could possibly be. "You're being weird. I don't have time for weird." With that, she brushed past him and strode out of the house, shouting a farewell to Marlon.

Bracken beat her to the car, an amused grin on his face, and opened the rear door for her. Then he hopped into the passenger side just as Zander slid into the driver's seat. They rode in silence . . . until Bracken starting chuckling. Zander shot him a dark look, but the other wolf just kept on laughing to himself.

"I'm not finding anything fucking amusing," Zander growled, but Bracken just laughed harder.

Soon enough, they arrived at Half 'n' Half. As they exited the SUV, Gwen noticed Brandt standing on the other side of the parking lot with his friends. He glared right at her, but that glare morphed into a confused frown as he looked at Zander and Bracken.

"That Brandt?" Zander asked.

"Yep," she replied. "Don't approach him. Even if you handed his ass to him, he'd be smug because he'd managed to cause a scene outside my place of work."

It went against Zander's nature not to act, but he knew that if he didn't respect her wishes, she'd insist that he not come with her in the future. He wanted her to trust him. So he contented himself with doing as his wolf had done—he merely tossed a snarl at the human.

Inside Half 'n' Half, Zander claimed the same booth as last time. After taking their orders, Gwen disappeared. Wearing a knowing smirk, Bracken made a show of ogling her as she walked away, which nearly got Zander's fist planted in his face.

"On the one hand, Z, I'm glad she didn't listen to you and cover up. On the other hand, a part of me doesn't like that every guy here will be imagining having those legs wrapped around his waist while he—"

"Don't," Zander bit out. He really didn't want to hit his friend.

"I should have seen this coming. Physically, she's not your type. But she has the other qualities you go for. She's smart. Confident. Capable. Stubborn enough to deal with you and your bullshit." Putting down his beer, Bracken sobered. "On a serious note, don't act on whatever you're feeling. She's got a shitload of stuff going on right now. I don't think she's got time for someone who is awful at being part of a couple even when the relationship isn't serious.

"Don't get me wrong, Z, there's nothing I'd like more than for you to let someone in your life. You've been on your own too long, and you're getting too used to it—and yeah, your wolf's partially to blame for that. But this would be a really bad time to do anything about it."

Honest with himself about his limitations, Zander could admit that he'd never been good at relationships. It wasn't just because his wolf fought him so hard. The simple truth was that he'd never found relationships fulfilling. Probably because he typically didn't connect with people.

"So, we're agreed that you'll just content yourself with staring at her legs?"

Zander sighed. "Are we really having this conversation?"

"It would seem so."

"Well, it's ending. Now."

"Fine." Bracken took another swig of his beer and stood. "I'll be five minutes. I need to—"

"I really don't want to know what you'll be doing in the restroom, Brack." Ignoring his pack mate's chuckle, Zander chugged down more of his own beer. That was when he scented Gwen approaching, and his wolf retreated again.

Gwen set two plates of food on the table. "Here. Enjoy." She was about to walk away, but then a large hand rested on her leg. She froze, watching as Zander used his thumb to scoop a little red sauce from her thigh. She had no idea why the movement seemed almost . . . sensual.

"You had something on your leg," he told her. "Of course, if you'd been wearing jeans . . ."

"Are we still on that?" she snapped, impatient.

"Yeah, we are."

Gwen stifled a smile at his hard tone. "Hmm. I see."

"See what?"

"You're one of *those* people."

"What people?"

"You can't let it go when you don't get your own way. You can't just chuck shit in the 'Fuck It' bucket and get on with your day."

His mouth curved, and he shrugged one shoulder. "I like to get my own way."

Well, Gwen could see that. She could also see that although he sat alone, he didn't *look* alone. Maybe because he dominated his space so completely. He appeared at ease with his own company, not lost or lonely the way many pack animals did. "I realize that shifters are tactile, but could you move your hand?"

"You don't need to be so uneasy. I won't bite. Yet."

"Whatever," she scoffed, going for aloof. He slowly removed his hand and then licked the sauce from his thumb, holding her eyes the entire time. She swallowed hard. "Enjoy your meal."

"I will." Zander's eyes followed her as she walked away, only shifting from her when Bracken returned and blocked his view.

Immediately, Bracken dug into his food. "Damn, this is good. I wish we could take the chef home."

The door swung open, and in walked a male who, going by his uniform, was the sheriff—the same male who'd been standing on Gwen's porch when he and Bracken first arrived at the B&B.

Zander noted that none of the patrons greeted the sheriff warmly. They either gave him a simple nod or avoided his gaze. Most of them sneered at his back. It seemed that the guy wasn't well respected at all. Maybe if he wasn't looking down his nose at everyone, it would be different.

Zander tensed when the sheriff made a beeline for Gwen. Spotting him, she simply greeted, "Sheriff." There wasn't an ounce of respect in the title, which was probably why the human narrowed his eyes.

"I heard two strangers are hanging around you." The sheriff adjusted his gun belt. "Yvonne said they're wolf shifters. They're staying at the B&B for a while, and they've offered to help with the Brandt situation." Suspicion laced every word.

Zander suspected that Brandt had contacted the sheriff, which led him to then call Yvonne. She'd probably told the sheriff they were shifters in the hope that it would scare him and the Moores.

Gwen nodded. "Yep."

"What do they want in return? No shifter does something for nothing."

That was true for the most part, thought Zander.

"They never asked for anything," said Gwen. "*Some* people actually help those who are being wrongly persecuted. A novel thing for you, Colt, I'm sure."

A muscle in Colt's cheek ticked. "Are you paying them?"

"Mostly with sex," she said, deadpan. "Turns out shifters *are* fond of threesomes."

The sheriff's lips thinned. "Don't be crude, Gwen. Why would they help you?"

"Ask them. They're over there." She gestured at their booth.

"Sheriff's on his way over," Zander said only loud enough for Bracken to hear.

"Yeah, I heard him and Gwen talking." Bracken's response wasn't surprising. No matter how absorbed he was by something, the enforcer wolf was always aware of his surroundings.

The sheriff arrived at their booth, planting his feet. "I'm the sheriff here." Like that was some sort of achievement. The noise level of the entire place lowered as people subtly tried to eavesdrop.

Zander's wolf took an instant dislike to him and stalked forward, teeth bared.

With a fry, Bracken gestured at himself. "I'm Bracken. This is Zander."

The sheriff's mouth twisted. "Where are you from?"

"California," Bracken replied.

"I see. What pack?"

"The Mercury Pack."

The human adjusted his hat. "So, you'll be staying until the Brandt situation is resolved."

"That's right."

"Sadly for you, I don't approve of that." His eyes narrowed as they danced from Bracken to Zander. "Not because you're shifters, but because this situation is already heated—I want things to calm down, not worsen. Shifters aren't known to be diplomatic. You'll just aggravate the entire situation."

Zander leaned back in the booth. "Sadly for you, your disapproval means nothing to us."

"Not a thing," confirmed Bracken.

The sheriff's eyes tightened. "It should, considering what position I hold in this town. I could have you thrown out."

"You could *try*," said Zander. "It won't work out well for you."

Bracken's mouth curled. "I'm kind of hoping he does try, Z. My wolf's itching for some action. We should probably cut this guy some slack though, right? I mean, he must be under a lot of pressure right now. He has those Moore people bugging him to side with them."

"Yeah, Brack, you're right. If he had even a little of Gwen's strength, he might just be able to pull his head out of his ass and stand up to the pricks." Zander tilted his head, staring at the sheriff. "I guess you're one of those 'If you can't beat 'em, join 'em' guys, right?"

His face flushed. Eyes hard, he cast them each a menacing glare. "I want you both out of my town by tomorrow morning."

"And I want you to keep the Moores away from Gwen." Zander shrugged. "We don't always get what we want, do we? There's no sense in pushing this. We don't answer to your laws. That shiny badge means nothing to me."

For a long, tense moment, the human just glared at them, face like a thunderstorm. Then he crossed to the door and wrenched it open, yanking out his cell phone as he did so. Zander noticed that many of the patrons smirked, happy to see their sheriff's butt shot down.

"He's no doubt calling the Moores," said Bracken.

Gwen's scent slid over Zander moments before she appeared—and, predictably, Zander's wolf annoyingly retreated again. Sighing, she scratched her nape. "That was pretty much how I expected things to go."

"He's not going to make us leave," Zander told her, but she didn't look convinced. As she moved to leave, he grabbed her hand. "Hey, we're not going anywhere."

"Good," she said, but she still didn't seem entirely certain of that.

CHAPTER SIX

At the end of Gwen's shift, Zander drove her home with Bracken riding shotgun again. Back at the B&B, they all parted ways, and Zander went straight to his room. He made himself a coffee and sat on the balcony, but he couldn't relax. He felt irritable and restless. The same tension rode his wolf, who paced within him, feeding Zander's edginess.

He closed his eyes, seeking calm and peace. He concentrated on the feel of the light breeze on his skin and the sounds of the crickets and—

"*Zander.*" The floaty whisper was accompanied by the brush of fingers across his forehead.

Eyes snapping open, he jumped to his feet. No one. Like last time, there was no one there. And, just like last time, he didn't *feel* alone.

Deciding to go for a run—no, he wasn't freaked out and fleeing from nothing—Zander headed downstairs. But he didn't go to the front door. No, he stalked into the kitchen as a familiar scent caught his attention. And there she was, cleaning the coffee maker.

Tense now for a totally different reason, his wolf withdrew. Well, at least he'd stopped pacing.

Somehow sensing she wasn't alone, she looked over her shoulder. "Hey."

Zander planted a hand on either side of the doorjamb. "Hey."

"Going for a run or something?"

"Yes." He looked at the now–immaculately clean coffee machine. "Do you ever do anything but work?"

Brow furrowing, she turned to fully face him. "Sure. I was just cleaning up after myself."

"What do you do when you're not working?"

Gwen gave a little shrug. "Stuff."

"What sort of stuff?"

"Just stuff."

"Like what?" he persisted.

Gwen tensed as he walked farther into the room. His gaze was locked on hers, searching her eyes for . . . something. She didn't like it. He looked too hard, watched her too carefully. And her mouth dried up under the scrutiny of those brooding winter-gray eyes.

Even with all that distance between them, she felt overwhelmingly aware of him. Her stomach knotted at the vision of him standing there, head up, chest out, feet wide apart. That powerful, authoritative stance totally revved her engines.

She didn't *want* to react to this guy she had no chance of having. But he was the living embodiment of raw sex appeal, and she was apparently helpless against it. Need churned in her stomach, her blood thickened, and her nipples beaded.

"Tell me," he coaxed.

"You wouldn't get it. You're a shifter; you guys are all about action." And she'd sound utterly dull to him, which wasn't on her agenda.

"Maybe I would. Tell me."

Fine, it wasn't like she had to impress him. "I just like to sit outside. Sometimes on the porch. Sometimes on the swing. Sometimes on my balcony. I find peace in just sitting around, soaking in the view and the quiet, and admiring the wildlife. Not thinking, not talking, not listening to trivial conversation, just *being*. That will no doubt seem boring to you, but—"

"It doesn't. When I'm on pack territory, I like to sit on my porch and just be alone. It's not that I need time to reflect and meditate or some shit like that. Sitting back, listening to sounds of nature, is a good way for me to wind down." When he was alone, he could relax and recharge. You didn't get much time alone when you were part of a pack, though.

Zander's eyes involuntarily dropped to her mouth. How hadn't he noticed how lush it was before now? He couldn't help picturing her on her knees as he wrapped her braid around his fist and fed her his cock. "Do you like working here and at Half 'n' Half, or do you just do it to support your family?"

She tilted her head. "You're pretty nosy, aren't you?"

"Only when something interests me."

Gwen did a double take. "I interest you?" It came out a skeptical statement.

"Yeah."

Bullshit. She narrowed her eyes. "What do you want?" He had to be sweetening her up to get something.

Zander's lips twitched. "So suspicious. I thought we were just talking."

"No, you were quizzing me."

"Go ahead and ask me a question."

She lifted her chin. "All right. I always wondered . . . You don't have to answer if it's personal, but . . . does it hurt to shift?"

"A little, but not enough to matter."

"Do you have to do it, like, daily?"

"I don't have to, but it's good to let my wolf free often, especially when he's somewhere new—he needs to know the territory to feel secure." Zander closed some of the distance between them in two slow strides. "My wolf likes it here; he likes the marsh." She smiled at that. Not a distantly polite smile—a real, genuine smile that lit up her face and should have knocked him on his ass. How had he ever thought her anything close to plain? She was stunning.

"I've always loved the marshland," she said. "It's peaceful. Lots to see and do."

"I guess you've explored every inch of it over the years."

"To Yvonne's consternation, yes."

"Maybe you can give me a tour." He'd seen boats at the dock.

"It's mostly Marlon who gives tours," she said, smile slipping from genuine to professional as she seemed to subconsciously adopt her receptionist tone. "We hold them on Mondays, Wednesdays—"

"Don't do that."

A line formed between her brows. "What?"

Zander prowled toward her, backing her against the fridge. "I don't want to talk to Gwen the receptionist. I want to talk to you." But she looked like she had no idea what he meant.

As he pulled the tie out of her hair and began loosening her braid, Gwen tried jerking away. He didn't even seem to notice. Shit, she really needed him to back up. She didn't want him to sense how fiercely her body reacted to him. "What are you doing?" And why wasn't she slapping him or something?

"You always braid it."

She frowned at the softly spoken complaint. "Is playing with people's hair something you do often?"

"No." Zander slid his fingers through the glossy cinnamon-brown curtain of silk. He almost moaned. It felt decadently soft against his skin, sending little electric shocks to his nerve endings. He expected his wolf to pull his usual shit and snarl at Zander for paying such attention to a female. This time, the wolf stayed in his hidey hole.

The beast didn't seem happy with the situation, but he'd apparently decided to stay out of it.

Gwen stood completely still as Zander toyed with her hair with a look of concentration on his face, like he was utterly absorbed by it. Her mouth twitched. "You're making me think of a cat with a ball of yarn."

His eyes slid to hers. "A cat?" He gave a slight punishing tug on her hair.

"Ow." But she chuckled. She got the feeling they were . . . playing. She knew shifters loved to play.

Zander brought her hair to his face and inhaled deeply. *Vanilla and coconut.* "Smells almost as good as your scent."

"I'm not going to ask what I smell like." But she was curious.

"You smell . . . tempting." Zander hadn't meant to growl it, but it was hard not to when the spice of need was currently warming her scent. Even his wolf was affected.

"Tempting? That must be weird for you, considering you're gay."

"What?"

She winced. "Sorry, were you planning to stay in the closet a while longer? I won't tell anyone, I swear. Although, honestly, you shouldn't be embarrassed to tell people. There's nothing wrong with being gay."

Zander almost gaped. "I'm not gay." Where the fuck had she gotten that idea?

"Okay."

He clenched his jaw at her placatory tone. "I'm not gay."

"Like I said, okay. We can forget this conversation ever happened."

Zander pressed his body against hers, shoving his rock-hard cock against her. "If I was gay, would I want to take you upstairs to my room and fuck you raw? Would I want to know what every inch of you tastes like?"

Gwen swallowed, taken aback. "I guess it would depend on how gay you were." Right then, there was something on his face she'd never expected to see—sheer unadulterated need. Just that look had her senses flaring to life.

"Not gay, Gwen. But I should still let you walk away." Zander didn't like getting involved with humans. They didn't always understand the ways of shifters. They didn't always understand that casual sex wasn't taboo to his kind, which meant that humans sometimes read more into it. Also, shifter sex could be rough and intense; humans were physically weaker and could be hurt easily.

None of those things held him back at that moment. It was something else. Something he couldn't quite name—a primitive warning of danger that made no sense but sure as fuck gave him pause. Still, as she stared back at him with eyes that glittered with a need that matched his own, it was so fucking hard to let her go. Somehow, he managed to force his hands to release her hair, but it was a few moments before he could force himself to back up.

Gwen rolled back her shoulders, a little shaken by the heat in his eyes and just how much it seemed to physically *hurt* that he'd let go, but she wouldn't let him see that. "Have a good night and enjoy your run."

Zander narrowed his eyes. The words were cool, calm . . . like he hadn't just had her trapped between him and the fridge. Like there wasn't so much sexual tension in the air that it sat heavy on his chest. And that just pissed him off.

He took in her scent, needing it even as it drove him crazy. The spice of arousal was still there, just as compelling as the tension that pulsed between them. A tension that was electric. Hot. Basic. So powerful, it was crushing. It had him in a tight grip and was heating his blood like a fever, making his cock so hard it hurt. And as her even pearly-white teeth dug into that lower lip he wanted to bite, something in him just snapped.

"Fuck." He was on her, hands sifting through her hair as he ravaged her mouth. She tasted of coffee and cream, and he needed more. He angled her head, going deeper, exploring every crevice of her mouth. She kissed him back, fingers digging into his shoulders . . . but there was a hesitancy there—he didn't like it, wanted it gone.

Growling, he snaked his hand under her thigh and curled her leg around him, groaning at the feel of that soft skin. He rocked his hips into hers, grinding his cock against her, swallowing her gasp. She didn't shy away. She tightened her leg around him, drawing him closer. Yeah, that was what he wanted.

Fuck, he couldn't get enough of her taste. Couldn't stop touching her. She had to use some kind of lotion because he'd never felt skin this soft. He wanted to lick it. Suck it. Mark it. Wanted to be sure no other male dared to touch her.

Gwen let her head fall back as he kissed his way down to her neck. She gasped as his teeth grazed her pulse. Then he bit it. *Hard.* Was he marking her? She hoped not. She didn't entirely understand the whole marking thing, but she knew shifters were possessive beings, and they marked what they didn't want to share. It should have snapped her out of the sexual fog, but she was too far gone.

She'd never known anything like this. Zander didn't kiss, he feasted. Every flick of his tongue, every nip of his teeth, every tug on her hair, every knowing touch of his hands—it was all a ruthless demand for more. No one had ever made her feel so wanted, so needed.

His powerful body was aggressive and dominant as it pushed against hers, crowding her, reminding her how much stronger he was. But she wasn't scared. Her frustrated body screamed with the need for more. His touch somehow both soothed the ache and drove her wild.

Hell, no wonder there were shifter groupies out there. She no longer judged them. *At all.*

Zander snapped open the buttons of her shorts, shoved his hand down her panties, and smoothly thrust a finger inside her. He groaned. "So fucking wet." Curving his finger just right, he worked her pussy hard, greedily swallowing every moan, loving the way she clawed at his back. "Come for me, Gwen. Come hard. Now." He caught her strangled cry with his mouth. As her slick pussy rippled around his finger, he wished like fuck he was deep inside her. He *had* to have her right then.

Gwen's heart jumped as she heard him unzipping his fly. Awesome. She was about to shove down her shorts and panties when a chiming sound filled the room. Zander swore against her mouth.

She blinked, dazed, as he backed up and fished his phone out of his pocket. And as the lust fogging her mind completely cleared, she wanted to curse. She was in her kitchen, where anyone could walk in and see her having a fumble against the fridge. Not smart. But, honestly, she probably wouldn't be regretting it if it wasn't for the way her throbbing pussy ached to be filled and fucked.

She fastened her fly and, hoping to look dignified, wiped all emotion from her face as she calmly said, "I'll leave you to take your call."

Zander watched as she walked past him, the image of nonchalance. "I'm gonna want more, Gwen." She didn't even break stride—just headed down the hallway and up the stairs. Cursing, he looked down to see Nick's name flashing on the screen of his cell. Zander answered, "Yeah?"

"Thought you might want to know that, as you predicted, Rory's being an asshole."

Fuck.

The next morning, footsteps along the tiled kitchen floor were quickly followed by a dreamy sigh. "Damn, Devlin has a great butt."

Returning spices to the revolving spice rack, Gwen flicked Marlon a brief glance. “Mmm-hmm.”

“And those abs are impressive—you can see them right through his shirt. I briefly considered spilling coffee on him to see if he'd whip it off and I could get a good look at what was beneath.”

Gwen widened her eyes. “You might want to lower your volume,” she hissed. “The guy's a shifter; he could hear you.”

“Over the dishwasher and the range-hood fan? I don't think so. I *do* think you should jump him.”

She did a double take. “I'm sorry?”

He shrugged. “In your shoes, I would have. Gwen, the guy likes you.”

Grabbing the broom, she began to sweep the floor as she quietly spoke. “I thought he was gay.”

Marlon looked at her like she'd suggested stripping naked and having a mud fight. “Why would you think that?”

“He barely paid any attention to Julie. That's not normal.”

Marlon's expression softened. “Aw, sweetie, not all guys want to use you to get to Julie.”

“I know that. But he didn't even take a moment to ogle her. What straight male wouldn't be attracted to Julie?”

“She's beautiful, sure, but so are you. Julie's beautiful in an in-your-face way. With you, it's more understated, but it's still there. Me and Julie always say we wish we had your eyes. And your skin—it tans easy and looks so smooth.” He gave her a stern look. “I don't like that you put yourself down.”

“I'm not doing that. I don't think I'm ugly, but I know I'm not beautiful either. I'm not the kind of girl who's someone's type. Zander could have anyone. Until last night, he didn't show a lick of interest in me.”

His eyes twinkled, and she wanted to slap herself for saying too much. Marlon skidded into her space. “What happened last night?”

"Nothing."

"Gwen, don't make me ask Zander. You know I will."

He *so* would. "It was just a kiss. No big deal."

"No big deal? And yet, you're avoiding him this morning."

"I am not." She totally was.

"And you ate junk food for breakfast—you only do that when something's bugging you. On a side note, you need to find another form of comfort. I've told you before, you are what you eat."

She threw him a dirty look. "That must be why you're such a dick."

"Ho, ho, ho, that was bitchy." He kissed her cheek, laughing. "You're all prickly because you don't like how close to the truth I am. Admit it, the kiss *was* a big deal."

"It was not."

"Then go collect whatever empty plates or mugs are left. I'll finish cleaning up." It was a dare.

She straightened her shirt and handed him the broom. "Okay. I will."

"Of course you will, because it was no big deal." He swept out a hand toward the doorway. *Bastard.*

Grabbing a tray, she headed into the dining room.

"Rory did *what*?"

Zander forked his last piece of bacon. "Put firecrackers in one of the large tin barrels around the construction site—the echoes were loud, and the builders thought it was gunshots and dove for cover." And since the construction site was the pack's partially built motel, all the Mercury members were exceptionally pissed. Particularly since the sounds could be heard from the main lodge and had terrified the pups.

The pack had done the emergency drill, hiding the weaker members while the others went to deal with the threat . . . only to realize that someone had been fucking with them. Knowing Rory as well as he did, Zander suspected the guy had watched from afar as the pack rallied to fight. He'd no doubt found it hilarious.

Bracken chugged down some coffee. "Nick's sure it was Rory?"

"Caught him on the security cameras." The pack had cameras all over their territory. "Jesse watched the footage. The figure was dressed in black, wearing a cap and sunglasses, but he's pretty sure it was Rory. There's no other person who'd want to toy with us for their own amusement." That was what Rory was doing—it was what he always did when he didn't get his way. He'd keep on doing it until he *did* get his way.

"Fucker. Has he been detained yet?"

Zander ate his bacon before answering. "Derren, Ally, and Jesse went to his address, but he wasn't there. His closet and drawers were empty, and the apartment was a mess. It looked like he'd packed up and left in a hurry."

"He's probably staying in a hotel somewhere." Bracken leaned back in his chair. "I doubt he's still here in Oregon. It makes no sense for him to go back and forth. I doubt he knows you're still here either, or he'd play his games near the B&B."

Zander's gaze sliced to the doorway as Gwen entered. Instantly, the memory of their little encounter leaped to his mind. His cock twitched as he recalled her taste, her raspy moans, how hot her pussy was, and the feel of her body perfectly molded to his.

He'd dreamed of her last night, dreamed of his hands fisted in her hair as he fucked her hard and deep. It had felt unbelievably real. But then he'd woken, full and aching—and seriously pissed off that it had been no more than a dream.

Bracken exhaled heavily. "Okay, what did you do?"

Zander slowly cut his gaze back to him. "Do?"

"Yesterday, you were looking at her like you wanted to know what she tasted like. Now you're looking at her like you already know, and you just want another taste."

"I didn't fuck her." But it hadn't been for lack of trying.

"I didn't ask what you *didn't* do."

"Drop it, Brack."

"I told you not to start anything with her."

"And we both know you were using reverse psychology."

Bracken looked ready to object, but then he sighed. "All right, maybe I did want you to make a move on her—*eventually*, when things had settled down. Now is not a good time. And you should bear in mind that she's human. She may not have the same casual attitude toward sex that we do, and she's not used to our level of intensity. As dominant males go, you're not very controlling. You keep *yourself* tightly controlled, but that's different. Still, my guess is you'll seem very demanding and controlling to Gwen, since she's not used to our ways. You'll need to take things slow."

Maybe he was right, but Zander knew there was no point in fighting himself on this or in trying to make himself wait for her. It wouldn't work. He was too fucking hungry for her.

He needed to know what every inch of her tasted like, how it felt to be deep inside her, and just how good those legs would feel curled around him. In his dream, he'd watched her come, heard her scream. That wasn't enough. It was never going to be enough. He wanted the real thing.

"You're not going to back off, are you?"

"No." It was too late for that.

Bracken pushed his empty plate aside. "I have to wonder what it's like to be a person who's so sure of their choices. Once you make up your mind, you never doubt your decision. You stick with it. Normally, I admire that. But in *this* instance, you've made the wrong decision, and you need to reevaluate it." He leaned forward. "Give her some space. Revisit the whole thing later."

Draining his coffee mug, Zander placed it on the coaster. "Are you done now?"

"Look, I get that you're your own man, but she's—"

"You're done."

"I'm not, actually. What about your wolf? You can't tell me he's going to like your decision."

"He's not pushing me to leave her alone. He's not interfering at all . . . it's like he's detached himself from the situation." And Zander was baffled by it. "You could be worrying for nothing. She might not want to be involved with anyone right now."

"No," allowed Bracken, "but rejection doesn't faze you."

He was right. Zander couldn't recall ever being personally threatened by criticism or rejection. He was comfortable with who he was, despite his faults.

Jasmine, orange blossoms, and wild berries.

The scent swirled around him moments before Gwen appeared at the table, tray in hand . . . and his wolf returned to his hidey hole.

"Morning," she said with a smile, but it was that formal smile that he didn't like. She stacked the plates and cutlery on the tray, cool as a fucking cucumber. No nervousness, no awkwardness, no blushing. Her hands were perfectly steady, her expression was calm, and her voice was even. And damn if that didn't rankle. Zander wanted her to be as affected as he was.

"More coffee?" she asked.

"I'm good," said Bracken.

Zander gave a quick shake of the head before asking, "You working at Half 'n' Half tonight?"

"Nope. I only work there three days a week." Then she was gone.

Smiling, Bracken sank into his chair. "Huh. Well, whatever happened between you two doesn't seem to be on her radar, does it?"

Ignoring Zander's glare, he went on, "Damn, it seems like you didn't make much of an impression, Z. You must be losing your touch."

Zander glowered at him. "You always were an annoying motherfucker."

"Hey, is that any way to speak to one of your best friends?"

"Couldn't care less."

Bracken just chuckled.

A little while later, Zander went into the kitchen to find Gwen with a small sheet of paper clamped between her lips as she slipped on a jacket. "Where are you going?"

She took the paper out of her mouth. "Grocery shopping."

He nodded. "Then let's go." Before she could object, he added, "Bracken will stay here in case the Moores show up." Zander wanted time alone with her.

Behind him, Bracken said, "I will?"

"You will."

"I will." But Bracken didn't sound happy about it.

Gwen shook her head. "That's okay. I'll be fine."

"We're here to look out for you, remember," said Zander.

Apparently uninterested in arguing with him, she waved a hand. "Fine. Whatever. Let's just go."

CHAPTER SEVEN

Why did she always end up with the cart that had squeaky wheels? Chewing the tiny cube of cake she'd gotten from a sample station, Gwen pushed the half-full cart down the aisle. Zander walked beside her, a silent sentinel. And she . . . well, she was pretty much acting as if she were alone.

It was rude, sure, but she suspected that the reason he wanted Bracken to stay behind was so that he could talk about last night. He probably wanted to ensure she understood that the little fumble they'd had in the kitchen didn't mean anything, that she shouldn't read anything into it. And how embarrassing would *that* conversation be?

In the car, she'd spoken only to give him directions to the grocery store. She'd stayed quiet, hoping he'd see that she didn't need a *talk*, and that she wasn't mistaking the fumble for anything other than a drunken mishap. God knew she'd had plenty of those herself over the years. He'd get no judgment from her.

Humming along with the music coming through the speakers, she did her best to drown out the irritating squeaky wheels. If she could just—

"You're good at ignoring people, aren't you, Gwen?"

"Dude, I'm so good at it, I can make people doubt that they're actually alive."

Zander's mouth quirked, even as his nose wrinkled in distaste. Most guys didn't like shopping. For Zander, it wasn't the stores themselves that annoyed him. It was the fluorescent lighting and the clash of scents—fruit, meat, detergent, flowers, bread, soaps. The smells didn't mix well at all. "You haven't checked your list once."

"I have it memorized." Not really. She just liked to browse and grab some impulse buys. Spotting Marlon's preferred brand of hot chocolate, she sighed. It *had* to be on the top shelf, didn't it? Gripping one of the metal shelves for balance, she reached up to grab the tub. No joy. She glared at Zander. "Are you going to watch me struggle?"

"That position pushes out your tits and your ass, so, yeah."

She rolled her eyes. "Boys. You're all the same." But he reached up, nabbed the hot chocolate, and dropped it into her hands. "Thank you," she said.

"You're welcome." As they began to walk again, Zander spoke, "Last night—"

"We don't need to talk about it." It was both a statement and an assurance.

"Yeah, we do."

She clenched her hands around the cart handle. "You don't need to gently tell me that it was a one-time thing. I already get that. I'm sure I looked damn stunning while you were wearing Beer Vision, but I know the reality is very different."

Zander frowned. "The reality?"

"You'd been drinking, you—"

"I wasn't drunk. I knew what I was doing. I knew what I wanted. If my Alpha hadn't called last night and interrupted us, I'd have taken you right there."

She bristled. "I wouldn't have fucked anyone in the kitchen, right where any number of people could have walked in."

"Don't kid yourself, Gwen. It would have happened." He paused as she stopped to grab milk. "Unfortunately, it didn't. But it will." He'd make sure of it. "I have to know."

"Know what?"

"What it's like to be in you. Taking you. Tonight, I'll have you under me. Why do you look so shocked?" He leaned forward. "I like sex, Gwen. I like it a lot. I like having it often. I intend to have it with you. Repeatedly."

More than a little surprised by the direction the conversation had headed, Gwen exhaled raggedly. While the thought of being under him held some appeal, she knew better. Careful not to squash the brownies, she placed a heavy jug of milk in the cart. "It's not gonna happen." The words came out hoarse, so she cleared her throat and firmly added, "It's just not."

The hell it won't, thought Zander. He put his face close to hers. "You think I can't tell that you want me?"

Oh, Gwen knew he could sense it. He was a shifter, so he'd be able to scent that she wanted him. And that left her feeling vulnerable and exposed. Grabbing the cart, she hastened her step as she took a sharp turn around an aisle . . . and shuddered. She hated walking down the frozen-food aisle; the chill always gave her goose bumps. Well, at least it might cool her down and calm her libido. That would sure be helpful.

Seizing the cart, he dragged it to a halt. "Look at me, Gwen. Come on, baby, look at me."

She met his gaze . . . and swallowed at the sheer intensity there. "What?" she rasped.

"You're running from me. From this. Why?" He cocked his head. "Is it because I'm not human? Does that freak you out?"

"No," she said immediately, not wanting him to think any such thing. "You don't freak me out in any way."

"Then what's the problem?"

She jutted out her chin. "I don't get involved with people who're spoken for."

"Good. Neither do I."

But he *was* spoken for, because . . . "You're a shifter."

"I'm well aware of that," he said, impatient. He had no idea where she was going with this. He thought it best not to comment on how cute she looked when she lifted her chin like that.

"You have a true mate waiting for you somewhere out there. Kissing you last night . . . I feel like I touched something that belonged to someone else. And now I feel shitty about it."

Understanding, Zander sighed. He hadn't expected the true-mate thing to be an issue. It wasn't something that had ever bothered anyone before now. Given that Gwen Miller was a female with principles, it would have occurred to him to expect that response *if* she'd been right. But she was human and didn't seem to properly understand the way it worked.

He rested his hand in the crook of her neck and caressed the column of her throat with his thumb. "You're right that I have a true mate, but who says she's waiting for me, Gwen? She could be imprinted on another. She could be someone who doesn't want a mate. She could be someone I never meet for any number of reasons."

Gwen frowned. "Imprinting is when two people who aren't true mates form a mating bond, right?"

"That's right. It happens more often than you'd think. I know several imprinted couples. One of my closest friends imprinted on a female not so long ago; their bond is as strong as any I've seen between true mates." He skimmed his finger over her cheekbone. "My uncle died recently."

She winced. "Sorry to hear that."

Zander shrugged. "I didn't know him well. He searched for his mate all his life. He never found her, and he died alone. He told me in a letter he'd written shortly before his death that I shouldn't spend my life doing the same. I never intended to anyway because, for me, searching for my mate would be pointless."

She tilted her head. "Why?"

"Several things can block the frequency of the mating bond, including doubts and fears and mental walls. Did you know that?"

She shook her head. "Let me guess. You have mental walls that are sky-high."

A smile tugged at his mouth. "You could say that my boundaries are more extensive than most." And he feared mating, in part, because he liked to be in control of himself, his life, his choices. Finding his true mate would take some of that control away.

"Those walls I have will block the bond," Zander continued. "That means I can't even be sure I'll recognize my predestined mate if I cross her path. We could pass each other in the street and never know. Hell, we could know each other for years and never realize we're mates. Unless she and I bond, I don't belong to her any more than she belongs to me. If it worked any other way, shifters would never be able to form a mating bond with someone who wasn't their true mate." He tugged on her braid. "In other words, I'm just as free and single as you are."

She looked away. "I don't understand. You're . . ."

"What?"

Gorgeous, edible, out of my league. Gwen slid her gaze back to him. "You didn't show the slightest bit of interest in me until yesterday, and now you're all up in my space."

Yeah, well, he hadn't admitted to himself just how much he wanted her until yesterday. He moved aside her collar so he could look at the bite on her neck. Masculine satisfaction flared through him—perhaps more satisfaction than he should be comfortable with. He brushed his thumb over the imprint of his teeth. "Do you know what that is?"

"I'm pretending it's not there."

Zander fought a smile. "But it is there."

"No, it's not."

"I'm looking right at it."

"At what? There's nothing to look at."

Mouth curving, he cupped her jaw. "That mark tells others that you're taken. Not by someone who considers you a simple possession—shifters won't mark people they don't respect, and they don't do it on a whim or for shits and giggles. The mark says you're taken by someone who respects, protects, and values you. Someone who, yeah, will be up in your space. Right now, while you have a threat hanging over your head, you need someone that close."

He respected and valued her? "You don't even know me."

"I like what I know. I know you're smart, resilient, you stand your ground, and you'll be a voice for people who can't speak up for themselves. It takes a strong person to do that." Even his wolf liked her strength, though he still held her at a metaphorical distance.

"You say all that, but you're still suspicious of me for a reason you haven't yet explained."

"I'm suspicious of *whatever* I don't understand. You, Gwen, are a mystery in many ways." It was the truth; it just didn't fully answer her question. But Zander didn't think that telling her of his wolf's struggles would help. Before she could question him further, he said, "Now let's finish up here and get back, yeah? There are too many scents in this place."

She let out a breath. "All right. I'm almost done."

As they'd each said their piece, the tension between them disappeared. But things sort of weirdly . . . shifted. She'd thought he'd been up in her space before, but she quickly realized he'd actually *given* her space. Now that the air was clear, he apparently saw no need to hold back.

He stroked her hair. Doodled patterns on her nape. Breathed her in. Nipped her earlobe. Swept a hand down her back. Pressed the occasional soft kiss to her neck.

Every touch was possessive and playful. She wasn't sure anyone had ever paid her that level of attention before. It was like he honed every sense on her, making her feel like the center of everything as he touched and crowded her. He was everywhere, and it was as overwhelming as it was thrilling. It was also a problem, because it was firing her libido.

As they were nearing the checkout stand, he let out a low growl that made her think of an idling motorcycle. She threw him a questioning look, surprised to see his nostrils flaring.

"You're wet," he said in a low, deep voice.

Her cheeks reddened. "You have no one to blame for that but yourself."

Once they'd bagged the groceries, they loaded them into the trunk of his SUV. She'd wanted to take her truck, but he'd rightly pointed out that as the Moores knew her vehicle, they'd know to look for her if they saw it around. Unable to argue that, she'd agreed to let him drive her to the store. Done loading the trunk, Zander drove en route to the house.

Resting one hand on her thigh, he asked, "Did Yvonne officially adopt you?"

Gwen sighed. "You're so damn nosy."

"Answer my question, and I'll answer one of yours."

"All right. No, she didn't. She just fostered me, the same as she did Marlon and Julie. Your turn." She lifted a brow. "You ever had anal sex?"

He did a double take. "What?"

"I'm curious. How'd it go?"

Zander gritted his teeth. "I know what you're doing, Gwen." She was trying to make the conversation superficial, trying to keep him at a distance. That wasn't going to happen. He wasn't interested in fucking a stranger, and he wanted to know her better. "No, I haven't. Shifters tend to save anal sex for their mates. Now, I have another question for you."

"That doesn't surprise me," she mumbled.

"How long have you lived with Yvonne?"

"Since I was eight. Now you. What do you prefer—tits or ass?"

"Gwen."

She turned to the window. "Fine, don't answer."

"I'm more of an ass-man. And you, by the way, have a hot little ass. One last question." For now, anyway. "What happened to your foster father?" he asked softly, already suspecting the male was dead.

"The first one died in a car accident."

He frowned. "There was a second one? What happened to him?"

"Karma." She sighed. "So, you like to use toys in bed?"

Zander grinned wickedly and lightly squeezed her thigh. "You'd be my toy, baby."

Her whole body seemed to flush at that. She'd heard about sex with shifters. Heard it was rough, intense, mind-blowing. What was the dumb phrase the shifter groupies used? *Once you go shifter, you'll never go back.* She'd always snickered at that. But while Zander's potent sex appeal swamped her, and she fairly ached for him, she suspected that he would leave a lasting impression on her. She couldn't decide if that was a good thing or a bad thing.

As they pulled up in front of the B&B and she spotted a familiar Audi, Gwen's libido instantly cooled down. The owner of said Audi was standing on the porch with Marlon, and they were having some kind of standoff.

Zander studied the thin, lanky male standing on the porch. Zander didn't recognize him from Half 'n' Half, and he was pretty sure he hadn't seen him around. "Who's that?"

She unbuckled her seat belt. "My ex-therapist, Aidan."

Zander's brows snapped together. The idea that she might have suffered some sort of trauma made anger surge through him, but he kept his voice even. "Why did you have a therapist?"

"For therapy."

Impatient, he pushed, "Why did you go to therapy?"

"Because Julie wouldn't go unless I did."

He gritted his teeth at her evasiveness. *"Gwen."*

"Do you have to be so fucking nosy?"

"When the fucking subject's you, yeah."

Huffing, she hopped out of the SUV and slowly climbed the steps onto the porch. She felt Zander's body heat, knew he was close behind her despite his not making a sound.

Aidan's face softened in a way she couldn't help but find creepy. "Gwen." His eyes slid to Zander, who now stood at her side so close their arms touched. And the therapist clearly didn't like it. "I'm Aidan Rogers. You are?"

"Why are you here?" Gwen asked, tone flat. Aidan would just love to get some sort of emotional reaction from her to *evaluate* it. She'd give him nothing.

"I wanted to check on you. Julie told me that you declined my offer of support and didn't want to see me. I respect that—"

"Do you?" rumbled Zander. "Because if you did, you wouldn't be here." He didn't know anything about this asshole, but he did know that the human felt *something* for Gwen. It was plain to see, and it rubbed Zander the wrong way. His wolf stalked forward and pressed against Zander's skin, taking a good look at the male. *Weak,* the wolf decided. *No threat.* Still, the beast wanted him gone. So did Zander.

Aidan ignored him, keeping his attention on Gwen. "Could we speak privately?"

"No," she said.

Aidan's mouth flattened. "Julie mentioned that you have guests offering to help. Shifters. I'm guessing the man beside you is one of them."

Folding his arms across his chest, Marlon asked, "Should you be sharing anything that Julie said to you, given it's all supposed to be private between you and your patient?"

Turning to him, Aidan raised a placatory hand. "I just want to talk to Gwen. That's all."

"Here's my problem, Aidan," said Zander, face hard. "I don't like the way you look at her. Not at all. Your voice changes, softens, when you say her name. Did you know that? No? Well, it does. And, yeah, I don't like it."

Twin spots of color stained Aidan's cheeks. "She's one of my patients. I'm fond of her."

"No, she's not," said Marlon. "She hasn't been one of your patients for a long time."

"That doesn't mean I no longer feel any concern for her."

Zander cocked his head. "Do you always chase down patients who choose to end their sessions with you?"

Aidan gave a dismissive snort of laughter that was clearly false. "I'm hardly chasing her."

"But you did at first," said Marlon. "Isn't that right?"

"At the time, I was worried," Aidan defended. "She left therapy before we could make any real progress."

"She left? I wonder why that was." The sarcasm in Marlon's voice made Aidan flush.

Done with the whole thing, Gwen said, "Go home, Aidan." She didn't need this shit. "And don't come back."

"I just want to help you," he said, looking the image of what she believed was false concern. "Everything that's happening with the Moores has to be tearing open some wounds."

God, the guy was dramatic. "It's not," Gwen said truthfully.

"Witnessing violence, feeling unsafe, the pressure to keep secrets—it must be like reliving your childhood," he insisted.

Gwen glared at Aidan, pissed that he'd pretty much exposed the bare bones of her childhood to Zander. The asshole was wrong. It wasn't like reliving that time. This situation wasn't about *her*; it was about Andie—an innocent female who'd been drugged, beaten, and terrorized.

"You want me to be this fragile person who needs your help to heal," said Gwen. He'd even tried to convince her that she was. "Maybe you like the idea of being someone's savior, and it makes you feel powerful, I don't know. But I'm *not* fragile. I *don't* need you. And I have *no* wish whatsoever to speak to you as a therapist or as a fellow human being."

"In other words," began Zander, closing in on him, "you aren't welcome here, and you need to fucking go. You also need to stay the hell away."

Gwen swallowed. The words had been spoken low and soft, and that seemed to make them all the more menacing.

"What are you going to do if I don't?" Aidan challenged, voice shaky. "Rip my throat out?"

Zander smiled. "That would end the fun all too quickly."

"Way too quickly," agreed Marlon.

Aidan looked from one male to the other. "I only came here to help her."

"You don't want to help her," said Zander. "I doubt that you ever did. No, I think you get off on making women dependent on you—and I think you should note that that is just plain fucked-up. You should also note that if you come back here, you won't leave unharmed."

The therapist's fear was clear to see. "You can't threaten me."

"I can and I did." Zander went nose to nose with Aidan. "In sum, you'll stay away from Gwen. You'll stop passing messages through her sister. And you'll get it out of your fucking head that Gwen could ever be yours. In fact, don't even think about her at all. We clear?"

Drawing himself up straight, Aidan licked his lips. "I have places to be."

"That's good. Bracken will walk you to your car."

Aidan's brow furrowed. "Who?"

"That would be me," said Bracken, standing directly behind him. Aidan whirled with a sound of alarm, and Bracken gave him a shark's grin. "Jumpy little thing, aren't you? I've been here for a while. You didn't know I was there? Hmm. Well, lead the way to your car." Before Aidan could object, Bracken shepherded him to the Audi by the scruff of his neck. "Here, let me get your door for you." He sharply yanked it open, making it smack Aidan right in the face. "Shit, sorry about that. Sometimes, I forget my own strength."

Hand covering his face, Aidan slid into his car. "I'm fine."

"You have a good day now." Bracken slammed the door shut, waving with a smile as the therapist drove off.

"Huh," said Marlon, eyeing the wolves. "Looks like you two might be useful to have around, after all. I have to admit, I wasn't so sure. I want to be as convinced as Yvonne that you'll see this through to the end."

"We'll be here until the entire issue has been fully resolved," Zander firmly stated. "Our Alphas won't call us home, if for no other reason than that a fellow shifter was assaulted and deserves justice." Nick might wish he could summon them back to pack territory, but Shaya would fight him on it. Her soft heart wouldn't allow her to ignore Gwen or Andie's plight.

After a long moment, Marlon nodded. "Fair enough."

Releasing a heavy sigh, Gwen turned to the wolves. "Let's take the groceries inside. Then I think it's time for you both to meet Andie."

Zander stayed beside Gwen as she expertly navigated the boat along the murky river, avoiding shrubs, logs, tall stalks, and old beaver dams. It was obvious that she'd done it dozens of times.

Despite the sun beating at his skin, Zander found himself lulled by the sounds of the boat motor, the flapping of wings as birds dove at the water, and the various wildlife scurrying through the high grass.

The marsh might not be what anyone would term *colorful*, but it was still scenic and peaceful. It was also thriving with wildlife. When he'd explored the marsh, his wolf had picked up the scents of many animals—foxes, otters, beavers, raccoons, mink, and deer, to name a few. His wolf had enjoyed playfully chasing some of them.

As a bird swooped down and caught a fish, a light spray of water hit Zander. "I've never seen so many types of birds in one place." Ducks, geese, herons, kingfishers, hawks—the list went on.

"Well, there's a whole lot of insects and fish for them to feed on," she said. "You don't like birds?"

"I like them just fine." It was the insects that he didn't like, especially the dragonflies flitting through the reeds. They looked like they'd been taking steroids or something.

Hearing Bracken chuckle from the other end of the boat, Zander looked to see that his attention was on his cell phone. He guessed that Bracken was texting Shiloh again only to receive yet more insults. Zander wondered if the female knew she wasn't discouraging the male whatsoever.

Taking advantage of the alone time that gave him with Gwen, Zander quietly asked, "What did that fucker Aidan mean when he said this must be like reliving your childhood?"

"How did I know you'd bring that up?" she muttered drily. "I'd rather not talk about it."

"Baby, I just heard you had one shitty childhood. Going by the things that asshole said, I'm guessing that one or both of your parents were violent and that you were forced to keep your mouth shut about it. I'm fucking pissed that that happened to you." It would surely leave any child feeling helpless, terrified, and unsafe. "And I can't help but wonder just how bad it was—my imagination is coming up with all kinds of shit. Give me something."

Startled that he'd actually care one way or the other, Gwen threw him a sideways glance. "I had a shitty start to life, yes, but so did lots of people—it doesn't make me anything special. It's over now; it doesn't matter anymore."

"It matters to me."

Gwen doubted that. Shifters liked casual sex; they liked to keep it simple. It was more likely that his natural curiosity was bugging him, she decided. In any case . . . "Zander, as someone with extensive boundaries, you should be able to accept when another person doesn't want to share their personal business."

Zander couldn't deny that she was right. He should back off, give her the emotional space she was asking for, but instead, he found himself saying, "My mother abused my father. Not physically, but emotionally. She was much more dominant than he was, and she used that strength to subdue and control him. She did it right up until the day she died—or so I heard, anyway. I hadn't spoken to them in years." He raised an expectant brow. "Now it's your turn."

The determined look on his face told her he wasn't going to drop this. Gwen inwardly cursed. If she told him about her biological father, she was pretty sure he'd look at her differently. No, she'd keep that part to herself, but she could at least tell him a little something. "My stepfather liked to drink, but that wasn't why he hit my mother. Drunk, sober—it didn't matter. Hanna didn't cower when he yelled. She stood up to him, argued with him. But the moment he hit her, she just crumbled. I often wondered if she *wanted* him to hit her." Why else would she have provoked him? "Over time, the beatings got worse. A lot worse. But even then, she forced me not to tell. She told me she'd lie to protect him if I did."

And then Zander got it. He understood exactly why she was so set on speaking up for Andie. As a child, she'd been unable to stand up for her mother—most likely also forced to lie and make excuses to anyone who asked about it. Now, as an adult, she wasn't backing down while someone needed help she could provide. "How did you end up in foster care?"

"That's as much as you're getting out of me today." She jerked her head back a little as a mosquito came too close. "Why don't you tell me why you and Bracken came all the way to Oregon? I doubt it was to test if the house is haunted. But if it's personal, just say so."

"I told you, my uncle died recently." A slight breeze brushed over Zander, giving him a reprieve from the harsh glare of the sun. "He wanted the beneficiaries to meet at his attorney's office for the reading of the will. That's where Bracken and I went yesterday."

Zander wasn't entirely surprised when she didn't ask how it went. She'd successfully changed the subject, which was clearly all she'd hoped to do. "You're an expert at dodging personal topics, aren't you, Gwen?"

"Yep. Believe me, Zander, my story isn't interesting."

"I'm not asking because I think I'll find it interesting; I'm asking because it's you."

She flicked him a confused look, noticing he was purely focused on her in a way that only a shifter could center their attention on someone. "Is this because you marked me? You feel the need to know everything about a person you mark?"

She didn't get why he'd care. He didn't know her. He'd claimed to respect her, sure, but she respected plenty of people—that didn't mean she had an urge to learn their personal business. In any case, she couldn't tell him more about her background. There were too many things that it was best he didn't know. It wasn't like they were in a relationship where they needed to get to know each other anyway, was it? He'd go back to his pack after the hearing.

Zander closed the gap between them and gently fisted her braid, but she didn't look at him. There was tension in every line of her body. "Baby, why is it so hard to believe I simply want to know you? Why does there have to be some sort of technical reason behind it? I told you in the grocery store, I like what I know about you. I want to know more."

She kept her gaze firmly ahead. "You don't need to know more."

"Never said I needed to. I said I wanted to. But maybe your mother trained you so well to keep secrets that you instinctively shy away from people who try to get close." She inhaled sharply. "Not trying to hurt you, Gwen. Just want you to ask yourself if you're so highly private for the wrong reasons." Noticing they were nearing a dock, Zander whistled at Bracken. "Almost there."

Tucking his cell in his pocket, Bracken sidled up to Zander. He must have sensed Gwen's tension, because he frowned. "Everything okay here?"

"Fine." She slowed the boat and steered it toward the dock, wincing at the grating sounds of reeds scraping along the side of the boat. Once she'd parked and anchored it, she said, "Let's go."

Nobody spoke as she led them across the marshland, but they didn't move in silence, thanks to the sucking sounds of their boots traipsing through the mud.

She hadn't introduced the wolves to Andie before now for two reasons. One, she'd needed to see that they were trustworthy. Two, she'd wanted to be sure they'd stick around—and that they'd be truly helpful if they did. If the way they'd dealt with Aidan was anything to go by, they would be . . . even if Zander *was* a nosy bastard.

Reaching the trees bordering their land, she led the wolves through the woods. Finally, a simple cabin came into view. Donnie had used it as a decoy to fool the mysterious *they* into thinking it was his home. Since Gwen doubted there was anyone actually searching for Donnie, she figured Andie was safe enough there.

As they neared the cabin, Bracken broke the silence. "The cougar's been staying here?"

"It was her choice," said Gwen. "She didn't want to stay at the house." Urging them to halt, she asked, "Is she inside?" As shifters, their hearing would be advanced enough to sense any movement.

"No," replied Zander. "But she's close. I can scent her."

"Then we wait," said Gwen.

It was mere moments before a cougar appeared—golden, graceful, with big, intelligent brown eyes. She gave them a snarl of warning before entering the cabin. Soon enough, Andie hesitantly came out in her human form, wearing jeans and a tee.

"Hey," said Gwen, "how much do you know of what's been going on lately?" Because Gwen was pretty sure that Andie would have kept a close watch, especially since she didn't look startled to see either Zander or Bracken. She did appear slightly nervous, though. That might have been why the wolves seemed to be making a conscious effort to appear relaxed and nonconfrontational—their stances open, their hands hanging loosely at their sides.

"I heard plenty," Andie replied, scratching her arm in a fidgety movement. She looked at Zander. "I saw you chase off Ezra. You and your pack mate want to help."

"Did you hear me tell Gwen about the shelter?" Bracken asked, his tone calm and easy. She shook her head, and he then asked, "You ever heard of the Phoenix Pack?"

"No."

"They're good people," Zander told her. "One of their wolves, Makenna, used to be a lone wolf and helps run a shelter for lone shifters. They're given protection, food, a roof over their heads, counseling, and any education they might need. Then, when they're ready, Makenna rehomes them. You could stay there rather than hiding out here. You'd even be welcome to stay there once this shit is over."

Andie squinted. "Surely if such shelters existed, I'd have heard of them."

"From what I understand, there aren't many," Zander told her. "That's probably why I hadn't heard of them either."

"You'd be in a place filled with people just like you, and you'd be safe," said Bracken. "The place is secure, and the Moores wouldn't think to look for you there anyway. I don't mean to scare you, but it's only a matter of time before they come searching the marsh, hoping you're here. You could run, sure. But where?"

Andie scraped a hand through her short red hair. "Look, I'm not stupid. I know I can't keep living like this. But I don't know how to be part of a pride. I was raised by humans—they adopted me without knowing I was a shifter, but they kept me."

Bracken shrugged. "A lot of loners at the shelter want to live among humans. Makenna helps them find a residence of their own, along with a job."

She looked from Zander to Bracken. "I'm nobody to you. Why care?"

"We learned that not all lone shifters are bad," said Bracken. "In fact, our pack adopted a little girl from the shelter."

Andie blinked. "You . . . adopted a loner?"

Bracken nodded. "The Phoenix Alphas gave Makenna and four other loners a place in their pack."

Her eyes widened. "Four?"

"Only one of them was related to a Phoenix wolf. The other three were strangers, and each had a shitty story of their own, but they were offered a place there." Bracken tilted his head. "The shifter who runs the shelter is a cougar, if that makes you feel more comfortable."

Andie bit her lip, still uneasy.

"I get that you have no reason to trust us," began Zander, "but what do you have to lose at this point? If you want the truth, my main reason for proposing you go there is that I'm hoping that, with time and space, you'll find the strength to go before the council and speak up for yourself. You should. You deserve justice. And I don't want Gwen doing it alone."

Andie's hands balled up. "I told her she should just back down."

"I won't let Brandt get away with what he did," Gwen declared. "I couldn't live with myself if I did."

Sighing, Andie rubbed her temple. "I need some time to think about it."

Zander inclined his head. "Take a few days to consider our offer. Come by the house when you've decided."

At Andie's nod, Gwen threw her a supportive smile. "You know where I am if you need anything." With that, they returned to the boat.

CHAPTER EIGHT

Lounging in the rocker on the B&B's porch later that day with a cold beer in hand, Zander gave Makenna a call and relayed the cougar's situation. He was glad when she confirmed there would be room at the shelter for Andie if she needed it. He was just ending the call when a small van came toward the B&B. Instantly alert, he slowly rose to his feet. As the van pulled up outside the house, Zander noticed it was a delivery van.

Soon, a young male wearing a baseball cap came jogging up the steps and onto the porch with a bag in hand that carried the scents of spicy food. He froze at the sight of Zander, but then the front door opened and a smiling Yvonne stepped out, holding a wad of cash.

"Keep the change," she told the human, who hurried away.

Zander followed Yvonne inside, down the hallway, and into the kitchen. Gwen, Marlon, and Bracken looked at the bag with covetous eyes as Yvonne placed it on the table at the center of the kitchen and pulled out several takeout boxes.

"What's this?" he asked.

"Chinese," said Marlon, sliding a pile of plates on the table. "Grab whatever you want."

After they'd all plated some food and settled on the stools at the table, Zander turned to Gwen. "I spoke to Makenna. She said there's room for Andie at the shelter." Gwen nodded but didn't appear relieved. "Not totally sold on the idea of the place, are you?"

She shrugged. "I just want to be sure she's somewhere safe."

Yvonne swallowed a chunk of curried chicken. "Aidan called me. Said he came by earlier and was chased away." She gestured at Zander and Bracken with her fork, adding, "He's concerned that you two aren't what Gwen needs right now."

Little bastard. "Is he?" Zander said evenly.

"What did you say?" Bracken asked her.

"I told him you're exactly what Gwen needs and that he shouldn't worry." Yvonne looked at Gwen. "He wants me to convince you to resume therapy."

Zander, Bracken, and Marlon all cursed.

Yvonne jerked back. "Am I missing something?"

Gwen didn't answer, not wanting to bother Yvonne with it.

Marlon scooped more food onto his plate. "Gwen ended the sessions because he declared that he loved her."

Yvonne gawked. "*What?*"

Gwen shot her foster brother a hard smile. "Thanks, Marlon."

Yvonne dropped her fork. "Why didn't you tell me, Gwen?"

"She was embarrassed," said Marlon.

Gwen widened her eyes at him. "Seriously, Marlon, you can shut up now."

Yvonne looked at her in disbelief. "Why would you be embarrassed?"

"Because she didn't see it coming, and she's totally weird," Marlon explained.

Gwen threw a handful of white rice at him. "I'll destroy your new shirt, I really will. Right now, I'm seeing red."

"You are? What's it like?"

She growled. "You are *not* color-blind."

"And you can know this how?"

Yvonne rubbed at her arms. "You should have told me, Gwen. *Aidan* is the one who should be embarrassed, not you. You need to tell Julie."

Gwen had seen this coming. "No. He really does seem to help her. She never spoke of her childhood until she started her sessions with Aidan. Now she talks about it all freely, and Chase says she rarely has nightmares these days."

"She should still know," Yvonne insisted.

Zander leaned slightly toward Gwen. "He might have done to her what he did to you."

Gwen shook her head. "If he'd told Julie he loved her, she'd have freaked out and told Chase."

"I don't mean that." Zander took a swig of his beer. "I mean he might be trying to make her dependent on him, like he tried with you."

"I thought of that, which was why I asked her a few questions to get a feel for how he treated her. I never got the impression that he was anything but professional with her." Or Gwen would definitely have told her. "If anything, he's made her feel like she can lean on Chase and confide in him."

"I'm still telling Julie," Yvonne announced. "She needs to know."

Gwen rubbed her temples. "She'll be pissed at me."

Marlon waved a dismissive hand. "Julie can't be mad for more than ten minutes at a time."

The back door opened, and Donnie strolled into the kitchen, no doubt lured by the smell of food. Without a word to anyone, he took a seat and dug in.

"Back to the matter of the shelter," said Marlon. "Do you think Andie will actually agree to stay there?"

Gwen puffed out a breath. "I don't know."

Donnie's brow furrowed. "What shelter?" After Bracken quickly explained, Donnie said, "Your kind is gonna need to build more of those shelters. Maybe underground. You'll need them for the casualties."

Yvonne blinked. "Casualties?"

"A war between humans and shifters will happen one day," said Donnie. "Not out of prejudice, but out of fear. Humans have always feared what they don't understand, but they didn't feel too threatened by shifters when they thought there was only a handful of breeds. Each year, it becomes clear that more and more exist. They're starting to worry they're outnumbered and outmatched. The war will eventually happen, and we're all being trained for it."

"Trained?" Marlon echoed, doubtful.

Donnie's lips thinned, a signal that a paranoid rant was coming on. "Have you not noticed how many video games are war-themed these days? It's the government preparing kids for war. The kids play online with their friends, communicating using headsets—similar to what soldiers do in the field. The games are always graphic, getting the kids used to blood, guts, and gore. The games don't just feature simple guns; no, there's a whole array of guns available to the kids—the government is actually educating them on weaponry!"

Gwen spoke, "Donnie—"

He slapped a hand on the table. "I'm telling you, the powers that be are basically creating soldiers and assassins. And look how many of those war-themed games are focused on killing zombies. The government is training kids to kill monsters, and then they send the message that *shifters* are the monsters. It's all propaganda. The kids are being brainwashed and—"

"Donnie."

His expression cleared as he looked at Gwen, all anger gone. "Hmm?"

She sighed. "Are you all right?"

He shrugged one shoulder. "Fine." He went back to his food.

Looking at Donnie in pure fascination, Bracken told him, "You made some good points." The two males then went on to further discuss the matter.

Amused despite herself, Gwen inwardly rolled her eyes. Feeling the heat of Zander's gaze, she looked to see him once more completely focused on her. His face was blank, but his eyes were alive with an almost electric intensity that gave her goose bumps. Heat rose to her cheeks, and her lower stomach fluttered and clenched as a sliver of need snaked through her. His mouth quirked, as if he'd sensed it.

Well, if he could sense her need, Bracken would soon sense it too—yeah, that would be too embarrassing. Done with her food, Gwen pushed to her feet. "I'm gonna take a shower and then head to bed. 'Night, everyone."

Zander gave her a look that said he'd see her soon. She nodded, letting him know she was done running. Personally, she still found it baffling that he seemed so attracted to her, but she wasn't going to fight it. A girl had to eat.

Upstairs, Gwen took a long, refreshing shower, trying to ignore the giddy flutters in her stomach. It wasn't easy. She could honestly say that she'd never been *giddy* at the prospect of sex before. Enthusiastic, yeah, but not giddy.

Maybe it was because Zander was a shifter, and she knew she was about to experience something wholly new. Maybe it was because he wasn't a virtual stranger to her—she didn't *know* him, true, but she also didn't have the emotional distance from him that she liked to keep between her and her partners. He'd been doing his best to eat up that distance, to *get* to know her. While part of her panicked at that, another part of her liked it . . . mostly because not many outside her foster family had ever cared to really know her.

Once she'd finished her shower, she stepped out of the stall and wrapped a lush towel around herself. After towel-drying her hair and dragging a brush through it, she walked into the bedroom. And stopped dead. Sitting on the edge of her bed, like he belonged there, was Zander.

Her stomach bottomed out. He looked . . . hungry. Ravenous, even. And so completely out of her league. Yet, he was here. For her. And as he stared at her like a predator measuring its prey, her mouth dried up and her nipples tightened.

She cleared her throat. "I locked that door." Which meant he had lock-picking skills. She'd have to note that for future reference.

He slowly leaned forward, resting his arms on his thighs. "Drop the towel." It was a soft, rumbly command, and the sheer power and authority in it almost made her jump.

Gwen swallowed. *Wow.* He'd switched all his natural intensity on full blast, and the room suddenly seemed too small. Too hot.

"Drop the towel, Gwen," he ordered, his tone low, deep, almost hypnotic; it also brooked no argument. There was a glint in his gaze that could only be described as dangerous. There was also the promise of something more there. The promise of a sense of satisfaction that she'd probably never experience from one of her own kind. All she had to do was drop the towel.

It would be hard to do that, since she sort of had a death grip on it. Why? Because she sensed now that taking this further would mean handing a good deal of control over to Zander. She wasn't good with that. But wouldn't it be nice to let go for a little while? Everything had been so tense lately, so serious; she wouldn't mind a little escapism.

Her heart stuttered as he rose from the bed and slowly began to stalk toward her. He had this cool, dominant, forceful energy going on that made everything in her stand up and pay attention. Heat and intensity drummed at her skin as he came to stand before her.

His finger traced the edge of the towel, breezing over the swell of her breasts. "I want to know what's under this towel. Show me, baby."

Pushing all self-conscious thoughts aside, she loosened the towel. Approval glinted in his eyes. And when the towel dropped to the floor, those eyes raked over every inch of her, smoldering and glittering with a raw, powerful need that made her breathing deepen.

A growl seemed to vibrate in his chest. "Beautiful."

Um, no, she wasn't. Never would be.

He skimmed his nose along her jaw, breathing her in. "And mine to play with." His eyes tracked his movements as he drew his fingers along her skin, tracing and shaping her, hands lingering on every curve just to tease her.

Honestly, Gwen wouldn't have expected such a light, noninvasive touch to rev her engines. It was like her skin was supersensitive. She was hot. Edgy. Needed more. And when his hands slid down to lightly cup her ass, she arched into him. "Zander—"

His mouth landed on hers. He didn't devour her like he had the night before. The kiss was soft. Sensual. Almost leisurely. But even as he sipped from her mouth, Gwen felt his need hammering at her. Somehow, he was keeping it in check. She didn't want that. She was human, but she wasn't made of porcelain.

Gwen caught his lip with her teeth, not biting but holding it captive. She slowly pulled back, letting his lip slide between her teeth. Hey, she liked to play too. A growl rumbled out of him, and his fingers bit into her ass. Then he was kissing her again. There was nothing sweet or gentle about it this time. Awesome. She sifted her fingers through his hair, raking his scalp with her nails, as she kissed him back. His hands seemed to be everywhere, driving her insane.

Releasing her mouth with a nip to her lower lip, Zander moved to stand behind her, admiring the sleek line of her back and her perfect ass. Like last night when he'd kissed her, his wolf had withdrawn, but he wasn't growling any objections.

Pressing his front to her back, Zander roughly fisted her damp hair and snatched her head back. Her soft gasp shot to his cock, which was already full and heavy. He put his mouth to her ear. "Who's my baby?"

Gwen swallowed. His hot breath on her ear gave her the chills.

"Who, Gwen?"

"Me." She shivered at his low growl of approval.

"That's right. And do you know what I want my baby to do?" He closed his hand possessively around her breast and thumbed her nipple. "I want her to come for me."

Well, Gwen was sure it wouldn't take much for that to happen. She'd always had a quick trigger, and she was already wet and aching.

He let her hair slide through his fingers and released her breast. "On the bed." Zander watched as she walked to the bed and then smoothly slid onto the mattress. "That's my girl." Crossing to her, he leaned his upper body over her, planting his fists on either side of her head. "I told you I'd have you under me tonight."

She licked her lower lip. "So you did."

Zander noticed that she hadn't spread her thighs. She wasn't submitting just yet. Good. He liked a little defiance.

He found his eyes drawn to the bite on her neck, felt his cock throb at the mere sight of it. His eyes dropped farther, drinking in the sight of her breasts. "So pretty."

Gwen sighed happily as he licked and sucked at her nipple, sending little electric jolts to her pussy. She slid her hands over the solid bulk of his shoulders, luxuriating in the attention he lavished on her breasts . . . until she felt the edge of his teeth. "No marking this time."

He cupped one breast. "But I like biting down on this soft skin."

"Then just don't bite too hard." She moaned as he sucked her nipple back into his mouth and then flicked it with his tongue. He pinched her other nipple, and she hissed at the double assault, digging her nails into his shoulders through his shirt.

"Harder."

Knowing his skin was tougher than hers, she gave him what he wanted and dug her nails in harder. He thrust his cock against her folds, bumping her clit. Fuck, that was good. She didn't mind the friction from the denim of his jeans. She *did* mind that his teeth grazed her nipple again. "Teeth," she reprimanded.

Zander licked his way to the side of her breast. Pinning her gaze with his, he bit down hard. She jerked, hissing. He swirled his tongue over the mark to soothe it. "I told you that you'd be my toy."

She might have balked a little at the word "toy," but he'd said it softly and with . . . affection. A possessive affection. Instead of making her feel disrespected or degraded, the word gave her a thrill.

Straightening, Zander stepped back a little. "I want to see how wet you are. Show me." She slowly opened her legs, and her scent flooded his lungs. "My baby has such a pretty pussy." Pink and plump and slick. "I knew you would."

Gwen swallowed at the hungry, possessive look on his face. He stared at her pussy like he wanted to own it. Like he wanted to ram his cock inside her and stay there. Awesome. Sounded good to her.

He tapped her thigh. "Wider."

She arched an imperious brow at his order. "If you want me to spread them wider, you'll have to work for it."

Taking that as the challenge it was, Zander roughly thrust a finger inside her, gratified by her strangled moan. "You're dripping wet." Because of him. All that cream was for him. And though his wolf stayed back, *he* also released a self-satisfied growl.

Zander began to thrust his finger in and out of her. Fuck, she was so hot and tight, and he couldn't wait to feel her stretching around his cock. But she wasn't ready to take him yet.

He sank another finger inside her, gritting his teeth as her pussy fluttered. He fucked her with his fingers, loving the breathy little moans she made, loving the way she tilted her hips for him, giving him perfect access.

Her hands fisted the sheets, and her eyes—those big, blue, beguiling eyes—never left his. It was so fucking intimate. Should have made him uncomfortable. It didn't. That wild look right there on her face—that was his. If he ever saw her look at another male like that, he'd kill him.

Hooking his fingers, Zander thrust harder. Faster. Her moans deepened, became little pleas for release. And when he pressed down on her clit with his thumb, she came. Her pussy and thighs clenched, and she let out a choked cry that almost had Zander coming in his jeans. "That's my baby."

He wasn't sure if she even knew she'd spread her thighs wider for him, but he took advantage. Crouching, he pulled her toward him so that her ass was hanging over the edge of the bed. Just as he'd imagined himself doing a dozen times since he'd first seen them, he hooked her perfect legs over his shoulders. "Yeah, this is what I want."

He slowly parted her folds with his thumbs, watching her glistening pussy quiver. Need roared inside him. Need for her. Need for her taste on his tongue.

With a growl, he fell forward and lapped at her pussy. Fuck, she tasted as good as she smelled. He sipped from her, drowned in her, all the while digging his fingers into the soft flesh of her ass. Every soft moan spurred him on and fed his own desperate need to come.

He lashed her clit with his tongue, felt her hips jerk. He sank his tongue inside her, drank from her, fluttered his tongue along her walls just to drive her insane. "You're going to come for me again, Gwen. Hard." He stabbed his tongue deep. Again. And again. And again. Until, finally, she gave him what he wanted.

Breathing hard, Gwen watched as Zander got to his feet and deftly shed his clothes, revealing a body that was all solid muscle, sleek skin, and buzzed with raw animal energy. She bet she could bounce a brick on those abs.

Her stomach twisted as she caught sight of his cock. So the rumors were true. Shifters *were*, in fact, well endowed. She had the feeling she was going to be sore tomorrow. And that was not a complaint.

She pointed at her dresser. "Condoms are in the top drawer."

Leaning over her, he flicked her taut nipple with his tongue. "Shifters don't carry STDs, and we can only impregnate the female we're mated to."

"Then we're good to go."

Straightening, Zander groaned as she curled her luscious legs around him—yet another fantasy he had. "That's it, wrap them around me." Angling her hips just right, he bumped her folds with the head of his cock. "I'll go slow while I slide inside you." He wanted to be sure he didn't hurt her, and he also wanted her to feel every inch of him going in. "After that, I want to take you hard, Gwen. If you can't handle that, tell me now."

She gasped as he lodged the thick head of his cock in her opening. The pressure was amazing. "I can take it."

Zander sank inside her. Slowly. Smoothly. Almost lazily. And, *fuck*, her hot pussy felt so good stretching around him. Even though she was deliciously tight, she was so slick he slid in easily. Still, he watched her face for signs of pain, but all he saw was a need for more.

Finally, balls-deep in her, he groaned. She felt like sheer fucking heaven. "You sure you can take it hard?" He damn well hoped so, because he wasn't sure he had it in him to give her slow and gentle. Not right then. He could keep in mind the relative differences in their strength so he didn't hurt her, but he couldn't give her gentle.

"I wouldn't have said it if I wasn't."

Taking her at her word, he reared back and slammed home. Her pussy clamped down on him, squeezing and rippling. *Fuck.* Zander pounded in and out of her, yanking her to him each time he thrust forward, driving as deep as he could possibly go. "Swear to God, never had a pussy this tight."

And she'd never had a cock buried so deep inside her. He was hitting all kinds of interesting nerve endings that Gwen hadn't known she had until now. She'd never felt so full, so *taken.* Truly, no one had ever fucked her like this; no one had ever paid so much attention to her body or ever been so intent on making sure she got off.

She hadn't actually been certain that she could come a third time, but the friction was building inside her. Building. Swelling. Inflating like a balloon until she couldn't stand it. Feeling his cock throb and pulse only made it worse. Gwen reached down to finger her clit, knowing she'd go off like a rocket. She gasped when Zander softly slapped her hand away.

"Mine."

Bristling, she clipped, "Um, no, it's not."

He stilled, eyes blazing. "What did you just say?" It was a menacing whisper.

She lifted her chin, refusing to be intimidated. "I said, no, it's not."

Zander leaned forward. "Whose cock is buried in you right now?"

She gritted her teeth. "Yours."

"That's right. Whose come will soon be filling this pussy?"

"Yours."

"Correct again. So, who does this body belong to right now?"

Well, that was easy. "Me." He pulled out. Just pulled out of her. Then she suddenly found herself on her stomach as a hand came down sharply on her ass. *Twice.* She glared at him over her shoulder. "What *the fuck* do you think you're doing?" Her curt tone was totally lost on him; he was too busy staring at her ass in fascination.

"Such a pretty shade of pink."

"Your goddamn face will be a pretty shade of pink if you spank me a—" He did it again. *Motherfucker.* Gwen rolled onto her back and slapped at the offending hand. "If you think that because I'm human I'll be intimidated into doing and saying whatever you want, you've got another thing coming."

"Oh, we'll both be coming." He gave her his weight, hiked her legs high, and drove his cock deep in her pussy. A shocked gasp flew out of her. Eyes shooting a fire that made his cock throb, she cursed a blue streak. He caught her wrists and pinned them to the mattress, and her pussy spasmed around him. He smiled. "My baby likes being pinned down."

Yeah, she did, but Gwen wasn't going to admit that aloud. "Just fuck me, Devlin."

Zander pounded into her, keeping her hands pinned in place. All the while, he kissed her—tasting, dominating, and swallowing her moans. Her pussy became hotter and tighter.

He shifted his angle, hitting her sweet spot. "Look at me when you come, Gwen." He needed to *see* that moment when her eyes went blind and . . . yeah, there it was. Her mouth opened in a silent scream, her back arched, and that sweet little pussy contracted around him.

Zander's own release tore through him, rushed through his blood—a blinding pleasure that went on and on as her pussy milked him dry. He collapsed on top of her, burying his face in her neck. He felt spent. Sated. At peace.

As he rolled onto his back and draped a limp Gwen over him, his wolf took a cautious step toward her. And another. And another. Pausing, the beast greedily took in her scent and then settled down, resting his chin on his legs. Again, he watched her, still slightly wary.

Progress, Zander thought with a smile.

CHAPTER NINE

A few days later, Gwen stood at the reception desk, writing down all the cancellations she'd made—it seemed smart not to have innocent people around if the Moores were going to cause more shit. Concentrating on what she was doing would have been a lot easier if she hadn't had a hard body curled around her from behind while Zander nuzzled her neck.

A hand snaked under her shirt and settled on her stomach, warm and possessive, and she sighed. "What are you doing?"

Zander traced a circle on her skin with his thumb. "Touching you."

She jerked a little as he nipped her nape. "Well, you can't."

"Already did," he rumbled. "Touched you. Tasted you. Fucked you. Multiple times. And I'm gonna do it again."

"I meant, you can't do it right *here*. Don't growl at me, Devlin." But she was chuckling. "The new guests should be arriving any minute now." They would be their last guests until after the hearing. "I don't look very professional with you caging me against the desk."

"But it's fun."

She snorted, turning to face him as he stepped back. "Fun? *You* didn't have a hard cock trying to jam itself between your ass cheeks."

"It was one way to stop you ignoring me. Were my questions really bothering you?"

"Bothering me?" Gwen waved a hand. "No. I stopped listening a while ago."

A throaty chuckle was followed by the appearance of Bracken, who strolled out of the kitchen and leaned against the desk. "I like that you don't make things easy for him. He's too used to having his own way." Zander flipped him off, but Bracken just grinned and added, "On another subject, Gwen, have you heard anything from Andie?"

"Not yet. Hopefully we will soon." She sighed. "I've decided to go with her and check out the shelter. Then, if she doesn't like it, I can bring her back home. If she knows she has that option and has someone with her who she trusts, she's more likely to be open to the idea of staying there." As Zander clenched his jaw, Gwen cocked her head. "You don't want me going to the shelter, do you?"

Zander hooked his finger in the belt loop of her shorts and tugged her to him. "I intended to stay here with you while Bracken took her."

"Why? Do the people at the shelter have something against humans?"

"Anti-shifter humans, yes. People like you, no."

"Then what's the issue?" But she could guess. "You said your pack is closely allied with Makenna's. If she sees the mark you left on my neck, she'll tell your other pack mates, won't she? You don't want them to know about it."

Bracken grinned at Zander. "Must be hard dealing with a female who can read you like a book."

Zander ignored him. "No, I don't want them to know about the bite. Not because you're a dirty secret or something. It's because my Alpha, Nick, might not like that I'm involved with someone I'm protecting."

"He'll worry that you'll ignore his orders for me." Gwen understood. "I'll cover the bite with makeup . . . What's with the growling? It's a perfect solution."

Still grinning, Bracken explained, "He wants you to wear his mark with pride, not hide it. It's a shifter thing."

It was a pride thing, in Gwen's opinion.

Bracken's head tipped to one side. "A car's coming." He stalked to the door and opened it wide, looking all intimidating as he filled the doorway. "You've gotta be shitting me."

Gwen tensed despite the note of amusement in Bracken's voice. "What? What is it?" But Bracken loped outside.

Zander crossed to the door. His jaw hardened as a familiar vehicle pulled up outside. "Whose name is the next reservation in?"

"Derren Hudson. Why?" He cursed, and Gwen added, "I take it you know him."

"Oh yeah, we know him." And there would be no way that Zander could hide his involvement with Gwen from the couple currently exiting their SUV. Not when Gwen's mark was clear to see and her scent was all over him.

Gwen stayed behind the desk as Bracken entered with a dark-haired couple behind him. More shifters, she sensed as they exchanged greetings with Zander, who then turned to her.

"Gwen, this is Ally and Derren. They're the Betas of my pack."

"I've heard a lot about you, Gwen." Ally moved to the desk, emerald eyes gleaming. "So, *is* your B&B haunted?"

Zander sighed. "Of course it's not." Even if the place was sometimes chilly and eerie, and even if sometimes things happened that he couldn't explain.

Gwen blinked at him. "You don't think it is? Huh."

His brow furrowed. "What do you mean, *huh*?"

She shrugged. "I just didn't think you were the kind of guy who blinded himself to the obvious. It's okay. Lots of people only see what they want to see."

Zander's frown deepened. "I don't blind myself to anything."

"So nothing at all has happened here that's spooked you?" He didn't answer, and Gwen smiled. "Thought as much." She turned back to the Beta pair only to realize that they were both staring at the mark on her neck. Busted. Before they could comment on it, she checked them in and slid their key across the desk.

"What floor are they on?" Zander asked.

"Same floor as you."

"I'll show them the way."

Gwen was totally fine with that. "Okay." She cast the Betas another smile. "There's a Welcome Hamper and leaflets with all you need to know in your room—Zander will fill you in. Hope you enjoy your stay."

Ally's mouth curled. "Thanks."

Derren looked at Gwen, eyes narrowed, jaw hard. But at Ally's urging, he followed Zander and Bracken up the stairs.

Blowing out a breath, Gwen turned back to the desk.

As the four of them gathered in Ally and Derren's room, Zander folded his arms. "So, why are you here?" He sincerely doubted that Nick sent them as backup, given things had so far been uneventful.

"A couple of reasons," said Derren. "Someone made an anonymous call to the police to say that Harley sells drugs at the club to humans. Even though it's a club exclusive to shifters and all shifter territory is beyond their jurisdiction, the police turned up anyway. Nothing came of it, but it was a pain in the ass. Our guess is that the anonymous caller was Rory."

His brother was *such* a fucking asshole. "You could have told me this on the phone. What's your other reason for coming here?"

"Nick wanted us to check on you."

Zander slid a brief look at Ally, who was sitting on the bed, looking awkward. "You mean he wanted Ally to get a read on Gwen."

Derren's brow arched. "I'd be surprised by how much that seems to piss you off if her scent wasn't all over you, and I hadn't seen that brand on her neck. At what point were you going to mention that you're involved with the human?"

At no point, really. "There's no need. It's my personal business. It doesn't affect the pack."

Derren sighed. "Look, I appreciate what the human is doing for the cougar. I respect it. And, yeah, where you choose to dip your dick is your own business. But there are things you don't know."

It wasn't just Derren's words that made his hackles rise. There was something in the Beta's tone that told Zander he *really* wasn't going to like this. "What does that mean?"

"I asked Donovan to do some checking on Gwen. If you and Bracken were going to spend time out of your lives protecting her, I wanted to be sure she was on the level. Has she ever spoken to you about her parents?"

"I know her stepfather is a drunk who abused her mother."

"Fucker," muttered Bracken, who was leaning against the wall.

"He is a fucker," agreed Derren. "And apparently the woman's a glutton for punishment because they're still together, and he still beats her ass. She's a stripper. The strip bar is owned by Kenny Cogman, a seedy bastard who's a drug dealer and a big sponsor of the extremists."

Yeah, Zander had heard of him.

"Cogman likes to *sample* his employees. Zander, he's Gwen's fucking father."

Everything in Zander stilled. "You're sure of that?"

"His name's not on her birth certificate—the father's name came up blank. But it's pretty much common knowledge down there that he's her father. He has the same big Prussian-blue eyes that your human down there has."

Gut clenching, Zander silently cursed. Should he feel betrayed that she'd kept it from him? Probably not. He wasn't an open book either, and it wasn't likely to be something she was proud to share—especially with a shifter. Still, that sense of betrayal beat at him.

Bracken spoke. "It's not a point against Gwen, Derren. She doesn't use his name. She clearly doesn't think like him or she wouldn't be helping the cougar."

The Beta shrugged. "Maybe. Maybe not."

"Are she and Cogman in contact with one another?" Bracken asked.

"From what Donovan gathered, no," replied Derren. "But she's in contact with Cogman's other daughter. If you've heard of him, you'll have heard of Geena."

Zander *had* heard of her. Heard that she was stone fucking cold and even more ruthless than her father.

"Geena plays a major role in the family business," Derren added, upper lip curling.

"That doesn't mean Gwen plays any part in it," said Zander.

Derren sighed, impatient. "Zander, Geena Cogman is not someone who'd give a shit about a half sister and be sure to stay in contact with her for any warm, fuzzy reasons. If they're in contact, it's for business reasons only."

Face hard, Bracken asked, "How often are they in contact?"

"On a monthly basis." Derren turned back to Zander. "Nick sent us here to get a feel for her. He's worried that your feelings about what happened to Shelby are coloring your reading of Gwen. Given that you've marked her, he was obviously right that something's coloring it."

Bristling at that, Zander took a step toward Derren. In a flash, Ally was between them.

"Now hang on a minute." Planting a hand on Derren's chest, she said, "I picked up no disgust or prejudice from Gwen. She was a little nervous, but that's it. I didn't get any bad vibes from her, and my wolf didn't pick up anything either. As such, I think we can safely say she's not anti-shifter." Ally turned to Zander. "I realize that Derren's coming across as an asshole right now. Admittedly, he does that a lot. The point he's trying to make is that you don't *know* Gwen, so we should be careful here."

By his own admission, Zander was a jaded bastard with serious trust issues. Although he couldn't deny that he didn't know her well, everything he *did* know about Gwen Miller told him that she was nothing like her father or half sister. Of course, that distrustful part of him wondered if he was wrong, wondered if the reason his wolf was wary of her was that he'd sensed a prejudice that Zander himself had failed to see. But his gut instantly dismissed that theory.

"I'm not saying she's anti-shifter," said Derren. "I'm saying that there's a very strong possibility that she's into illegal shit, and I have *a lot* of reservations about you getting involved with her. When it comes to my pack, I don't take chances. Hearing you're involved with the daughter of Kenny Cogman . . . I don't like it."

"With all due respect, Derren, you don't have to like it."

Derren arched a brow. "So that's the way it is? Now, see, *that's* what I was afraid of."

Zander's jaw clenched. "Not going to argue with you about this, Derren. Leave it alone. When I want your approval about who I have in my bed, I'll let you know."

The Beta snorted. "Don't be an ass, Zander. I had a point. I made it. You want to ignore it? That's your call—you're a grown fucking man. But it's not like you to give people the benefit of the doubt, which makes me think that either you're in deep with this human or you have a blind spot here because you're mixing Shelby's situation with this one. Whatever it is, be careful . . . because both those scenarios could bite you on the ass."

◆ ◆ ◆

Gwen hadn't heard him coming. Even as she sat on the wooden swing hanging from the tree, surrounded by only the evening quiet of the marsh, she hadn't heard him stride down the boardwalk. It was truly eerie.

Still, she sensed she wasn't alone and opened her eyes to see him standing beside the swing. His face was in shadow, but she somehow got the feeling that he was frowning.

She hadn't seen him since she'd checked his pack mates into their room earlier that day. From what she could tell, he'd spent the entire day with them—exploring the marsh, showing them the borders of the land, going on a pack run.

He'd then gone to a local restaurant with them for dinner—something she'd discovered from Marlon, since Zander hadn't even bothered to say goodbye. Marlon was unhappy with Zander for not inviting her to join them. As she'd already planned to go with Yvonne to Julie's house, Gwen would have declined anyway. Still, Marlon felt his behavior was rude. For Gwen, *ducking* her was rude.

She refused to acknowledge that she'd actually missed him a little—apparently, she'd gotten too used to him being around her all the time. Gwen raised a brow. "So . . . are you done pettily avoiding me for a reason you haven't cared to share with the class?"

Zander's jaw hardened. Had he been avoiding her? Yeah. He'd needed time to think shit through and to work it all out in his head. So many things made no sense, and the only person who could really make him understand was Gwen. "You ever seen your birth certificate?"

Stilling the swing with her foot, Gwen blinked. He could be so damn random at times, and she didn't see where he was going with this. "Of course. I have a copy."

"So, you know that your father's name isn't on it." A muscle in his cheek ticked. "But you know who he is, don't you?"

It wasn't so much a question as it was a dare for Gwen to deny it, to lie to him. And if he thought she'd have reason to lie about it, he obviously knew the truth . . . which meant he'd done a thorough background check on her. She figured she should have expected that. There was no reason for him or his pack mates to trust her. Still, it stung. What hurt worse was his stiff behavior and curt voice. "Now you think that I, what, work with Kenny Cogman?" She'd tried to keep her tone even but failed by a *mile*.

"Why didn't you tell me he was your father?"

The note of betrayal in his tone made her spine lock. "Oh, I'm sorry, have you told me everything about you?"

"I spoke to you about my family," Zander pointed out. "I told you more than I've told most people."

Okay, well, that sort of caught her off guard. "Kenny isn't my family. I don't even consider Hanna my family. I haven't seen her since the social worker took me away when I was eight." And Gwen had absolutely no issue with that. "Kenny's sperm had fun with Hanna's eggs—that's the extent of his role in my life."

Yeah, thought Zander, but Kenny wasn't completely out of her life if she was linked to him through her half sister. "Do you consider *Geena* family?"

Gwen stiffened. She wasn't touching that one. The subject of Geena was off-limits.

"We know you're in contact with her."

Then they'd certainly run an extensive search. "If by that you mean you had someone check my phone records, you and your pack are creepy motherfuckers because *that* is going way too far."

"Given how different you are from Geena, given that *you* actually have a fucking conscience, I fail to understand why you're in contact with her."

Well, given he and his pack had invaded her privacy in such a way, Gwen failed to understand why he thought she'd tell him shit.

"Look, if I wanted your opinion on everything, I'd have married you, okay." She held up her hand when he went to speak. "Climb back out of my ass, Zander. My business is exactly that—*mine*."

His fists clenched. "She's as bad as Kenny. Worse in some ways. Why would you have anything to do with someone like that? Make me understand, Gwen, because I don't fucking get it."

"I don't need you to *get* it." Gwen rose from the swing. "And I don't have to explain or justify myself to you—and definitely not to your nosy-ass pack. I've got an idea. If you have such a problem with me and what I do with my life, get the fuck out of it and go back to California."

"Is that what you want?" he clipped. "For me to leave?"

No, she didn't. Nonetheless . . . "Tell me something, Zander. If I did a background search on you that totally invaded every inch of your life and then I expected you to *explain* your choices, would you actually care to do that?"

He sighed. "Gwen—"

"Would you want me around, knowing I have so little respect for your privacy?"

"I wasn't the one who ordered the background search, Gwen. No one did it to hurt you—my pack's intention was to be sure that Bracken and I knew everything we needed to know. They did it out of concern for our safety."

"But you *didn't* need to know all of that, Zander. And I sure as hell don't need to defend any of it. You don't like that? Go Yahoo, *Who gives a rat's ass?* I can promise you won't find my name." She turned to march down the boardwalk, but a hand pulled her up short.

"We're not fucking done," he growled.

She pulled her arm free. "Don't fucking curse at me, Devlin, I'm not in the goddamn mood for this fucking shit. And we're *so* done." Hearing the front door slam shut, Gwen looked to see Ally rushing off the porch.

"Ally, wait!" Derren called out, hot on her heels with Bracken right behind him.

Zander prowled toward them, abruptly alert, as their footsteps thundered along the boardwalk. "What's going on?"

"Get her in the house!" Ally shouted, urgency in every syllable. "She's not—"

The breath left Gwen's lungs as something heavy crashed into her back, knocking her down. Fire blazed along her shoulder blades as razor-sharp knives stabbed and tore through her skin like butter. Not knives, she numbly realized as a short, shrill shriek split the air. Talons.

Even with pain beating at her back, she tried to get up. However, she only managed to roll onto her side as, in a mad rustle of wings, a flock of large birds descended on her. Glaring at her through deep red eyes, they shrieked and bit and raked their talons, leaving trails of white-hot pain in their wake. She kicked her legs and swiped out at them, but they were too damn heavy to move. It all happened within seconds.

There was a loud, guttural roar. Then something larger jumped into the fray. And something else. And something else. Shrieks of alarm and pain mingled with furious growls and snarls. Unable to move, Gwen stayed curled up in a protective ball as a fight *literally* went on around and above her.

Suddenly the birds were gone in another rustle of feathers, and she heard the click of claws as the wolves gave chase.

"Gwen?" said Ally, shakily, as she dropped to her knees at Gwen's side.

She lifted her head, and there was a large wolf, his fur a mix of brown and gray. "Zander?" The wolf snarled, golden eyes hard and . . . distrustful. More pain tore through her, but it was emotional pain this time. The wolf raced off in the direction the other wolves had headed.

"Gwen," Ally repeated, "can you stand? We need to get you inside."

With Ally's help, Gwen rose to her feet. For a long moment, she stood still—baffled, speechless. Then the blazing pain from her wounds *really* kicked in, and she snapped right out of her shocked state. Noticing two gray birds lying dead on the boardwalk, she blinked. "Shit, what the fuck?" She touched her throbbing cheek, felt something warm and wet.

"Inside," said Ally, gently drawing Gwen along the boardwalk. Ally led her into the house and through to the living area. The lights flickered, and doors banged shut all over the house. Ally's brows almost hit her hairline. "I don't think the ghosts like that you're hurt. I'd ask you to lie on your back, but I think it would hurt like a bitch. Just sit on the floor for me."

Gwen did so. "What are you going to do?"

The Seer fell to her knees at her side. "Sorry if this hurts." She rested her hands over a wound on Gwen's back.

Gwen flinched, hissing in pain, but otherwise remained still. Soft, preternatural energy flowed through her like warm syrup, soothing and healing. If she wasn't having her own personal crisis in her head, she'd have been utterly absorbed by what she was feeling. It was one thing to know that some shifters could heal, and a whole other thing to experience it.

At that moment, Marlon came rushing into the room. "I heard all the—" His eyes bulged. "What. The. Hell?"

"Marlon, get over here and hold Gwen's hand."

Marlon did so, demanding, "Will someone please tell me who the hell did this to you? Was it Brandt? I will seriously shoot the little bastard myself if—"

"It was a flock of birds," said Gwen, tone flat. "Big birds with red eyes." Initially, she'd been numb with shock, unable to properly process what happened. But the shock had given way to a controlled anger that left her able to think more clearly. "Shifters."

"Shifters?" echoed Marlon, incredulous. "That's—" Noticing that Gwen's wounds were healing, Marlon said, "Wow."

"Yes, shifters," Ally said to Gwen with a sad sigh. "It's shifters like those birds who give our kind a bad rep and make humans distrust us." After a few moments, she sat back on her heels and puffed out a long breath. "You may feel a little drowsy, but I doubt you'll lose consciousness."

Yeah, "drowsy" was a good word. Gwen's body felt limp and featherlight, like she could happily doze off. She probed the area where she'd had a long rake mark on her arm, surprised to find it wasn't even tender.

Marlon frowned at Ally's pasty face. "You don't look too good yourself. Stay there, I'll be right back."

Gwen sat on the sofa, her movements sluggish. She took a deep, shuddering breath. "Thanks for healing me."

"How do you feel?" Ally asked.

Gwen snorted. "Like I was attacked by a flock of birds. You came running outside as if you knew something was wrong. Did you?"

"I'm a Seer. I had a vision that you were attacked by goshawks."

"Goshawks?" Gwen shook her head. "I've seen goshawks. They're big, and some of them have red eyes, sure, but they're not *that* big."

"Shifters' birds are often much bigger than their avian counterparts. Our pack had a run-in with harpy eagle shifters not so long ago. That was bad. One struck Zander hard from behind, barely missing the back of his neck—that move might well have killed him. Another actually tried to carry him off; it probably would have carried him high and then dropped him."

Gwen's chest tightened. She was pissed at him, but that didn't mean she was okay with hearing he could have been seriously hurt or killed.

Marlon reappeared and handed both Gwen and Ally a bottle of water and a granola bar. "Here. Now, tell me exactly what happened."

Gwen gave him a nod of thanks and unscrewed the lid of the bottle. "They just came out of nowhere. Zander, Derren, and Bracken shifted and attacked them while I pretty much lay there, unable to do a fucking thing. Ally thinks they were goshawks."

Marlon swore. "The Moores will be behind this."

"I should have expected Ezra to hire shifters to hurt me." Gwen sipped her water. "No one would suspect him of that."

"Bastard," Marlon spat. He shot Ally a weak but grateful smile. "Thank God you were here."

Gwen sighed down at her ruined, bloody clothes. "I really liked this shirt. Yvonne bought it for me. I'm so glad she decided to stay at Julie's for the night. This would have sent her in a blind panic."

Frantic footsteps were quickly followed by the door bursting open and Andie dashing into the room, breathing hard. "I saw the wolves running around like their asses were on fire." She noticed the blood on Gwen's torn clothes, and her eyes flashed cat.

"I'm okay. Ally healed me."

Andie carefully eyed the she-wolf, who was munching on her granola bar.

"I'm no threat to you," said Ally. "I'm one of Zander and Bracken's pack mates."

Looking a little mollified, Andie shifted her focus back to Gwen. "Did Brandt come back? Was it one of the Moores?"

"In a sense." Gwen explained what had happened, leaving Andie gaping at her.

"God, I really hate that family." Andie nostrils flared. "I think I smell fire."

Marlon cleared his throat. "That happens sometimes. We'll smell things like perfume or smoke or aftershave. Blame the ghosts."

Looking fascinated, Ally went to speak. But then her head tilted. "Sounds like the boys are back."

Silently, Derren entered first, scratches on his face. “They got away,” he bit out. “We followed them as far as we could, but . . . well, we can't fucking fly.”

“At least we killed two of them before the others flew off,” said Bracken. “We dumped the bodies in the river.”

Zander stalked inside and made a beeline for Gwen, neck corded, nostrils flaring. Fury was stamped into every line of his face. A frisson of fear trailed down her spine.

“She's fully healed,” Ally reassured him.

Zander sank onto the sofa and drew Gwen onto his lap, holding her tight against him. He breathed her in, using her scent to calm him. But the scent of her blood was still strong in the air, thanks to the stains on her clothes and skin, and it was hard to regain his composure.

He wanted to punch and bite and claw and mangle and *kill*, but most of the bastards had gotten away. He needed to see them pay, needed to tear them apart, needed the smell of their blood to replace the smell of Gwen's.

He ground his teeth until his jaw ached. There was a tightness in his chest—unfamiliar and insidious, leaving him with a thick ache in his throat. He could see that she was trying to relax against him, but she couldn't stop the delicate tremble that ran through her limbs. Couldn't erase that her face was pale or that her eyes were wide and glassy.

Adrenaline still coursed through him, making it even harder for him to cool his anger. If she was close, if he could scent and feel her, just maybe he'd get through the night without losing his mind.

Gwen squirmed. “You can let go. I'm fine and—”

A growl rattled his chest. “Shut up and let me hold you.”

She pinched him, but the big bastard didn't even flinch. “I don't need your attitude right now, Devlin.” But she didn't push him away, because she sensed he was on edge. She was still pissed at him for earlier. In fact, she was pissed at the other three wolves in the room too—they had no right to invade her privacy. But since one had healed her and the others had just risked themselves to hunt a flock of bird shifters who'd attacked her, she couldn't really complain right then.

"Why can I smell burning?" asked Bracken.

Marlon quickly explained, only to receive skeptical looks from Bracken and Derren.

"The birds were goshawks, weren't they?" said Ally.

"Big-ass goshawks," said Derren. "Most flocks of their species are available for hire." The light flickered, and he tensed as he glanced up at it. "There aren't many of the flocks around these parts. We'll find out which one it was, and they'll pay one way or another."

Gwen twisted as much as Zander's grip would allow so she could look at Andie. "I don't mean to scare you, but you could be next. If you're not going to go to the shelter, at least move in here. You'd be safe inside the walls."

Andie bit her lip. "About the shelter . . . I was thinking that maybe it might not be such a bad idea to check it out. I'm just a little worried that it's not even real. It's hard to believe a place like that exists."

"It exists," Ally assured her. "I think it would be a good place for you."

"I could go with you to see it," Gwen offered. "If you don't like it or you feel it won't work for you, we'll come right back here."

Zander didn't argue. It would be good for Gwen to get away from Oregon, even if only for a day. He was no longer concerned about trying to hide his involvement with her from his pack, beyond caring whether they would approve of it. Human or not, Kenny Cogman's daughter or not, she was his. Since Ally and Derren already knew, it was likely that they'd told Nick anyway, so it made no difference if Gwen stayed behind.

"We can take you there as soon as tomorrow," Bracken told the cougar. "In my opinion, the sooner you leave, the better."

Andie took a long breath. "I'll go and check it out tomorrow, but I want Gwen to come."

"That's fine," said Bracken. "We'll leave in the morning. I really think you should stay here tonight, just to be on the safe side."

After a long moment, Andie nodded. "I'll go pack my stuff in the morning, just in case I decide to stay at the shelter."

Relieved, Gwen smiled. "The only guests we have at the moment are Ally and Derren. There are plenty of free rooms—take your pick."

"Marlon can help her find a room." Zander stood, cradling Gwen against him. "You need rest."

"I'm just a little drowsy—Ally said it's normal."

Ignoring that, Zander carried her out of the room and up the stairs. He heard Donnie enter the house, but he kept walking. The others would reassure Donnie that Gwen was fine and explain what happened. She needed peace and quiet and rest. And he needed to be alone with her.

Zander never resorted to panic. He was always the practical voice of reason in a dangerous situation. But as they'd stood on that boardwalk and he'd seen those birds descend on her and he'd smelled her blood, he'd sure as fuck panicked. That panic hadn't yet left him; it still slithered through him, tormenting him. She was really the only thing keeping him from losing his shit, and he doubted she even knew it.

Inside her room, Gwen squirmed. "Put me down. I can walk on my own steam."

"Don't, Gwen," he clipped. "Just let me have my way right now."

Gwen sighed inwardly, not really sure what to do with him. She'd never seen him this way before—edgy, vibrating with suppressed anger. So Gwen didn't say a word as he took her into the en suite bathroom, where he gently set her down and stripped off their clothes. She didn't say a word as he opened the frosted glass door of the shower stall and ushered her inside. Still silent, she shampooed her hair as he soaped her down, careful to wash away every bit of dried blood from her skin, utterly focused on his task.

When they stepped out of the shower and he wrapped a lush towel around her, she said, "Your wolf doesn't like me, huh?"

He blinked in surprise. "He didn't like seeing you bleeding and in pain. The smell of your blood made him crazy."

She snorted. "He snarled at me, Zander. He doesn't trust me. I could see it in his eyes."

Patting her dry, Zander explained, "My wolf is a tough fucker. Nothing fazes him. Something about you makes him wary, but I'll be damned if I can figure out what. He doesn't dislike you; he's just on his guard."

She didn't like to think that his wolf felt that way about her. "Suspecting I'll do what?"

"I don't know. He's gotten better as the days have gone on. He doesn't mind you being around; he's not uncomfortable with you. In fact, he enjoys your company and *wants* you around. He's also protective of you. But he's still on his guard." Now that she was dry, he used another towel to dry himself off. "You shouldn't take his negative behavior personally. My wolf generally doesn't like female attention."

She paused in pulling a brush through her hair. "Why?"

"It's just the way he is."

"Maybe he gets aggravated by it because the only attention he wants is that of his true mate," she suggested.

Zander frowned thoughtfully. He hadn't considered that before. "Maybe." Right then, it didn't matter. He cupped her jaw, letting his gaze roam over her face. "Such big eyes."

She swallowed at the possessiveness in his voice. "Aren't you supposed to be pissed at me for not pouring out my life story?"

"You're not going to cause an argument, baby, if that's your game."

"I don't have a game. I have a problem with people thinking I have to justify myself to them. There's a good reason why I don't tell people shit about my past—there's nothing good to share from before I went into foster care."

"Gwen—"

"When people learn that my mom's a stripper, my stepdad's a drunk, and my dad's a drug dealer, they look at me differently. I'm the same Gwen you impaled on your cock last night. But because you discovered my biological father is a drug-dealing equivalent of a Nazi, you were looking at me like you'd never seen me before." And that hurt, even as she wished it didn't. "You know what? It doesn't matter."

He crowded her, shaking his head. "Oh, no, you don't."

Her brows snapped together. "What?"

"You're pouncing on this as an excuse to push me away." He could literally see her bolstering her defenses. "Let's get a few things perfectly straight. You're right; you don't have to justify yourself to me. I was mostly mad because I didn't like learning something so significant about you from my Betas. I would rather have heard it from you. It hurt, so, yeah, I overreacted a little.

"I understand your privacy is important to you. Neither me nor my pack meant to hit any hot buttons. But I'd do the same search on any stranger that hung around you . . . because you matter, and I'd put your safety before another person's right to privacy. I won't apologize for that, so I can't expect my pack to apologize for putting my safety first either. Also, I don't believe you're anything like Cogman. I'd have already sensed it if you were."

"Maybe I'm a good actress."

"And maybe you're someone who's trying to atone for the sins of her father—that's not something you need to do."

Gwen perched her hands on her hips. "I'm not trying to atone for Kenny's fucked-up mistakes. No amount of good deeds from me would manage that." The guy was plain cruel. "This isn't about me or anything I went through. It's about *Andie*. I'm helping her because I *want* to, because she deserves justice, and because Brandt needs to pay. That's it. My childhood . . . it's not relevant here. None of it matters anyway. It's in the past."

Oh, it matters, thought Zander. If it hadn't, she'd have looked her cool and casual self. Right then, she looked like someone who'd been jammed in an elevator too long. He'd have expected defensiveness or anger, but not the panic he could scent. And then he understood.

Zander framed her face with his hands. "It's not just that you're highly private, is it, baby? It's not even that your natural instinct is to keep things to yourself. You avoid talking of your childhood because you never feel far enough away from it." Her eyes flickered, and he knew he'd hit the nail on the head. "I didn't see that before. Should have. I blame your legs. They're too damn distracting. Your eyes too. And your mouth."

He kissed said mouth, indulging in a long, thorough taste of her. His cock, already hard at just the sight of her naked, throbbed painfully. But she needed to rest, not to get fucked into the mattress. So he settled them both in bed, curving himself around her. "Sleep, Gwen."

Gwen licked her lips. She should probably tell him to go after the shit he'd pulled earlier. But, well, she didn't want to be alone right then. She was still a little shaken from the attack, and he made her feel safe. Still . . . "I'm not sure I can sleep."

"It's not complex, baby. Close your eyes. Relax. Don't think." He almost smiled at her long-suffering sigh. Within minutes, her breathing evened out, and she sagged into the bed. Only then did he close his eyes, but sleep didn't come to him. It probably wouldn't come for a while.

His anger was still too hot, his need for vengeance still too strong. He was also mad at himself for pushing her buttons earlier, for being too wrapped up in his own hurt to truly consider both sides of the situation. It was all part of empathy not being his strong point. Still, he'd been an asshole, and he knew it.

Zander wouldn't allow her to push him away, though. He wouldn't let them go back to square one. He *definitely* wouldn't pack his shit and leave. She was stubborn as hell, but he could be very persuasive when he wanted something. He'd use those powers of persuasion tomorrow.

CHAPTER TEN

She was in a good mood. Mostly because she'd woken to a tongue stabbing inside her. Better than any alarm, in Gwen's opinion.

Of course, she'd known it was an attempt to soften her up so that she didn't insist on Zander and his pack mates leaving. It hadn't worked. Really, it was the apology he'd delivered straight after making her come that earned him her forgiveness. It hadn't been a long, heart-felt apology. It had been quick, straight, and offered no excuses—she respected that, and she preferred it to soppy words.

Not that she thought for a single moment that he wouldn't ever again push her buttons. He'd even do it purposely if he thought it was necessary. He'd continue to shove his way into her business because, as she'd quickly come to learn, Zander Devlin was a nosy and often interfering bastard who had absolutely no quit in him.

He might not be a born Alpha, predestined to lead a pack, but he was the typical alpha male that could be found in most species. That meant he came with some traits that were often problematic for females. Dominant. Assertive. Persistent. Stubborn. Controlling in his efforts to protect and defend.

Gwen didn't see the point in expecting anything different from him; she'd only be driving herself insane if she did. And holding grudges was a lot like swallowing poison—you were only hurting yourself.

Besides, he'd . . . well, he'd been good to her last night. He'd not only killed two of her attackers and then tried to hunt the rest of the flock, he'd comforted her, cleaned her up, taken care of her, and held her while she slept. Yeah, okay, he partly did the latter things to help himself calm down, but there were plenty of other ways for a person to calm down. He'd chosen to be with her.

Due to her good mood, Gwen didn't complain at the way Zander hovered around her as she and Marlon cleaned the kitchen after breakfast. He was still on edge, and she didn't want that. She knew that touch soothed shifters, so she let him crowd her, play with her hair, nibble her earlobe, lick over the mark he'd left on her neck.

It wasn't exactly a hardship to have six and a half feet of gorgeousness take up her space.

It *was* hard to clean with three dominant male shifters in the room—it was a whole lot of testosterone. Marlon seemed to bask in it. Ally seemed perfectly used to it.

"Andie's been a while," said Marlon. The cougar had gone to the cabin to grab her things. "Do you think she might have changed her mind?"

"I doubt it," said Ally. "When she left this morning, I didn't pick up any indecisiveness from her. Just determination and a little nervousness."

A cell phone beeped. "That's mine." Marlon dug his smartphone out of his pocket. "Yvonne wants me to pick her up from Julie's. Do I tell her about the goshawk attack?"

Gwen bit her lip. "It would be wrong to keep it from her. Just downplay it a little. Make it clear that I wasn't on death's door or anything."

"She's still going to freak out," said Marlon.

Zander stilled. "Someone's coming." He stalked out of the kitchen and down the hallway. His pack mates stepped onto the porch behind him as a car pulled up outside. Zander didn't recognize the black Audi, but he did recognize the male wolf who slid out of it. He was not a person who Zander would have expected to see at all.

Ally blinked at her foster brother—her somewhat sociopathic brother and, no, that wasn't an exaggeration. He wasn't a bad guy, but his moral compass was off course. "Cain? How did you know I was here? Is everything okay?"

Cain stopped in his tracks, looking surprised to see her. Recovering, he bounded up the steps and eyed them all curiously. "What are you guys doing here?"

Ally snorted softly. "Well, hello to you too. I know you're not a hugger or one for gushing, but you could at least look happy to see me."

Cain rolled his eyes. "I saw you a week ago. Don't be dramatic."

"If you're not here looking for me, why are you here?"

"I need to speak with the woman who works here. Gwen Miller."

Zander wasn't comfortable with that. "Why, exactly?"

Cain blinked. "Why the suspicious tone? Is something going on?"

At that moment, a chuckling Marlon came jogging out the door, off the porch, and down the steps while Gwen came striding down the hallway, shouting, "*You are not color-blind!*"

Giving Zander and the others a quick wave, Marlon jumped into his car—no doubt intending to collect Yvonne—just as Gwen reached the door, huffing.

Zander threaded his fingers through hers. "Gwen, this is Ally's foster brother."

Gwen blinked and then gasped. "Shit, Cain, I forgot you were coming. Hey, I didn't know you were related to one of Zander's pack mates."

Zander tensed. She knew Cain? And she knew him well enough to be on a first-name basis with him? It had taken constant pushing on Zander's part to make Gwen use *his* first name. He noticed that the others looked just as surprised and intrigued.

Cain crossed to her, frowning as Zander moved protectively closer. "Jesus, Zander, I'm not going to hurt her. Gwen, what's going on?"

Derren's gaze slid from Gwen to Cain. "So, you two know each other? How?"

Cain shrugged. "I stay here sometimes."

Ally snorted. "You really think I don't know when you're lying? Come on, Cain, tell us. You know you can trust us. You know you can trust me." She sounded hurt that he'd hesitate to tell her.

Cain's lips clamped together as he looked from Gwen to the wolves, seeming torn over whether to answer honestly. Gwen held up her hands, gesturing that she'd leave the decision up to him. She would rather keep the matter quiet, but she had the feeling that Ally would keep hounding her foster brother until he told her *something*.

Done with waiting for the wolf to make up his damn mind, Zander growled, "How do you know Gwen? And why are you here?"

Cain sighed. "We need to talk somewhere we won't be overheard."

"My room," Zander proposed. If they were in the living area and Donnie entered the house, he'd likely hear them talking. But if they were upstairs, they were more likely to have complete privacy.

Zander kept possession of Gwen's hand as they all headed up the stairs. He didn't speak again until they were inside his room and he'd closed the door behind them. "Now, answer my questions, Cain."

The male gave him a pointed look. "This can't go any farther than this room."

"You can't expect us to keep secrets from our Alphas," said Derren.

Cain raised a brow at him. "Oh, so you've told them absolutely everything about you?"

Derren shrugged one shoulder, mouth twitching. He and Cain had known each other a long time. If Cain hadn't asked Derren to play Ally's bodyguard for a short while, the mated couple might never have met. Even though Cain liked and respected Derren, he also had a big problem with *any* guy being with Ally, so he had little patience for Derren these days.

"If any of you don't feel comfortable keeping quiet, leave the room," said Cain. When no one made a move to leave, Cain rolled back his shoulders. "Gwen's an informant for The Movement. Has been for the past six years."

A shocked silence hit the room. Cain was part of The Movement, and he even pretended to be one of the key players so that the true masterminds could act without being closely monitored by human law enforcement and the extremists themselves.

"An informant?" Derren slowly echoed, and Cain gave a curt nod.

It quickly clicked into place for Zander. Gwen didn't know anyone involved with the extremists . . . but her half sister did—the same half sister whom she was in regular contact with. Zander hadn't understood why the hell Gwen would have any contact whatsoever with someone like Geena Cogman, but if Geena was feeding her information about the extremists . . . yeah, that made sense.

Zander swallowed, touched that Gwen would go to such measures to help his kind. On the other hand, he was pissed because it put her in a whole lot of danger. If they hadn't been in a room full of people and Cain hadn't had a lot more talking to do, Zander would have pulled her to him and kissed the breath out of her.

Derren looked at Gwen. "Huh. Didn't see that coming."

Zander gave him a look that said, *I told you that you'd gotten her all wrong.* The Beta inclined his head.

Cain turned to Gwen. "Now, explain why you have Mercury wolves guarding you."

"Well, it all started with a bunch of delinquent assholes." Gwen told him everything, starting with the assault she witnessed and ending with the goshawk attack.

Cain scraped his hand over his jaw. "I've said it before and I'll say it again—you've got some balls, Miller. Not a lot of people would be so determined to see this through to the end."

"How many people know you're an informant?" Ally asked her.

"In my life? One," replied Gwen.

Ally lifted a brow. "Marlon?"

Gwen shook her head. "No. No one here knows, and it needs to stay that way. If they knew, they'd be in danger." And likely try to talk her out of helping the group.

"Your secret's one hundred percent safe with us," Bracken vowed.

"Do you think the goshawk flock was hired by Moore?" asked Cain.

"Yes," said Zander as he absentmindedly toyed with Gwen's braid. "It's a smart way to target Gwen. People would never link a shifter attack with him."

Cain turned to Gwen. "I don't like this. I can set you up in a safe house."

"I appreciate the offer, Cain," she told him. "I do. But I won't let them chase me away from my own home. Nu-uh. Besides, my leaving won't stop them coming here."

"So bring your family with you."

"Donnie won't leave. He's more likely to rig the place and blow them all to pieces, sacrificing himself in the process." She sighed. "My point is that a safe house isn't the answer."

Zander nodded. "I agree."

Cain snickered at him. "Of course you do—you've marked her, and your scents are all over each other. You want her where you can see her."

"Yeah, I do," Zander admitted. "I respect you, Cain, but I don't trust you or any of your people to protect her better than me."

"Really? Then why do you feel that you need Bracken, Ally, and Derren here as backup?"

Bracken bristled. "I'm here because I want to be."

"Nick sent me and Derren," said Ally. "Zander didn't ask us to come or to stay."

"So why are you *still* here, knowing shit is going down?" growled Cain.

"Because Ally wanted to know if the damn place was really haunted," said Derren.

Bracken gave the Beta male a daring look. "And you're bored."

Derren sighed. "And I'm bored."

Done with the conversation, Zander opened the door. "I need a minute alone with Gwen. We'll meet you downstairs." One by one, the wolves filed out. Zander closed the door, waiting for the sounds of footsteps to disappear down the hall before he spoke to Gwen. "Geena passes you information about what Kenny is getting up to with the extremists, and then you pass it on to Cain."

Gwen rubbed her nape. She'd hoped he wouldn't guess, but there was clearly no such luck. She supposed it wasn't a big leap to make.

"Does she know that you feed Cain information?"

"I'm trusting you not to repeat this." Which was a big deal for her, because trust didn't come easily to Gwen. At his nod of reassurance, she said, "Yes, she knows. Geena's not a saint. She is involved in Kenny's business, but she has morals. She's firmly against the extremists, and she doesn't like that money from the business is funding their shit."

So Geena's motives were partly selfish, Zander mused, because she was protecting her money. Still, she was also risking her life, because if Kenny discovered what Geena was doing, he'd probably kill her. "How long have you been in contact with her?"

"Since I was fourteen. She found out about me and wanted to be sure that I was okay. I think she's just surrounded by so many jaded people who she can't trust or relax with that she just wanted someone in her life who didn't want anything from her. Someone who wouldn't judge her for where she came from." Gwen could understand that. "She's not all bad. She keeps up the cold-bitch reputation because, in many ways, it protects her. For all her faults, she isn't prejudiced against anyone or anything."

"Have you two ever met in person?"

"Sure. Kenny knows. He doesn't care. He'd never guess that she tells me stuff."

Zander settled his hands on her hips. "Does he want contact with you?"

"No. He'll be glad I'm not coming to him, looking for money."

"She doesn't pass on anything that can shut him down and put his ass in jail?"

Gwen shook her head. "She loves him, in her way. She wants Daddy's approval. Unless he does something truly horrific, I don't think she'll ever move against him. For now, this is enough."

Zander twisted his mouth. "If The Movement is repeatedly crushing the extremists' plans, he must be considering that there could be a leak."

"Too many of them work together for anyone to have a specific idea of where the leak is. According to Geena, Kenny thinks some of the extremists are having their calls monitored and being watched constantly. He's too arrogant to think he's the weak link."

Zander caressed her hip bones with his thumbs. "You could have told me all this."

"You know why I didn't." She was protecting her sister.

"If he finds out you two are working together like this . . ."

"We each have our reasons for taking that risk."

Zander rested his forehead on hers. "I want to spank your ass for putting yourself in the line of fire this way, even though I appreciate everything you're doing. I don't like the idea of you in this kind of danger." Hated it, in fact. His wolf didn't like it. He was pacing, agitated.

"You can't tell anyone what I told you, Zander. Not about me. Not about Geena."

He combed his fingers through her bangs. "I can't guarantee that my pack mates won't guess some of it, but I won't confirm or deny any theory they run by me. I won't repeat anything you've told me."

She nodded, knowing that would have to be enough.

"Gwen, Andie's here!" Bracken practically bellowed from downstairs.

Gwen winced. "That guy has got a big set of lungs on him."

Grunting, Zander slid his hand around her nape and then took her mouth. The kiss was soft but deep as he devoured her, needing her taste on his tongue. "Let's go. Makenna's expecting us."

A few hours later, Gwen frowned up at the basic redbrick building. It didn't have a sign or in any way identify itself as a shelter. "It's . . . unobtrusive. Not the sort of place that would snatch your attention as you walk by."

"Maybe that's sort of the point," suggested Andie, flexing her fingers nervously.

"Yeah, maybe." Gwen shot her a supportive smile as they followed Zander and Bracken up the path. Derren and Ally had decided to stay at the B&B to keep watch over Marlon, Yvonne, and Donnie, which Gwen sincerely appreciated.

Cain had left with the envelope of information she'd given him that she'd gathered from Geena, but not before making yet another offer to set her up at a safe house. Again, she'd declined. Running and hiding wasn't the answer, and it wouldn't solve anything.

Zander knocked on the glass door and then turned to Gwen. "You okay?"

"Sure. Why wouldn't I be?"

Bracken leaned against the wall. "I guess some humans would be nervous about entering a building full of lone shifters."

Gwen's nose wrinkled. "Nah, I have you three to kick asses and take down names and all that stuff."

Andie shook her head, amused. "How is it that you always manage to make me smile, no matter the situation?"

"I don't know."

The door opened, and a slender, quirkily dressed female with long hair made up of gold, copper, dark-red, and plum-purple streaks smiled at them. She also wore a baby sling. As the sling faced inward, Gwen could only make out tiny limbs and a little mop of short, dark curls.

"Zander, Bracken, hi." She looked at Andie, who was tense as a bow. "I'm Makenna. You must be Andie."

The cougar nodded and flashed Makenna a quick smile.

Makenna's gaze then sliced to Gwen and turned assessing. "And you must be Gwen."

Gwen gave her a polite smile. "I am. I can only see a little of your baby, but it sure does look cute."

"Aw, thank you. Come on in." Makenna stepped back, allowing them to enter a small, bright reception area. She twisted to give them a better view of her baby. "Meet Sienna Rose Conner."

Gwen smiled. "She's so sweet."

Makenna gestured toward a broad, grumpy-looking male who stood a few feet away, exchanging nods with the Mercury wolves. "That's my mate, Ryan. The scowl is permanent, so don't take offense. He's extra grouchy today because he doesn't like me or the baby leaving our territory." Ryan grunted, and Makenna crossed her eyes. "No, I'm not. Stop being a brat."

At Gwen's confused frown, Zander explained, "Makenna claims she can translate his grunts."

"Ah," said Gwen with a slow nod.

Makenna pointed to the small, round brunette who was standing behind the reception desk with a guy who seemed to be sorting through one of the lockers lining the wall. "That's Dawn. She owns and runs the shelter."

Hearing her name, Dawn turned. She gave the Mercury wolves a gorgeous smile. "Boys, it's good to see you."

Ignoring the way his wolf's mood typically soured at the presence of the females, Zander inclined his head at Dawn. He liked her. The born Alpha had dedicated her life to the running of the shelter, even though it was a nonprofit organization and it had to be difficult for her inner cat to be without a pride. She'd done her best to find sponsors, grants, and also funding from the shifter council. Even with the additional help of both financial and practical donations, it wasn't easy, but she ran the shelter without complaint. He respected the sacrifices she'd made.

His wolf snarled at him, wanting to leave. He didn't like being around females who weren't from his pack, just as he didn't like all the strange scents of varying shifter breeds. Zander drew Gwen's scent into his lungs, drowning out the other smells. His wolf settled a little, finding an element of comfort in her scent.

"This is Gwen," said Makenna. "And behind her is Andie, who I told you about."

Dawn beamed. "Great. We've been waiting for you. This here is Heath. He works at the desk for us." She gestured to the male at her side who Zander noticed was busy staring at Gwen's legs. It wasn't entirely surprising to Zander, given that she was wearing shorts.

When she'd pulled them on that morning, she'd said, "Don't whine about the shorts, Devlin. It's too hot to wear anything else."

Actually, Zander found he didn't mind the shorts so much now that he knew he'd be the only person touching those legs. He got a strange kind of kick out of knowing others wanted what they didn't have a prayer of touching because she was his. He didn't need to be told that wasn't particularly normal.

Dawn rounded the desk, her smiling eyes on Andie. "I must say it'll be nice to have another cougar around. There aren't many here."

Andie stepped out from behind Gwen and shook Dawn's hand. "Um, hi." She exchanged a nod with Heath, who was now staring at Andie like she was food.

"I know a little of your story, but only the basics," Dawn told her. "You're more than welcome here. All we need is for you all to sign in, and then I can take you for a tour." Dawn handed a pen to Bracken, who quickly jotted down their names in the book on the desk.

Having finished reading the "Rules and Regulations" sign on the wall, Gwen turned to Dawn. "This place is safe, right? I mean, I noticed you don't have guards."

"This place is as safe as we can make it," said Dawn. "The Phoenix Alphas offered to post guards, but I don't want people to mistakenly think that the shelter is run by the pack. Loners would never feel they could come here for sanctuary if it wasn't run by other loners."

Gwen nodded, getting it. "Do the security cameras work?"

"Yes. They're relatively new, courtesy of the Mercury Alphas, and each of the cameras provides live feed to the monitors in my office. The Mercury pack also installed software on my phone that gives me a panic button. If there's a problem and I press it, both the Phoenix and Mercury Packs will be alerted."

Andie seemed to relax a little at that, Gwen noticed . . . as if the cougar realized that Zander had been telling the truth when he told her about their acceptance of loners.

"Why don't you wait in the common room while I take Andie for a tour?" Dawn suggested to Gwen.

Yeah, right, like *that* would happen, especially since Andie didn't appear fond of the idea. Gwen smiled. "Thanks, but I'd be interested in coming along to look around, if that's okay with you." She thought that sounded a lot better than, *"I don't trust Andie's safety with you yet."* But Dawn's eyes narrowed, as if she'd easily read between the lines. Still, she didn't seem offended, just understanding.

Zander sidled up to Gwen, his arm brushing hers. "Bracken and I will come too."

"All right," said Dawn. "We can—"

Bracken suddenly shuddered. "Whoa, just got a horrible chill down my spine."

"Someone walked over your grave," both Gwen and Makenna said in unison. Then the two females looked at each other, chuckling.

Zander frowned. He'd expect that from Makenna, since she was incredibly superstitious, but not Gwen.

Bracken held up a hand. "Wait, you really think me feeling a chill means someone walked over my grave?"

Makenna snorted. "Obviously. Jeez. Come on, Gwen, you're going to love this place."

Gwen listened avidly as Dawn told them about the shelter while they walked. Apparently when her mother started it thirty years ago, it had been just a day center—a place loners went to simply sit, drink coffee, eat a decent meal, and talk with other loners. With the help of funding, Dawn's mother had gradually expanded it. It was certainly expansive.

Dawn guided them around each of the floors, except for the attic, since that was where Dawn lived. The first floor had a common room, cafeteria, communal toilets, and private rooms for those with children. Females slept on the second floor, and males slept on the third—both floors were dormitories. All supplies were kept in the basement.

Gwen had been surprised to learn that many slept in the dome-shaped tents that were scattered around the land at the rear of the building near the children's play area. Dawn sure made use of every inch of space, both inside and outside the shelter.

"How long are people allowed to stay here?" Gwen asked.

"There's no time limit," said Dawn, pausing in a hallway. "Although Makenna can attempt to get them a place somewhere, like with relatives or with Alphas that are willing to adopt or foster loners, many prefer to remain loners. We do what we can to help them find an apartment and blend into the human community, but some wish to stay here long term."

"You allow that?"

Dawn nodded. "In exchange, they work here—there are always plenty of things that need doing at a shelter, like cleaning, cooking, and laundry. It's understandable that they might wish to stay. You're a human, so you may find it difficult to understand just how isolating the loner lifestyle can be. Shifters aren't built to live alone. Some residents find the same comfort in running the shelter as they'd find in belonging to a pack or pride, for instance."

Dawn turned to Andie. "I want you to know that you're not the only person here who's had problems with humans—not by a long shot. Being without a pack, pride, or whatever it may be means that loners are vulnerable to other shifters and humans. People often assume that a shifter would only be a loner if they were cast out by their Alphas. Not always. Some are runaways, others are in hiding, and many are simply lost after the death of their mate. Many loners here will be able to relate to your situation."

Makenna tilted her head at Andie. "How did you become a loner, if you don't mind me asking?"

Andie cleared her throat. "I was adopted by humans as a baby. My parents didn't know what I was. When they realized, they kept me."

A bell suddenly chimed, and Dawn smiled. "Time for lunch. You should eat with us."

Minutes later, they claimed one of the plastic tables in the school-like cafeteria. Gwen was surprised to find that the food wasn't bad. Thankfully, Andie seemed to enjoy it. When they headed to the water fountain after they'd eaten, Gwen asked her quietly, "Well, what do you think?"

"It's restful here," replied Andie, her voice just as low. "I didn't expect that. It's kind of nice not to be looked at with scorn for being a loner."

"It's got to be a hell of a lot better than the cabin in the marsh, but if you don't want to stay, that's fine."

Andie twisted her mouth. "My cat likes it here. She's intrigued by all the strange scents, not nervous. I didn't expect that."

"Why don't you give it a trial run?" suggested Gwen. "Stay here for a few days, see what it's like. If you can't settle here, if you want to come back to the marsh, all you have to do is call, and I'll come get you."

Andie's face softened. "You really would do that, wouldn't you?"

"I would." The girl had been through enough. Reaching the water fountain, Gwen filled a plastic cup and passed it to Andie before filling a cup for herself.

Andie rolled back her shoulders. "I'll stay, give it a shot."

"I thought you might." And Gwen was glad, because she liked the shelter too. It was clean, secure, and well run. The people looked relatively relaxed.

Andie leaned into Gwen. "I wasn't gonna say anything but, um . . . taking on Zander? Bold move. He must be a handful."

Gwen's mouth curved. "He has ways that compensate for that."

Andie chuckled. "I'll bet he does."

◆ ◆ ◆

"Aw, look, Andie's smiling," said Makenna, sitting beside Zander at the table. "That's a good sign."

Zander's gaze had been on Gwen. He liked to watch her. Liked to see her big eyes light up. Liked to see that lush mouth curve, and watch how she used those elegant hands as she spoke. Liked knowing he was the only one who touched her.

He *didn't* like that she was wearing a shirt that covered his mark, but he suspected she'd done it so that Makenna wouldn't tell tales to his pack. He'd told Gwen that he didn't care if they knew, that it was likely Derren would have told Nick anyway. But she clearly hadn't been convinced.

"I think it's likely that Andie will stay," hedged Bracken.

"Me too," said Dawn. "I'm relieved. She's been through a lot, and she deserves to finally feel safe."

"She does," agreed Makenna, taking a little peek at Sienna Rose, who was now being held by Ryan. "Gwen's cool. I have to say, I wasn't sure if I'd like her."

Zander couldn't help but frown, affronted on Gwen's behalf. "Why?"

"Her name's Gwen."

And that explanation was apparently supposed to make sense to him. "So?"

"So I know three other Gwens, one of whom is Ryan's mother—I can't stand any of them." Makenna shook her head in distaste. "I don't associate the name with anything good. Personally, I think it's odd that I know several Gwens; it never struck me as a popular name. But now there's yet *another* Gwen. Odd, right?"

Because she already knew people by that name? "I have an uncle called Ryan, an old pack mate named Ally, and my great-grandmother's name was Dawn."

Her eyes widened. "Really? Weird, huh?"

"No."

Ryan grunted, seeming amused, but Makenna just rolled her eyes.

At that moment, Zander's cell phone beeped. He fished it out of his pocket and saw that it was a text message from Nick: "Make sure you stop by on the way to Oregon. Shay won't stop whining that she wants to meet Gwen."

Tucking his phone back in his pocket, Zander looked at Bracken. "Nick wants us to make a pit stop at our territory so that Shaya can meet Gwen." Although the Alpha female was good at getting her way, Zander hadn't thought she'd win this one.

Bracken's brows raised slightly. "Well, that's a surprise. Gwen's not only an outsider, she's an outsider who happens to be a human that's currently in the kind of trouble he wouldn't want on our doorstep."

It made Zander wonder if Derren had contacted Nick with news of Gwen being an informant, despite giving his word to both Gwen and Cain that he wouldn't. But no, the Beta wouldn't break a promise. He would, however, assure Nick that Gwen could be trusted. There was, of course, another possibility . . .

Cutting his gaze to Makenna, Zander said, "I noticed you texting someone earlier. Would that have been Nick?"

"No," Makenna denied with a sniff. In a quieter voice, she added, "It was Shaya." She shrugged. "Roni and Harley too. I just wanted them to know that I think Gwen's cool. I get a lot of shifters coming here with one bad story after another. Never before has anyone told me that a human went to bat for them. It's natural for most to look the other way and stay out of people's business. That made some suspicious of Gwen's motives. I'm not, and I wanted your pack to know that." She patted Zander's arm. "It'll all be fine. You'll see."

He hoped she was right, because the one thing he wouldn't be able to tolerate was his pack treating Gwen like shit. Not just because she was important to him, but because now he knew the truth of just how brave and selfless she actually was. The last thing she deserved was their mistrust.

Honesty was important to Zander. Gwen could have spun him a pretty story to get him off her back—God knew he'd driven her crazy with his questions—but she hadn't lied to him; she'd respected him enough not to do so. That got to him, just as it had that she'd trusted him with her secret.

He'd always had difficulty sharing things—his past, his feelings, his goals. He'd only shared pieces of himself with Gwen so that she'd share pieces of herself in turn, but that meant he'd inadvertently opened up to her. He'd unknowingly let her in. And she'd also done the same with him. She'd trusted him with the truth of her and her half sister. As someone with trust issues, he knew how difficult it was to rely on another person not to betray you. To him, that trust she'd shown in him to keep her secret safe was a gift. One he had no intention of abusing.

He hoped his pack didn't put him in a position where he had to defend her to them. Maybe the reason he'd always worried about Nick discovering he was involved with Gwen was because he'd known even then that he couldn't obey any order to abandon her while she needed his protection.

Zander had always been unwaveringly loyal to his pack. But if Nick put him in a position where he had to choose between them or Gwen, Zander couldn't be sure that he'd choose his pack . . . so it seemed that Derren was right and that Zander was in much deeper with Gwen than he'd thought. What worried Zander was that Derren could also be right in predicting that the scenario could bite him on the ass.

CHAPTER ELEVEN

As she slid out of the SUV, Gwen glanced around Mercury Pack territory. There were several vehicles, including a Winnebago, of all things, in the parking lot. Tall, majestic trees were everywhere, creaking with the breeze—all territorially marked by claws. But it was the impressive building in front of her that held her attention.

As Zander rounded the hood of the SUV, his wolf stretched within him, happy to be back on his territory, and inhaled the comforting wild scents of nature and home. "This is Nick and Shaya's lodge. They're my Alphas."

Gwen gave him an incredulous look. "This isn't a lodge." It was *huge*. Okay, it had that rustic feel going on, but only the second and third levels had timber frames. The first level was made with large stone, and those glass dove windows were not typical of a lodge *at all*.

"Well, we call it the main lodge."

"I wouldn't have expected the fairy lights." They hung on the trees around what was more of a mansion. They would look awesome in the evening. Right now, they weren't needed while the glaring sun beat down on them. The hot breeze gave no reprieve from the heat.

"Yeah, most people don't," said Bracken as they walked onto the wooden porch.

Gwen probably should have been nervous. She was a human on shifter territory, after all. But she was actually kind of excited. Coming here was a little like stepping into the shoes of a shifter for just a few hours. There were so many times as a kid that she'd found herself wishing she was part of her neighboring wolf pack, and now maybe she'd have a little idea of what that would have been like.

The front door opened before they reached it. A redhead with elfin features stood there, smiling. "Boys, I have to say I kind of missed you."

"Just kind of?" asked Bracken.

"Shaya, this is Gwen," said Zander. "Gwen, this is my Alpha female."

Shaya gave her a welcoming smile designed to put her at ease. "I heard all about you from Makenna and Ally—it was all good stuff. Come in."

"Thanks." As they walked into a large rustic and very contemporary kitchen that led into a roomy dining area, Gwen glanced at Zander over her shoulder. "Yeah, Zander, this is so *not* a lodge."

Shaya laughed. "Pretty spacious, isn't it?" She gestured for Gwen to follow her into the dining room, which Gwen quickly realized was attached to an expansive living area. She loved how the three rooms were one huge, open space.

Several people rose from the luxurious sofas and plush armchairs. One male was already standing, leaning against the wall near the stone fireplace. One muted the TV—the entertainment system was state-of-the-art shit, Gwen noted—and Zander came to her side while Bracken stood close behind her. They didn't move from her as they exchanged greetings with their pack mates.

Zander knew his body language was protective as he shifted slightly in front of Gwen, taking up her space, but it was automatic—some unwelcoming faces stared back at her, and that rankled in a big way. His wolf didn't like it either. Both man and wolf wanted her in easy reach, despite knowing the pack wasn't a physical threat to her.

Nick took in his body language and arched a brow, but he didn't seem surprised by it. And when his gaze flicked to Gwen's neck, Zander knew that Derren had told the Alpha about the mark. *Chatty bastard.* Not that Zander cared if they knew. Still, he resisted—barely—the urge to possessively cup Gwen's neck and make a point to the others that she was taken. He didn't want her to feel awkward in front of his pack mates.

Shaya began the introductions. "Everyone, this is Gwen. Gwen, this here is my mate, Nick. Ignore the scowl. It's nothing personal. He's just not much of a smiler."

Gwen just nodded at the blond, indomitable-looking male near the fireplace, refusing to be intimidated by the alpha energy emanating from him. She turned back to Shaya. "I've been around Zander for a few days, so I'm sort of used to the intense stares at this point."

Shaya's smile widened. "Good, that helps. Near the window are Eli and Roni, Nick's siblings."

Gwen met Eli's analytical gaze, thinking he was just as daunting as his brother even though he wasn't quite as tall. "I see you've got the scowling thing going on too."

Roni snickered, flicking long ash-blonde locks over her shoulder. "He's not upset with you. I put salt in his coffee."

Gwen's mouth curved. "I did that to my brother once. It's every sibling's right."

Roni smiled. "I totally agree."

Shaya pointed to a small brunette standing at the rear of the room, arms folded in a way that was almost petulant. "That's Nick's mom, Kathy. As you can see, she's good at the scowling too. Lastly, we have Jesse and Harley over there by the door. They're a mated pair."

Gwen could already sense they were mated by how intimately close they stood. She studied the golden-eyed female closely. "You don't seem like a wolf."

One dark, perfectly plucked brow arched. "I don't?"

"Walking around the shelter—which I think is pretty awesome—I noticed different kinds of shifters seem to have different . . . airs about them. You have a feline air."

Harley's mouth curled and she bowed her head slightly, making her dark hair fall forward enough that Gwen noticed the burgundy highlights. "Very good," said Harley.

"Perceptive," agreed Jesse.

"She reads Zander so well it's not even funny," said Bracken, a smile in his voice.

Zander shot him a hard look, but the enforcer just smirked.

"Did Andie settle at the shelter okay?" asked Shaya.

Gwen nodded. "Yeah. She said she'd give it a try but that if she changed her mind she'd give me a call."

"Give you a call?" echoed Zander.

"So I can go pick her up and bring her back to Oregon," Gwen explained. "I don't think that'll happen, though. She seemed comfortable there."

"I was thinking the same thing." Bracken yawned. "Any chance of a coffee before I go pack more of my shit, Kathy?"

The woman humphed as she crossed the room. Her eyes danced from Gwen to Zander. "I suppose you both want one too?" she said snottily.

"No, thanks." Gwen touched her stomach. "I'm bloated after my meal at the shelter."

Shooting Kathy a "back-off" look that she was wise enough to heed, Zander said, "I need to go to my lodge. I don't want to stay here long in case the Moores or any people they hire turn up at the B&B while we're not there." Ally and Derren would need backup.

Bracken nodded. "I'll go get my stuff once I've had my coffee."

Zander cupped Gwen's elbow, ready to lead her out of the lodge. "Anything more from Rory?" he asked nobody in particular. His wolf curled his upper lip at the mere mention of Rory.

"No," replied Jesse. "We left a camera at his apartment. He returned to it yesterday and took a few things. He was gone before we got there."

"We haven't seen him lingering around," Eli added. "Derren told us about the goshawk attack." His eyes cut to Gwen. "Must have been pretty scary for you."

"I'm not gonna admit to fear in front of a bunch of predators," she said with a smile.

Eli's mouth twitched. "No one would blame you for being freaked by such an attack."

Zander looked at his Alpha. "I want to know what flock it was."

"We'll find out, and they'll pay," Nick stated firmly.

With a satisfied nod, Zander ushered Gwen outside. He had to admit that she'd handled his pack like a pro. She hadn't let the unwelcoming vibes faze her or bristled at the scowls directed her way. She'd let it all wash over her, dismissing the behavior but not in a way that was snarky or disrespectful. His wolf was impressed.

As they crossed the lush land toward the woods, grass rustling beneath their feet, Zander noticed her looking at the outdoor play area on their far left. "Shaya designed that. We all pitched in to build it for the pups."

"How many pups are there?"

"Two. Both girls."

"It's pretty cool. I'll bet the kids love it." She took a long breath. The air was so fresh here, so alive with various scents. Wildflowers. Pine. Moss. Sun-warmed earth. It all spoke to her on some level. "I like your pack."

"There's a lot more of them." He glanced back at the lodge. "It doesn't bother you that some were a little curt?" It had bothered him. It had bothered him more when Eli's eyes took a long scan of Gwen's legs, although some weird part of him had gotten off on it too.

"This is their home. They're protective of it. I wouldn't expect them to welcome someone here who they didn't know or trust." Gwen jerked back at the whine of a bee as it rushed by. She didn't like anything that buzzed. It just wasn't normal.

As they walked into the trees, escaping the glare of the sun, she exhaled a happy sigh. "Listen, I got the impression by what was said that your pack's having trouble with some Rory-person. If so, maybe you should stay here with them. I can have Marlon come pick me up." She didn't realize how much she wanted him to decline her offer until he actually shook his head. Relief poured through her. Too much relief. It was disconcerting.

"They don't need my help dealing with Rory."

"Is he an Alpha of another pack?"

Pleased that she'd asked a question without adding something like 'You don't have to answer,' Zander replied, "He's not an Alpha. He's my identical twin. Lives in another pack."

"Really? Huh." Gwen skimmed her hand over a birch tree, feeling the rough bark. She liked it. Liked the sound of the twigs crunching beneath her shoes, the twittering of the birds, and the branches shuddering. Noticing Zander was looking at her funny, she frowned. "What?"

"I'm waiting for you to ask me dumb questions."

Her frown deepened. "Like what?"

"Like can me and Rory hear each other's thoughts? Can we feel each other's pain? If you pinch me, will he feel it?

"I'm assuming by the cynical note in your voice that those things definitely don't apply to you and your brother."

"Your assumption is right, but people tend to automatically assume we have some kind of mystical connection. They're often surprised to hear we don't get along, let alone that we don't find it hard to be apart."

"I always figured it would have been fun to have an identical twin."

"It isn't always as much fun as people assume." He paused as they stepped over a crumbling log. "Think of someone who pisses you off easier than they can breathe. Now imagine living with them, seeing them every day, sharing a room with them, having to deal with them doing whatever they can to irritate and goad you."

Oh yeah, that would have been a level of hell. Fingering a berry bush, she asked, "Have you ever gotten along?"

"I don't remember there being a time when we ever did. Even when we were toddlers, I remember him always trying to be the leader because he was born first. But I didn't want a leader, and I didn't want to lead him. His first word was 'mine.' Apparently, my first word was 'shush.' Even then he must have annoyed me."

"There was never any rivalry between me, Marlon, and Julie. None of us fought for Yvonne's attention or anything."

"Good. People say that sibling rivalry is normal . . . a rite of passage that builds character. Maybe it is healthy when you're a kid, but it sure never felt that way." He neatly sidestepped a patch of spongy moss. "What fed the rivalry was that we were each other's measuring stick. The first thing people seemed to do was tally our differences. When people talked about us, it was often comparing us rather than describing us as individuals. Who was born first? Who crawled first? Who walked first? Who spoke first?"

She nodded in understanding. "Ah. I can see how that would make things worse."

"Plus, we were expected to share everything. We didn't always have our own stuff. He didn't like to share. When people bought us gifts, they often got us the same thing in an effort to be *fair*. That didn't help. He'd always *lose* his stuff and swear that I'd taken it.

"When we got older, we'd have our own things, but he hated that. He believed whatever I had was better simply because I had it, so then he wanted it. I was often told to give him stuff just to keep the peace. But there was no real peace in that house."

Pissed on Zander's behalf, she asked, "What did your parents do?"

"Nothing. Mom would always excuse his behavior, so he was never held accountable for anything. If you're not taught something's wrong, how can anyone expect you to regret it? Why would you ever feel the need to change? I'm not saying it's completely her fault that he is the way he is. We each have our own mind. But that's the mental path he went down. If he's ever in his life felt guilty for anything, I'd be surprised."

"But . . . why did she excuse his behavior?"

"He was Mom's golden boy, and she felt guilty for him almost dying after he donated a kidney to me when we were kids. Dad thought it was normal for us to *battle it out*. Did you know that sibling competition begins in spotted hyenas at birth? At least twenty-five percent of their pups are killed by siblings. It's the Cain Complex, right? The unconscious, secret wish to kill your sibling."

She blinked. "You think he'd like to see you dead?"

"I think he wouldn't care if I was. I don't know how much money Rory was expecting to inherit from our uncle—probably all of it, since he has that sense of entitlement—but he wasn't happy whatsoever to hear he'd been left a dollar."

She couldn't help that her mouth quirked. "Wow. Your uncle pissed him off even after his death."

"Rory wants half of what I inherited. He thinks it's his due. He'll toy with the pack until I give him what he feels he's entitled to have."

"*Will* you give it to him?"

"No. He's *not* entitled to it, and he wouldn't use it smartly anyway." Zander gestured at the lodge ahead of them. "Here we are."

It was a hell of a lot nicer than the cabin on her property, she thought. In fact, it was more like a miniature version of the Alphas' lodge, except that there were only two floors, and the frame was all timber. Still, it was big and bold in its way.

To the side of the lodge was a cutting stump and woodpile. "I have a sudden vision of you shirtless and sweaty, chopping wood with an ax. Don't know if you do it shirtless. That's just the image that my dirty mind came up with."

Zander chuckled. "Your mind can't be half as dirty as mine, baby." He led her onto the porch and then into the lodge, closing the door behind them.

The interior was exactly like him, Gwen thought. Masculine. Organized. Stylish in a simple way, no frills or splashes of color.

Like the Alphas' lodge, it had an open-plan living, dining, and kitchen area. The dark-cream oversize sofa and recliners looked damn comfortable—she'd test that theory in a minute. The weathered coffee table was a rich, oiled wood that gleamed as the sun shone through the windows. The stone fireplace should have been the focal point, but the wide-screen TV stood out more. It seemed to be the most expensive thing there, but she could see that the style of the furniture was deliberately understated.

"Nice," she said, turning to face him. "Suits you."

She suited him, Zander thought. He drew her to him and kissed her, practically pouring the possessiveness he'd bottled up right down her throat. She kissed him back with a soft moan that was like a stroke to his quickly hardening cock.

He'd meant to keep the kiss slow and easy, since they couldn't stay long and needed to get back. But he found himself gripping her braid and angling her head to deepen the kiss. His wolf pushed him to take her right there in his lodge. The beast wanted her scent to be all over it.

Zander snapped open her fly and shoved his fingers inside her panties, pausing as soon as he found her clit. She bucked against his hand, but he did nothing other than circle her clit with the tip of his finger. He swiped his tongue over her lower lip. “Such a gorgeous mouth. It deserves to be fucked, don’t you think?”

“Not really.”

He fought a smile. “Yeah, you’ll put that pretty mouth on my cock one day. Not today.” He flicked her clit. “Today I want to feel my baby’s sweet little pussy squeeze my dick like it’s hers.” He took her mouth again, feasting greedily as he played with her clit. “Shirt off, Gwen.” She quickly shed both her shirt and bra. “Good.” He thrust one finger inside her, rewarding her. “Now the rest.” Breathing hard, she kicked off her shoes and then shoved down her shorts and panties. He traced the shell of her ear with his tongue and whispered, “So good for me.” He sank another finger inside her.

Splaying his free hand on her lower back to still her, Zander fucked her with his fingers. Hard. Fast. Growling at the prick of her nails on his nape. He kept his mouth pressed to hers, tasting every moan and gasp. Soon, her pussy fluttered around his fingers. “That’s it. Give me that come, baby.” He kept his fingers buried deep as she came, growling into her mouth as her cream soaked his fingers.

Shaking a little, Gwen double-blinked, caught up in her post-orgasm buzz. She couldn’t take her eyes off Zander as he withdrew his hand from her panties and, holding her gaze, sucked his fingers clean. *Damn.* She tore open his fly and wrapped her hand around his cock. He was long and hard, and he seemed to thicken even more as she pumped him with a tight fist.

“I can have you any way I want,” he rumbled, closing his hand around her breast. “Tell me. Say it.”

Her eyes narrowed. “Actually—”

He yanked hard on her hair. "Don't get bratty with me. I don't reward bratty." He pinched her nipple. "Tell me."

Gwen almost shivered at the growl that rattled his chest. Sensing he wasn't going to give in because, yeah, he was a total asshole sometimes, she relented, "You can have me any way you want."

"That's my baby." He walked her backward, spun her around, and then bent her over the plush arm of the sofa. "Spread those legs for me. Very good." He punched his hips, driving his cock inside her. She was so tight and swollen that he only made it halfway. "Take it all, Gwen." He reared back and thrust hard, burying every inch of his cock deep in her pussy. Her slick walls clamped down on him, squeezing him so tight he was surprised he didn't see stars.

"Zander," she breathed, "I'm not gonna last long. Just saying."

He doubted he'd last long either. She felt like liquid fucking fire, and it almost ate at what little control he had. "Tell me if it gets too much." He rode her hard. Took and fucked and possessed her body, driven by something dark and primal inside him. Only *she* touched that part of him. Only *she* woke and taunted it until his control was close to being nothing but a distant memory. No one had ever called to him on such a primitive level before, and he was past the point of caring.

Gwen closed her eyes, letting him sweep her away. Before Zander, she'd never had sex so intense in her life. It was always rough and carnal. Probably should have been a little too rough, but she loved every moment of it. Her eyes snapped open as a wet finger probed the rim of her ass. "Zander—"

"Nobody's ever had this, have they?"

"No."

"I will."

She wanted to deny it, but then his finger slid inside and her breath caught in her throat. She didn't think it would feel good, but it did. Waves of sensation overwhelmed her—his cock stretching her walls, a strong hand holding her in place, a finger thrusting in and out of her ass. She could feel her release barreling toward her, knew it would hit her any second now.

Zander wrapped her braid around his hand and yanked hard. "Up."

But it was too late—the bite of pain to her scalp had thrown her over, and white-hot pleasure whipped through her. She felt Zander's weight on her back as he sank his teeth into her shoulder and rammed his cock deep, felt the hot splash of his come as her pussy contracted around him, as if greedy for every drop. And then her strength just left her.

She slumped over the sofa, breathing hard. God, the guy was good. It was like he'd taken a crash course on how to play her body or something.

Zander hummed against her neck. "I needed that."

She snorted. "You say that like you've gone without sex for months. We had it this morning."

"And you've been parading those legs in front of me all morning and afternoon."

Her head snapped up. "Parading?"

"Yeah, parading." Pulling out of her, he helped her straighten and then turned her to face him. "I love seeing your eyes all sex-drunk."

She chuckled. "Sex-drunk?" Well, she kind of liked seeing *his* gaze the way it was now . . . all lazy and languid. "I need to clean up."

"Bathroom's upstairs."

Once they were done and they'd righted their clothing, Zander said, "I'm going to pack my stuff so we can leave. Sit. Relax. Or go take a look around—whatever you want. I won't be long."

Deciding to wait downstairs so that they wouldn't end up testing the endurance of the bedsprings, Gwen crossed to the recliner and sank into it with a groan. Oh yeah, it *was* as comfy as it looked.

Sprawled there, she read the spines of the books that were lined up neatly on the oak shelf, but she soon found her eyes drifting shut. Maybe it was that she felt safe here. Maybe it was that it had been a long morning and afternoon. Whatever it was that made her feel so relaxed that she could just nap, she wished she could bottle it up.

Sometime later, she felt a tug on her braid and opened her eyes. "How do you move without making a sound? I have to know."

Duffel in hand, Zander pulled her out of the recliner and drew her close. "Training." He pressed a kiss to her mouth, breathing in her scent—there was still a slight spice of need to it, and it shot straight to his cock. *Fuck.* "Ready?" She nodded. "Then let's go get Bracken."

"I was thinking that . . . Never mind."

"Thinking what?"

She waved a hand. "Nothing. It's fine."

"Gwen, finish the sentence." Before he went insane.

"Really, forget it."

"Tell me."

She lifted her shoulders. "But it doesn't matter."

"Just fucking tell me what you were going to say."

"Jesus, Zander, I hope there's a way to block you in real life because you're a pain in my ass." She held up her hand when he went to argue. "I'll pencil in some time to hear you whine about it later. Let's just go."

He breathed deep. "Fine."

They were walking to the door when her cell phone rang. Gwen halted when she saw the identity of the caller. "It's Geena."

Zander's brow creased. "Answer it."

She swiped her thumb over the screen. "Hey."

"I heard you were hurt last night," said Geena. She wasn't much for pleasantries. "Are you okay? What happened?"

Gwen frowned. "I'm fine. How did you find out?"

"One of Dad's contacts called—the guy's friends with Ezra Moore. Apparently Ezra found out that Kenny's your father, and he wants him to *talk* to you about going before the shifter council and ask you to *see reason*."

"I shouldn't be surprised that Ezra dug into my past, given that he very easily obtained my bank-account details and all that shit." Gwen told her about the goshawk assault, smiling at the string of curses her sister let loose. "The Moores have to be behind it."

"Probably," said Geena with a weary sigh. "Dad plans to contact you to set up a meeting. You should know that he thinks he can talk you out of speaking against Brandt."

Gwen narrowed her eyes. "He can't."

"I know that. You know that. But maybe you should let him believe that he can."

Pride made her bristle at that. "Hell, no."

"I get that it would be hard to act like you're *bowing down to his greatness*, but it would be harder to deal with constant attacks from the Moores. Pretend to fold. Agree to cooperate. Then go before the council and tell them the fucking truth. But if you're going to tell the truth, you need to be sure you're ready for what comes next."

Gwen rubbed her temple. "Someone offered to put me in a safe house."

"It won't make any difference. They'll just go after your foster family to flush you out of hiding." There was a pause as voices mumbled in the background. "I've got to go," said Geena quietly. "Call me if you need me. And be careful."

"You too." Gwen looked up at Zander. "Did you hear any of that?"

He nodded. Neither Zander nor his wolf wanted Gwen anywhere near Kenny. "Your sister's right. It might be a good idea to let him believe he's talked you out of it. I'd say he's arrogant enough to think that you'll give in to him."

"He is, but it will gall me to let the Moores believe they've made me cower."

Zander smoothed his hands up and down her arms. "Yeah, but just think how much fun it will be when Brandt goes to that hearing feeling smug as all shit . . . only to then sit there and listen to you tell the truth."

Gwen couldn't help grinning as she imagined the look on Brandt's face. "He will hate that."

"Of course he will. No one likes being tricked. And if he believes you are going to change your statement, he won't do anything stupid like run before the hearing. In a sense, you'd be setting a trap for him."

"And he's arrogant enough to walk right into it."

"Exactly." Zander kissed her. "You'll get the last laugh, baby. Do what you gotta do to get it."

CHAPTER TWELVE

Zander stretched across the table and took his shot. There was a loud, satisfying smack as the white ball connected with another. Straightening, he watched the second ball smoothly roll across the table and then tumble into a corner pocket. Zander's mouth curved.

Derren tossed him an aggravated look, gripping his cue stick. "I hate playing pool with people better than me."

Sitting on a high stool, watching the game, Ally snorted. "You're such a sore loser."

"I haven't lost yet."

They'd claimed the pool table in the far corner, which gave them the best view of the large space. It also allowed Zander to track Gwen's movements as she worked. Watching her walk around in shorts and a tank top was distracting, to say the least. Still, he was kicking Derren's ass at pool. But then she bent over to pick up a coaster from the floor, and Zander understandably missed his next shot—it was the black ball, to make matters worse. Derren was immature enough to smirk about it.

Zander propped his cue against the wall as he downed a gulp of his beer. Hearing Bracken curse, he looked to see that the wolf was finally abandoning the pinball machine. Good, because all its bleeping and blooping was getting on Zander's damn nerves.

"What time is Gwen meeting Kenny tomorrow?" Ally asked.

"Midday," replied Zander, voice unintentionally hard. He didn't want Gwen anywhere near that son of a bitch, but he knew the meeting needed to go ahead. They'd arranged it a week ago during the call she'd received from Kenny, which had been the day after she'd gotten her warning from Geena. "I don't like it."

"You were the one who said Geena's suggestion was a good one, remember."

"Doesn't mean I like that Gwen and Kenny will be in the same room together."

Overhearing that, Bracken sighed as he reached them and said, "Yeah, I don't like it either."

"Hey, who is that guy that keeps staring at Gwen?" asked Ally. "Is he one of the Moores?"

Zander didn't need to look to know whom she was talking about, because he'd already noticed. Placing his bottle on the tall, high table where the other drinks rested, Zander said, "No. That would be Aidan, Gwen's old therapist."

Ally sneered, no doubt remembering all he'd told his pack mates about the human. "Asshole," she muttered.

"Yeah, he's definitely that," agreed Bracken.

"Clearly my warning to stay away from Gwen didn't penetrate," clipped Zander.

Careful not to knock the rack of pool cues, Bracken leaned against the wall. "Well, to be fair, he's in a public place, and he's on a date."

"Sitting in Gwen's section of the bar," Zander pointed out. "He thinks that being in a public place means he's safe."

"Damn," cursed Derren. "Your shot, Z."

As he got a good look at the table, Zander understood Derren's frustration. The wolf had managed to pot all balls but the black, and the white ball was lined up perfectly to hit it. Zander effortlessly sank the black and then leaned the cue against the table just as Gwen approached to take their empty glasses and bottles. That lush mouth kicked up into a smile as her eyes met his.

"Come here," he growled. She did, and he pulled her close, splaying his hand possessively on her lower back. He kissed her, growling in satisfaction as her body fairly melted into his, fitting against him a little too perfectly. His wolf took in her scent, letting it drown out the distasteful smells of dry chalk and green felt.

Gwen smoothed her hand over the solid bulk of his shoulder. "Why are you so tense?"

"I don't like that Aidan's here."

She shrugged, nonchalant. "He always comes here when he's on dates."

"Does he always sit in your section?"

"Yes. But if I ask him to move or for one of the other waitresses to switch with me, he'll think he bothers me. He'll get a kick out of it." Gwen nipped his lip, smiling at his low growl. "Now let me go. I've gotta work."

Zander put his mouth to her ear. "If we were alone right now, I'd have you flat on that pool table with my dick in you." He snaked his hand under her tank top just to feel all that soft skin. "On second thought, it wouldn't be so bad if Aidan was here. Then he could see me taking you. He'd get that you're mine."

She arched an imperious brow. "Yours?"

"Mine." He stroked the mark on her neck with his thumb. "Another shifter would see this and understand exactly what it meant—that you're off-limits, that you're not to be touched, that there's someone who'll raise fresh hell if you're harmed. But a human . . . they know what the mark is, but they don't get the true extent of how serious it is. That makes me antsy."

"Zander, I think the humans here know that you consider me taken, since you're rubbing yourself all over me like a cat."

"*Again* with the 'comparing me to a cat' thing," he complained.

"You know what I mean." Gwen straightened, pushing against his chest. "Now I really have to work. Be good." Collecting the empty bottles and glasses, she said a quick "Hi" to the other wolves, took orders for more drinks, and then disappeared.

Ally twisted on her stool. "Now there's a guy staring at *you.*"

Zander followed her gaze. A tall, burly male was studying him closely through narrowed eyes. "That's Gwen's future brother-in-law, Chase. He owns this place. From what I understand, he's protective of her."

"And part of you is offended by that," Ally sensed. "You feel that protecting her is *your* job. There's no point denying it, Zander. I can sense what you're feeling." She crossed one leg over the other. "I like Gwen. She's good for you."

Yeah, she was, but Zander wasn't the heart-to-heart type, so he said nothing.

"She doesn't have any emotional expectations of you. She doesn't pressure you to open up. You needed that at first. It was the only way you were ever going to know that, really, you *don't* want distance."

What he really didn't want was to have this conversation. It felt like he was being profiled. Made him feel exposed to know someone could read him so well. Gwen was good at reading him, but he didn't mind that so much—it didn't feel like an imposition, though it probably should have. So Zander concentrated on the game that Bracken and Derren were playing, hoping Ally would take the hint.

"Marlon's told me a lot about her," continued Ally, unfortunately. "Enough for me to realize that, like you, she doesn't give much of herself to people. You both seem to back away from anyone who pushes. But you didn't like that she backed off and gave you space, did you? You wanted her to push. You wanted to know her, and you wanted her to *want* to know you. Over time, she stopped backing off and dropped her guard a little. But the irony is that if she hadn't given you space in the beginning, if she hadn't fought to keep a distance from you, you might never have seen that you *don't* want it because your defenses would have stayed up."

Zander sighed. "Are we done with the amateur psychology?" He tried to sound bored, but they both knew she'd interpreted the situation too well for his liking.

"No. Now, as I said, neither of you give much of yourself to people. You both seem that way for different reasons, though. With you, it's because you find it instinctively uncomfortable to connect with people, probably because the connections you had with your family, particularly with your twin—a person who should have been closest to you—were weak and, in Rory's case, warped. I wouldn't want to let people close either." Ally propped her elbow on the table and rested her chin on her hand. "You confuse Gwen."

That made him frown. And intrigued him, which was no doubt Ally's intent. "Confuse her?"

"The level of attention you pay her. The possessiveness. The way you try to preempt what's best for her. It baffles her. That's how I realized that the reason she doesn't give much of herself to people is that she doesn't think they want it—and she definitely doesn't trust that they'll want to keep or protect her."

That made sense, he thought. Gwen's mother and stepfather were too wrapped up in their own drama to care about her. Her biological father hadn't even acknowledged her.

"I think a big factor was that some of the boys who pursued her over the years were really just trying to get to her foster sister."

He scowled. "Why?"

Ally pointed at him. "That right there is why you're so confusing to her. She knows it's not about looks for you. She doesn't *get* what it *is* about. It's not that she has a low sense of self-worth. She doesn't. She's confident, bold. She's at ease with who she is; she just didn't expect anyone else to be."

"You said she doesn't give much of herself to people, but she let Yvonne, Marlon, and Julie get close."

"Ah, but have you noticed that she sort of mothers them?"

Thinking on that, Zander realized she was right. Gwen put them first, protected them, and was a rock to each of them. In a way, she'd fostered that family—not the other way around. "She's strong for them. The dominant force of the family, really."

Ally nodded. "You don't need her strength, you don't need a rock, and that makes you unfamiliar territory for Gwen. She's not used to being around people who are as equally strong as she is. She doesn't quite know how to deal with someone who'll want *her* to rely on *them*. Everyone wants to know there's someone they *can* rely on, even if they never intend to do it. She's never had a rock. The idea of having one will be as alluring as it is scary."

Because to rely on someone, you had to trust them, Zander thought, and trust was hard for Gwen. "Okay, Dr. Ally, I got a question for you."

"Dr. Ally," she echoed with a smile. "I like that."

"She invested some trust in me. She's let me in a little. She's let me know her. But she still holds back. Why?"

"This confuses you?" Ally rolled her eyes. "We're shifters, Zander. What are shifters most known for doing?"

He shrugged. "Mating."

"Yes. We're most known for having true mates and metaphysical bonds."

"I already explained to Gwen that having a true mate doesn't mean I'm spoken for unless I've bonded with them."

"Which is likely the only reason she let you in her bed. But this is what she'll be thinking: that once the Brandt situation is over, you'll go back to your pack and she'll never see you again—that this is a . . .

holiday romance for you. If this is more, you need to make that clear to her." Ally tilted her head. "Would your wolf fight you on it?"

"No. He adores her. It took a little while for him to warm up. At first, he backed away from her—practically hid from her. Little by little, he closed the distance he kept from her, though still not all the way. Gwen thinks he's weird with women because he's not interested in any female but his true mate. I don't know. In any case, she won him over."

Ally gaped at him. "Good God, Zander, you're lucky you're hot."

"What?"

She plonked down her glass and leaned across the table. "Maybe it's because you're too close to the situation, I don't know, but you're missing some things here. Right, let's imagine that there's this wolf. He's strong. Fierce. Hard. Wounded, though. He was shot a couple of times. He recovered, but he has scars. Now, he's not afraid of guns as a result—no, he's too brave for that. But he is wary of them, so if he sees one around, he's going to be on his guard in case the damn thing goes off. Now, *your* wolf wasn't shot, but he *is* wounded. What wounded him, Zander?"

He frowned. "The people who were important to him."

"Right. So let's say your wolf comes across someone else who's important to him—maybe the person that's the most important of all. How the hell do you think he'll react?"

"He'd be wary." Zander swore as realization slapped him right over the head. His mouth went slack, and his whole body stilled in shock. Hell, even his heart seemed to stop—then it was pounding in his chest like a drumbeat.

His wolf did a sheepish, metaphorical shrug. The beast had known Gwen Miller was their mate from minute one; he'd simply been too wary of having a mate to accept it—even now, the wolf was still slightly wary.

Zander gave a slow, incredulous shake of the head and almost laughed. Not with euphoria, but at his own stupidity. He should have known. He snapped his gaping mouth shut and drew in a breath through his nose. "Why didn't I see it?"

Ally's smile was sympathy itself. "Maybe because your wolf isn't the only one who's wounded. Maybe you're wary of finding your mate too. Who isn't? A mate will want everything from you. But not to take and keep those pieces of you, Zander. To protect them, to love them. She's the one person who'll make everything worth it for you."

He stood there, reeling as several emotions overwhelmed him. Astonishment. Disbelief. Satisfaction. Pride that the female heading toward them belonged to *him*. He carefully masked his expression as she neared, keeping his smile hidden. Still, she saw something on his face that made her frown. He bit down on a smile of pride—his mate was incredibly observant.

Gwen set their drinks on the table as she asked, "You okay?"

"Fine." His world had been rocked, of course, but in a good way. Zander drew her close, drinking in every little detail of her face, quietly savoring the knowledge of what she was to him. "I'll be even better when your shift is over and I can get you home."

"Not long to go."

As Gwen walked away, he said to Ally, "I have no idea how to tell her that I believe she's my mate. She's not a shifter; she wasn't raised knowing that she'd one day be mated. She won't be prepared for it or for how much the mating bond will demand of her."

Ally gave him an understanding smile. "Yeah, it will come as kind of a shock. This isn't going to be easy. I don't envy you having to explain it to her."

"And if she were to ask me to confirm that she was, without question, my true mate, I wouldn't be able to prove it until we felt the pull of the mating bond. I don't know if my *belief* that she's my mate would be enough for her. Not when she still holds back from me."

"She only holds back because she doesn't realize this is serious for you."

Zander ground his teeth. "I marked her. I told her that she's mine."

Ally snorted. "Everyone knows shifters are territorial over pretty much everything, even over what we consider temporarily ours. Unless you've told Gwen in no uncertain terms that you want something long term with her, she's unlikely to be aware of it."

Well, no, he hadn't been clear about it. He was regretting that now. "There's so much shit going on around her. The question is . . . if I tell her she's my mate, will it make her happy, or will it make her feel like yet more stuff is being piled on her?"

"I don't know." Expression thoughtful, Ally worried her bottom lip. "Look, I know this will be hard on you, but maybe . . ."

"What?"

"Maybe it would be best to keep the true-mate thing to yourself for now. Tell her this is serious for you. Make her believe it. Let her see that she's important to you. If she's secure in what you feel for her, she's more likely to accept that you're mates than if you simply blurt it out at a time when she's still unsure what's going on between you."

Zander scrubbed a hand over his jaw, knowing Ally was right but not liking it because . . . "Not telling her, resisting the urge to claim her, will be extremely difficult for me and my wolf."

"Yes, but with all this crap going on, she needs something good in her life right now. At the moment, that's you. Keep being that good thing that's distracting her from the bad. Keep being the person she can relax with. When she's ready to hear it, you'll know.

"You've already lured her to you, Zander. Now you just need to keep her with you. Use everything you have in your arsenal, including your pack mates. We'll be behind you on this. If she's yours, she's also ours." She patted his arm. "Congrats. Your days as a bachelor are long gone."

"Why are they long gone?" asked Bracken as he and Derren joined them.

Zander told them his belief that Gwen was his mate. All the while, he kept his eyes locked on the source of his current emotional mayhem, letting the knowledge that she was his mate sink in and fill him up.

"Makes sense." Bracken took a swig of his beer. "Just because you can't feel the pull of the bond doesn't mean it isn't there, Z."

Derren nodded. "It just means something's blocking it, and that could be any number of things. Do you think she'll react well to being part of a pack?"

Ally drummed her fingers on the table. "According to Marlon, when Gwen was a kid, she used to wish that she was part of the pack that occupied the land near the trailer park where she lived."

"Marlon really does like to chat," mused Zander.

Ally shrugged. "He wants her happy. He thinks you could make her happy. Anyway, my point is that I think it would help if we all sort of embrace her and make her feel like she's one of us, which she is—though she doesn't know it yet. If she can associate our pack with safety and security, she's less likely to freak out when she realizes she will be part of it."

"I'm not so sure Nick will be happy to embrace her," said Zander. Before he'd left pack territory after their brief visit, Nick had pulled him aside to talk about Gwen.

"I have it on good authority that Gwen's not a threat to the pack—if I didn't believe that, I wouldn't have let her in the same house as my mate and daughter. Derren won't tell me why she can be trusted, only that it wasn't his secret to tell. I don't like that, but I respect it. Still, I'm hoping that you'll tell me at some point, because it has to have been something

big for her to have won over four of my wolves, especially Derren—he's almost as jaded as you are."

"It's not my secret to tell either," said Zander. "It's hers. I won't break a promise. I gave her my word, and that means something to me."

Nick lifted a brow. "And the fact that I'm your Alpha doesn't?"

"Why don't you just say what you really want to say instead of asking probing questions."

"All right. You've marked her. Earlier, you glared at us all like you'd gut us open if we did a single thing to upset her. This isn't some casual thing for you, especially if her feelings come before our concerns. So, I have to ask myself if this means you now have divided loyalties. She already has you keeping secrets from me for her, so you can't say my concerns aren't valid."

"If Shaya asked you to keep something quiet from the pack, would you?"

"Yes . . . but Shay's my mate, Zander. Gwen Miller is just someone you marked. Unless there's something else you're not telling me?"

Zander gave a quick, sharp shake of the head. "She's not just someone I marked. She matters to me. Do I have divided loyalties? Depends on what it is you'll ask me to do."

"And if I asked you to stay home, to send Eli to Oregon in your place, would you?"

"No. I promised her that I'd see this whole thing through with her to the end."

"Something you shouldn't have done, since you initially agreed over the phone that if I asked you to come home, you would."

"Bracken agreed," Zander corrected. "I didn't."

Nick thought about it for a moment and then shot him a glare. "You're a sneaky fucker, Zander." Then he sighed. "Go. Keep me updated. It was good to see you."

◆ ◆ ◆

Zander snapped out of the memory and said, "The one thing Nick didn't want was this shit making its way to the pack. If Gwen's one of us, her shit becomes our shit."

"It's not ideal that your mate has trouble dogging her heels," said Derren. "But that doesn't mean Nick won't want her to be one of us. Harley had trouble with extremists, but he didn't ask her to leave—he knew Jesse wanted her as his mate, and that was enough for Nick. Hey, don't worry so much about that. Concentrate on Gwen."

Like Zander could do anything else. As the hours went on, he kept watch on her. Now that he knew she was his mate, it was as if he was looking at her through a different lens. A lens that wasn't clouded by uncertainties, mistrust, or a need to guard himself. He saw her so clearly.

She was no longer someone who simply mattered to him, no longer someone he simply felt possessive and protective of. She was more. She was everything. And that knowledge seemed to take down every defense he had. It wasn't that his walls were gone. No, but she was inside them now. Safe and close to him. Closer than anyone else had ever been.

It was hard to stand there and do nothing, to act as though his life hadn't just been upended. His muscles fairly quivered with the effort to remain where he was instead of following the primal urge to cross to Gwen and claim her. Soon. He'd claim her soon. It had to be at a time when it was right for both of them.

Later, shortly before her shift ended, Zander turned to Derren. "Watch over Gwen for me while I use the bathroom."

It was as he was washing his hands in the restrooms that Chase entered, the smells of greasy food and cigarette smoke clinging to his clothing. Zander turned to face him, meeting his gaze head-on. The bold stare pissed Zander off, but he didn't want to hurt the man who would soon be his brother-in-law.

Chase crossed his arms over his chest. "I could start this by casually introducing myself, asking your name, and then subtly quizzing you while also doing my best to look all intimidating. But I don't play games. I know who you are. I'm pretty sure you know who I am. I'm also pretty sure you know what brought me over here."

Zander liked his directness. "Gwen."

"Gwen," confirmed Chase. "If you know who she is to me, to my fiancée, you know exactly why I'd be concerned about her."

"I'm not going to hurt her."

Chase snorted. "I doubt you even could. Gwen's an emotional badass. It's more likely that she'll hurt you."

Zander couldn't even argue that.

"No, what worries me is that you marked her. I may not understand all the ways of shifters, but I do know that branding someone is no small thing. Does she know that?"

"You're insulting Gwen's intelligence by asking that question."

Chase made a sound of impatience. "Gwen isn't a person who lets people *mark* her as theirs in any sense of the word. She runs a mile from possessiveness. Did you play it down and tell her it was a hickey?"

"Why don't you ask Gwen these questions? Probably because she'd tell you to mind your own business. Tell me why I shouldn't say the same thing."

His jaw hardened. "She's practically my sister-in-law. I look out for her."

"Yeah? If you're so protective of Gwen, why haven't you thrown Aidan out?"

"Because you're here, and I knew you were involved with her. I figured it would be a good thing for him to see her with someone. Then maybe he'll let her go. At some point, I will punch him in the dick. For now, I'll teach him the same lesson you're teaching him."

That Gwen was taken. "If you don't have an issue with Gwen being with me, why does the mark bother you so much?"

"Because the Gwen I know would *never* say she belonged to anyone but herself."

"Then I guess you don't know her as well as you thought. You made assumptions based on how she acted with her past partners. I'm not them." Zander strode past him, heading right for the door. As he was leaving, he heard Chase's voice behind him.

"I hope that's true, because those were all assholes. She doesn't need another asshole."

Speaking of assholes . . . the moment Zander stepped out of the restrooms, he saw Aidan making a beeline for Gwen near the bar. *Son of a bitch.*

"Do you not like breathing? Is that what this is?" asked Gwen. Why else would Aiden try talking to her when four shifters would happily take him down for even sharing her air? Gwen didn't fail to notice Zander signaling for the others to hang back, gesturing that he'd deal with it. "Really, Aidan, you should go."

"I saw the bite," Aidan clipped.

Yeah, it had gotten a lot of people's attention. The other waitresses fairly swooned at the sight of it. Chase had glowered like she'd petitioned to cancel Christmas. And now Aidan was staring at it, face scrunched up in revulsion. But she sensed that the revulsion wasn't born of any antipathy toward shifters. No, the glitter of bitterness in his eyes told her he just didn't like what the mark represented—essentially, that she was no longer single.

"Are you mated to him now?"

"Aidan, do you honestly think it's a good idea to confront me like this while Zander can see? I'd say use your brain, but, well, that's a little like telling Colt to find his balls—utterly pointless."

"Unless he's taken you as his mate, you're nothing to him but a body he doesn't want to share. Like a kid with a new toy. Is that what you want? To be his toy?"

She smiled wickedly. "Oh yeah." It was certainly fun.

Aidan's lips thinned. "This isn't a joke, Gwen. You think I'm wrong? That he'll stay with you? Are you really that naive?"

She snorted softly. "Apparently not as naive as your parents since they didn't use a condom. Aidan, seriously, just back the fuck off and go back to your date—this isn't fair to her." But he didn't, and it was too late anyway because two arms curled around her from behind and held her gently but possessively.

Zander nuzzled her. "How's my baby doing?"

"Fine," she assured him, knowing he was pissed despite how carefully he handled her.

Releasing her, Zander then edged around her—placing himself in front of her like a barrier, forcing Aidan to back up. "Didn't I warn you to stay away from Gwen?"

Aidan spluttered. "You can't stop me from talking to someone."

"Really? Let's take a walk."

"Yeah, a walk sounds good."

Gwen almost jumped at Bracken's voice. She hadn't even realized he was behind her until he spoke. He followed Zander, who fisted Aidan's collar and dragged him out the door.

She stood there, torn over whether to follow and be sure they didn't kill Aidan. Not that his life meant anything to her, but being an asshole wasn't a reason to die. Still, if she did anything to defend Aidan, he'd see it as a green light to keep badgering her. Maybe she should just let him learn his lesson the hard way.

Decision made, she headed into the kitchen. Damn, it was hot, despite that they'd stopped serving food, since it was near closing time. As per usual, she helped the staff clean up and carried the garbage bags outside into the side alley. She tossed the first bag in the dumpster, then the next, and was just about to toss the third, when she heard the slight scuff of a shoe.

Whirling, she dropped the garbage bag . . . and then sagged in relief as she saw it was Zander. She frowned, opening her mouth to ask why he'd gone down the alley instead of just reentering the building through the front door. But then he smiled, and Gwen tensed. Zander didn't smile. Not like that. His mouth curved and quirked, but never spread into a huge toothy smile. He also didn't wax his eyebrows or slick back his hair. And then she noticed his clothing was now different. Which could mean only one thing.

She was about to say, "You must be Rory." But the guy that Zander had described would *love* to know that Zander talked about him. So, instead, she frowned. "For a minute there, I thought you were someone I know. I'm guessing you're related to Zander Devlin."

His smile faltered. "I'm his brother Rory."

"Damn, I can't believe he never mentioned he had an identical twin. Does he know you're here?"

"No, I was hoping to surprise him."

Yeah, she was just betting he was. She wondered if he'd been hanging outside the front of the building but scampered down the alley when Zander hauled Aidan outside. If so, it was most likely pure chance that he'd managed to confront her here.

"Well, I'm sure he'll be thrilled to see you." Her pulse jumped as Rory began to advance on her. Keeping her eyes on him, she leaned down to grab the bag, discreetly slipping her other hand into the pocket of her shorts to feel for her switchblade.

"You're not my brother's usual type. Far from it. But I can see why he's trying a new flavor."

Flavor? What was she, ice cream? She smiled, as if flattered. "Aw, thank you. You should go on inside and talk to him. I'm sure he'd love to see you."

"No, I don't think he would." Rory tilted his head. "And I think you know that." In a flash, he was right in front of her, both hands gripping her hips—and one of those hands had clearly unsheathed its claws, because the razor-sharp blades dug into her side threateningly. "Walk with me."

She snickered. "God, you're dumb."

"Excuse me?" He froze. Well, of course he did. What sane man would move when someone was pressing the tip of a switchblade against their ball sack?

"I suggest you sheathe those claws, Scooby."

Nostrils flaring, he bared his teeth. "And I suggest *you* drop that fucking knife." He dug his claws tight enough to break her skin.

Hissing at the sting, she pricked his ball sack with her blade. He inhaled sharply, clamping his lips tight. "You should really let me go, Rory. I get nervous when I'm threatened, and nerves make my hands twitch. I don't think you want me feeling nervous right now."

He lowered his arms with a harsh curse. "Drop the knife."

"Hands up first. Call me weird, but I don't trust that you won't—"

His eyes snapped toward the door and widened a little, and she got the feeling he heard something that she didn't. He leaped backward so fast it took her breath away. He backhanded her, sending her crashing into the dumpster. Her head hit the metal so hard she was surprised she didn't hear something crack. He fled like hell's army was on his heels.

"Bastard." She struggled to her feet, dazed and *pissed off*.

The door swung open, and Zander came rushing out with the other wolves behind him.

She pointed down the alley in time to see Rory disappear. "That way! The motherfucker went that way!"

If she hadn't swayed, making his stomach bottom out, Zander would have joined the others in pursuing his twisted brother. Instead, he grabbed his mate by her elbows, steadying her. "Gwen, baby, where did he hurt you?" His voice shook with barely contained fury and a need to *hurt*. But she came first.

"I'm okay. Really. Banged my head, though." She prodded the back of her skull and winced. "Gonna have a goose egg for sure."

He growled, gently probing the area she'd touched. "I can smell your blood." There was only a hint of it in the air, but it was enough to send yet more rage coursing through him. His wolf paced within him, growling and snarling.

"Oh yeah, he pricked my side with his claws." She peeled up her shirt and saw small, shallow puncture marks—blood had seeped to the surface, but it wasn't pouring down her side or anything. "Your eyes just flashed wolf."

"My beast is pissed right now," Zander told her. "He wants to hunt and kill the fucker responsible."

"It was Rory," she said quietly, hating that the knowledge might hurt him.

Zander tore a strip off the bottom of his shirt and pressed it against the punctures even though the wounds weren't bad. "I know," he rumbled. He took a long breath, seeking a calm he knew he wouldn't find for at least a few hours. Gwen didn't need his rage right then. "Ally had what she calls a flash-vision. Most of the time, her visions are at least a couple of minutes long. But occasionally she just sees a single flash of the future—like a photograph. She saw him putting you in a car."

"We didn't get to that part." Ally sure was handy to have around.

Zander clasped her nape, vowing, "I'll kill him. When they bring him to me, I'll kill him." Slowly. Mercilessly.

Gwen saw the Mercury wolves returning. "Not sure you're gonna get the chance." Because Rory wasn't with them.

As Zander turned to them, Derren said, "The asshole sped off in his car before we could get to him. No point trying to chase him—he has too much of a head start, so he'd easily lose us."

"Trying to snatch me was a half-assed plan," said Gwen as Ally came to her and laid a healing hand over the punctures on her side.

"It was a test," Bracken corrected. He looked at Zander. "It was a test to see if you'd be upset if something happened to her. You remember the threat he made."

Derren frowned. "What threat?"

"Yeah, what threat?" asked Gwen.

Bracken explained, "When Zander refused to give Rory any of his inheritance, Rory said, 'If you don't give me what's mine, I'll take from you what's yours.'"

And Gwen was definitely his, thought Zander. He doubted that Rory had any clue that Gwen was his mate, but he was clearly aware that she was someone to him. "Do you think he followed us to Oregon? He could have been lingering around our territory, saw us leave, and then followed."

"It's possible," said Bracken. "Or maybe he's here to see the attorney—Rory wanted to contest the will, right? I doubt he could. He's probably just hoping that if he bothers you with legal shit, you'll give in just to get him off your back. But he could have come to see the attorney, spotted us somewhere around town, seen you with Gwen, and then waited for a chance to test you."

Zander wasn't sure. Right then, while the scent of Gwen's blood tainted the air, he couldn't think straight. He only knew one thing . . . "Rory won't get to you again," he promised her. "I'll find him."

Shaking her head, Gwen fisted his shirt. "If you go hunting him, it will divide your resources."

"You think I should let this go?" he asked, voice soft and filled with disbelief.

"Yeah, I do. Bracken said it was a test. If you don't go after him, he'll think this didn't affect you that much. It isn't all that different from me pretending to cower over the Brandt thing—which is something I'll have to do tomorrow when I meet with Kenny. If I can do that, you can do this."

The problem was . . . Zander wasn't sure if he really could. "Maybe I should take you to my pack's territory. You could stay there." Where she'd be safe and he wouldn't have to smell her fucking blood every five minutes.

"And *that* isn't all that different from me going to a safe house." Gwen lifted her chin. "I'm not leaving here."

Zander planted his hands on her shoulders. "Listen to me. You matter to me, Gwen. You don't see that, I know, but it's true. I have to know you're safe and protected."

"Yeah? Then pretend you don't give a shit what Rory did. That's what will protect me from him."

Derren sighed. "I hate that she's right, but she is. He'll get what's coming to him, Zander. He won't get away with this. Not in the long run. We just have to be choosy about when we strike. Besides, one thing we can be sure he'll do is come back—he's intent on fucking with you. But now we know to keep an eye out for him. He won't touch her again."

Sensing that Zander wasn't even close to calming, Gwen leaned into him and slid her arms around his waist. Resting her cheek on his chest, she said, "I really want to go home. Can we make that happen?"

Fighting to keep his touch gentle, Zander brushed her bangs away from her face. "Yeah. We can make that happen."

CHAPTER THIRTEEN

Kenny dabbed his mouth with a napkin and then wiped his fingers. Smiling, he leaned back in his chair and gestured from him to her. "This is nice, isn't it?"

No, it wasn't. Gwen just looked at him. It was the first time that he'd spoken since they'd chosen a table. They'd eaten in silence as customers chattered, oven timers beeped, cutlery clattered, and frothing machines whirred.

The bell repeatedly chimed as more and more people filed in. It was a busy place. Despite the long line to the register, the stainless-steel counter and bistro tables were always clean and clear of crumbs. Kenny had wanted them to meet at a local, upscale restaurant, but Gwen had declined. Instead, she'd chosen this bakery-slash-coffeehouse.

She loved the scents here—bitter coffee, donuts, fresh bread, and the various baked goods kept within the glass case. Any other time, she would have dived on her Danish and enjoyed it with relish, but she'd only managed to eat half—and it sat like lead in her stomach.

It was harder than she'd thought it would be to sit opposite the man in front of her and pretend she had no idea that he was an absolute monster who sponsored extremists. How Geena managed to be around him each and every day, Gwen didn't know. But then, Geena saw something different when she looked at Kenny. She saw a father, *her* father. Gwen just saw a twisted asshole.

As he'd carefully eaten his apple pie like it was a rare delicacy, she'd studied him. She'd seen Kenny several times before, of course, though mostly from afar. There'd even been times when he'd come to the trailer to speak with Hanna. The first time he'd come, Hanna had afterward said dispassionately, "That was your dad, by the way."

Gwen didn't like that she had his eyes, but she was thankful they didn't otherwise look alike. Tall and muscular, he seemed in pretty good shape for his age. His narrow face was shaven and carried scars that said he'd led a rough life. His stylishly cropped short dark hair was thin and dusted with gray; it kind of worked for him. Add in the tailored suit, and he looked more like an average businessman than a seedy, conscienceless drug dealer.

Two of his *friends* sat at the table adjacent to theirs. Zander and the other Mercury wolves were sitting at a corner table, subtly keeping an eye on her. She didn't think Kenny was aware that they were there, or that he'd recognize them if they earned his attention. Despite the large distance between the wolves and Gwen, she was quite sure that the shifters would overhear her conversation with Kenny easily enough.

"Your mother's mad that I'm meeting you today." He crumpled up his napkin and set it on his empty plate. "She thinks we should leave you to have a good life."

Officially abandoning her Danish, Gwen picked up the porcelain mug and sipped at her milky latte. A little powdered sugar still clung to her fingertips. The tiny napkins were shit. "I came here today because you said you had something important to tell me. You said it was about Geena." He'd said what he thought would make Gwen meet him—she knew that. Still, she needed to play the game or he'd know that Geena had warned her.

"I may have lied about that." The cell phone on the table chimed. He tapped the screen with his finger, quieting the device. His phone hadn't stopped ringing since he'd arrived, but he canceled the call each time—giving her a pointed look that said this meeting was more important to him. Whatever.

"So, what do you want?"

He managed to look offended. "Is there something so terrible about a man wanting to know his daughter? I thought it was about time we finally met officially." He picked up his mug. He was drinking iced tea, of all things—she hadn't expected that. "Geena's been better since making contact with you. Less mercurial. More composed and efficient. I like that. It made me curious about you."

Not curious enough for him to get in touch until he wanted something, though.

"I recently learned that you and one of my acquaintances have mutual friends. The Moores. They're not happy bunnies right now."

Good. "They're also not my friends."

"Yes, I heard that you're not too fond of the boy, Brandt, after stumbling upon him in a rather tricky situation. But you know, there are two sides to every story."

"Shame Brandt's a prick in both of them."

His mouth curved. "If he's anything like his father, who I've heard plenty about, then he *is* a prick and probably always will be. But he's also the son of a friend's friend." Kenny sipped his iced tea. "You know, I'm confused. According to Geena, you're an intelligent girl. So why would you stand up for a shifter and, in doing so, vilify your own kind? And don't give me something about it being the right thing to do. Ethics don't keep people alive. *Smarts* keep people alive. And me, well, I'd rather you were alive."

Pissed that he'd pretend to care about her, she set down her mug and leaned forward. "Let's just be honest, shall we? You don't want me in your life. I don't want you in mine. You're not a faithful friend to your friend of the Moores or to anyone else. In fact, you probably fuck people over so often that you have to carry lube in your pocket. If you want me to back off, it must benefit you in some way—I don't care what it is. The point is that you haven't done a single thing for me in my entire life, so give me one good reason why I should do a damn thing for you."

His eyes narrowed, but they sparkled with amusement and . . . approval. He gave her a slow smile. "Interesting. You have spine. I expected you to be more like your mother. It's nice that you and I have something in common, don't you think?"

No, she didn't.

"I did do something for you, Gwen. I did what your neighbors didn't have the balls to do—I called Social Services."

She almost drew back. "You're lying." She'd always wondered who'd called them, but she'd never once considered that it could have been him.

"What went on in that trailer . . . It wasn't a good environment for you to grow up in." His voice took on a haughty, judgmental tone. "I warned your mother that I'd take steps to have you taken from her if she didn't get rid of that useless excuse of a human being. She should have put you first."

"But you didn't want me either, so what makes you better than her?"

"It was nothing personal, Gwen. I don't like kids."

Well, she didn't like drug dealers.

"I didn't want my kid growing up around that shit. You'd have ended up just like Hanna. Weak. Dramatic. Self-pitying." He shook his head in disgust. "I got you out of there."

"Which could have been a case of tossing me from the frying pan into the fire—foster care is no walk in the park for most people. Sometimes it's worse than where they came from."

"Ah, but you went to a good family. I saw to that." He smiled at her start of surprise. "Money talks, Gwen. Always has. Always will."

She wanted him to be lying. She really, really did. Otherwise, she'd have to be at least a little grateful to him for her ending up with the Millers. Gwen didn't want to be grateful to him for anything.

"There's nothing glamorous about your life, Gwen, but it was a good one, for the most part. You have a job, a family, friends." He drained his cup and put it down. "So, you see, you were wrong in saying I've never done a single thing for you. I took care of you in my way. Granted, I did it from afar, but I still did it. I've never walked into your life, asking anything of you, but now I am. I'm asking you to do this one little thing for me and just alter your statement. Tell some sweet little lies for Brandt. From what I've heard about him, he doesn't need you to ruin his life—he'll manage that all by himself."

She narrowed her eyes. "How do I know you're not just saying that you called Social Services so I'll feel that I owe you?"

"I suppose you don't. But you could always check with Social Services. I never made any secret of my interest in being sure you were placed somewhere safe. I also didn't call them anonymously. My name and my involvement should be on record."

She slowly sank back into her chair. "So you want me to cower before the Moores as a thank-you to you for getting me out of that trailer?"

He pursed his lips. "Well, it would be nice if you did it for me purely because I'm your father, but I'd be disappointed in you if you showed any respect to someone who hasn't earned it. So, yes, doing it as a thank-you would suit me fine."

"It's not that simple. They didn't just hurt the shifter. They invested months of their lives into fucking up my life. Brandt even came close to beating me with a bat not so long ago."

Kenny's face hardened. "Did he, now? I can guarantee that won't happen again."

"No, you can't. Brandt doesn't listen to anyone. He doesn't heed warnings or threats. Hell, he doesn't even heed common sense."

"I'll make it clear to his family that any trouble he causes you will be revisited on all of them."

Since she couldn't afford to look as though she was giving in easily, she continued to argue. "My point is that I'm not just gunning for that family because of what they did to the shifter—I want them to pay for the shit they've caused for me. Altering my statement and saving Brandt from the wrath of the shifter council doesn't really appeal to me."

Kenny actually smiled, the weirdo. "You get that vengeful streak from me."

Um, no, she didn't.

"He'll pay for what he did to you, and I'll make it clear that you're not to be harassed or touched. In exchange, you'll change your statement. Everybody wins."

"Except for the shifter."

Kenny flicked his hand. "She's not more important than your life, Gwen. And that's what we're talking about here. Your life. If you go ahead with frying Brandt's ass, the anti-shifter extremists might find out. If they do, they will leap on the situation. They wouldn't just go after you; they'd go after your foster family. So ask yourself, Gwen . . . is one shifter more important than the lives of you and those closest to you?"

She gritted her teeth against the urge to point out that he could probably put a leash on the extremists if he really wanted to—telling them he'd withdraw funding would most likely go a long way toward making them let the situation alone.

"If you're going to keep yourself and your foster family safe, you need to take action. It's best not to delay. I understand that you don't know or trust me, so of course you'll struggle with doing what I'm asking of you. But the truth is that if you change your statement, you'll be doing it for yourself and for your foster family too."

For a very long moment, she said nothing. Let the silence stretch out. Ensuring that she sounded begrudging, she said, "I'll do it. For *my family*."

He smiled again. "Excellent." He pushed out of his seat. "It's been nice talking to you, Gwen. I have to say, I wasn't expecting that." He did sound genuinely surprised. "You, Geena, and I will have to get together sometime."

Hell, no.

"I'll be in touch." He and his cronies then left.

Remaining seated, she watched through the window as they disappeared in a black BMW. That was when the Mercury wolves joined her.

Zander took the chair beside hers and angled it so that his front was pressed to her side. Even sitting down, he managed to crowd her. His spread legs bracketed her chair while one arm draped over her shoulders and the other reached across her body to smooth his hand over her thigh. "You okay?"

"Kind of." She sighed. "I didn't think he'd try the concerned-father routine. I thought he might play on my concern for Geena and pretend that any trouble I had could bleed over onto her."

Zander kissed her temple. "Instead, he appealed to your sense of fairness."

She nodded. "He made out like I owed him a debt, somehow sensing I was the kind of person who'd repay one." She could see why Geena cared for Kenny—he was manipulative, played on a person's weakness. He'd know that Geena wanted his approval, and he likely used that to keep her loyal to him. Gwen didn't like to think of her sister being played that way.

"I think he really did call Social Services," said Ally. "I heard the ring of truth in his voice. Not that I'm saying you owe him anything, Gwen. You don't. I just figured you might prefer knowing."

Gwen nodded her thanks. "It doesn't change anything. He wasn't a father to me. And you're right. I owe him nothing. But he thinks I should feel that I do, so I don't think he'll doubt that I'm truly backing down."

"He'll believe it," agreed Zander, stroking a hand over her hair. It had been damn hard to remain in his seat, leaving her to deal with Cogman alone. He'd wanted to be close, wanted to give her support as a mate should. Instead, he'd had to watch her sit opposite that motherfucker. His wolf had growled and snarled and brooded, not wanting the male anywhere near her.

Zander had also kept watch on Cogman's bodyguards, wanting to be sure they didn't touch Gwen. If they'd even *tried*, Zander's shifter-speed would have had him at her side in an instant. Cupping her chin, he brought her face to his. "You won't have to deal with him again."

He kissed her, and Gwen almost moaned. He tasted of cream, fluffy pastry, and sugary glaze. As he pulled back, she took a long breath and said, "So now we put the next part of our plan into action. I need to speak to Colt."

Zander brushed his thumb over her chin. "I'll be with you."

"You can't come into the station with me."

His grip involuntarily tightened on her jaw. "Why not?"

"Because it wouldn't make any sense for you to keep protecting me if you thought I was giving up on Andie. Colt will think it's weird that you'd stay at my side. I have to lie to him and say that you don't know why I'm there."

Zander swore, releasing her. He hadn't considered that.

She rubbed his thigh. "You can stay in the SUV. I'll give some spiel to Colt about wanting to keep you guys around for my family's sake. I'll be okay on my own. Nothing's going to happen to me in a police station."

Zander clenched his jaw. She was probably right. Still . . . "I don't like it."

"Trust me, I'll be fine."

"I do trust you."

Gwen's breath caught in her throat. Considering she'd opened up to him at a snail's pace, it was the last thing she'd thought he'd say. Especially since he was, by his own admission, extremely guarded. Lost for words, she leaned into him, letting him know she appreciated and valued his trust in her.

He pressed a lingering kiss to her hair and squeezed her nape. "Let's get this done, yeah?"

"Yeah," she said softly.

A short while later, Derren whipped the SUV into a parking space outside the sheriff's department. Zander immediately noticed the sheriff's car. Through the large windows of the office, it was easy to see that the chairs in the reception area were vacant. Good. Zander didn't want Gwen to have to hang around awhile, waiting for her chance to speak with Colt.

"Hopefully I won't be long," said Gwen.

Zander grabbed her braid, keeping her in place as he gave her a light kiss. "We'll be here. Call or text if you need me."

With a faint smile, she slid out of the SUV. Staying in his seat, watching her walk into a messed-up situation alone, went against every protective instinct he had. And it gutted him.

"She'll be okay, Z," said Bracken. "The sheriff might not like her, but he's not a physical threat to her."

Derren nodded. "Besides, she's tough."

"She's also mine." This was twice in one day that Zander couldn't be at her side while she went through a shitty experience. He hated that.

"She's been through worse alone," Ally pointed out.

Zander clenched his fists. "Reminding me of that does not help." His pulse spiked as Gwen disappeared into the sheriff's department, out of his line of sight. He took a long breath. "This plan better fucking work."

Gwen stepped into a clean, sterile reception area, nose wrinkling at the scents of coffee and bleach. The room was empty, apart from the janitor, and—as luck would have it—the sheriff. He appeared to be bullying the janitor, just as he did everyone else . . . which was likely why the poor guy looked close to ramming his cart into Colt's gut.

She took a few steps toward them, snatching the sheriff's attention. He straightened to his full height, brow creased. To her amusement, he also seemed to be struggling not to bare his teeth.

"Why are you here?" he asked.

"Such commendable people skills," she said drily. There was no sense in acting pally with him. That would only make him suspicious.

"Just answer the damn question, Gwen."

Before she could speak, the front door swung open, and a scantily dressed woman crossed to the sheriff on high heels, leaving the faint scent of marijuana in her wake. She also had some serious bruising on her face.

"Where is he?" she demanded, her voice a whip.

Colt sighed, bored. "Sandra, I'm going to have to ask you to stay calm."

"Where's Jim?"

"Where he normally is, Sandra—the drunk tank. And I suppose you're going to tell me that the bruises on your face aren't his artwork."

She shifted uncomfortably. "I fell. You know I'm clumsy."

"Clumsy. Right."

"Let him go, Sheriff. *Please.*"

Gwen's stomach plummeted. The scene was too close to home—or to the home she'd had during her childhood, anyway. How many times had her stepdad's ass ended up in the drunk tank? How many times had Hanna pleaded with the police to let him go, always equipped with inventive excuses to explain the bruises? She'd even taken Gwen along for sympathy, encouraged Gwen to back up her lies. And Gwen had.

"He assaulted a police officer while in custody," said Colt. "That means he isn't leaving for a little while. You go on home, Sandra."

"No. I want to speak to Jim!"

A muscle in Colt's cheek ticked. "If you insist on sticking around, that's fine. Maybe we could do a little drug test while you're here."

Sandra instantly drew back, paling. "Fine. I'll go home."

"Thought you might."

Spinning on her heel, Sandra made a dramatic exit—much like Hanna used to do.

Colt cleared his throat. "Well, Gwen, what kind of complaint do you have now?"

Gwen balled up her hands. She wasn't sure she could do this. Wasn't sure she could again lie to protect an abusive son of a bitch . . . she'd done enough of that as a kid.

But this time it would be different, she reminded herself. This time, the son of a bitch wouldn't go unpunished. He'd eventually get what he deserved. Still, a part of her felt shamed by what she was about to do. It didn't make much sense, but that shame was there all the same.

She lifted her chin. "We should talk alone."

Whatever he saw in her expression made his confrontational stance ease. "Come to my office."

She followed him into what was essentially a box room, but he'd made the most of the small space. At his gesture, she took the seat opposite him. "I'm here to alter my statement," she said through her teeth.

Colt stiffened, surprised. "Really?"

"I'm not doing it for Brandt or any of the Moores—let's just be clear on that. I owe someone a favor, and they've called it in. I repay my debts."

He leaned forward, bracing his elbows on the table, looking rather satisfied. "All right. Why don't you tell me what you really saw that night?"

Gwen narrowed her eyes. He knew her version had been the truth—the issue was that the truth simply didn't suit him. "Don't push it. Before we get started, I have a condition. I'll do this, but I don't want the news to make its way around town. The shifters can't know."

He abruptly straightened. "They're still here?"

"My family needs protection right now. I was attacked by a flock of avian shifters the other night. There's no way I'll believe that the Moores weren't behind it—there's no one else who'd mean me the kind of harm that the shifters caused."

"They could have been enemies of the wolves you've got hanging around you."

"If that was the case, they wouldn't have attacked me."

"Maybe the extremists got hold of the story and sent someone to hurt you."

She rolled her eyes. "Believe what you want. The point is that I want to keep the shifters around for protection. I'll give the Moores what they want and alter my statement, but they need to keep it to themselves."

Colt twisted his mouth. "The shifters will find out at the hearing."

"But by then, the Moores will be happy and willing to leave me alone."

"And what about the shifters? I don't think they'll like that you've used them."

"I know." She sighed, as if troubled. "I'm thinking it might be best if I act like I'm having second thoughts the night before the hearing. I could act afraid and stuff. Then they'll just think I fell at the last hurdle. They'll be upset and pissed, but not as much as they'd be if they found out how long it had been my intention to back down."

He lifted his brows. "Sounds like a good plan."

"It's not a plan I intend to put into action until the Moores confirm they'll keep my cooperation quiet."

"They'll be willing to do that."

"Call them. Ask. I'm not saying a word until I have their agreement."

He picked up his cell phone. "You'll trust their word? They might not stick to their end of this bargain."

"If they don't, I can always change my mind again at the hearing. This is their one and only chance to gain my cooperation. They can take it or leave it."

Colt swiped his thumb over the screen of his cell and then sank into his chair. "Hey, Ezra. I think you'll be rather interested to hear who's sitting opposite me right now. Gwen Miller." Colt told him about her offer, advised him to take the deal. Then he held out the phone. "He'd like to speak with you, Gwen."

She took the phone and, not bothering to greet the asshole on the other end of the line, simply said, "What?"

"I must admit," began Ezra, sounded smug as fuck, "you took longer than I thought to fold—"

"I'm not folding, Moore," she snapped. "I'm not doing this for, because of, or out of fear of *you*. You're really not as special as you seem to think you are, so tone down the narcissism a little bit. I'm repaying a debt that I owe to someone else. But that arrogant tone of yours is pissing me off enough to reconsider just how important that debt is."

There was a long pause, and she could almost sense him backing down. "I'll agree to keep your cooperation quiet," he said finally in a businesslike voice, all trace of smugness gone.

"Then it's a deal."

"It is. Take care, Miss Miller."

She handed the phone back to Colt. "Ready when you are."

He led her into a plain, basic interview room. The hard, plastic chair was as uncomfortable as they came, but she didn't let her discomfort show.

"Would you like a coffee?" asked Colt. It was a genuine offer.

"No." She rolled back her shoulders. "Let's get this over with." She gave him a statement that corroborated Andie's second one, said that she couldn't be sure that Brandt hadn't simply stumbled upon a hurt and bruised Andie, and that it was possible that he'd even been trying to help her.

After they were done, Colt walked with her to the reception area. "You did the right thing, Gwen. It's not easy to back down. And it takes strength to back down from people you despise. You did the right thing."

"Not the right thing."

"The smart thing."

Outside, Gwen headed straight to the SUV and slid onto the rear passenger seat. No sooner had she shut the door than Zander pulled her to his side and gave her a quick kiss.

"You okay?" he asked, smoothing her bangs out of her face.

"Better now that I'm out of there." Even better now that they were driving away.

Zander massaged her nape. "Did he buy it?"

"Yep." Her upper lip curled. "Ezra sounded like the cat that got the cream."

Riding shotgun, Bracken twisted to look at her. "The lie will keep you safe."

"For a while," she said. "When I blurt out the truth before the council, things will go to shit *fast.*" Gwen turned to Zander. "You sure you want to stick around for that? Ow!" She rubbed at her scalp, scowling at the asshole for pulling her hair.

Zander put his face close to hers. "Then don't ask stupid, bullshit questions. I'll be at your side the entire fucking time."

"So will I," said Bracken.

"And me," added Ally.

Derren glanced at her through the rearview mirror. "Me too, Gwen."

She swallowed hard. Their show of support might have been partly for Andie, but it still touched Gwen. Still meant a lot to her. She gave a nod of thanks, speechless.

Back at the house, she went upstairs, intending to take a relaxing bath. Zander followed her into her room and helped her undress. Somehow, they ended up in bed instead of the bath. Still, the result was the same—the tension left her muscles, and her mood lifted.

Afterward, as they lay in bed watching TV, Zander said, "You know, for someone who spends a lot of her time cleaning, you have a surprisingly messy room."

Snuggled into his side, Gwen shrugged one shoulder. "I'm a rebel that way."

The sound of the floorboards creaking above them made him frown. The person who stayed up there was constantly a noisy bastard. He knew none of his pack mates were up there. "Is that Marlon's room?"

"No, he's down the hall."

"Yvonne's?"

"Nope. Her room is near his."

Unease slithered down Zander's spine. Snorting at his body's dumb reaction, he picked up the remote. "I'm turning over."

"Hey! I want to see which pack she chooses!"

He sighed at her. "You do know that this movie is *nothing* like real life for shifters, don't you? The pack dynamics, the mating bonds—the scriptwriters got it all wrong."

Gwen rested her chin on his chest. "What *are* mating bonds like? I know they're metaphysical and stuff, but that's pretty much it."

"I can't really know what they feel like. I've never had one. I can only tell you what others have told me. A mating bond connects you to someone on a level that nothing else will. It's intense. Powerful. It allows you to *feel* your mate. Feel their emotions, their pain. You can use the link to bolster their strength by pushing energy down the bond. Your scent mixes with theirs and becomes one unique scent. And if one dies, it's very hard for the other to survive the breaking of the bond. But I'm told that the bond is special enough to be worth the risk."

Zander wished she was ready to hear that he believed she was his mate, but his gut told him to keep quiet for now. He continued, "Most mated couples I've come across seem happy and stable. The pairs balance each other out, accept each other for who they are, and seem content in a way I can't imagine ever feeling. I guess you'd have to experience the bond for yourself to really know."

Gwen gave him a faint smile, unable to suppress a twinge of envy. She wasn't a soppy person, but she did like the idea of predestined mates—thought it was a beautiful thing. "Has anyone ever told you what it feels like for the mating bond to form?" she asked, relaxing as he ran his fingers through her hair.

"I've heard it hurts at first, but then the pain gives way to a sort of euphoric sense of peace. It usually takes certain steps for a mating bond to fully snap into place. First, the couple has to be open enough to each other to sense the bond. Only after they've overcome certain obstacles will the bond strengthen and their scents mix. But they still need to be absolutely solid before the mating bond's complete and fully working."

"Must be nice to know you'll have that one day."

"Not sure I'll make a good mate."

She frowned. "Why?"

"I know myself, Gwen. I know I'm intense, even for a shifter. I know I'm shit at connecting with people and have all kinds of issues." He figured it was only fair that he warn her. "I was harsh on you that night at the boardwalk, so I'm sure you've noticed that I also lack in the empathy department. I'm not good at understanding people's problems or seeing their point of view. It doesn't make me a great confidant or partner—people can get upset when they don't think you appreciate how bad their situation is or how they're feeling."

Given all she'd learned about him, Gwen didn't think it was all that surprising that he struggled to connect with people or that his ability to trust was all fucked-up. She instinctively knew that he wouldn't be an easy mate. In fact, she doubted he was familiar with love or emotional expression. But she also knew he was someone who'd always be there for the people he cared for, no matter what. Someone who'd be unwaveringly loyal. That was pure gold for a woman like Gwen, so she didn't doubt that there would be other females out there who'd feel the same way.

She jabbed her finger into his chest. "You're not the bad catch you seem to think you are. You have plenty of good qualities. Lots of people have issues. I don't think I've ever met a single person who doesn't. If your mate turns out to be a fussy bitch who can't accept you for who you are, fuck her—she doesn't deserve you."

She deserved him just fine, Zander thought. Suited him perfectly. Would complete him in a way that words would never explain. Although he hadn't sensed she was his mate on even a subconscious level before Ally knocked some sense into him, there had always been that primal warning of danger around Gwen. Now, he understood it. Zander didn't like vulnerabilities, and he'd instinctively known that she could become one. Known that she could become an addiction. Addictions fucked with a person's self-control, and Zander needed control. He just needed Gwen more.

He dragged her on top of him. "You do realize that this—you and me—won't come to an end once the trial's over, don't you?"

Gwen stilled, though her heart slammed against her ribs. It hadn't been a flippant remark. There was a fierce determination in both his tone and expression. "You have a pack to go back to."

"I didn't say I'd leave the pack."

"Long-distance relationships are hard. Putting in the effort when it's just a long-distance fling seems pointless."

He lightly tapped her ass. "We both know this is more than a fling. I told you last night, you matter to me."

"Well, this can't be anything other than a fling. I'm not your mate."

His wolf snapped his teeth at that remark. "How do you know?"

She spluttered. "Because . . . I'd know."

"Would you? I already told you, the frequency of the bond can be blocked by lots of things. I'm not saying you are my mate." But his wolf urged him to do so. "I'm just making the point that it makes no sense to end something good on the premise that I should be waiting for a mate that could be lying right on top of me. A mate that could have walked past me yesterday or bumped into me another day. I've told you before, Gwen, I'm not going to spend my life searching for someone I may never recognize as my mate."

She went to sit up, but Zander wrapped his arm around her to pin her in place. "I like what we have, Gwen. You like what we have. Why end it without a good reason? Do you have a good reason?"

Gwen licked her lips. She could point out that she was a pain in the ass, that he could have any woman he wanted, that surely a shifter would suit him better. But she said, "No." She made a big deal out of him being nosy and pushy, but she really didn't mind it so much—she just pushed right back, stood her ground, snorted at his nonnegotiable tone. The truth was that Zander was exactly her type. Loyal, trustworthy, honest, sexily assertive. He listened, paid attention. He was also an absolute rock star in bed. The kind of person who'd leave a mark wherever he went.

As a rule, Gwen didn't trust any situation in which she got what she wanted. She'd been confused by his interest, hadn't trusted it, so she'd slammed up her guard. Now? Now there seemed no point. Holding him at a distance hadn't worked. Trying to push him away hadn't worked. Feigning disinterest in him and his life to offend him hadn't worked.

He was like a freaking emotional tank. Solid. Resilient. Just kept on forging ahead, able and willing to smash whatever obstructed his path. If he said she was who he wanted, fine. She wasn't gonna argue. Not anymore.

"Do you *wish* you had a good reason?" Zander asked carefully.

Gwen took a long breath. "No."

Triumph surged through Zander, and his wolf settled a little. He tightened his hold on her. "Then don't fight this. Let it happen. Go with it. Let yourself be fucking happy."

"Want the truth?"

"Let's hear it."

"You do make me happy . . . and not only because you make a pretty picture naked beneath me." She smiled dreamily. "Very, very pretty."

His mouth curved. "And you make me happy. But I'm not pretty. I am, however, naked. As are you." He rolled them and urged her to wrap her legs around him. "I think we should make the most of that."

"I think it would be a crime not to."

"Good." He angled her hips and drove his cock deep.

CHAPTER FOURTEEN

Joining his pack mates on the flattened grassy area not far from the rear of the house, Zander asked, "Any sign of him?"

"Someone's been creeping around the southern border of the land," said Derren, "but I can't be sure it was Rory."

Zander lifted a questioning brow at Bracken. "What did you see?"

"There were some wolf paw prints on the eastern side," began Bracken, "and they were too big to be those of a full-blooded wolf. My guess is that it was Rory."

Zander clenched his jaw. His blood boiled at the thought of his brother anywhere near Gwen. It had been more than a week since Rory had tried to take her, and they'd checked the land daily for signs that he'd been nearby. Today was the first time that they'd found any, which likely meant that Rory was done waiting for Zander to hunt him.

Shaya had been furious to hear that Rory had harmed Gwen. She'd taken an immediate liking to Zander's human, apparently. And when Zander had shared that he and Ally were certain that Gwen was his mate, the rest of his pack became just as pissed about Rory's *test*.

Given the shit that Nick had previously spouted, Zander had expected the Alpha to be disappointed to hear that Gwen was his mate. If he was, he'd given no indication of it. He'd simply said, *"Keep her safe, Zander. Take it from someone who watched his parent fall apart after she lost her mate—you'd be a shell of a man without her. I don't want that for you."*

His Alpha was right on that score, but Zander was resolute that he'd never know how that felt. He'd never have to be without her. No one would take her from him, especially not Rory. The asshole had hurt her once—he wouldn't get another chance. Zander would make sure of it.

Ally took a step toward him. "I know your instinct is to hunt Rory and eradicate the threat to your mate, but it won't be that simple. For one thing, he's your twin."

"Don't think that means anything to me right now," Zander rumbled. "Blood doesn't make family. Rory isn't my family. Never was. Gwen—she's everything. If I have to kill him to keep her safe, that's what I'll do." His wolf was behind him all the way.

"Gwen won't like to think that you killed your twin for her," Ally gently pointed out. "She's the type of person who'd worry that it killed something inside you and that you'll one day hate her for it."

"She's also the type of person who fully understands that sharing someone's DNA doesn't have to mean anything."

Ally inclined her head, conceding that. "While we're on the subject of Gwen . . . have you decided when you're going to tell her that you believe she's your mate?"

He sighed. "I'm working up to it."

"She's a lot more relaxed with you now. She seems really happy."

Bracken slipped his hands in his pockets. "Do you think it will be hard to convince her to leave here and move to pack territory? She works for Yvonne and her soon-to-be brother-in-law, and she keeps a close watch on the whole family. She might feel like moving away would be abandoning them."

"I worry about that." Ally paused to swat at a mosquito. "But Marlon and Yvonne will bodily throw her out if it comes to it—they want her happy, and they think Zander can give it to her. I haven't told them that she's your true mate, just in case you're wondering."

"She'll join the pack," said Zander, confident.

Derren tilted his head. "What makes you so sure?"

"She's full of questions about the pack, our culture, the laws we abide by." She quizzed Zander daily. "In my opinion, she's always been fascinated by wolf shifters for a reason—deep down in her soul, she knew she belonged to one. She subconsciously knew she'd be part of a pack one day. She's ready for it. *Hungry* for it on some level."

"He's right," said Ally. "When she's with us, when we're together as a group, something in her sort of . . . settles. I can't explain it. But it makes me think that joining our pack won't be a big problem for her. Leaving her family will be, though. You can't ignore that, Zander. You have to face it so you can think of the best way to deal with it."

A cool breeze slid over Zander, bringing with it the scents of wet grass, salty water, and . . . *human males*. He stiffened. "We have visitors."

Derren's nostrils flared, and then he tensed. "Where's Gwen?"

"She's inside the house; she'll be fine," said Zander.

Bracken lifted his brows. "You sure?"

"I'm sure."

Suds splattered on the ground as Gwen scrubbed the side of the truck with the wet sponge. Soapy water pooled at her feet and dotted her legs. Her tank top and denim shorts were wet with soap and water, but the air was so hot and dry that they wouldn't be damp for long.

Her sunglasses protected her eyes from the shards of sunlight that bounced off the wet, clean paint.

Washing her truck was *not* her favorite pastime, but she'd needed something to do. She was used to new guests arriving at least once a week—used to having rooms to clean, linen to launder, Welcome Hampers to prepare, and people to take on tours around the marsh.

It was strange to have so much time on her hands. Hell, she'd been so bored, she'd even cleaned her own room. Marlon and Yvonne had made it worse by fussing over her. Needing some air and space, she'd turned to her dirty truck.

Having something to do also helped distract her from thoughts of Kenny and the Moores. On the evening of the day she'd met with Kenny, Geena had called to say that he'd seemed very happy after the meeting. He'd supposedly contacted Ezra Moore and instructed him to back off.

So far, his *instruction* had worked. There had been no more attacks or problems. Gwen wasn't confident that things would remain so calm, though. Not when the people in question were laws unto themselves.

Zander's tension hadn't eased either, but she suspected that was partly due to the lingering threat that Rory presented. She wasn't worried about that moron because, well, he was a moron. But she could happily shoot him right in the dick for toying with Zander and using her to do so.

It was laughable to be protective of someone who was a gazillion times stronger than she was. If anyone could take care of himself, it was Zander Devlin. He didn't need her. It was both strange and . . . uplifting to be around someone who didn't need her to be *the strong one*.

Hanna, Yvonne, Julie, and Marlon had all used her as a crutch to some extent. Hanna was a lost cause, but Gwen had shaken free of her as a child. The others didn't need her so much anymore. Julie now had Chase, and Marlon's inner strength had bloomed once he'd admitted he was gay and stopped forcing himself to be something he wasn't. Now that Yvonne no longer had her husband browbeating her, she was better too. Oh, she still liked burying her head in the sand, but she didn't lean so much on Gwen anymore.

Gwen loved her family, had no problem being there for them, but she'd never really realized just how tired she'd been of always being their rock. Not until Zander came along, offering his support, protection, and strength. It had been so tempting to just accept what he offered and let him take the weight of everything, but she'd resisted at first. Really, he'd just seemed too good to be true—definitely too good to be truly interested in someone like her.

She'd given up resisting, and she felt lighter for it. She still thought that a female shifter might suit him better, but who was she to tell another person what was or wasn't good for them? Or what they did and didn't want? It was insulting, really. Zander was a full-grown man who had his own mind.

Done scrubbing the window, she swiped her forehead with the back of her hand and then dropped the sponge in the bucket. Iridescent bubbles slithered down the red paint and onto her shoes. Nice. Picking up the hose, she turned it on. Water blasted from it, rinsing the soap from the car and dripping on the ground. It was as she turned off that hose that she heard the chuckles. Familiar, irritating chuckles.

Gwen spun on her heel. Brandt was leaning against Marlon's car, arms crossed, smirking smugly. He obviously knew about the deal she'd made with his father, and he was here to gloat. Yeah, she'd figured he'd do something stupid sooner or later. He just couldn't help himself.

Rowan and Mack stood a few feet behind him, eyeing the hose nervously—they apparently had the sense to consider that she may want to use it on them. Brandt . . . he was too caught up in this "I have the upper hand" moment. It pissed her off that she'd have to let him think he did. Inside her, pride warred with the need to be smart, and *smart* barely won out.

Brandt lifted his hands. "I'm not here to give you trouble, Gwen."

Well, that would be a first. "If you have any sense in your head, you'll leave *now*."

"I just wanted to say that I'm glad you finally saw reason, that's all."

"Saw reason?"

"I get that you're upset about the stuff I did to you. What's sad is that we could have avoided all that if you'd just seen reason a lot earlier." He shook his head with a sigh, as if she'd been acting like a brat all this time.

Anger surged through her, hot and sharp. He could not be believed. "I'm not sure if you genuinely believe that all you did is *my* fault and not a consequence of you being a fucking turd. I also don't care. Just. *Go.*"

His smirk died a quick death. "There's no call for speaking to me like that, Gwen. I would have thought you were smarter than that." Like he was someone big and important whom she should quiver before. Unreal.

"You think you're tough and scary, Brandt? Is that what it is?" She snickered in disbelief, giving him a withering look. "It doesn't take a gynecologist's opinion to know you're a pussy."

Eyes blazing, he pushed off Marlon's car. "What the fuck did you just call me?"

"I don't see you going around harassing male loners. Oh, no. You went for the female. Know why? You're *weak*, Brandt. You'll always be weak. That was why you drugged Andie before you attacked her—you were too chicken shit to take her on while she was at full strength. You go around town, acting like a first-class asshole, and then hide behind Daddy. So, yeah, you're a pussy."

He balled up his hands. "Didn't Rowan once warn you that your mouth was going to get you in trouble one day? You should've listened, Gwen."

Rowan quickly slid in front of him and put a hand on his chest. "Brandt, you heard your dad—you can't touch her. If she reneges on the deal, you'll be on Shit Street."

Mack nodded. "Come on, man, this ain't worth it."

Brandt hissed at them through his teeth. "*No one speaks to me like that.* She's gonna damn well pay for it." He shoved Rowan aside, only to come to an abrupt halt. Gwen frowned, confused, but then Zander's hand smoothed up her back as he silently sidled up to her from behind.

"Everything all right here?" he asked.

"Fine," she said, gaze still locked on the asshole in front of her. "You know, I had no idea that pussy lips could talk. My mind is blown."

Brandt sneered as he studied them. "I heard you were rubbing yourself all over some shifter at Half 'n' Half. What does it say about you, Gwen, that you gotta fuck other species because your own doesn't want you? How's that bestiality thing working out for you?"

Zander looked at her. "I'm confused. Is he trying to be funny or intimidating?"

She shrugged, scratching her nape. "I always struggle trying to figure that one out. Either way, he fails dramatically, so I don't suppose it matters."

Zander took a slow, predatory step closer to the human boys, and they each shuffled backward—he wasn't even sure if they'd done it consciously. As he'd crept up to the house, he'd heard enough of the conversation to know the visitors were Brandt and his friends. *Pissed* didn't begin to describe how he felt as he stared at the male who'd harassed and almost assaulted his mate. His wolf swiped at Brandt with his claws.

Arching a daring brow at Brandt, Zander said, "You're not going to give *me* shit? You only mouth off when you're dealing with females?"

Brandt swallowed hard and then jutted out his chin. "This is between me and Gwen."

"No, kid, it's not. You got a problem with Gwen, I become *your* problem. You piss her off, you deal with me. And trust me, kid, you *don't* want to deal with me. You can't. I can see in your eyes that you know that."

Brandt's breathing sped up. "There're three of us. There's only one of you."

"No, there really isn't," said Bracken, coming up behind the boys. They whirled to face him, wide-eyed. That was when Derren and Ally came out from behind the SUV and moved so that the humans were then surrounded by the four shifters.

Brandt spun back to face Gwen. "Call off your guard dogs."

"You think I don't know that you're terrified?" Zander asked. "I can smell your fear." His wolf relished it. "So there's no point in making ballsy little comments. You're just making yourself look stupid."

"Maybe he simply is stupid," suggested Derren.

"It's a strong possibility," allowed Zander. "I tell you what, kid. You and me can take care of this right now. We'll battle it out here. Your friends can even join in and help you. My pack mates will stand back; I don't need the backup. What do you say?"

Rowan grabbed Brandt's arm and whispered, "Dude, we need to go."

Brandt glowered at his friend. "You're scared of some fucking animals?"

"Yeah," said Rowan, unashamed. "And so are you."

Mack shifted from foot to foot. "I knew we shouldn't have come. Let's just go."

Brandt's eyes sliced back to Zander. "You wouldn't be protecting her if you knew the truth."

Rowan's eyes widened. "Fuck, Brandt, use your head and stop!"

Shooting them a bored look, Zander lifted a brow. "You kids going now? Pity."

"It would have been fun to watch you kick their asses, Z." Bracken moved aside, letting the humans pass. Brandt did so reluctantly, but his friends couldn't seem to get away quickly enough.

Tossing Gwen a glare over his shoulder, Brandt said, "I'll be seeing you soon."

"Not if you want to live, you won't," growled Zander. That made all three boys hasten their steps. When they were finally out of sight, he said, "Bracken, follow them to the border; make sure they leave the land." With a nod, the enforcer did. Zander turned back to Gwen. "You were supposed to be inside the house."

She arched a brow. "And you assumed this because . . . ?"

"Dammit, Gwen, you said you'd stay home."

Her spine snapped straight. "No, I didn't. I said I wouldn't go trekking through the marsh. I didn't say I would stay inside those four walls—I'd go crazy if I did. I should be perfectly safe in my own damn driveway. *Brandt* was in the wrong place, not me. And I'm not going to sit behind closed doors because of assholes like him and Rory. *You* wouldn't."

"We're not talking about me."

"That empathy deficiency is interfering here. Imagine how you would feel if the situation were reversed. Would you stay inside?" He didn't answer her question, but his expression said it all. She resumed rinsing the car as she asked, "Now, did you find any sign of Rory out there?"

"He's been here. He hasn't come close to the house, but he's come close enough."

"I don't think he'll make another try for me. It's too obvious a move. He doesn't seem like the kind of person who likes to be predictable. That, oddly enough, makes him a little predictable." She looked at the Beta pair. "He's more likely to strike out at one of you next time. Probably you," she told Ally.

Derren's eyes narrowed in interest. "Why do you say that? I'm not disagreeing, I'm just curious."

"Well, if he targets your mate, wouldn't your instinct be to hunt him?" At his nod, Gwen continued, "Then I'm guessing that Ally wouldn't want you doing that alone. That means that she'd either go with you or insist on someone else doing so. By making that move, he'd be dividing your group. And that would make Zander a clearer target." Gwen looked at Zander. "I know that so far he's focused on others, but you're the ultimate target."

"We can't split up, no matter what he or anyone else does," Ally insisted.

"We won't," stated Derren.

Noticing that each of the shifters had dirty boots from walking around the marsh, Gwen asked, "Want me to give your boots a quick rinse?" At their nods, she used the hose to quickly wash off the mud before the water could soak through the leather.

The Beta pair headed up the porch steps, promising to take off their wet boots before entering the house. Zander remained where he was, and now he was looking at her with such intensity that her stomach twisted.

"What are you thinking about that has you staring at me like that?" she asked.

"Baby, you're standing there wet in a tank top and shorts. What do you think is going through my head?"

She rolled her eyes. "One-track mind."

"And you just noticed?"

The front door swung open, and Yvonne leaned out. "Dinner will be ready in twenty minutes. If you need to shower, go now!"

With Zander's help, Gwen quickly finished washing her truck and then took a shower. He joined her, of course. Conserving water was important. The brief bout of sex was just a bonus.

After dinner, they settled on Zander's balcony with her sitting on his lap. At her request, he called Dawn to ask about Andie. Gwen had called Andie a few times herself, and though the cougar claimed to be okay, Gwen wanted to be sure. According to Dawn, Andie had settled in fine and was spending a lot of time with Heath—the male she'd met on the first day.

"I'm relieved she's doing okay. And I'm super glad she left here before Rory showed up. He might have seen and hurt her."

Zander skimmed his hand up and down her leg. "Probably. He's an asshole that way."

She sifted her fingers through his hair. "He never did even one thing good for you in his life?" she asked, sad at the idea. Even Hanna, neglectful and selfish though she was, had done the occasional good thing for her.

"He gave me a kidney, but my parents had to bribe him to do it."

"*Bribe* him?"

He nodded. "He also tried to make me feel bad about it afterward. He still says I *stole* his kidney. He even said it in the attorney's office." Zander almost smiled when she leaned farther into him, giving him comfort. "You know, when he told me he'd take from me what's mine, I dismissed the threat. At the time, I had nothing for him to take."

She frowned. "You have your pack and your home."

"Yeah, but they're not something that's mine and only mine. You are. In a sense, he'll see you as an impostor."

"Impostor?"

"He's the same way with Jesse and Bracken. See, in some fucked-up way, Rory sees me as belonging to him. He doesn't care about me. Doesn't want me in his life. But he doesn't want others to care about me—not even our sister—and he really doesn't want me caring about others. He was always jealous of my friendships with Jesse and Bracken, and he'll be jealous of what I have with you."

"Tough," she snapped.

Zander smiled. "Yeah, tough."

"Tell me more about your sister. You've never really talked about her much."

"Remember I told you that I know someone who'd once needed someone to stand up for them the way you're standing up for Andie? I was talking about Shelby."

Gwen gaped in horror as he told her about the shootings and how the witnesses had been bullied into silence. "No wonder you and Bracken offered to help me. You're doing it for Shelby."

Zander skimmed his fingers down her face. "No. I'm doing it for you. I told myself it was for Shelby. But it wasn't. Not then, not now."

She swallowed. "Thank you."

"No thanks needed." Zander reached back and yanked the tie out of her hair. He gently unraveled the intricate braid, unsurprised by her exasperated sigh.

"You need to stop taking out my braid."

"I love your hair. Playing with it relaxes me." With a firm grip on her hair, he tugged her head back and kissed along her neck.

Gwen let her eyes drift closed as he used his lips, tongue, and teeth to devastate her neck. "This relaxes you too?" It fired up her libido *big*-time.

"This makes me hard as a rock." He swiped his tongue over the mark on her throat. "It also makes you wet." He could smell it.

Hearing a familiar chiming coming from inside Zander's room, she rasped, "That's my phone." She'd left it inside.

"Ignore it."

She did, but it just kept on ringing. "Let me answer it. It could be Andie or Julie." He reluctantly let her go and gave her a firm spank on the ass as she passed. "Hey!" She fished out her phone, but didn't recognize the number. A little cautiously, she answered, "Hello?"

"Miss Miller, it's Ezra."

Her grip tightened around the phone as irritation blasted through her. She was about to ask how the hell he'd gotten her number, but then she supposed it couldn't have been too hard for him, given he had people who'd electronically messed with her life.

"Rowan told me what Brandt did today. I wanted to apologize—"

"Aren't you tired of apologizing for him, Moore?"

He sighed, sounding . . . weary. "It won't happen again."

"It better not." She paused as Zander strolled into the room. "Brandt almost let the cat out of the bag earlier right in front of the shifters."

Ezra whispered a curse. "Like I said, it won't happen again."

"Glad to hear it." She ended the call. "That was Ezra, apologizing for Brandt."

"I suspected he might contact you."

She placed her phone on the dresser. "I don't like that he called my cell."

Zander crossed to her. "I don't like that he called you at all."

"Hopefully he'll find a way to keep Brandt on a leash. It's a vain hope, though."

Softly, Zander brushed his mouth over hers. "Don't let them mess with your mood."

"Hard not to."

"Forget about them." He grazed her lower lip with his teeth. "I don't want to talk about them."

"Really?"

He snaked his hand around her throat and gave it a gentle squeeze that made her pupils dilate. "Really. Know what I do want?" He kissed his way up her neck, along her jaw, and over to her ear. "I want to play with my baby."

She shivered as he sucked on her earlobe. "Then play with me."

He kissed, no, he *feasted* on her mouth—barely even stopping as he stripped off her vest and bra. A big believer in fair play, Gwen gathered his T-shirt in her hands and slid it upward. He helped her whip it off, and then she smoothed her hands over his warm chest. Damn, he was amazing. Solid. Edible. Perfect.

Driven by an urge she was too turned on to overthink, she grazed his chest with her teeth. He growled and fisted her hair, pushing her head closer. She bit. Hard. Sucked to leave a mark.

Gripping her hair tighter, Zander snatched her head back and kissed her as he clutched and squeezed her breast. She was the softest, sweetest, most perfect fucking thing. And when her hand cupped his cock over the denim of his jeans, he groaned. She was looking down, watching as she rubbed the heel of her hand over his dick. "Something you want, Gwen?"

Well, now that he'd mentioned it . . . Gwen sat on the bed, putting her head level with the cock that was rock hard within the confines of his jeans. She deftly tackled his fly, and his cock sprang out—long, thick, and ready. Her pussy fluttered. Her hands tingled with the urge to fist him tight and pump hard. But she found herself simply staring at him.

"Well, go on, then."

Gwen slithered her tongue up from base to tip, and then swept it over the head. There was no way she'd be able to take all of him in her mouth, but she was happy to try. Not yet, though. First, she wanted to tease him. Wanted to hear him groan as she pushed him to the edge. Zander was always so attentive, so damned determined to make sure she got off that Gwen wanted to return the favor. So, well, she went to work on his cock.

Zander watched in sheer fucking awe as his mate went down on him. She licked and stroked and played, like he was something to explore and savor. Every now and then, her eyes would flick to his—eyes glittering with need. He felt that look in his balls. Balls she cupped and rubbed and licked.

"Baby, take me in your mouth." She didn't. The little witch kept on playing and teasing and generally driving him out of his mind. *"Gwen."* She blew a cool breath on the head of his cock while lightly grazing his thighs with her nails. He bit out a curse. "Gwen, if you don't quit fucking around . . ." She fisted his cock and took him into her mouth. "That's it. Good girl."

Zander sank his fingers in her hair, groaning as she sucked him hard and fast, like she was trying to drain the come from his balls. Nails dug into his ass, pulling him forward as she took him deeper. Her throat contracted around his cock as she swallowed, taking even more of him. *Fuck.*

Seeing her there, lips wrapped around his cock, cheeks hollowed and flushed, her breasts and hard little nipples bared . . . Zander knew he was gone. "Swallow it all, Gwen." His orgasm pulled him under, sending pleasure spiraling through him. He gripped her hair tighter as he exploded inside her mouth, shooting jets of come down her throat.

"Jesus, Gwen." As he stood there trying to find his composure, his dick still in her mouth, her eyes snapped to his, expectant, waiting for direction. He liked that a fuck of a lot. "I think you deserve a reward for that."

In complete agreement, Gwen slowly slid him out of her mouth, kind of pleased with herself. How he was still half-hard, she didn't know, but she sure did appreciate his excellent recovery time. He didn't move. Just raked his gaze over her, like he was taking a moment to appreciate a view that was his. "Something you want, Zander?" she asked, throwing his earlier words back at him.

"I have what I want right here. Stand up." She did, and Zander slid down her shorts and panties while she kicked off her shoes. "I can smell how wet you are," he growled. The scent of her need made his dick throb. His wolf inhaled it with a contented growl.

"I do hope you're going to do something about it," said Gwen. He tossed her on the bed, and a laugh bubbled up. She blinked, bracing herself on her elbows . . . just in time to watch the show as he made quick work of his clothes. Damn, the guy was a delicious sight to behold.

"Spread your legs, Gwen." Holding his gaze, she did as he asked. "My baby's being a good girl for me. I like that." He knelt on the bed and spread the folds of her pussy with his thumbs. "Slick. Plump." He sank a finger inside her. "I bet you like to play with yourself, don't you?"

"Don't need to. I have a vibrator to do the work."

Zander stilled as all kinds of graphic images exploded in his mind. "Watching you fuck yourself with a vibrator has its appeal. *But* . . . I find I don't like the idea of anything being in this pussy but me." He added another finger, smiling at her sharp gasp.

"The vibrator doesn't make me come as hard as you do," she said, surprised she could speak while his fingers were thrusting in and out of her, hitting her most sensitive zones with unerring accuracy. "But it also doesn't make me do things I don't want to do."

"What do I make you do that you don't want to do?"

"You make me say I'm yours."

"You are." He thrust his fingers deep to punctuate his point.

"I don't like to say it."

She didn't like to *admit* it, Zander thought. There was a distinct difference. "Why? Is it because you worry I'll one day give you back?"

Gwen shrugged one shoulder. "Maybe."

He withdrew his fingers. "Baby . . . I couldn't give you up even if I wanted to." He tilted her hips toward him, hooked her legs over his shoulders, and swiped his tongue between her slick folds. Her taste blasted through him, and he groaned. "I love going down on you."

Zander ate at her pussy, licking and suckling while she bucked and moaned. He growled each time he was rewarded with more of her cream. She tasted so fucking good, *smelled* so fucking good. As her moans turned into curses because he wouldn't let her come, he scooped up some cream with his finger and slipped it into her ass.

Gwen's back bowed a little. "Jesus, Zander, you need to give a girl some warning before you go shoving things up her—" She cut off as he lightly suckled on her clit. "Fuck. Don't stop." But of course he stopped, the jerk.

"I want to be in you when you come." Zander lowered her legs, satisfied when she locked them around his waist. He curled his tongue around her nipple just because, and her fingers delved into his hair. Those fingers tugged hard when he plucked the taut bud with his teeth.

"No biting," she hissed.

So he bit her. Right on the swell of her breast. "You like it when I bite you." His wolf fucking loved it. Zander grabbed her wrists and pinned them above her head, staring into blue eyes that were hazy with need. The sight made his balls ache. "I'm going to hold you down."

Gwen swallowed, totally mesmerized by the stamp of feral possessiveness on his face.

"No struggling. Just take it." Zander slowly sank into her, gritting his teeth as her pussy squeezed his cock. Fuck, she was so damn tight. Yet, he always slid smoothly inside . . . because she was made to take him. Once he'd buried every inch of himself inside her, he groaned into her ear. "Gonna make my baby come long and hard, until she can't even breathe."

"I am *totally* up for that, just in case there was any doubt."

His lips curved as he reared back. "Good." Zander slammed home, driving himself deep. Heels dug into his ass, and her pussy rippled around him. Grunting into her neck, he pumped his cock in and out of her body. Every stroke was hard, wild, possessive. She didn't struggle against his hold on her wrists. She took what he gave her, and that sent his pleasure soaring.

"Do you have any idea how hot you looked with my dick in your mouth? Any idea how hot it was when I came right down your throat and you swallowed every drop I gave you?" He bit her earlobe. "Know what else you'll do one day? You'll take my cock up your ass."

Gwen shook her head, even though she knew she'd let him do it. Hell, she'd let him do just about anything as long as he made her come.

He lifted his head to pin her gaze. "You will, Gwen. And you'll love it. If I wasn't so possessive of this pussy, I might have considered sticking your vibrator in it while I take your ass." He plunged harder, drove deeper, took everything she had to give. Every moan spurred him on. Every flutter of her pussy pushed him closer to coming. And he was so close now . . .

He kept on slamming into her, until her pussy became so tight and hot that it was almost too much. He knew she was hanging on that same edge, knew exactly what would throw her over. Because as much as she pissed and moaned about him biting her, she fucking loved it.

Zander sank into his teeth into her throat, growling as her pussy clamped down on him and she came with a choked scream—back arching, heels digging into his lower back. He rammed his cock deep again and again until, spine locking, he exploded inside his mate.

As always, a sense of peace crept over him. He might not have claimed her yet, might not have the bond, but she still got to him in a way that no one and nothing else ever could. There was no doubt in his mind that she was his mate. He just needed to find a way to make sure there was no doubt in hers.

CHAPTER FIFTEEN

Jaw clenched, Zander drew in a breath through his nose, seeking calm. "I asked her to stay inside."

An amused Marlon bit his lip as he wiped down the kitchen counter. "But did she say that she *would*?"

No, she hadn't. Gwen had done that thing where she nodded her head, and made an *mm-hmm* sound. It was a sound that usually meant she was going to do whatever the hell she wanted, which was exactly why he'd pushed her to agree to remain inside until he got back from his morning patrol. Her response had been, "If you need me to stay inside, I'll stay inside." Yet, she was gone.

"To be fair, she hasn't exactly gone shopping or anything," added Marlon. "And there was no way she was ever going to sit around relaxing when she knows she has the hearing tomorrow. She's actually been pretty calm this past week, all things considered. Plus, she has Ally with her. They only left, like, a minute ago. You could probably catch up with them."

"Where are they headed?" asked Derren.

"To see Donnie at the outdoor shooting range."

Zander had seen the range during his patrols. It was a pretty sweet setup. Donnie had constructed a simple outbuilding with a short row of shooting benches on the firing line. Various homemade targets had been set up at different ranges. The closest was approximately twenty-five yards away, and the farthest was more than one hundred yards away. At the back of the range was a wall of rubber tires to stop projectiles.

Zander gave Marlon a curt nod and then strode out of the house, with Derren and Bracken close behind him. As they approached the range, his wolf snorted at the scents of gunpowder, hot metal, and lead. They were faint, which suggested no one had shot anything recently. Apparently, Donnie hadn't yet begun.

Rounding a cluster of trees, Zander saw the two females crouched near a huge black case, which Gwen was looking through like it was a treasure trove.

When his mate pulled out a whopper of a gun, Zander growled, "What are you doing?"

Chewing gum, she gave him a cursory look, then focused on the weapon. "Flossing my teeth. What does it look like I'm doing?"

Even from there, he could smell the gum on her breath—it was strawberry flavored. "Put that down before the damn thing goes off. I thought you were inside the house."

She sighed. "This again?"

"Gwen."

"I can't talk. I'm introverting right now. You're disturbing me. That's not good, because I'm already pretty disturbed."

"Gwen."

"Stop being snippy." She eyed him, dubious. "You've been moody lately."

He had. It was wearing on both him and his wolf that they hadn't yet claimed her. Especially because they knew she would be *safer* with the bond. Zander would be able to sense her and feed her energy if need be. "You said that you'd stay inside."

"No, I said that if you *needed* me to stay inside, then I'd stay. But you didn't need me to; you just wanted me to—there's a difference."

Zander opened his mouth to argue . . . but he couldn't. It had been a sneaky move on her part—a move similar to those he'd seen Shaya use on Nick dozens of times. He should have recognized it. He shot Ally a hard look. "I would have thought you'd have kept her inside."

Ally shrugged. "I didn't really want to bring her out here, but I couldn't claim that she was breaking a promise to you. Plus, she has her own mind. I'm here to protect her, not smother her or tell her what to do."

"Awesome," breathed Bracken, staring at the array of weaponry in the box. Zander didn't have a clue what the models were—he fought with tooth and claw. But Bracken was a Call of Duty addict, so he probably had a fair idea of what he was looking at.

Zander turned back to his mate. "Not sure if Donnie will like you touching his stuff, Gwen, but I *really* don't like it."

She pursed her lips. "Hmm."

"Gwen."

"Don't interrupt me while I'm ignoring you—that's just rude." Gun in hand, she clicked the mag into place and then swerved to face the targets. "There are ear and eye protectors in the box, if you want to use them."

Wait, she was planning to *shoot*? Before Zander even had the chance to object, she fired. Several times, in fact, sending shiny casings scattering across the ground. By the end, Zander was gaping, because she'd hit every single target dead-on.

Bracken gave an appreciative whistle. "Wow."

Derren tilted his head, grinning. "You can shoot?"

Gwen shrugged. "I'm not as good a shot as Donnie, but I'm okay."

"That's better than okay, Gwen," said Bracken.

Gwen carefully put down the gun and then looked at Zander. "I don't know *what* will happen when I tell the council the truth at the hearing tomorrow, but I know the aftermath will be bad. I intend to be ready for it—hence the target practice. You can stay and watch and frown as if I'm a kid playing with her daddy's shotgun, or you can go, and I'll see you in an hour or so."

Zander crossed to her and gently pulled his mate to him. "You're a woman with hidden talents." He kissed her neck, breathed her in. While a part of him balked at the idea of her holding a dangerous weapon, the rest of him—his dick included—was totally turned on by how competent and badass she looked when she aimed and fired. He knew exactly when she realized just how hard he was, because she smiled up at him.

"Zander Devlin, you're a weird one."

"What's in the other box?" Bracken asked.

Gwen moved to the smaller box and unlocked it, revealing plenty of self-defense items—some legal, some not so legal. "Donnie believes in being prepared, as you may have noticed."

As Zander settled on the gun bench, Gwen reset the targets and then switched weapons. He watched as she dug some bullets out of a box of ammunition with utter ease and confidence and quickly and expertly loaded the gun. "It's wrong just how hot I find it to watch you do that."

Gwen laughed. "You sure you guys don't want to wear ear protectors? This must be hard on your enhanced hearing."

"I doubt it's much harder for us than it is for you. Noise is noise. Besides, I'm not going to use ear protectors when my woman isn't wearing them—I'll just look like a pussy."

She laughed again. "Zander, you could never look like a pussy." Gun ready, she turned to face the targets. As taught by Donnie, she automatically shifted her weight to find her balance and let that familiar sense of calm wash over her as she steadied her breathing. Narrowing her focus on the target ahead of her, she pulled the trigger. Adrenaline spiked within her as the bullet tore through the center of the circle.

Again and again, she fired, hitting her target every time. Appreciating her handiwork, she smiled. Yeah, she still had it.

While the Mercury wolves sat back and watched, Gwen used a series of guns to hit her targets. It was as much about blowing off steam as it was about practicing to keep her skills sharp. She needed time to just filter out all the bullshit by having a task that required her complete focus. This way, she didn't have the time or opportunity to sit and contemplate the hearing.

A little while later, Donnie kicked aside a few casings as he approached. "You done?"

She rolled back her shoulders. "Yeah. Just keeping my skills sharp. You ready for whatever comes next?"

"Born ready." Donnie crossed his arms. "Traps are all set. I already showed your friends here where they are so they know to avoid them."

"Good."

"That wolf was damn lucky he didn't fall into one or set any off." Donnie huffed. "He'd better not come back. He'll get a shock if he does."

Zander's heart slammed against his ribs. He slowly pushed to his feet. "What wolf?"

Brow furrowing, Donnie replied, "The one I saw round these parts last night. Didn't Yvonne mention it? I called the house. I told her to tell you."

Gwen puffed out a breath. "Ah. The thing is, Donnie, you probably shouldn't have relied on a shitfaced woman to pass on an important message." Anxious about the hearing, Yvonne had poured herself a glass of wine to "settle her nerves." That would have been fine if she hadn't kept refilling the glass until it was a true wonder she hadn't passed out right there at the table.

"I thought it was one of you at first," Donnie told the Mercury wolves. "But it didn't move like it was patrolling or investigating. It was hunting. When it sensed me there, it growled, the little bastard. I shot it in the flank, but it rushed off. I was just changing out of my wet clothes, and I wasn't about to chase it through the marsh while I was only wearing my boxers and shower cap."

Zander blinked. "Shower cap?"

"I don't like getting rain in my hair."

Lost for words, Zander just looked at him.

Ally forced a smile and said, "Who does, right?"

"Right," said Donnie. Turning to Gwen, he studied her expression. "You all prepared for tomorrow?"

"As prepared as I can be," she replied, cleaning one of the guns.

Donnie's gaze cut to Zander. "Tell me about the shifter council."

"There are four members," said Zander. "The council was, for the most part, created to appease humans. It aims to resolve issues between shifters before violence can occur. It's a good thing. It helps people like Andie. It helped the shelter when an Alpha wolf tried to take it. In cases where humans have harmed shifters and not paid for it according to human laws—like with Brandt—the council has the right to step in and administer punishment."

Donnie pinched his lip. "Could it rule for Brandt to be killed?"

"I doubt it," said Zander. "He hurt Andie badly, but he didn't kill her—the council is unlikely to choose a punishment that outweighs the crime. But the council won't go easy on him. They can't be seen to go easy on anyone."

"Can we be sure they'll take Gwen's word as gold?"

"No." Zander had warned Gwen of that, but she'd insisted on speaking up for Andie anyway. "They may have already looked into the matter discreetly, though. They may already know most of the answers to the questions they ask her. In fact, they may have already made up their mind what they're going to do, but they'll have the hearing just the same."

"What's likely to happen?"

Tapping his fingers on the bench, Zander said, "If all goes well, they'll charge Brandt and detain him. He'll be punished and later released."

"And if all doesn't go well?"

"They'll find him innocent—something which is extremely unlikely, especially given the case that Gwen is able to put forward to support her testimony."

"But either way, the Moores will retaliate somehow." Donnie twisted his mouth. "They may wait for you to leave here and return to your pack before they make a move."

Zander wouldn't be leaving Gwen. He looked at her. "I still think you should take your family and go stay on my territory after the hearing. Me and my pack mates can deal with the—"

"I'm staying," she insisted.

As she walked off to pick up the casings from the ground, Donnie spoke to Zander. "You won't get her to leave. Gwen doesn't run. She fights."

Yeah, Zander had already learned that. He loved it about her. He just didn't want her to *have* to fight. He wanted her to be happy and safe. His wolf didn't like it that there were threats to her safety out there, and he wanted to tuck her into his lodge back on their territory, where she'd be out of reach from said threats.

When his pack mates and Donnie left, Zander remained with Gwen as she packed away the weapons. "I didn't mean to snap at you for leaving the house," he told her. "I just like to know you're safe when I'm gone. I don't ask you to stay inside permanently, just when I'm not around."

It was a half-assed apology, thought Gwen, but she'd take it. "If the range was near the border, I would have waited for you. But it's pretty much smack bam in the middle of the land. Intruders would have a hard time getting that far undetected—which you know full well. Besides, it's not like I gave Ally the slip or anything. I took her with me." Locking the gun storage box, Gwen said, "As much as I appreciate that you're protective, I'm looking forward to having a break from the weight of it. It'll ease off when all this shit's over."

Zander frowned. "I will never be any less protective of you, no matter what is going on."

"But you won't be here every day, growling orders at me." Gwen refused to admit how much it would hurt when he went back to California, even though it wouldn't be the end of their relationship. "I don't know how often you plan to come down here—"

"It doesn't have to be a long-distance relationship, Gwen. You could come live with me; you could join the pack." Zander held his breath, waiting for her response, hoping she didn't freak out. His wolf waited, anxious. For a long moment, she just looked at him steadily.

"Is that what you want?"

"Fuck, yes. I want you with me. I want you in my pack. I want you to be there when I wake up. I don't want to see you on weekends or whenever either of us have free time. That won't be enough for me. I'd like to think it won't be enough for you."

She rubbed her forehead. "I don't know, Zander. It would be a major decision. And it would surely involve you taking me as your mate, because I'm doubting your Alphas would take in a human for no good reason."

He placed his hands on the bench and leaned toward her. "I've made it clear countless times that this is more than a fling. I told you I was keeping you, I told you that you're mine. This is not a temporary thing for me. I want you with me. Not just for now. For good."

"You also told me that imprinting can happen without the conscious decision of the couple, and you said it can happen fast." Gwen had waited, reasoning that if she and Zander really had something deep and true, imprinting would have begun, but . . . "It hasn't happened for us."

"I also said that it can take months."

Gwen folded her arms. "Where's your wolf at?"

"He adores you. He wants you happy and safe and at our side. He wants you as our mate." Zander rounded the bench and closed the distance between them. "I know you've gotten used to people turning away from you or giving you up, but I'm not going to be one of those people. I'm here for good."

"I know."

The total confidence with which she'd spoken both relieved and satisfied him. "Good. You're it for me." He flicked her bangs out of her face. "But I need to be it for you. I'm not saying I'll leave if I'm not. That's not going to happen. I just want you to know that I *need* that. I need to be as important to you as you are to me."

She tossed him an impatient look. "You know you're important."

"How important?"

"Important enough that I'm considering moving to California. Be fair, Zander, it's easy for you to suggest it—you're not the one who'd have to make all the changes."

He'd figured out in advance that she'd say that, so he had his answers prepared. "You're right. I'd be asking you to move out . . . but really, Gwen, did you imagine yourself living in that house forever? You might not have planned exactly when you'd leave, but you knew that you'd move out eventually. I'm not asking you to do something you wouldn't have done at some point anyway. Okay, yeah, my territory isn't exactly down the road from here, but take the distance out of the way for a minute. Can you envision yourself living in a place that's more beautiful to you than my territory?"

No, Gwen couldn't, but . . . "It's not the only change I'd have to make."

"You'd have to give up your jobs, I know. But those are jobs that you do for your *family*, not for you, not because you enjoy them. You can't honestly tell me that you'd miss either position."

That was totally true, Gwen conceded to herself.

"And yes, living with me would mean leaving your family, but it's not like they'd be on the other side of the globe. You could visit them anytime, and they could come visit you. Plenty of people live far away from their relatives. My sister lives a fair distance away from me. It's not ideal, but it's not soul-destroying either. I know you feel that they need you, but you can't sacrifice your own happiness so that they have your company regularly. It's senseless. They'll tell you the same thing." He cupped her face. "Just say yes, Gwen. It's real easy."

Easy? Gwen snickered. "You have to see this from my point of view. You're not just asking me to move in with you. You live on pack territory. You and all your pack mates live virtually on top of each other and are probably constantly in each other's business. In some ways, it's the human equivalent of living in a house with most of your relatives. Moving in with you would mean moving in with them, in a sense."

Zander brushed his nose against hers. "Baby, you're not fooling anyone if you think I don't know how much the idea of belonging to a pack appeals to you. The idea of being surrounded by people who will care for, support, accept, and protect you is drugging to you. You're hesitating right now because you're scared to reach for it. I don't like how scared you are of reaching for happiness."

"I reached for you, didn't I?" she shot back.

Satisfaction roared through Zander at that. His mouth curved. "Yes, baby, you did. And you have no idea how glad I am of that. But I'm greedy—I want all of you. I want you with me every day and every night." Neither he nor his wolf would settle for anything less.

"Who says your pack would want me anyway? Your Alpha male didn't seem too enamored of me."

"They'll welcome you because you're mine. The females like you a lot, especially Shaya. Stop looking for excuses and just agree." His wolf growled when she backed up a step and bowed her head, eyes to the floor. Zander didn't like it either, but he understood that she just needed that moment to think, needed that little bit of space. So he held himself still, waiting.

Finally, Gwen raised her gaze to his. "You have to be positive—*positive*—that this is what you want."

"I am absofuckinglutely positive."

She let out a long breath. "I need to speak with Yvonne and Marlon about it first. I'm not saying I won't act without their approval. I just want to talk with them."

"You're stalling."

"Why does that make you smile?"

He crossed to her and cupped her chin. "Because if you're stalling, you're scared. And I've come to learn that the only thing that *really* scares you is happiness. The idea of saying yes to me would make you so happy that you're afraid to risk it."

Gwen narrowed her eyes at the smugness in his voice. "I preferred it when you were moody." He just shrugged.

"You know, I was thinking . . ."

"What?"

She shook her head. "Never mind."

"What were you going to say?"

She sniffed. "It's nothing, really."

Zander ground his teeth. "Tell me."

"It doesn't matter."

"Will you just fucking tell me," he clipped. "I can't stand it when you start a sentence and don't finish it."

Bristling at his tone, Gwen lifted a brow. "Yeah? You know what that sounds like? Your problem, not mine."

Growling, he fisted her shirt, pulled her close, and gave her a hard kiss. "No one gets my blood boiling like you do."

"Aw, that's such a nice thing to say."

He just shook his head.

With nothing to do and nowhere to go, the day was a fairly boring one for Gwen. But having so much unoccupied time gave her the chance to think about everything Zander had said, to realize just how much she wanted to reach for what he was offering, to concede that, yes, she was stalling. However, she really did want to talk to her family about it before making an informed decision.

So, later that evening when the Mercury wolves went on their nightly patrol, she settled at the kitchen table with Yvonne and Marlon. As they drank coffee, Gwen engaged them in a little chitchat, not wanting to just blurt it out. Surprising her, Yvonne mentioned the wolves first.

"I've gotten used to having Ally and the boys around," she said. "It'll be strange when they're gone."

Biting the bullet, Gwen confessed, "Zander wants me to leave with him."

Yvonne didn't seem the least bit shocked or even disappointed. "I thought he might."

"What do *you* want?" asked Marlon, who also didn't look surprised.

"There isn't an easy answer to that question." Gwen cradled her hot mug in her hands. "Leaving with Zander would mean leaving here." She sliced her gaze to Yvonne. "You'd only have Marlon to help you with this place."

Yvonne set down her cup. "I'm actually thinking of selling it."

Gwen blinked. "You serious?" She hadn't seen that coming at all.

Yvonne glanced around. "I've run this place for a long time. I've loved every minute of it. But I'm tired. And not all the memories here are good ones. I've been looking at houses online. I saw this gorgeous little house by a lake. There's room for you and Marlon there if you want it, though the rooms are a lot smaller than the ones here. And it has plenty of land so that I can build a cabin where Donnie can grow old. You're not mad at me, are you?"

Marlon's brow creased. "Why would we be mad?"

"This is your home."

"Dylan asked me to move in with him," Marlon admitted. "I'm not ready just yet, but one of the reasons I held back was that I didn't want to leave you."

Yvonne huffed. "I'm not an invalid."

"No," allowed Gwen, "but this place isn't something you could run on your own."

"Don't worry about me." Yvonne leaned her elbows on the table. "I never intended to spend the rest of my days here. You two need to live your own lives."

Marlon shifted in his seat. "It would feel like I was abandoning you."

Face softening, Yvonne put a hand on his arm. "You know how it feels to be abandoned, and you don't want to repay me for giving you a home by leaving me. I understand, but that's a load of crap. Fleeing the nest is a normal step in life. And I'm sorry to say this, kids, but you're murder on my sex life. You scare away every guy who shows any interest in me. I know you do it to protect me, but . . ."

"A girl's gotta eat," Gwen finished.

Yvonne laughed. "Exactly. If you're not ready to move out, fine. But don't stay for me. You have no idea how happy it will make me to see you taking such a natural step in life. It means that I didn't screw you up when I married husband number two."

"We prefer to call him Asshole," said Marlon.

"An apt description." Yvonne sighed. "Zander's good for you, Gwen."

Yeah, but . . . "A relationship with a shifter would be far from simple."

"Sweetie, no relationship is simple. They're what you make of them."

"But it's not like I could leave if things didn't work out. Zander and I would have to mate. You can't escape a mating bond."

Yvonne looked at her like she was crazy. "Why would you want to escape it? He adores you. Protects you. Looks at you like you're some kind of gift to him."

Marlon nodded. "He's good to you. Good *for* you. I think if you don't leave with him, you'll always regret it."

And that was what made up Gwen's mind. She *would* regret it if she said no. She didn't want to live with regrets. She also didn't want to live a life that didn't have him in it.

When she gave Zander her answer later while they lay in bed, he smiled and crushed her to him, eyes glinting with triumph and contentment. His eyes flashed wolf, and she saw that same satisfaction there. Both man and beast were smug bastards at times.

CHAPTER SIXTEEN

Gwen did her best not to fidget nervously when Derren turned the SUV down a dirt road that led to the building where the hearing would take place. The large piece of territory was bordered by three mountains and had a lot of forested area. "Do the council members all live on this land together?"

Beside her, lightly digging his fingers into her skin as he massaged her nape, Zander replied, "No. It belongs to one of them, Parker Brant."

"He's the eldest of the four members, right? The one you said is pretty fair and neutral."

"That's him." Zander had told her about the council. Harrison Whittle and Landyn Green were also known for being relatively impartial, albeit not quite as diplomatic as Parker. But Emilio Mendes was something of an asshole who didn't like loner shifters much. It was possible that Emilio wouldn't give much of a shit about Andie's attack.

Finally, Derren parked the SUV in a little parking lot. Moments later, Marlon's car whipped up into the space next to theirs. Riding with him were Yvonne, Julie, and Chase. Donnie had opted to stay at home to *guard* and *patrol.* That was no surprise to Gwen.

No sooner had they gotten out of the vehicles than four guards came and escorted them to a small courthouse-type building.

Glancing around the empty reception area, Gwen said, "There's no sign of the Moores. Maybe they won't come." One could but hope.

Zander spoke into her ear. "Opposing parties use separate entrances."

Hearing a door creak open at the other side of the room, Gwen turned to see a beefy, official-looking male. He ran his eyes over them all as he said, "The council is ready."

With Zander practically fused to her side, Gwen crossed to the door and walked into a partially wood-paneled room. As courtrooms went, it had the basics down. A gallery, a walkway that ran between the pews, a simple chair that seemed to pass as a witness stand, and even a wooden bar with a gate that divided the gallery from the council's space. But there were no desks for the plaintiffs and defendants. No lecterns, no jury box, no state flags. Four men sat at a raised bench, facing them. They weren't wearing black judge robes, but they each had that judge-type frown going on.

At the beefy wolf's urging, Gwen and Zander strode down the gleaming, polished floor to the front of the gallery. Instead of sitting, though, Zander stopped and urged the others to slide into the left-side pew-style bench. Once they were seated, Zander and Gwen joined them, which placed her at the end of the row.

"Is the left side of the gallery for *applicants* or something?" she asked him quietly.

"No. The party that arrives first is taken through the front entrance and asked to sit on the left. The other party will then come in through the back and sit on the right." Zander gestured to a door on the other side of the room. "The Moores and their supporters will enter through there."

Not liking the smells of lacquered wood and citrus cleaner, Zander kissed her shoulder and took a long, savoring breath—letting her luscious scent override them. She brought him a peace that couldn't be equaled. Right then, though, he wasn't feeling peaceful. Unease and anticipation hummed through him, leaving him edgy. He tried hiding it, though. He knew she was nervous and didn't want to make it worse for her. But it was hard, especially while his pacing wolf was urging him to get her out of the building and take her someplace safe.

"I'm thinking they'll bring Colt. Probably the families of Rowan and Mack too." Gwen suspected that Ezra would want the boys to back Brandt's story. She just hoped that the council didn't put much stock in their versions of events.

As everyone waited for the other party to arrive, the council members chatted quietly among themselves. Not the most patient person when she was nervous, Gwen found herself repeatedly grinding her teeth. Her muscles were so tight with tension that they actually ached. Every little noise grated on her nerves—the ticking of the clock, the rustling of papers, the whooshing of the air conditioning, and the creaking of wood as people shifted on the benches.

Zander pulled her closer, but it only annoyed her. He made absolutely no effort to give her any room. In fact, as he sat with his head up, chest out, gut sucked in, and legs spread, he took up the space around him as if he belonged there. More to the point, he took up *her* space. She already felt smothered by the tension in the atmosphere. She jabbed his arm with her elbow. "Move over."

He nuzzled her. "Why?"

"Because I need a little space."

"You need to know someone's here for you. That you're not alone and someone has your back. That's me." Truth be told, Zander needed the contact as much as she did.

"Stop saying nice stuff or I can't stay mad." She glanced down the bench to check on her family. Yvonne gripped her purse tightly, offering Gwen a strained smile, as Marlon eyed each council member. An anxious Julie was leaning against a rigid Chase, whose mouth was tight with annoyance. Yeah, she was annoyed herself. The Moores seemed to be deliberately making them wait—probably to convey a message that they didn't find the hearing important.

It was a further ten minutes—literally *one* minute before the hearing was due to start—that the door on their far right opened and the other party filed out, led by Ezra. Aside from a snarling Brandt, the others cast smirks at Gwen. Ezra and his supporters all settled on the benches at the front of the gallery's right side.

Ezra placed himself on the edge of the bench, meaning he was almost within touching distance of Gwen. He shot her a smug smile. Well, he wouldn't be so pleased when he realized she was there to damn his precious and exceedingly stupid son.

The gray-haired council member cleared his throat. "I am Parker Brant." After introducing the other members, he rested his gaze on Gwen. "According to what I have read, you witnessed a shifter, Andie Windsor, being attacked and are here to tell your version of events—a version that massively conflicts with that of the accused." His eyes then cut to Brandt. "Before we go any further, I must ask if you still wish to plead your innocence."

Brandt lifted his chin, looking like a petulant kid. "I did nothing wrong." The thing was . . . he probably didn't think he *had* done anything wrong.

Parker turned back to Gwen. "We would like to hear from you first, Miss Miller. Please come forward."

It went against everything in Zander to let her walk away. He wanted to scoop her up and take her home. Instead, he lightly squeezed her shoulder and spoke into her ear. "You'll be fine, baby."

Gwen nodded, blowing out a breath. On legs that were surprisingly steady, she moved through the gate and crossed to the chair at the right side of the panel. Feeling all eyes on her made her skin itch. She shifted on the uncomfortably hard seat.

"Please tell us what happened that night," said Parker.

She took a deep, preparatory breath. "I heard laughing. Loud, boisterous laughing. Straight away, I knew someone was either on our land or nearby. It wouldn't be the first time that teenagers had gathered there to get drunk or smoke cannabis. I grabbed my shotgun, and I followed the sounds. Soon, I heard the cries, the horrible sounds of metal hitting bone. I hurried, and then I saw them. Andie was on the ground, her face all messed up and her clothes dirty. She was trying to crawl away from someone—he kept hitting her with a metal pole while his friends laughed and urged him on. I shot at the ground near their feet to make them run off. Then I helped Andie back to my house and called the sheriff to report the incident."

"Can you identify this male that you saw assault Andie Windsor?"

"Yes." Gwen glared at the asshole in question. "His name is Brandt Moore."

Curses and abrasive mutters came from Moore's group. Only Ezra and Colt seemed unsurprised that she'd reneged on her deal. They'd probably half expected it, given that Brandt had turned up at her house again.

Emilio studied her carefully. "This is the same account that you gave to Sheriff Johnson the night it happened, but you recently altered your statement."

Gwen straightened her shoulders. "It was made clear to me that it was the only way I would keep my family safe. I didn't see the harm in giving a different statement to the sheriff—he hasn't exactly had any official involvement in the case, so I doubted he'd care."

Harrison narrowed his eyes. "What do you mean when you say the sheriff had little involvement?"

"Sheriff Johnson didn't hold the boys for more than an hour. He seemed skeptical when he took Andie's statement, he didn't do a drug test to corroborate or even dismiss her story, he didn't take photos of her injuries, and he wouldn't have even taken my statement to support her story if I hadn't insisted on it. He was also of no help to her when Brandt and his friends terrorized her, harassing her into altering her statement. Finally, she did."

"As did you," Emilio pointed out. "And you say it was to keep your family safe?"

"Brandt and his friends harassed me to change my statement." She told them how the harassment had begun as pranks and steadily got worse. "Brandt didn't once plead his innocence to me or insist that I'd seen someone else that night. Brandt confessed that he wasn't sorry for what he'd done and that, in his view, Andie's nothing more than an animal.

"After one particular night when Brandt almost assaulted me with a bat, his father showed up at my house and tried to bribe me into changing my statement. Like his son, he's very much anti-shifter. When I refused, he threatened to make me pay."

Landyn flicked Ezra a brief glance. "And did he?"

"A couple of weeks later, I was attacked by a flock of goshawk shifters."

From his seat, Ezra snickered. "I don't associate with shifters. How can I have had anything to do with that attack?"

Parker shot him a hard look. "When I want to hear from you, I will say so." His eyes returned to Gwen. "Please continue, Miss Miller."

"They came out of nowhere. Knocked me to the ground. Descended on me. Clawed and bit at me. If it wasn't for the Mercury wolves, I don't know if the goshawks would have stopped. I believe Ezra Moore hired them. I've heard many goshawk flocks are happy to sell their services."

Harrison rolled a pen between his fingers. "Yes, that is true."

"I didn't just fear for myself, I feared for my family and for the Mercury wolves who were living with us to offer protection. So I altered my statement to keep us safe."

After a long moment, Harrison said, "You may sit down, Miss Miller."

Well, thank God for that. Ignoring the glares that she could feel coming from Moore's side of the gallery, Gwen returned to her seat beside Zander. He kissed her temple and rubbed her nape, and she leaned into the contact, needing it.

Parker looked at Brandt. "Please take a seat over here, Mr. Moore."

Brandt's stride was cocky as he made his way to the chair. He didn't sit on it; he lounged on it like it was a park bench or something.

"Tell us your account of what happened."

"Me and my friends found the cougar crawling through the marsh on Miller land. We tried to help her, but she seemed confused and scared. Looked at us like *we'd* been the ones who'd hurt her. When Gwen shot at us, we ran—who wouldn't when bullets are flying? I'm not saying the cougar was lying when she pointed fingers at me; I think the drugs just muddled up her mind, and she confused me with the person who'd hurt her. I think she later realized she was wrong and that's why she changed her story. She herself says it wasn't me. There's really no reason for this hearing."

"There is every reason for this hearing," clipped Parker. "Don't make the mistake of thinking this operates like a human hearing. If we believe a matter needs exploring, we'll explore it."

The door opened, and the beefy-looking guy from earlier crossed to the panel. He whispered something to the council members.

Gwen leaned into Zander. "Did you catch that?" He shook his head.

Once Beefy was gone, Parker spoke again to Brandt, "So, you believe that the cougar was possibly so confused by the drug that she mistakenly blamed you."

Brandt nodded. "It's what makes most sense to me."

Harrison sighed. "I won't deny it's possible that Miss Windsor was confused by the drugs, but it wouldn't account for Miss Miller seeing the accused beating the cougar with a pole. From what I understand, Miss Miller wasn't drugged."

"Considering that Miss Miller changes her mind so often and feels it is no problem to do so, I would say it's obvious that she's not a credible witness," said Moira, Brandt's mother. A harsh look from Parker made her mouth snap shut.

"Mr. Moore, you may return to your seat," said Parker. "Sheriff Johnson, I would like to hear from you." Once the human was seated, Parker said, "You questioned Mr. Moore and his friends, but you didn't feel it necessary to charge them. Why?"

Colt lifted his chin. "There was no evidence that Brandt was the cougar's attacker."

"There was a pole, which I'm assuming had fingerprints on it."

"Brandt admitted to picking up the pole when he found it on the ground, but he maintained that he didn't strike her with it."

Emilio's brow lifted. "And you believed that?"

Colt's jaw hardened. "Two witnesses upheld that Brandt was not the attacker. The cougar said she'd been drugged, so I couldn't be sure if her testimony was reliable. It was also very dark out there, so I couldn't be sure that Gwen truly did see Brandt attacking anyone. The bottom line is, there was no evidence."

"Did you make any effort to find out who the attacker might be?" asked Parker.

Colt's mouth opened and closed like a landed fish.

Ezra slowly rose. "May I please speak?"

Parker sighed. "Fine."

"I know exactly why Miss Miller claims my son was the cougar's attacker. She is trying to pin the attack on Brandt to get back at him for ending their relationship."

"*What?*" Gwen burst out. She looked at Zander. "He can't be for real."

Even as a growl of rage built in his throat and his wolf swiped his claws in anger, Zander clasped her nape as he whispered, "Shh. You don't want the council throwing you out of the room, and you definitely don't want to give the Moores the satisfaction of seeing you pissed off."

No, Gwen definitely didn't want either of those things. Feeling her nails stabbing her palms, she relaxed her clenched hands and took a deep breath.

Ezra continued, "I asked him to end it because, since she is much older than he is, I felt their relationship was quite inappropriate. She is angry with me for that." Ezra spared her a brief glance. "She claims our family is anti-shifter, but it is in fact *she* who is prejudiced."

Landyn slowly lifted a disbelieving brow. "You believe Miss Miller is anti-shifter?"

Ezra jutted out his chin. "I can prove that she has connections to the extremists. Kenny Cogman—a man who we all know is rumored to sponsor extremists—is her biological father."

Well, shit. Gwen somehow kept her expression blank and held her tongue. Zander went rigid beside her, and a low growl rumbled out of him.

Landyn's brow pinched. "It's my understanding that she lives with her foster family and has since she was eight years old."

"But she is in contact with her father. In fact, they met up very recently. I can prove it." Ezra signaled to a man who Gwen recognized as his brother, Gerard. The male riffled through a briefcase and retrieved a brown envelope. He pulled out of a bunch of photographs.

"May I hand one to you?" Gerard asked the council. At Parker's nod, he opened the gate separating the galley from the council's space and crossed to the bench . . . but not before handing Gwen a photograph.

Gritting her teeth, she took it. The enlarged photograph was cool and smooth to touch, and it showed both her and Kenny sipping drinks. He was smiling at her. She had to admit, the scene looked pretty cozy.

"Miss Miller, what do you say to this?" clipped Emilio once Gerard returned to his seat.

Gwen rose to her feet. "Kenny Cogman called me a couple of weeks ago. He said that he was contacted by someone who is friends with the Moores, and he believed that me and my family were in danger."

Harrison frowned thoughtfully. "Cogman was the person who warned you that it would be best to alter your statement?"

"It was more that he was asking me to do it as a favor to him, but he did point out that it was the best way to keep my family safe. The latter was my only interest." With that, she sat.

"A pretty story," said Ezra. "But it's just that—a story."

Landyn leaned back in his chair, expression skeptical. "Why would an anti-shifter human stand up at this hearing and speak against her own kind?"

"As I said, to punish my son for dumping her." Ezra sighed. "She attacked him not so long ago. He went to her house to try to reason with her, to apologize for hurting her when he ended the relationship, but she attacked him with a bat—a bat she scrolled his name on, thinking she could pass it off as his. I have photos of his injuries." The asshole signaled Gerard again, who then handed out said photographs. The whole time, Ezra continued to speak, "Brandt returned to her house a few days ago to try once again to make amends. He was threatened by the wolves over there."

Parker spared the wolves a brief look, but then turned his attention to Rowan and Mack. "Both of you stand. Do you support your friend's account of what happened?"

Mack cleared his throat and nodded. "Yes."

“That’s exactly how it happened,” said Rowan.

Brandt nodded. “I’m sorry that the cougar shifter was hurt, but I’m not responsible for it. I shouldn’t be at this hearing.” He looked at Gwen with heartbreak in his eyes. “Gwen . . . I don’t know how you could do this. You know I never meant to hurt you. He’s my dad—I have to honor what he says.”

Oh, for the love of God. *Someone* had better see through this shit or she was going to lose it. If it wasn’t for Zander touching her, keeping her calm, she’d have already snapped by now.

Parker gestured for everyone to sit and sent Colt back to the bench. “It seems extreme to me that someone would pin the blame of an assault on an ex out of spite.”

“Hell hath no fury like a woman scorned,” said Ezra.

Parker’s gaze slid to the wolves. “I know much about your pack. And I believe that you, Ally Marshall, are a Seer. Correct?”

“I am,” said the she-wolf, voice clear.

“Please come forward.” If the council member heard Derren’s low growl of objection, he didn’t show it.

Gwen and Zander stood so that Ally could shuffle past them. Shooting Gwen a reassuring smile, she then crossed to the chair beside the panel.

Parker clasped his hands. “As a Seer, you are able to sense the emotions of others. If Miss Miller was prejudiced toward our kind, you would sense it. Correct?”

Sitting, Ally nodded. “I would. I can firmly state that Gwen is not prejudiced toward shifters.”

“What about Brandt Moore?” asked Emilio.

Ally looked at the boy as she answered, “Around our kind, he feels hate. Repugnance. And fear.” Ally’s gaze met Parker’s once more. “My pack mates and I were there the day that Gwen met with Mr. Cogman. We heard the entire conversation. I can verify that Gwen was telling the truth when she spoke of her conversation with him.”

Harrison nodded at Ally. “Thank you, Miss Marshall.”

Ezra, ballsy as ever, stood. “I’d like to ask Miss Marshall a question, if I may.” He smiled at her. “You claim you can sense the emotions of others.”

Ally narrowed her eyes at his skepticism. “I can tell you what you’re feeling right now as a demonstration, if you’d like.”

Ezra’s smile faltered. “If you believe it is true, I shall take your word for it. But is it not worth considering that not all extremists are prejudiced? It’s not always that they dislike shifters as a race. Some humans simply don’t like how much land the shifters take up. Others may not like that shifters are so secretive that we don’t know enough about them to understand them. That’s not something you would pick up, is it?”

“I would pick up any emotions associated with those issues. In any case, I’ve spent a lot of time around Gwen Miller—day in, day out. If she felt anything negative toward shifters, I would have sensed it.”

At a gesture from Parker, Ally returned to her seat.

“The situation is as simple as this,” said Ezra. “It is Gwen Miller’s word against that of the three young men you see here. And let’s face it, her *word* keeps changing. I do not dispute that the cougar was attacked, though there is no evidence that she was ever injured, but it was not by my son.”

“She was a mess,” Gwen gritted out.

“But you have no proof that there were any injuries,” Ezra said with a smirk.

Gwen lifted a brow. “You sure of that?”

Ezra’s eyes flickered. “Photos can be doctored.”

“Then maybe the photos you provided of me and Kenny Cogman shouldn’t be considered reliable.”

“If my son were responsible for those injuries, the cougar would be here now, seeking justice.”

Parker inhaled deeply. "As it happens, she is here. She arrived not so long ago, and she would like to speak." He gestured at a wolf manning the door on their right to open it.

Gwen's heart pounded hard and she sat up straighter. Andie walked in, head high, shoulders back. Warmth and pride rushed through Gwen, and she couldn't contain her smile—even though it was a little on the smug side as she noticed the sheer and utter dread on Ezra's face.

Andie took a moment to seek Gwen out with her gaze. She shot her a smile that held only a hint of nerves. It was clear to see by the determination in her eyes that Andie was there for justice. Awesome, because it was exactly what she deserved.

At Parker's invitation, Andie took the chair near the panel. He then said, "Tell us what happened that night, Miss Windsor."

Placing her hands on her lap, Andie licked her lips. "It was the anniversary of my parents' death—my human parents, I mean. They adopted me when I was little, not knowing I was a shifter, but they kept me. I was upset and I went to a bar, had a few drinks. Brandt Moore and the two young males who sit with him today . . . they approached me. Brandt flirted with me, tried to get me to leave with him, but I refused. Then things got . . . foggy. My cat went crazy inside me, but I couldn't shift. I knew then that I'd been drugged.

"I remember that they shoved me in a car, drove to the marsh, and dumped me on the land. Brandt beat me. Badly. The others mostly just laughed and encouraged him to keep going, but they kicked me in the ribs and the back once or twice. They wouldn't stop, and I was too weak to stop them.

"Then bullets hit the ground, sending mud everywhere, and they ran. My savior was Gwen Miller. She took me back to her house, took photos of my injuries before they healed, and then helped me get cleaned up. She called the sheriff. Not that that did much good. It was clear that he didn't believe I had any rights."

Harrison spoke. “The Moores claim it is *Gwen* who is anti-shifter.”

Andie gave a startled chuckle. “Gwen couldn’t be further from it.”

“Were you aware that her father is Kenny Cogman?” sniped Ezra, the shit-stirring bastard.

Andie gaped for a moment. “No, I wasn’t. But I don’t see that it matters.” She looked back at the council members. “She’s not him, and she’s nothing like him. Gwen was there for me all the way through this. She was willing to speak up for me when I wouldn’t speak up for myself. Even after I changed my statement, Brandt didn’t stop harassing me. Gwen gave me a place to stay. Helped me however she could. That kind of support can’t be faked.”

Touched by Andie’s complete confidence in her, Gwen swallowed hard.

Parker nodded. “Please take a seat, Miss Windsor.”

Pointedly ignoring the Moores and their supporters, Andie made her way to the bench behind Gwen. Leaning forward, she whispered, “Sorry it took me a while to get my shit together.”

Gwen frowned. “You don’t have to be sorry for anything. I’m really proud of you for doing this. I know it couldn’t have been easy.”

Andie glanced at the council members, who were now chatting quietly among themselves. “I can’t hear what they’re saying. Did Brandt come up with a decent case for his defense?” After Gwen debriefed her on all that had been said, Andie gawked. “The bastards tried to really imply that you were involved with that measly little fucker?”

Gwen silently chuckled. “Hopefully the council doesn’t buy it. Or buy anything else they said, for that matter. I got to warn you, though, they were quite convincing at times.” She gave Andie’s hand a supportive squeeze. “Even if the shithead gets off with it, he won’t get away with it, because I’ll shoot him in the dick.” She wasn’t even kidding. Hearing a throat clear, Gwen turned to face front.

Parker knitted his fingers together. "I agree with Mr. Moore that it doesn't look good that both females altered their version of events. It can be hard to decide which statement holds the truth. I must also say that it is quite odd that someone who would fight so strongly for a shifter would even give the time of day to someone such as Kenny Cogman, biological father or not."

Landyn nodded. "It would also be fair to note that it is the word of three against two—three boys whose stories never changed. They all come from respectable families and have never been in trouble with the law."

Gwen almost snorted. Well of course, they hadn't—Colt wouldn't have arrested them.

"But there are other things to consider," added Harrison. "Like that the Moores have a reputation in their hometown for being anti-shifter. The accused himself has a reputation for being violent and reckless."

Emilio stared at Colt as he said, "I find it curious that the sheriff did indeed mishandle this case—or, to be specific, didn't handle it at all. Nor did he handle it when the accused confronted Miss Miller at her home, bat in hand." He held up a hand when Ezra went to speak. "Yes, I did see the injuries. But I know the difference between bruising that's been done by fists and bruising done by blunt objects. Someone hurt your son, but it was not Miss Miller."

"I find it hard to believe that Miss Miller and the accused were in a relationship of any kind," said Parker. "I also find it difficult to believe that she could hide any prejudice from five shifters, particularly when one is a Seer. She has done our kind a good service, and I thank her for that."

Emilio looked at Colt. "If you had dealt with this matter and the accused had been punished by human law, he would not be in this room right now. In a sense, you are partly responsible for the punishment he will endure at our hands."

Ezra jumped to his feet, spluttering. *"Punishment?"*

"Brandt Moore, it is obvious to us that you are guilty of the assault on Miss Windsor," Parker declared.

Relief filled Gwen, and she felt like she'd taken her first real breath since yesterday. She squeezed Zander's hand and threw a smile over her shoulder at Andie, whose eyes were wet.

"We will detain and punish you, and then you will be released tomorrow," continued Parker. "Your friends will also join you and receive punishment."

Rowan's father grabbed his son. "Not a chance." And chaos pretty much broke out.

A defeated-looking Colt remained still and silent as the others shouted and cursed and protested. The council members merely left through a door near their panel, effectively dismissing them.

Brandt whirled on his father. "Do something! You can't let them take me!" By then, three stocky males had entered the room and were already heading his way.

Red-faced, Ezra promised, "I won't let him, I'll—"

"You said you wouldn't let this happen!" yelled Brandt. "You said you'd get me off!"

Arriving at the bench, the three males grabbed Brandt, Rowan, and Mack. As they were hauled away, their parents and Ezra's chauffeur, Thad, struggled to follow. More shifters piled into the room, forcing the humans to step back while the boys were shoved through the door that the council members had disappeared through.

"Let's leave now before their attention turns to us," said Andie.

Gwen nodded. "Good idea." But it was too late. No sooner had they all begun sliding out of the bench than Brandt's mother, Moira, came storming toward Andie.

"You lying whore! My son never touched you!"

Andie just regarded the hysterical woman steadily. "I can see in your eyes that you know that's not true."

"You're pinning it on him because you hate humans!" Moira screeched. "This is a hate crime! And *you* . . . you're not even a person! You're an animal!"

Andie gave her a brittle smile. "And yet, I'm not the one who drugged and beat someone with a metal pole while my friends laughed, am I? *Now back the fuck off.*"

Gently bumping Andie aside, Gwen said, "Move your ass, Moira; your time to embarrass yourself is up."

She raised her hand to slap her, but Gwen grabbed it. "No, Moira. Your boy made his bed. It's his own fault if he finds it lumpy."

"Get your hands off my wife!" Ezra bellowed. He tried shoving his way into Gwen's personal space, but Zander pushed him back.

"Fucking touch her and you're *dead*," Zander growled, eyes flashing wolf.

The asshole froze, gulping because, yeah, Zander could be a scary bastard at times. As he opened his mouth, no doubt to issue a threat, Gwen waved a dismissive hand and said, "Spare me the 'You'll pay for this' bullshit, Ezra."

"Take Andie outside, Gwen," said Zander, eyes on Ezra. He didn't move his gaze from the bastard as his pack mates and Gwen's family headed to the exit. His wolf lunged at the human, desperate to tear him apart. Zander barely kept him suppressed.

The last to leave, Yvonne lingered and said, "Emilio Mendes was right—it's partly Colt's fault that your son will pay at the council's hands. But you're at fault too, Ezra. In buying his way out of trouble his whole life, you taught him that he could do whatever he wanted and there'd be no consequences. Now he's learning the hard way that there are. So if you want to start blaming anyone for what happened here today, look at yourself first."

CHAPTER SEVENTEEN

Arriving back at the house, Gwen was surprised to see yet another SUV parked outside. Four people exited the vehicle—two of whom she'd seen before. She did a quick study of the unfamiliar tall, sable-haired female and the *huge* male at her side with perceptive brindle-brown eyes. As she took in the fluid way they both moved, Gwen was quite sure they were shifters.

"What are you guys doing here?" asked Bracken.

Jesse snorted. "What do you think we're doing here? There's a chance you'll need backup. We came. And, yeah, I'd like to get my fucking hands on Rory after he sent the cops to Harley's club."

Gwen waited with her family and Andie while the Mercury wolves and the newcomers exchanged greetings. It was obvious to her that they were all close.

Zander turned to her. "Gwen, you remember Jesse and Harley. This is Jaime and Dante. They're the Betas of the Phoenix Pack."

Gwen gave the new arrivals a quick hello and then introduced her family and Andie. "We appreciate you coming."

After greetings were exchanged, Yvonne and Marlon made everyone a light lunch. While they ate, Zander and Derren told the other shifters what happened at the hearing. A little overwhelmed by the number of people, Julie soon made her excuses to leave. Once she and Chase were gone, the others all went outside to look at the views of the marsh.

As Gwen stood with Jaime and Ally out on the boardwalk, she asked the Beta female, "How's Makenna and the baby?"

"They're both fine," said Jaime, eyes lighting up. "The baby is adorable, isn't she? Makenna won't agree to stay on our territory, so Ryan's constantly freaking out. In his head, I mean. You wouldn't know it to look at him."

Recalling that Ryan's default expression seemed to be a scowl, Gwen smiled. "Yeah, I can imagine."

"Roni and Shaya *really* wanted to come, but I'm guessing you can understand why they didn't."

"Of course," Gwen assured her. "It's vital that the Mercury Pack isn't left vulnerable. To be honest, I'm surprised Jesse and Harley came, especially after Rory pulled that firecracker stunt." Zander had told her all about it.

"Jesse, Zander, and Bracken are really close," said Ally. "I think it was hard for Jesse to stay out of this, so he'd have turned up here even if Rory hadn't insisted on being a shithead. Harley will have come along to get a shot at vengeance."

Gwen sipped at her coffee and then spoke to Jaime. "To be blunt, why are you and your mate here?"

Jaime tilted her head. "I'm not sure if Zander's told you that our packs are closely allied with each other. In fact, we share Roni and Marcus. See, she's a Mercury enforcer, and Marcus is a Phoenix enforcer, but neither wanted to switch packs. If either of our packs have trouble, one always has the other's back." She paused, her smile approving as she stared at Gwen. "What you did for Andie . . . it was a brave thing."

"It was the *right* thing," Gwen pointed out.

Ally nodded. "But sometimes the right thing is scary and difficult to do. You still did it."

"Although you didn't do it on behalf of shifters everywhere, I wanted to say thank you." Jaime lifted her mug to Gwen, as if in salute.

Uncomfortable with the praise, Gwen just nodded. Noticing Harley and Andie slowly heading down the boardwalk, she said, "They seem to be getting along well."

Ally nodded. "Harley spent the first half of her life in a pride, but she spent the second half in the human world—she lived with her aunt, who took care of her. She can relate to how Andie must feel, having lived among humans for a long time. Has Andie decided what she'll do next?"

Gwen shrugged. "I don't know. I hope to find out later."

From where he stood on the porch with Jesse, Zander watched Gwen interact with the other females. She seemed relaxed around them. He liked that. He wanted her to feel comfortable with them so that it would make the transition to his pack easier. He also wanted her to feel that she had friends when she moved there.

"When do you think the Moores will attack?" asked Jesse.

"It's possible that they won't. They hired goshawks to hurt Gwen not long ago." The memory made Zander's wolf snarl. The beast was brooding because he'd been denied the chance to attack and kill Ezra. "They might do the same thing again."

Jesse nodded. "Makes sense, since it's unlikely that they'll want to face you and a bunch of shifters. They have to know that you could beat their asses all on your own. If they do come here to take care of this themselves, they'll come armed."

"Probably. But it won't help them. They'll die either way." Zander wouldn't allow any threat to his mate to live. Speaking of threats . . . "I know you want to deal with Rory yourself. I get why. But if he comes here, he's mine. Not just because he deserves a ration of shit for all the things he's done over the years, but because he hurt my mate. He made her bleed. He would have taken her if Ally hadn't had a vision that warned us. I can't let that go."

Jesse gave a nod of acceptance. "Understood. Just make sure you hurt him. Badly."

That wouldn't be a problem. "Back to the subject of the Moores . . . I don't think there'll be an attack tonight. They'll know we're on our guard. But I don't think the Moores will be prepared to wait long—they're too hungry for revenge on Gwen."

"I didn't think I'd like her," Jesse announced. "Knowing what she's done for the cougar, I respect her. But you're one of my best friends. More like a brother. I knew I'd have trouble accepting your mate, whoever she was, because I'd need to be sure that she was good for you. We both know from watching our parents that not all mated pairs live a dreamy life."

Yeah, Jesse's parents had some serious issues. His mother dominated his father's behavior, but she didn't wish to do so, didn't like that he'd folded under her strength by his own choice. She wanted a partner, an equal, and her mate was no longer that for her.

Jesse sighed. "You and me . . . we're not easy people, and we're never going to be easy partners. Harley gets me and lets me be until I push too hard. I wanted to be sure that your mate was someone who got you and accepted you. From what I can see and from what Ally's told me, it's pretty clear that Gwen does."

"It's a good thing that you didn't run her through a gauntlet," said Zander. It was the kind of thing his pack mate would do. "I would have had to kill you for that."

Jesse's mouth curved. "She's got you all tied up in knots, hasn't she?"

"That's the way it should be, though."

"Yeah, it is." Jesse's frown returned as he looked back at the females. "They all look deep in conversation over there, don't they? I think they're talking about us. Typical. Just typical."

"*The Matrix* could *so* be real," insisted Harley.

Ally's nose wrinkled. "Some of your theories *do* have substance, but I'm not convinced."

"I think it's possible." Gwen paused to drink the last bit of her coffee. "Although, I once read an article somewhere that said if the world really was a simulation, it's doubtful that we'd be plugged into some kind of system. We'd most likely be more like virtual entities that were made at the same time as the simulation."

Jaime's brows lifted. "I never thought of it like that. Interesting."

"If *The Matrix* is real, let's hope the programmers don't press the 'Off' switch," said Andie dryly.

Jaime's brow pinched at something over Gwen's shoulder. "Who's that?"

Turning, Gwen smiled. "Oh, that's Donnie. My uncle." Gwen crossed to where he stood, eyeing the newcomers. "The hearing went well. The council remanded Brandt, Mack, and Rowan."

"Good," said Donnie. "I'm guessing the Moores didn't take it well."

"No, they didn't." She sighed. "And they didn't look as though they had any intention of letting this go."

"We always knew they'd retaliate. We're ready for them and that other wolf, Rory. He hasn't been back."

"How do you know?" asked Jaime from behind Gwen—her voice almost made Gwen jolt in surprise. Jaime moved as silently as Zander.

"I know," replied Donnie. He glanced around. "Who are these people?"

"More wolves," said Gwen. "This is Jaime. The guy standing with Derren and Bracken is her mate, Dante. The female coming toward us with Andie and Ally is Harley, and her mate is over there with Zander; they're his pack mates. Jaime and Dante are the Betas of the Phoenix Pack."

"Huh." Donnie's tongue poked the inside of his cheek.

"Seen any more of that wolf you shot?" Ally asked him.

"Already asked him that," Jaime told her. "He said no."

"If he's got any sense," began Donnie, "he won't come back."

"He doesn't have any sense," said Gwen.

Donnie sighed. "That's what I thought. Make sure you warn the new people to be careful if they go patrolling the area."

"Why?" asked Jaime.

He frowned, as if not understanding the question. "Because I got the place rigged. Why else?" With that, he walked off.

"He's . . . interesting," said Jaime.

Gwen smiled. "Ain't he, though?"

A little while later, the she-wolves and Harley went to chat with their mates, leaving Gwen and Andie alone.

Andie gently took her arm. "Gwen, I honestly can't thank you enough for everything you did and for all the support that you've given me and all the risks you've taken. I'm not much good at talks like this, but I wanted to say that you're the shit—just so you know."

Gwen's lips curled. "You don't have to thank me for anything I did. You helped yourself. And not just by turning up at the hearing today. You took a chance on the shelter, you got yourself together, and you found the strength to get justice for yourself. I'm proud of you. Speaking of the shelter . . . are you going back there?"

Andie bit her lip. "For a little while, yeah. Heath and I are thinking of getting an apartment together. I know it's fast. I know that. But . . . it just feels right. I'm not saying I think he's my true mate. I'm not totally sure about that yet, but I think it's possible. Either way, I want to be with him."

Gwen briefly glanced at Zander, who was currently talking with Bracken and Marlon. "Zander wants me to leave with him and move to his pack."

Andie snorted. "Well, of course he does. He's hardly going to want to leave his mate behind. In fact, he'd be more likely to stay with you than leave. Mates come first. I'm guessing it took a little while for you to realize you were true mates. Still, I'm surprised he hasn't claimed you yet. Are you reluctant to form the bond or something?"

Gwen didn't realize she'd been holding her breath until that moment. Clearing her throat, she asked carefully, "What makes you think he's my mate?"

Andie gave her a look that questioned her IQ level. "He looks at you with eyes that scream *mate.* He hardly ever leaves your side, he's constantly touching you, and his face softens when he sees you." She tilted her head. "He didn't tell you? Shit, I thought you knew or I wouldn't have said anything."

"Why would he keep it from me?" The words came out soft, quiet.

"You may have noticed that dominant male wolves are protective. They're hyperprotective of their mates. If he's kept it from you, it's most likely because he thinks it's not good for you to know yet. To be fair, a lot of stuff has been going on around you. Maybe he didn't want to add to that." Andie shrugged. "I don't know him well enough to make a good guess."

"He should have told me." All this time Gwen had been waiting for imprinting to begin, had panicked that the bond wouldn't form . . . and he'd secretly believed that there already *was* a bond. Or, at least, that the potential of it was there.

"Whatever the case, hold tight to him, Gwen. So many shifters would love to have what you've found in Zander. A mate is a special thing. Don't turn your back on it—especially just because you're a little annoyed with him for not mentioning it."

Honestly, Gwen wasn't sure what she was going to do. A lot of it would depend on his reasons for keeping it from her, and on just how sure he was that they were true mates. It was possible that he hadn't told her because he wasn't certain—*that* she'd understand.

As her head was figuratively up her ass, the day seemed to pass in a blur. She'd made an effort not to seem upset, knowing Zander would pull her aside and demand an explanation—that was a conversation they'd need to have in private at a time when they were unlikely to be interrupted.

Needing some time to herself, she was glad when he went on patrol that evening with the other shifters. She took a long bath and leisurely dried her hair before pulling on a peach silk camisole and matching boy shorts.

Sadly, the time alone didn't relax her. She found herself pacing up and down in her room, fists clenching and unclenching. When her door opened, she halted and turned to face Zander as he stalked inside and locked it behind him. His eyes raked over her and heated. Her body automatically reacted—knowing that look and knowing what it meant.

Every step fluid and silent, Zander crossed the room to her. He didn't try to pull her to him as he usually did. His hand gently smoothed her bangs aside, and he studied every inch of her face, searching. "You've been quiet. At first, I assumed you were worrying about the Moores. But looking at you now, it's clear you're pissed about something. Tell me. I'll fix it."

Her phone rang. If she hadn't been so tense, she might have jumped. Grabbing it from the bed, she frowned when she saw it was Kenny. Hesitantly, she answered. "Hello?"

"I heard you changed your mind about doing me that favor, Gwen . . . or did you never intend to do it?" Strangely, Kenny didn't sound upset or angry. He sounded relatively amused. But then, it wasn't as if the situation affected him *personally*.

"I never intended to do it." Yeah, she was hoping to piss him off. It didn't work.

He chuckled. "That devious streak is another thing you got from me."

"I wasn't being devious. I was being smart. You wanted me to do the smart thing, right?"

"I did," he said, a smile in his voice. "But it wasn't entirely smart. Not when it means you'll now have the Moore family on your ass." He sighed. "I'll give them a call. Warn them to stay away from you. But I can't guarantee they will. Unlike you, Ezra Moore doesn't appear to be smart at all."

"I can handle him."

"I'll bet you can, since you have the protection of shifters. Do you think that's wise? They're not known for being loyal to anyone outside whatever group they live in."

"They've protected me so far."

"Yes, it would seem they have," he mused. "Just be careful. I'd rather not have to wipe out an entire pack of wolves, but I won't hesitate to do so if they harm you." He ended the call before she could respond to that.

With a curse, Gwen tossed the phone on the bed. "I'm guessing you heard that conversation clearly enough."

"Maybe his warning will be enough to make Ezra back off for a while."

She snorted. "Even if Ezra was willing, Moira and Brandt wouldn't be. The moment Brandt's released by the council, he'll be demanding that someone make me pay. And if they don't do something, he will. In other words, *something* will happen."

Zander sighed. "Sadly, I can't disagree with you. Was this what was bothering you? Were you anticipating a call from Kenny?"

No." Gwen literally blurted out the question. "Why didn't you tell me you think I'm your true mate?"

He stiffened. "Who told you that?"

"According to Andie, it's pretty obvious." And if it was obvious to the cougar, Gwen had to wonder if it was just as obvious to the other shifters. If that were true, it would be both embarrassing and hurtful to think they'd all possessed that knowledge and she'd been oblivious.

"Before we talk about this, you have to promise me something." His gaze pinned hers. "Promise me that you won't walk out of this room, that you'll stay here until we've talked it all out." Zander still wasn't certain that she was ready to hear this yet. Nonetheless, part of him was glad that they could lay it all out finally. He *was* pissed that she'd heard it from someone else, though. Still, it was his own fault.

"Just tell me," she clipped.

"Promise me."

She unlocked her back teeth. "Fine. I promise. Now, why didn't you want to tell me?"

"I *did* want to tell you. You have no idea how much. No idea how hard it was to keep it from you. But you've got enough going on—I didn't want to pile something else on you. I had no idea which way this would go, whether you'd be pleased or freaked. I wasn't sure you were secure enough in our relationship to handle it. I won't take it well if you reject the bond, Gwen, and I didn't want tension between us at a time when you needed me here for you."

Gwen inwardly cursed. She was hurt that he'd kept it from her, wanted to be mad at him, but that response was impossible to be mad at. "How long have you believed we're mates?"

"Since the night that Rory attacked you." His wolf growled as he recalled what happened. "Do you remember I told you that my wolf was guarded around you at first?"

She nodded.

"You know he's not anymore. What you don't know is why he acted that way in the first place. It was Ally who worked it out. My wolf is . . . damaged, I guess you could say. The people who were important to him let him down. I can relate to that, and I think you can too."

She inclined her head.

"So, it stands to reason that he'd be wary of anything or anyone that had the potential to wound him that badly again. I didn't think of that. But once I did, once I put it all together, everything became perfectly clear. Like a veil had been lifted."

"You really think I'm your mate?" she asked. He shook his head, and her stomach dropped.

"I *know* you are." He rested his hands on her shoulders. "Think about how fascinated you've always been by shifters. Hell, you were even obsessed with wolves."

"I wouldn't say *obsessed*."

"Some part of you knew where you belonged. It all adds up. And if that isn't convincing enough for you, ask yourself this: How would it feel if I walked away from you? I know how it would feel, Gwen, because it would be the same for me if you sent me away. That's not a normal kind of hurt, is it?"

Considering her chest felt like it was on fire at just the idea, no it wasn't normal. "I know you said that it's not so easy to sense the bond. I know that. But we let our guard down with each other. Hell, I even committed to joining your pack, yet we haven't sensed anything."

"It's not just about mental walls, Gwen. So many things can block the frequency."

"Like fears and secrets," she remembered. "You know I fear happiness like a weirdo, and you know about Geena and that I'm an informant for The Movement. I don't have any other secrets."

"Sometimes a couple will feel the bond without baring that much of themselves—it can depend on a lot of things. But one thing is absolutely guaranteed to block the frequency."

"What's that?"

"The unwillingness to believe that it might be there." He slid his hands from her shoulders to her neck. "You have to let yourself wonder if it is, Gwen. And I know how hard that's going to be for you, because it will mean letting yourself hope. And you fear hope almost as much as you fear happiness, because the two are very much linked."

He was right. It might have been kind of backward to fear hope, but Gwen did. Feared hoping and reaching for something, only to be disappointed. She'd spent a good portion of her childhood *hoping*. Hoping that Hanna would love her, hoping that her stepfather would stop hurting Hanna, hoping she'd never be forced to lie to protect him from the police ever again. *Hoping* had done her a fat lot of good. She'd thought that just maybe fate or luck had intervened and led her to the Millers. But it turned out that *Kenny* had intervened.

"Until you can let yourself wonder if it could be true, we won't feel that bond." His wolf wanted Zander to bite her, claim her, so she couldn't get away. But, though it killed him, Zander said, "Take some time to think about it all. Think about what I told you. What you feel. What you need."

"Wouldn't it be hard for you to give me time? I mean, if you think I'm your mate, isn't it hard for you not to claim me?"

"Hell, yeah, it's hard. For me and for my wolf. He constantly pushes me to claim you. It's been killing me that I couldn't tell you about it, but I didn't know how you'd react. And giving you time won't be easy for me, but if that's what you need, I'll give it to you."

She raked a hand through her hair. "I don't want to give it time. I don't have the patience to sit around and ponder shit. I like to *know* the facts." But there was really only one way to know. "You really truly believe we're mates?"

"I don't have a single doubt in my mind." He rested his forehead on hers. "Just admit that it's possible, Gwen. That's all you have to do. You're already mine, and I'm already yours. Nothing will change that. Not a thing. I wanted you for keeps before I realized we were mates. I *am* keeping you, no matter what." He kissed along her jaw to her ear and whispered, "Admit it's possible. For me. For you. For us. Admit it." He and his wolf both stilled, holding their collective breath.

Gwen swallowed hard, wanting it to be true . . . hoping. "It's possible."

Zander's knees almost buckled as the mating urge kicked in hard and fast—lust slammed into him like a fucking freight train, and black spots dotted his vision. His blood thickened, and his cock went instantly hard. The need to take and mark and claim crawled over him, *demanded* him to act. The only thing that stopped him from leaping on her was that she looked a little disoriented.

A mating between true mates was supposed to be wild and explosive. He'd never lost total control with her before. He'd come close to it, but he'd always managed to retain that one bit of sanity and remember their difference in strength. He wasn't sure if he could do it this time—not while the mating urge was riding him and his wolf was going insane for her. But there was no way to fight it. Zander slid his fingers into her hair. "Gwen, I need to fuck you." The guttural words came out through his teeth.

She took a shaky breath, fisting his shirt. "Then fuck me." His mouth slammed on hers, and she moaned. The kiss was deep, hot, and hungry. Need was like a wildfire in her veins, burning and consuming every part of her. She felt shaky. Feverish. Desperate. Her nipples had tightened to the point of pain, and her pussy was already slick and quivering.

Stumbling around the room, they yanked off each other's clothes in record time—until he was naked and she was wearing only her panties. His skin was warm and sleek beneath her hands, and she dug her nails into his chest just to hear him growl.

The breath whooshed out of her as her back slammed into the wall. Opening her eyes, she found Zander staring at her, his face set into a mask of dark, primitive need. Her pussy clenched. He tore off her panties and cupped her hard, and she almost cried because she'd needed his touch *so* badly.

She'd never felt like this in her life. Never felt like she'd die if she didn't come just once. But even as she was out of her mind with need, it wasn't just anyone she wanted; it was Zander. It *had* to be him. Some primal part of her *needed* him, *needed* his come inside her. "Zander." It was a ragged plea for more, for anything. He drove a finger inside her, and she literally melted between him and the wall.

As he thrust his finger in and out, Zander licked over her bottom lip. "I love this mouth. It looked so very pretty wrapped around my cock." He sank another finger inside her, groaning at how wet and hot she was. "No other cock will fuck it again. Only mine."

Gwen licked her lips, remembering the feel of him in her mouth. "And your cock will never fuck any part of anyone else." She kissed him, trying to ride his hand. He let her. Growled encouragements. Sucked on her tongue. Then his free hand fisted her hair, snatched her head aside, and he bit her neck. Like that, she came.

"I love hearing my baby scream," he rumbled into her ear. Withdrawing his fingers, he sucked them clean. "I want more of your taste, but I can't wait—I need to be in you." Cupping her ass, he lifted her and poised her over his cock. "I'm going to fuck the absolute hell out of you. Right here, against this wall."

Curling her legs around him, Gwen sifted her fingers through his hair. "Do it." Instead, he lifted her a little higher and sucked her nipple into his mouth. Every tug on the taut bud sent a bolt of pleasure to her clit, making her pussy ache. She pulled on his hair *hard*.

"What do you want, Gwen?"

"I want to feel you in me. I want to feel you *come* in me—"

Zander slammed her down on his cock just as he drove upward, seating himself to the hilt. Her pussy contracted possessively around him. "Jesus, baby." He powered into her, unable to stop. Every thrust was hard and almost savage, driven by his wolf and the compulsion to possess what belonged to him, to claim this one thing that would always mean more to him than anything.

Her pussy squeezed and spasmed around him, so inferno-hot and deliciously slick that he'd never get enough. Never. Her nails raked over his scalp, and Zander growled. "Is this pussy yours? Is it, Gwen?"

Trick question, her foggy mind warned her. Defiance rose up inside Gwen, but it was immediately crushed by the primal need consuming her. "No."

"Then whose is it?"

"Yours." She moaned as he upped his pace, rewarding her. God, she was so close to coming. The friction kept on building and building, winding her tighter and tighter until she thought she'd implode.

"Can you hear that?" he hissed into her ear. "The sound of me fucking you? Owning you. I fucking love that sound."

She jolted as he slipped a wet finger in her ass. The burn felt good, like when he sank his teeth into her skin—a good kind of pain that just made her hotter. Her release crept that little bit closer, so close she could almost taste it.

"My baby wants to come for me, doesn't she?"

Hell, yeah, she did. But she was beyond words, so she leaned forward and dug her teeth into his neck. For a moment, Zander froze. Then he was ramming himself into her like his control was gone. Something primitive in her made her bite him hard, draw blood, and suck until she left a mark.

Zander shifted his angle to hit her G-spot. "Mine." He sank his teeth into her neck, and white-hot pleasure swept him under, made him explode in her pussy with a force that almost sent him to his knees. At the same time, she came with a choked scream of his name. He sank his teeth even deeper, tasting blood, and sucked hard to leave the ultimate, definitive mark that would brand her as his.

Licking her lip, Gwen panted. "Fuck. Jesus. Shit." She'd never in her life been so thoroughly fucked. "How long does it take for the bond to—" Her breath caught in her throat as a burning pain sliced through her head. It lasted only seconds, but it was like her world had tilted. She blinked, feeling off balance . . . and then her vision blurred around the edges, and darkness came.

As she sagged in his arms, Zander swore and scooped her up. Neither he nor his wolf panicked. They knew she was fine; they could feel her through the mating bond. Still, they didn't whatsoever like the sight of their mate unconscious. It was only then that Zander remembered hearing once that the intensity of the moment could be difficult for a human to bear. *Shit.*

Acting on instinct, he carried her into the bathroom and got into the shower with her still in his arms. He stood under the hot spray, hoping it would help her wake. It was no more than a minute later that she opened her eyes. His mouth curved. "Welcome back."

Gwen blinked. "What happened?"

"You passed out for a minute."

"I don't pass out."

"You did just now. I'd forgotten that the bond's formation could be hard on a human. You okay?"

She nodded, meaning it. Where before there had been pain, there was now peace and tranquility. The feelings washed over her, smoothing away all the tension in her mind and body. And there was the mating bond, so vibrant it almost seemed alive. "This is so weird. I can feel you." Inside her and outside her, like he was a shadow. She could feel Zander on the other end of the bond—a strong, solid presence. Even feel an echo of his emotional state.

"Our scents have mixed," he told her. His wolf rumbled in satisfaction. "That doesn't usually happen straight away. I'm guessing that *hoping* was so difficult for you that it gave the bond added strength. It's not fully formed yet."

"What will happen when it is?"

"Our connection will be more intense. We'll be able to feed each other energy."

Gwen quieted, letting herself get used to the bond. That feeling she'd always had that something was missing—a feeling she'd attributed to the absence of her biological family's love—was totally gone. "So, true mates really are two halves of a whole, huh."

"Yes. That feeling of completeness will get stronger when the bond is fully formed."

As they got out of the shower and dried themselves off, she asked, "Does it bother your wolf that I don't have, you know, a wolf for him?"

Zander snorted at the stupid question. "He adores you just as you are. He wants to rub up against you right now. You good with that?"

She swallowed. "Okay."

Once they were out of the bathroom and she was wrapped in a robe, Gwen stood back and watched as Zander shifted forms. She winced at the sound of bones popping and snapping. In a flash, Zander was gone. In his place was a large, familiar wolf, but he wasn't snarling like last time. Her heart pounded, though she felt no fear.

Gwen crouched down. "You're a handsome thing, aren't you?" The wolf padded to her and literally shoved himself right into her space, almost knocking her over. He rubbed his jaw against hers as she petted his neck. His fur was thick and much softer than she'd expected. Her nose wrinkled as he licked at her jaw. "Ew." She gave him a gentle shove, and he backed up with a playful growl.

She remained still as the wolf circled her, rubbing up against her just as Zander had warned her that he would. She smiled. But that smile soon faded when he started clawing at her door and furniture, marking his territory. “Hey! You’re going to wreck the room.” He either didn’t understand the words or didn’t care, because he didn’t stop.

When he was apparently satisfied that the space was well and truly marked, he padded back to her and licked at her face again. Before she could give him another playful shove, he backed away. Bones snapped and popped, and then Zander was in front of her.

“You weren’t exaggerating when you said he wanted to rub up against me.”

Zander drew her to him as she stood. “You’re gonna have him wrapped around your little finger.”

She smiled. “He’s a menace.”

“He’s happy.”

That made her chest ache in a good way. “What about you?”

“You don’t need to ask me that. You can feel through the bond that I’m happy.” He brushed his nose against hers. “And I can feel that you are too.” Which meant that all was good in Zander’s world. Not even the threat that lingered over them could spoil the magic of what he’d found in Gwen. Not a single thing could.

CHAPTER EIGHTEEN

"*Zander.*"

The whisper snatched him out of sleep a few nights later. Zander blinked. There was no one there, except for the female sleeping peacefully at his side. Still, tension began to creep into his muscles. Something felt . . . *wrong*. Like the air was charged with something.

The sound of fast footsteps was quickly followed by knuckles rapping on the door. "Zander, we got company coming our way," warned Derren, urgency in every syllable.

Motherfucker. Zander shot out of bed and reached for his jeans. "Ally had a vision? What did she see? Moore?"

"Shifters. Lots of shifters."

Zander stilled, frowning. "Shifters?" *Fuck.*

Gwen's eyes flickered open. "You okay?" Whatever she saw in his expression made her bolt upright, fisting the bed sheets. "He's here, isn't he?"

"No," said Zander, watching as she practically leaped out of bed and yanked on a tee. "The bastard must have hired shifters to do his dirty work for him again."

"Z, we have to go," Derren called out.

Gwen swallowed. "I'll be okay. Go."

He could hear in her voice that she didn't *want* him to go, but she wasn't going to ask him to be something he wasn't and remain behind. He couldn't leave his pack mates to face the trouble alone, but he didn't want to leave his mate either. His instinct was to stay with her, protect her. His wolf felt just as torn.

Gwen tugged on her jeans, noticing that Zander was staring at her, jaw hard. "Really, I'll be fine." Snatching her handgun from the top drawer of the dresser, she said, "I have claws of my own, remember."

Hooking his hand around her neck, Zander pulled her close and skimmed his fingertips along her jaw. She meant fucking everything to him, more than he'd thought anything could. "You know what to do."

"I know." They'd been through the plan countless times, and Gwen hadn't forgotten.

He gave a short nod of satisfaction. "Be safe for me, yeah?"

"If you get hurt, I'll be super pissed. Just note that."

He kissed her, clasping her nape tight. "I'll be back." Since he'd be shifting soon, Zander didn't bother dressing. He just headed out into the hallway, where his pack mates and the Phoenix Betas were waiting.

As they crossed to the staircase, adrenaline spiked within him, and his pulse began to quicken. He was ready for this. Wanted it over and fucking done with. "Did anyone wake Yvonne?"

"I knocked, but I didn't get an answer," said Jaime.

"Gwen says she often takes sleeping pills," Zander told her. Marlon was staying at his boyfriend's house, so that was one less person for Gwen to worry about. "What breed of shifter are we dealing with, Ally?"

"Multiple," she replied. "Seems like Moore hired himself a group of mercenaries. In my vision, they were coming from the east."

As they hurried down the stairs, Dante said, "Then we go east, cut them off."

Their priority was to make sure the trespassers didn't get near the house. Gwen and Yvonne would be hiding in the attic. But if any shifters got into the house, they would be able to follow their scents up there; they'd find them eventually. Zander needed to be sure that didn't happen.

He yanked open the front door, and they all filed outside onto the porch. The night air was cooler than usual, and a mist was rolling along the river. "How long do we have before they cross onto the land?" Sometimes Ally's visions were of something that would happen only minutes later; sometimes it was longer.

Ally pursed her lips. "I can't be sure, because—"

A loud rumbling sound seemed to vibrate through the air, and then . . . *boom*, followed by a pained roar. Which meant someone had set off one of Donnie's traps.

Harley hissed. "They're here."

As one, they shifted and ran toward the trespassers.

Stomach knotted, Gwen shifted from foot to foot as she stood in Yvonne's doorway while the woman quickly dressed. She flexed her grip on her Glock, finding comfort in it. She wanted to pace and curse and fidget with nerves, but she needed to keep cool. It was damn fucking hard.

The house was so deathly quiet that she could hear the explosions, growls, roars, and gunshots—which meant Donnie had clearly joined the fight. Her stomach churned. Knowing Zander was out there, fighting for her, maybe even bleeding for her . . . it was hard to keep calm.

"Yvonne, we gotta go. Now. Come on."

Yvonne placed a hand on her stomach and followed her out of the room. "I didn't think the Moores would be stupid enough to do this. The shifters will eat them alive. Literally."

"Ezra hasn't come. He sent a bunch of lone shifters." *Fucking coward.* Somehow, Gwen kept her shit together as she led Yvonne down the hallway. A smashing of glass from somewhere ahead of them made Gwen grind to a halt. Her pulse skittered. "Someone's inside. Must have broken through a terrace room." *Shit.*

"Go up," urged Yvonne. The attic had a secure door and, even better, a decent-size fire exit.

Heart pounding, Gwen grabbed her hand and pulled her toward the staircase. But they didn't make it. One of the bedroom doors swung open, and a heavy weight crashed into Gwen's side, tackling her. She landed awkwardly, wincing as pain struck her shoulder.

The male rolled her onto her back and straddled her, and it was only then that she realized it was Thad. His big, beefy hand snapped around her wrist and bent it awkwardly, trying to make her drop the Glock. She balled her free hand into a fist and slammed it into the bridge of his nose. There was a nauseating crack, and he bit out a harsh curse as blood dripped from his nose.

Yvonne came up behind him and yanked so hard on his collar that it dug into his throat. Making choking sounds, his hands flew to his collar . . . releasing Gwen. She dug the Glock into his chest, right above his heart, and fired. He paused, eyes widening in shock.

Gwen propelled herself upward, shoving him out of her way, and scrambled to her feet. Bile rose in her throat. She'd never killed anyone before. Shot them, sure, but never killed. Maybe she'd feel bad about it later, when adrenaline and panic weren't feverishly racing through her system. For now, getting Yvonne to safety was her priority.

"Let's go." Her hand hurt like a bitch, thanks to Thad, but she kept a good grip on her Glock as she ran for the staircase.

A door from downstairs crashed open. "That shot came from upstairs," said a familiar male voice.

A gasp flew out of Yvonne. "Ezra," she whispered shakily.

Yes, Ezra. Looked like he'd come, after all. He'd probably taken advantage of the moment when Zander and the others had hurried out of the house to face the trespassers.

"We have to keep moving," Gwen said.

She and Yvonne raced up the stairs to the third floor. They arrived on the landing just as Gerard came skidding out of the room near the smaller staircase that led to the attic, pistol in hand. Raising her Glock, Gwen squeezed the trigger twice, wincing as the flexing of her finger sent pain radiating through her hand and wrist. She'd aimed for his head, but the bullets collided with his arm and shoulder. *Dammit.* Still, the pistol slipped out of his fingers and fell to the floor—that helped.

Hearing footsteps stomping up the stairs behind them, Gwen dragged Yvonne toward the smaller staircase. She dragged too hard. Yvonne stumbled, falling to one knee on the first step.

Something wrapped around Gwen's ankle, and she looked down to see that Gerrard had crawled toward her. He tugged hard, but she gripped Yvonne's shoulder to steady herself and pulled the trigger. She'd aimed for his head again, but the bullet hit him in the throat. That would do. "Go, go, go." They climbed two steps when a series of bullets thudded into the wall and the painting above their heads.

"Don't move if you want to live!"

Gwen didn't freeze—she was too hyped on adrenaline to do anything except run. But then the bullet-ridden painting fell off the wall and crashed on top of her and Yvonne. Glass sliced into her face, and the Glock went flying out of her hand as she and Yvonne ungracefully crumpled to the floor and, of course, went rolling down the stairs. *Fuck, that hurt.* Sprawled on her back, she instinctively looked for the gun and spotted it a few feet away.

"Don't even think about making a dive for it," warned the same voice that had ordered her to freeze. Rowan's father, she realized. "Stay exactly where you are," he barked.

"Now that's unfair, Nelson," said another voice she recognized. "You can at least let them move that painting out of their way."

With an inward hiss, Gwen watched as Ezra climbed the last few stairs at a leisurely pace, wearing that slimy smile. Shoving the painting aside, Gwen spoke without moving her gaze from him. "You okay, Yvonne?"

Yvonne's chuckle was short and a little hysterical. "I've been better, sweetheart," she replied as she and Gwen slowly got to their feet.

Itching to act, Gwen spared her Glock the briefest glance, fingers flexing.

"Don't be stupid now, Gwen," Ezra cautioned.

Coming up behind him, Moira snorted. "I'm not sure she can help it."

Awkwardly walking beside Moira, using crutches, a massively bruised Brandt scowled at Gwen. Damn, he looked bad. Black eye, broken nose, split lip, swollen jaw, bruised cheekbone, a bandage around his head.

If he were anyone else, she'd have felt at least a *little* sorry for him.

Ignoring them both, Gwen spoke to Ezra. "How the hell did you get a bunch of shifters to fight for you?"

Still smiling, Ezra said, "I didn't. Our new friend Rory did."

Rory? *Son of a bitch.*

"He saw his brother haul Aidan out of Half 'n' Half and made it his business to find out who Aidan was," Ezra continued. "It became apparent that me, Aidan, and Rory have some common enemies, so Aidan passed Rory's contact details on to me. He and I had a very nice chat and came to an agreement that would be beneficial for us both. Rory hired the shifter mercenaries using my money. All he wanted in exchange was a shot at his brother . . . and for his brother's female to be killed."

Moira glared at her, eyes fairly sparkling with hate. "We're more than happy to see you dead."

Ezra nodded, chest puffing up. "Then justice will have been done."

Gwen couldn't help snickering. "Justice? You don't even know what that is."

"Look at what they did to me!" spat Brandt. "You think this is bad? They beat me and then healed me . . . just so they could do it all again. Over and over. The last time, they only healed me enough that I could stand up and walk out on crutches."

"You don't even see it, do you?" Gwen shook her head at him. "They gave you the same injuries that you gave Andie, only worse." When Gwen had helped the cougar reach her house that awful night, she'd had to support Andie's weight as her leg had been fractured. "It's called *karma*."

Brandt snickered. "Well, now you're about to know how karma feels. This happened to me because of *you*. Now you'll pay."

"But first," began Ezra, crossing to her, "I'll take out some of my rage on Yvonne here." His cruel smile was replaced by a glower. "I'll beat the shit out of her right in front of you, just like your stepfather did to your mother."

Fear scuttled down Gwen's spine. Fear for Yvonne. Pain, Gwen could take. But knowing that Yvonne was in pain? *Seeing* Yvonne in pain? Hearing it? Being able to do nothing about it? No. That couldn't fucking happen.

"Yes, Aidan told me about your childhood," continued Ezra. "He's been in my pocket for a long time. Sells me the secrets of those he counsels. I have a great deal of blackmail material, thanks to dear ol' Aidan."

As much as Aidan was a little weasel, it actually surprised Gwen to hear he'd stooped that low. She hated knowing that these people knew some of the dark facts of her childhood.

"If it makes you feel any better, he didn't want to tell me anything about you. In fact, he even lied at first that he knew nothing at all. But once he saw you with that shifter, he snapped. Coughed up your secrets." Ezra tilted his head. "But I'll bet there are more. Tell me, Gwen, did your stepfather ever turn on you? You said no to Aidan, but I'm not so sure. Tell me."

She didn't respond. Just glared at him.

He lifted a reprimanding brow. "You need to be cooperative, Gwen, if you want your death to be a quick one."

She gave him a mocking smile. Maybe if she pissed him off, his focus would remain on her and he'd forget about hurting Yvonne. "Oh, you're waiting for me to be scared and start to cry? You should have packed a lunch, Moore—this is gonna be a long night. Although I might have taken you more seriously if you hadn't raised a kid that tempts me to OD on birth-control pills."

Pain exploded behind her cheekbone as he slapped her hard enough to send her head whipping to the side. Brandt laughed. And for a reason that she couldn't explain, Gwen laughed too . . . which sort of cut Brandt's laugh short.

The lights flickered, and floorboards creaked. Nelson's eyes widened and darted around, searching for the source of the noise. The others looked just as uneasy. Ha.

"Kenny won't like this, you know," said Gwen.

Alarm briefly flashed in Ezra's eyes. "Yes, he made that clear. I agreed to leave you be. He'll never know it was me."

Was he for real? "He's gonna guess, Moore. It won't exactly take detective work to figure it out."

Sidling up to Ezra, Moira snorted. "It's not like you and he are close."

"But I'm still his daughter. He warned you to keep away from me, didn't he, Ezra? Warned you to keep Brandt away from me. So *this* . . . yeah, he *really* won't like it."

"Who's ever going to believe that *I* would work with shifters?" Ezra shook his head. "No, Rory will take the blame . . . though he doesn't know it yet."

"Rory didn't tell you anything about himself, did he, Moore?" Gwen gave him a look filled with pity. "He won't let you live to tattle on him. He won't honor any agreements he made with you. In fact, he'll probably kill all of you and any mercenaries who survive so he can then pocket your money and whatever else he can steal from you. The guy is fucked in the head . . . a little like your son, actually."

Moira slapped her, sneering, "Don't you talk about my boy. Because of you, he's in absolute agony as we speak."

Cheek stinging, Gwen sighed. "Moira, I'm gonna have to ask you to turn down the neurotic thing you got going on just a bit, okay. Seriously, there are such things called *consequences*. Brandt faced them for what he did. He was punished."

"Well, now you will be too," she spat. "You'll be punished for betraying your own kind."

As long as it wasn't Yvonne being hurt, Gwen could take it. Zander would come soon. He'd help her. "I'm sorry, I don't understand. What is this? Is it that you want to die? Is this, like, a suicide mission? Because I can get behind that."

"Shut up," Moira hissed.

"If you hurt me, you *will* die. Zander will never let it go. He will hunt and track and rip you into little pieces."

Ezra scoffed. "He won't live through this night. He'll be killed by his own kind, just like my son was betrayed by his own kind."

"Are we still on that? I didn't betray anyone's kind. *I told the truth.* You should try it some time." She tensed as Ezra raised his hand, but he didn't slap her this time. "Seriously, you really haven't thought this through, Moore. Let's say your plan works, all your mercenaries earn their pay, and you manage to kill me. Do you honestly think that

Zander's pack and their allies won't retaliate? They *will* kill you. All of you. Every. Last. One."

Unease rippled across Ezra's face. "If they come for anyone, it will be Rory."

"No, Moore, because they're not stupid like you."

Brandt snarled. "All we'll have done is killed two measly humans. You and Yvonne are no one to them. They won't bother avenging you."

"Yeah, little boy, they will . . . because I'm part of the Mercury Pack now too. I mated Zander."

Ezra's face went slack. "That's a lie."

Gwen smirked. "No, talking bullshit is your thing. I wear his mark. He wears mine."

Nelson hissed a curse. "She's no better than one of them now, Ezra. Let's get this done. We need to get on with this and leave. If she's telling the truth, he'll feel her pain through that weird mating-bond thing. He'll come for her."

Very true, and that made Gwen smile.

"I'm not rushing this," said Ezra.

"Then we need to go down to the second floor and do it there," insisted Nelson.

Ezra's face scrunched up. "Why?"

Nelson's Adam's apple bobbed. "I don't like it up here. I heard the third floor is haunted."

Ezra snickered. "Don't be so ridiculous." But his eyes darted around, wary.

Gwen hid her smirk, but Yvonne didn't as she said, "He's right, you know. This floor sees the most paranormal activity. Didn't you notice the lights flashing on and off? Don't you feel that draft? I don't think the ghosts like what you're doing."

"Ask them for me after we kill you and you join them," Moira snarled. And then she backhanded Yvonne so hard that the woman almost fell back against the wall.

Without thought, Gwen lunged for the bitch, but Nelson wrapped his big, thick arms around her and pulled her out of the way.

"Now you get to watch as they hurt her," Brandt said with a cruel smile. "You get a front-row seat."

Ezra's boot slammed into Yvonne's stomach, and Gwen tried lunging again. She failed again. One of Nelson's arms released her, and cold metal dug into her forehead.

"Try that again, and I'll shoot you right now."

Fuck.

The wolf clamped his jaws around the leg of the barely moving cheetah. He spun the cat, sending it sliding into the murky river. Then he stood, sides heaving. His fur was matted with blood, mud, and the odious marsh water. His injuries burned, but the wolf ignored the pain.

The mercenaries were strong. Fast. But they did not work as a unit—not like the wolf, his pack mates, and the Phoenix wolves. That made the mercenaries vulnerable.

Sharp teeth dug into his rear leg. The wolf whirled hard enough to dislodge the attacker. The fox tumbled, rolled. The wolf pounced, biting down on the fox's neck and raking open its stomach . . . watching as the life left its eyes.

At the sound of a roar, the wolf snapped his head up. A lioness was charging through the high grass, eyes blazing. The wolf braced himself, snarling.

Gunshot. The lioness stumbled. Staggered. Crumpled to the ground.

A shadow fell over the wolf. *The human.* Donnie. The wolf approved of him. He was fierce. Bloodthirsty. A predator.

"I don't know if you can understand me, but a few other wolves are trying to take down a grizzly over there. They may need your help."

The wolf did not understand the words. But his inner human urged the wolf to head in the direction that the human was pointing. The wolf ran, leaving prints in the mud, splashing the water pools.

Soon, he heard the distinct booming roar of a bear. The wolf skidded to a halt. Two of his pack mates were charging at the grizzly from either side—clawing and biting. The bear batted them away with its large paw, but it was bleeding heavily. Tired. Weak.

The wolf charged at the bear's front and leaped. Hit it hard. Sank his teeth into fur and flesh. The grizzly batted him away. The wolf hit the ground, but the mud cushioned his fall. He stood, shaking his head.

A margay dropped down from a branch above them and landed on the bear's back. The bear arched with a roar, and the wolf knew the margay had raked her claws down its back as she slid down to the ground.

The grizzly whirled to find the margay, who had jumped to expertly miss the human's trap. The bear did not see the trap. It fell right into it and disappeared into the pit. Its agonized roar told the wolf that the grizzly had fallen onto the bed of spikes.

The wolf turned. Looked for more enemies. There were many dead bodies. He could not see or hear—

He froze as hate rushed through him. Hate and fear. Echoes of his mate's emotions. Heart racing, the wolf whirled and ran for the house. He tasted his own fear. Fear for her. Fear of losing her.

As he neared the house, he heard human cries of pain. Female cries. But they were not coming from his mate. He knew through their bond that she was not hurt.

The wolf ran for the steps that would lead to the porch. A hard weight barreled into his side, sending him sprawling. The wolf crashed into the truck. Spots dotted his vision.

Rory stood over him. "Hello, brother. You're supposed to be dead by now. Shame. But I don't mind taking care of that problem."

The wolf growled. He did not understand the words, but he heard the cruel intent in them. The wolf stood, snarling. He did not care that the male was his sibling. He wanted him dead. Wanted to taste his blood. Wanted to watch the life leave his eyes as he had with the fox.

"I didn't want it to come to a fight between us. You're my twin, after all. We're part of each other in a weird way. Right? All you had to do was give me what was mine. I told you what would happen if you didn't. I warned you. But you didn't listen. You brought this on yourself, Zander. And now your little human will die, and so will you."

Rage exploded inside him—the emotion came from the man within the wolf.

"I can smell her on you. Your scents have mixed. Congratulations on your mating. A pity you had such little time to enjoy it." Rory lifted a gun, pointed it at the wolf. "I told Ezra that I'd let him have her, but . . . maybe I'll claim that pleasure myself once I'm done with you and—"

Another wolf launched himself at Rory, knocking him down. The gun slid under the truck. Zander lunged for the surface so hard that the wolf did not have the opportunity to fight him for dominance.

Standing, Zander glared down at his brother, nostrils flaring. "You'll never touch her again." He signaled for Jesse's wolf to back away from Rory—this was something Zander had to do himself. Jesse's wolf let out a disgruntled growl as he moved aside. Zander rolled back his shoulders. "You want to fight, Rory? No, I won't give you that. People fight to win. I don't want to win. I want to *kill* you. You know I can."

Rory staggered to his feet, putting a hand to the claw marks on his side. "You're bleeding—"

"Now, so are you." Not near as badly as Zander, but bad enough. "And how fucking typical is it of you that you wouldn't attack until you thought I was too weak to beat you. I'll always beat you, Rory. Every time. Because *you're* the weak one. You always were. A part of you even knows that. You'll just never face it because, as I said, you're *weak*."

Rory sniggered. "Not so weak that I didn't get dear old Mom and Dad to leave me everything."

"And what was it you thought I wanted from two people who were as equally pathetic as you? Abusive people are weak, and that was what Pearl was. Dad wouldn't stand against Pearl, not even to defend his own kids. He was spineless, like you. So, where's your victory?"

Rory's mouth bobbed open and closed. "You're saying I'm weak?" Nostrils flaring, he took an aggressive step forward. "If it wasn't for me, you'd be on dialysis—"

"This again? Honest to God?"

"That infection almost *killed* me!"

"Yeah, *almost*. Right now, I'm wishing it had, because then it wouldn't have come to this. Now, I'm done listening to your shit." Zander shifted just as his brother clawed off his clothes and then did the same.

The identical wolves circled each other, ears flattened. The only difference between them was the scar on the face of Zander's wolf.

The scarred wolf pounced. The other lunged. And they clashed, clawing and growling.

CHAPTER NINETEEN

Ezra cocked back his fist to hit Yvonne once more, but he froze at the sound of vicious growling just outside the house.

Gwen tensed, hope blitzing through her. There was so much noise out there, so many growls, roars, and screeches, that it sounded like a zoo gone crazy, but *those* growls . . . they were close. Very, very close. And Gwen would bet money that one of the wolves was Zander. She could feel his rage and determination, could feel that he was near.

She allowed a little smile to surface as Ezra looked at her. "I told you he'd come for me," she reminded him.

Nelson grunted in her ear and dug the gun harder into her temple. She barely held back a wince. The bastard's arm was like a thick rope around her chest, pinning her arms at her sides, and she felt like she couldn't get enough air.

Even with the gun pointed at her head, Gwen had fought him at first. But that had only made them laugh and hurt Yvonne more, so Gwen had quieted. She'd clamped her mouth shut to contain the pointless pleas for them to leave the woman alone. Now, Gwen remained perfectly still. But her muscles were tight, ready to spring at the slightest opportunity.

"We need to end this *now*," insisted Nelson.

Ezra didn't seem concerned. "That sounds like two wolves fighting to me. It's probably Rory tearing his brother to pieces . . . unless her mate's fighting one of his pack mates, of course, which is quite possible. Those animals know no loyalty."

Gwen bared her teeth. "*He's* an animal? You're the civilized one?" She flicked a meaningful look at a beaten Yvonne, who'd curled up into a protective ball—her nose was broken, her face was swollen and bruised, and there were scratches on her face from Ezra's ring. She no doubt had at least one broken rib and a dozen bruises beneath her clothes. Emotionally, Gwen had felt every slap, kick, punch, and whack of Brandt's crutch.

"You think *that* makes you strong?" Fists shaking, Gwen curled her upper lip. "You're a pussy, just like your son. Ah, Brandt doesn't like being called that either. It's only the truth."

"I'm telling you, Ezra, we need to get this over with!" asserted Nelson.

Brandt's fists clenched. "Aidan said it would hurt her most to see Yvonne hurt."

"Then your job is done, because Yvonne is out of it," Nelson pointed out. "Now, Ezra, just kill her now!"

The lights flickered again. Doors slammed all over the house. One. Two. Three. Four. Five.

At Brandt's panicked expression, Ezra assured him in a shaky voice, "It's just the wind coming through the windows."

"I can smell burning," said Nelson. "Can't you smell burning?"

"No," said Ezra, but he could. And so could Gwen, just as she could feel the chill in the air. Her muscles went taut, and the hairs on her nape rose.

Brandt jerked. "Shit, I just saw something move in the shadows."

Moira sighed. "You're being ridiculous." But she looked just as freaked.

"I did! I saw something! And it's not windy out there, so how can the doors be slamming shut?"

Nelson suddenly jumped and whirled, scrubbing at his neck with the hand holding his gun. "Something just breathed on me."

Taking advantage of his loosened hold, Gwen jammed her elbow into his gut and snapped back her head to connect with his nose. As he cried out in pain, she dived for her Glock. At the same time, Yvonne reared up and stabbed Ezra in the thigh with a thick shard of glass.

Gwen grinned in satisfaction as her hand wrapped around the butt of her Glock. She rolled onto her back, shot Nelson in the chest, and then aimed it at Brandt . . . who was about to slam his crutch over Yvonne's head. But then the painting on the floor whipped through the air and hit him hard, sending him toppling over the banister with a loud cry.

A screeching Moira grabbed Nelson's gun and fired blindly over and over. Unused to shooting, her body shook with the impact, and her shots went wide. Except for one.

Pain blazed across Gwen's temple. "Motherfucker." She aimed her Glock at Moira's head, but Ezra's body knocked Gwen to the ground before she could squeeze the trigger.

For the second time that day, her gun went skidding along the floor. As Ezra straddled her, she heard gunfire and then Moira screech, and she distantly wondered if Yvonne had shot her. But Gwen's attention was on Ezra as she scratched at his face and fought him like a wildcat. His hand fisted her hair, and he rammed her head on the floor. Once. Twice. Three times. He reached up, grabbed a heavy ornament from the round antique table, and smashed it right over her head.

Without mercy, the wolf stabbed his claws deep into his sibling's flank. He liked hearing his opponent's yelp of pain. Liked seeing that pain in his eyes. In retaliation, his opponent bit hard into the wolf's wounded ear.

The fight was fast and fierce. The wolf was brutal in his attack. Fury was in every vicious bite, every sharp lunge, every merciless swipe of his claws.

The wolf had fought his sibling before, but never like this. Never with the intent to kill. His sibling had not fought with honor then, and he did not do it now. Instead, he bit and clawed at the injuries the wolf had sustained in the battle with the trespassers. Fur already matted from blood, mud, and dirty water was now soaked with yet more blood.

The wolf's chest heaved, breaths sawing in and out of him. Every heave made the deep rake wounds on his sides burn. The wolf was tired from battle, and the blood loss was beginning to slow him down. But the wolf would not submit. Would not be pinned down. He fought harder.

His sibling's snarls and yelps filled his ears. The scent of their combined blood and rage filled his nostrils. There was something else he could scent: fear. It wafted from his opponent, inciting the wolf.

With a savage growl, his opponent tore a strip out of the wolf's badly injured side. Agony blazed through the wolf. Made his knees buckle. But he pounced at his sibling again.

A bullet fired inside the house. The wolf's heart jumped, and he froze. His sibling took advantage and lunged. Tried to wrap his paws around the wolf's neck. But the wolf fought him off and swiped at his head. His claws raked over his opponent's muzzle. Blood sprayed on the ground. The wolf bared his teeth in a feral smile as his sibling bounced back with a yowl.

Flattening his ears, his sibling sprang at him. They collided furiously. Brutally slashed and bit at each other. Teeth and claws tore through the wolf's skin and scraped bone. Pain rippled through him, but he pushed it aside as more gunshots rang through the air.

His mate was in pain. He needed to reach her.

With a newfound strength, the wolf wrestled his sibling onto his back, pinned him flat, and clamped his jaws around his throat. He sank his teeth down hard. Panicking, his opponent swiped at his bleeding sides, struggling. But the wolf used his rear paw to tear open his opponent's stomach and then clamped his jaws tighter around his throat.

Finally, his sibling's body went lax beneath him. Dead.

A dark satisfaction flooded the wolf. But he didn't take a moment to revel in victory. He needed to get to his mate.

He raced up the steps onto the porch and slammed his body at the door. Again. And again. And again. He heard his pack mates and allies howl as they came to join him. Finally, the door burst open. The wolf followed the sounds of a struggle. Bounded up the stairs.

More gunshots fired. The wolf kept vaulting up the staircase. He saw his mate. Saw the human "Ezra" straddling her. He was smashing something over her head over and over. The wolf heard the cracks, *felt* her pain, *felt* the darkness swallow her, and he slammed into the human with a furious growl.

The human screamed as the wolf savagely slashed and bit at him. The wolf did not stop. Not even when the human ceased screaming and the life left his body.

"Zander, I need you over here!"

The man inside the wolf battered at him, reminding him that his mate was in need. He fought for dominance, but the wolf refused to withdraw. He abandoned the dead human and padded to his mate's side.

She lay very still. Eyes closed. Their connection was weak. Too weak. He licked at her face, trying to wake her. She did not move. Fear struck him hard.

He could feel and hear her heartbeat slowing. Could see and feel her breathing becoming shallower. The man within him was terrified and beating at the wolf, demanding him to withdraw. The wolf didn't. He couldn't leave his mate.

The human female who had raised his mate held her hand. "Ally's gonna heal you, baby girl. Just hold on for us, okay?" She looked at the Seer. "Do what you can. Please. Don't let her die."

The Beta male spoke to the Seer. "Her head wounds are bad. He almost bashed in her fucking skull. Concentrate your healing energy there, Ally."

The Seer looked at the wolf. "Zander, I need you to shift back. She's barely hanging on here. You have to feed her your energy. I'm hurt and weak from healing other wounds—I'm not sure I can do this without your help." Her voice cracked, sounding sad.

The words were foreign to the wolf, but he could see that the Seer was weak, could sense her panic, and knew what his mate needed. But the wolf couldn't feed his mate his strength. Their bond was incomplete.

The man inside him was frantic, unsure of what to do. But the wolf wasn't blinded by issues. Wasn't knotted by emotions. He knew the problem. Knew he himself had held back from his mate out of fear. It shamed him. He pushed aside that fear now. It was easy, because he realized he feared being without her more than he feared the power she had over him.

Pain slammed into his head and chest. His vision darkened around the edges. As the pain faded, the man within him beat at the wolf so hard that the beast could fight him no longer.

Zander's stomach bottomed out as he looked down at his mate. He felt the blood drain from his face. Felt an all-consuming terror wrap around his heart tight enough to stop it beating.

He knelt beside her, speechless. Blood poured from a wound on the side of her head, drenching and matting her hair. But even with all the blood, he could see that her skull had caved in. "Jesus. Shit. Holy fuck." He scrubbed a shaking hand over his face. The panic within him swelled until his chest tightened and his lungs seemed to ache with the effort to breathe.

"Don't go crazy on us, Zander," said Bracken.

He couldn't promise anything on that front. Rage and despair filled every part of him. He could feel Ally's healing energy trickle through Gwen. Feel it soothe. But he didn't feel it *heal.*

As Zander reached out to take Gwen's hand, pain blasted through his shoulder. He'd forgotten his own injuries. They didn't matter. He pushed the pain aside. It wasn't important. *She* was important. Fixing the fucking skull that was caved in was important.

"Tell me you can heal that head wound, Ally," he said, almost choking on the words. "Tell me you can do it." Because he'd lose every bit of rationality left in him if she couldn't make him that promise. He'd seen Ally heal many wounds, but nothing like that.

Ally licked her lips, nervous. "Honestly, I've never healed a wound that bad before." Her voice shook. "That's why I need you. Feed her energy."

Squeezing Gwen's hand, Zander shoved energy down their mating bond, too frantic to celebrate right then that it was finally fully formed. He fed her strength and bolstered the bond that was currently as fragile as she was. Her heartbeat was lazy and erratic. Her breathing was steady but so damn shallow that he wasn't sure her lungs would keep working much longer.

The entire time, his pack mates and Yvonne alternated between whispering assurances to Zander and urging Gwen to hold on as they gathered around them. But the assurances didn't work, because she didn't seem to be healing. His raging wolf was in an absolute frenzy, clawing at Zander, demanding he do *something.*

Zander did all he could do—he kept on pushing energy down the mating bond, heart thudding in his chest, wishing he could do more.

He did it over and over, until his head began to spin and darkness crept around his vision. He was weak from blood loss, but he couldn't let that matter.

He'd never in his life felt fear like this. Hadn't known such a level of hellish, incapacitating, debilitating terror existed. It flooded him. Choked him. Ate at him.

"You need to feed her strength, Zander," Ally said urgently.

"I am," he clipped. "It's not making any fucking difference." Every bit of energy he pumped into her seemed to fizzle out. The head wound didn't seem to be improving, and her vitals were getting worse. At most, his and Ally's efforts were keeping her alive . . . but only barely. The weaker Gwen got, the weaker the bond became. Right then, it was threadlike.

Zander was just as weak. He felt hollowed out, like he didn't have much left to give. He suspected that the only thing keeping him conscious was the crazed terror that was like a band around his chest. "Why the fuck isn't it working?" he demanded through gritted teeth.

"There are some things that even a healer can't fix," said Derren, voice low.

Zander shook his head at the softly delivered warning. No. Gwen wasn't going to fucking die.

A crying Yvonne shot Derren a hard look. "She'll live."

"I'm gonna fix it," Ally insisted, sniffling. "I am. I *can*."

Derren rubbed her back. "Baby, you're wiped."

Ally shook him off. *"I can do it."*

Derren looked at Zander, his expression sympathetic. "If I wasn't feeding Ally my strength, she'd be unconscious right now. She's not going to last much longer."

Ally blinked back tears. "If Gwen were a shifter, it would be easier—she'd have accelerated healing, and that would help the process. But she's human, so she doesn't. All we can do is keep trying."

Zander *felt* as Gwen's heartbeat stuttered weakly. Panicked, he pushed a large pulse of energy down the bond so fast that he swayed. Light-headed, he blinked. He couldn't afford to pass out; she needed him. His wolf snapped his teeth at him, urging him to stay awake, to hold their mate to them.

"Jesus," breathed Bracken.

Tracking his gaze, Zander stared. What the fuck? Three people stood a few feet away, their eyes dull and concerned. Which would have been fine if they weren't partly transparent. He noticed then that their clothes and hairstyles were old-fashioned.

Yvonne shot to her feet, glaring at them. "No, you don't get to take her." Her voice broke, and a sob caught in her throat. "You can't have her."

But one of the teenage . . . entities, ghosts, whatever the fuck it was . . . slowly came toward them, her eyes resting on Gwen. Yvonne went hysterical. Bracken, Jesse, and Harley started swearing. Frozen, Zander could only stare at the . . . whatever it was.

She walked right through Yvonne, but she didn't go to Gwen. She went to Ally. Derren growled and pushed at her, which did absolutely nothing because his arm just went straight through her. The girl touched Ally's head. The Seer's hair went static, and her T-shirt ruffled, and the girl faded away . . . right along with the other two whatever-they-were.

Zander almost jumped as healing energy literally shot through Gwen. He was honestly surprised her back didn't bow with the force of it.

Double-blinking, Ally inhaled deeply. "We can do this. We can. Hold her here, Zander."

He held on to Gwen through their bond, giving her what little reserves he had left. His entire system seemed to shake with relief when her heartbeat picked up and her breathing improved. Their bond soon strengthened, and the color returned to her face. More important, the dent in her skull was gone.

Ally sat back. "She'll be okay." Then the Seer burst into tears and leaned into her mate, who held her close.

Zander slipped his arms under Gwen and gathered her to him, trying to keep his hold gentle when all he wanted to do was squeeze her tight. His hands were fucking trembling, and he knew his legs would have given in if he'd been standing.

Heat behind his eyelids, he buried his face in her neck and felt her pulse beat strong against his mouth. She was alive. She was with him.

He somehow swallowed around the painful lump in his throat. For a moment, when their bond had become so thin and fragile that he'd expected it to snap, he'd experienced a hint of the profound loneliness that would overwhelm him if he'd had to live without her. A hint of the emptiness that would have awaited him, that would have consumed him until there was nothing left for him. He couldn't live without her, and if it wasn't for Ally, he would have been forced to.

Zander looked up at Ally. "Thank you." The words sounded like gravel.

She gave him a wan smile. "You're welcome. Thank you for helping me help her."

Zander turned back to Gwen, drinking in every detail of her face even though he knew it by heart. His wolf pushed against his skin, rubbing up against her and breathing her in. Zander felt Ally then put a hand on him, felt her healing energy flow through him, warm and soothing, but his eyes were locked on his mate.

"I really thought we'd lost her," sobbed Yvonne, who kept stroking and kissing Gwen's hair even as Zander cradled his mate against him. She didn't try to take her from him, which was a good thing because it wouldn't have worked.

He felt Ally's hand leave him, and he guessed she must have then used her skills on Yvonne, because he heard the woman release a gasp of wonder.

Moments later, Ally sighed. "I got nothing left." And she slumped against Derren.

Jesse crouched next to Zander. "Come on. Me and Bracken will help you get back to the bedroom before you fall asleep right there." Before pride could make Zander reflexively jut out his chin, Jesse snorted and said without heat, "Just suck it the fuck up, asshole."

Too tired to argue, Zander sucked it up.

Eyes closed, Gwen stood under the hot spray. Shampoo bubbles and blood swirled together as they ran down the drain. It was the third time she'd shampooed her hair, and that seemed to be the last of the blood. *Finally.*

Nothing like your last memory being a large ornament getting smashed over your head.

As everything had started to go black, she'd known death was coming. She hadn't had even a moment to think about what she would be leaving behind. The world had faded too fast. All she'd felt was a *knowing* that this was the end. And then she'd woken up. Thank fuck for that, because she couldn't stand the thought of Zander being left alone.

He'd have senselessly blamed himself. Would have tormented himself about what he could or should have done differently. Worse, he wouldn't have known that she loved him. He'd never have heard the words. And, hey, just because neither of them were people who liked soppy words didn't mean she shouldn't have told him.

Awake, she resolved that she'd tell him at some point that very day—she wouldn't even let it bother her if he couldn't say it back. She'd tell him because life was too damn short.

Hearing the shower door open, she turned as a naked Zander stepped into the stall. She smiled. "Good of you to shift back." She'd woken on her bed next to a deep-sleeping wolf that was covered in blood and mud and that absolutely *reeked*. Still, she'd grinned, so fucking glad that he was okay.

Zander practically folded himself around her as he kissed her. Softly. Carefully. Like she was made of fine bone china. Yet, there was so much relief and desperation in the kiss—the emotions came from both her and him.

"My wolf was going crazy; he needed to rub up against you. I tried to shift back, but he wasn't having any of it. How long have you been awake?"

"About half an hour. I'm surprised you're on your feet—I can feel how tired you are. You were in a worse state than me, so that's probably why it took you longer to wake."

"I was in a worse state than you?" Zander echoed, the image of her head wound flickering through his mind. He'd been absolutely frantic. His mind had been in complete chaos because she'd been *dying*. And *he* was in a worse state? "Are you kidding me?" he growled.

Soaping him down, she said in a soothing voice, "I meant you had a lot more wounds than I did and that you lost a whole lot of blood. You fed me a lot of strength too—and that was after a battle *and* a duel with another wolf. It zonked you out." She gave him a quick kiss. "I didn't want to leave you in bed on your own, but I needed to get all the blood off me. My scalp was itching like crazy."

"I need a shower even more than you do." He grimaced at the stench. "I don't know how you slept next to me."

She chuckled. "I was totally out of it. You sure you have the energy for a shower?"

"I'll fucking find it."

Gwen chuckled again. "Our bond's complete now."

He nodded, stroking a hand over the curve of her shoulder. "My wolf's fear was in the way."

"Fear of me?" she asked, a little hurt by that.

Zander shook his head. "Fear of the power you hold over him. He's a tough motherfucker. Not used to feeling vulnerable. You're his only weakness, the only thing that could really hurt him. He feared that power you hold. Still does a little. I think it will take time for it to really fade."

"Then how did the bond . . . you know . . ."

"Snap fully into place?" Zander massaged conditioner into her hair. "He stopped letting the fear hold him back from you. He fears losing you more than he fears that power. That realization cleared the path for the bond."

Zander's breath caught in his throat as he remembered their bond weakening, remembered the feel of her energy fading and her slipping away from him. He hadn't truly grasped the extent of how essential she was to him until right then.

He buried his face in her hair. "When I saw the son of a bitch smashing your head . . . I'll never get that picture out of my mind. Never. I felt your pain. Felt everything go . . . dark for you. I've never been so fucking scared. No, not scared. Terrified. My wolf wouldn't withdraw at first, the stubborn bastard. I can usually fight him for dominance, but he was all about you."

She kissed his chest. "I was a little scared when I woke to see you covered in blood. Panicked. Even went banging on Derren's door to ask Ally to heal you. She assured me that she had healed you and that you'd wake soon. I could feel through the bond that you were okay, but the panic didn't ease off." Trying to keep her voice sensitive, she said, "I take it you killed Rory. I heard the two of you fighting."

"It had to be done."

She wrapped her arms around him. "I'm sorry he put you in a position where it had to be done."

Zander figured he should be feeling guilt or shame or *something* about having killed Rory. All he felt was relief, because it meant his mate was safe from the threat that Rory had presented. "Tell me what happened after I left here last night."

Gwen took a deep breath and told him everything, pausing only at moments when Zander took a second to spit out a harsh curse. "Ally healed Yvonne—that she-wolf is *the shit*, by the way. She also saved Bracken's life, you know."

Zander stiffened. "What happened to Bracken?"

"A coyote and a cheetah teamed up to try and tear him to pieces. He's okay now, though. Ally healed him before healing me. He's probably still sleeping it off."

Zander kissed her hair. "I should have known Moore brought the mercenaries to draw us away from the house. I should have stayed with you."

"No. Your pack mates needed you."

"You needed me."

"Yeah, I did. And you came. I knew you would." She nipped his lip. "So, no guilt."

He helped her rinse off the conditioner as he asked, "How about you? Are you stupidly giving yourself a hard time about hurting and killing those bastards?"

"Part of me is shook up by what I did. Feels bad, even. But then I remember that Ezra, Moira, and Brandt beat on Yvonne. I remember that Thad, Gerard, and Nelson shot at us, and that Ezra almost killed me. Then I don't feel too bad about it."

"Good." He kissed her forehead. "They don't deserve your guilt. They chose to come here, they put you in a position where you had to defend yourself and Yvonne, and that was exactly what you did. They put you in a position where you had to choose between their lives or yours and Yvonne's. You made the right choice, and it's not one you should feel any remorse over. Okay?"

"Okay."

He doubted it would be that simple for her, suspected there would be times when it tormented her a little. Zander took her mouth. He'd only meant to give her a swift kiss, but it quickly turned hot and hungry. Before long, he was fucking her against the tiled wall. Not hard and fast, but soft and slow. And when she came, he bit her neck to leave yet another mark. He rested his forehead against hers. "I love you, Gwen." He hadn't actually meant to say the words—they'd just popped out. But it was only the truth. Her winning smile made his chest tighten.

"And I love you."

"Good. Now let's finish here, get dressed, and go for breakfast."

Sounded good to Gwen. A short while later, she was walking downstairs, hand in hand with Zander. Her knees felt a little rubbery, but she seemed to be doing a good job of hiding it from him because he didn't comment. As they strolled into the kitchen, it was to find Marlon, Yvonne, and Donnie sitting at the table.

"Damn, I'm starving," Gwen declared.

"Thought you would be." Marlon jumped to his feet and hugged her tight. Then he started crying.

Alarmed, she exchanged a panicked look with Zander and patted her foster brother's back. "I'm fine."

Marlon actually slapped her arm as he pulled back. "Fine? You almost *died*. We could have been picking out your coffin and headstone right now."

"There's no need to say it like it was my fault."

He put a hand over his chest. "Sometimes I think God sent you here to test the strength of my heart."

"Then you're weird."

He snorted. "Says the person who always flushes the toilet twice—before *and* after she uses it."

"Says the person who stupidly lies that he's color-blind."

"I *am* color-blind."

Gwen rolled her eyes. "I'm too sober to deal with you. And stop with the dramatics."

"I'm not being dramatic. Yvonne thought the damn ghosts had come for you."

Gwen frowned. "Ghosts?" As Yvonne then told her what happened, Gwen gaped. "I don't get how the girl could have helped."

"Ally said the girl gave her a sort of . . . dose of preternatural energy," Yvonne explained. "It boosted her healing skills, because her healing energy is preternatural too. Or something like that. She said it better."

"Damn, I wish I'd been awake for that."

Marlon looked at Zander. "I heard you saved my sister and then practically ate Ezra Moore alive. For that, I will forever adore you."

Not really sure what to say to that, Zander just nodded. That seemed to please Marlon, because he beamed at him and then declared he'd make pancakes.

Donnie frowned. "I want Pop-Tarts."

Marlon sighed. "I'll get you Pop-Tarts."

Yvonne stood and drew Gwen into her arms, squeezing her tight. "I'm so glad you're okay. You scared me last night. I wasn't sure you were going to make it." Her voice broke at the end.

Gwen hugged her tight. "I'm sorry that Ezra, Moira, and Brandt hurt you and—"

Yvonne pulled back and gripped her face, pinning her gaze. "Don't you apologize. Nelson was restraining you and had a gun to your head." Ignoring Zander's growl, she continued, "There was no way you could have done anything, Gwen. Besides, you got free in the end. You saved us both . . . and then Zander and Ally saved you." Yvonne smiled at Zander. "Thank you. And thank you for not dragging her away from me—I can see you want to keep her close right now."

Zander ignored the teasing note to her voice. Besides, she was right. He needed to keep Gwen close, needed to breathe her in. He sat, and at his urging, Gwen settled on his lap.

"You okay, Donnie?" Gwen asked him as he bit into a Pop-Tart.

Donnie gave her a thumbs-up. "Nearly died." And for some reason, he sounded . . . cheery about it. Like it was the first bit of excitement he'd had in a long time. "If Ally hadn't done that healing thing, I'd have met the reaper and you'd be planting lilies over my head." He looked at Yvonne. "Make sure that happens when my ticker finally stops ticking, okay? Lilies. I want lilies."

"Lilies," Yvonne promised.

Donnie lifted a brow at Gwen. "What do you want planted over your grave?"

Zander growled. "Let's not talk anymore about Gwen dying, yeah?"

As Marlon made pancakes and Yvonne made coffee, more and more people came downstairs for breakfast. Considering the night before had been one hell of a fuckup, it was surprising that the atmosphere was . . . peaceful.

The arrival of a car ruined it.

"It might just be Julie and Chase," said Yvonne.

But as Zander stepped out onto the porch, it was to see that she was wrong. The sheriff slid out of his car, face grim. Beside him, Gwen quietly cursed. The others all emptied out of the house and spread out along the porch.

As Colt marched up the steps, Gwen lifted a brow. "Can I help you with something?"

"Where's Ezra?" he demanded.

Gwen blinked. "Ezra?"

"Don't play with me, Gwen," he clipped.

Zander growled, and his wolf swiped his claws. "Watch your fucking tone."

Colt's lips thinned. "Last night, I had several reports that there were all kinds of noises coming from here."

Yvonne snickered. "Kind of you to check on us the day *after* the reports came in."

Perching his hands on his hips, Colt jutted out his chin. "Shifter business is shifter business."

He had that right, thought Zander. "We went on a pack run. Things can get noisy."

But Colt wasn't buying it. "Ezra talked about coming here with his brothers, making you pay," he told Gwen. "I calmed him down, thought I'd made him see reason. But I went by to see him this morning, and he's gone. So are Moira and Brandt. His chauffeur and brother are nowhere to be found either."

Gwen frowned. "And you think they'll come here?"

"I think they *have* been here. I think you did something to them last night."

"Why?" she asked.

His face flushed. "Because they wouldn't just vanish like this! I want to search the premises. I want to get a crime-scene unit out here and—"

"That's not going to be possible," Zander told him, voice hard.

Colt did a slow blink. "Excuse me?"

"Well, see, you have no jurisdiction here anymore," Gwen explained. "Haven't you noticed all the shifter markings?"

Colt's nostrils flared. "That doesn't make this shifter territory."

"This does." Derren handed the sheriff some folded-up papers. He snatched them fast and began to read them. "These are the deeds to the house and land," said Derren. "As you can see, they no longer belong to Yvonne."

"Who's Nick Axton?" Colt asked.

"Our Alpha," said Jesse. "That makes this shifter territory, which means, as Gwen said, you have no jurisdiction here."

Gwen barely hid her smile as Colt glared at her, looking ready to explode. Nick had bought the house and land from Yvonne just days before the hearing to cover their asses in case such an event occurred.

Fisting his hand in the papers, Colt growled, "Your neighbors said they heard fighting!"

Gwen arched a brow. "Do we look like we've been fighting?" Thanks to Ally, the answer was no. And as they'd moved the cars so that they covered the bloodstains on the ground from Zander's and Rory's duel, there was no way to tell that there had been a battle without taking a stroll around the marsh.

The bodies of the dead shifters and humans had all been lumped together deep in the marsh near two of Ezra's cars. According to Zander, Cain would be sending some people from The Movement to collect them all. Collecting and disposing of bodies was apparently something they'd done for the Phoenix Pack before.

"The deeds," said Derren, holding out his hand.

Colt handed them back with a petulant frown. "Ezra and Moira wouldn't have just . . . left."

"They might have if they were worried that shifters would come hunting Brandt for what he had done to Andie," said Harley. "We've all heard of The Movement."

The sheriff shook his head. "Ezra would have told me if he was leaving. And he wouldn't run from *shifters*."

"But he might run from Kenny Cogman," Gwen mused. "Ezra said some pretty mean shit about me at that hearing. Told some lies about me too. Kenny wasn't too happy to hear that."

Colt's frown turned thoughtful. "If you have nothing to hide, prove it and let me inside."

Yvonne raised a mocking brow. "You sure you want to come inside, Sheriff? You never did like this house."

Zander folded his arms. *Like hell* was he letting this bastard enter. "This is shifter territory now. You have no right being here. And we sure as shit don't want you here."

"Even if the Moores did come here last night, it would be no business of yours," said Bracken. "We all know that if someone takes their chances trespassing on shifter territory, they can't expect to walk away unharmed. As you yourself said, shifter business is shifter business."

"They're my friends," said Colt.

Gwen shook her head. "Not friends, Colt. Not really. People like the Moores aren't friends with anyone. They're all about themselves. You lost the respect of a lot of people around here because of them. There had to have been times when you did want to arrest Brandt for one thing or another. After all, he was making your job harder for you. But you always had to let it go, didn't you? They didn't respect your authority, and soon other people stopped respecting it. At least you won't have that problem until they come back from wherever they've gone."

The sheriff sighed. "Just give me a straight answer. Did they come here last night or not?"

"If they did, I didn't see them," said Marlon, which was true as he'd been at Dylan's. "And I doubt they'd have come here just to hide in the trees. Besides, I think the noises this lot made on their pack run would have scared them off."

For a long moment, no one spoke. Colt pointed a finger at Gwen. "If I find any evidence to suggest they came here—"

"There'll be nothing you can do about it," Zander stated. The pack would never admit to anything. Explaining or justifying themselves to humans would be the same as answering to them. "And me, well, I'm not eager to talk to a person who didn't protect my mate or one of my kind when they were being harassed and persecuted. Now drop your fucking finger, get back in your car, and don't come back."

Looking strangely tired all of a sudden, Colt muttered to himself as he slowly returned to his car. Watching him drive off, Gwen said, "It really was smart of you to ask Nick to buy the house and land so that Colt couldn't insist on coming inside."

"I'm always full of smart ideas," said Zander.

As the others retreated into the house, Gwen slid her arms around him. "What does Nick intend to do with the place?"

"I don't know. You'll have to ask him." Zander brushed his mouth over hers. "You can do that tomorrow, when you come home with me."

She raised her brows. "Tomorrow?" That was a lot sooner than she'd expected, and she could admit, if only to herself, that it made her panic a little. But then, she supposed it was important to him to get back to his pack.

"Tomorrow," he stated.

She saw the dare in his eyes, knew he was expecting her to object and claim it was too soon. Instead, she sighed and agreed, "Tomorrow."

Mouth curving, Zander wrapped his arms tight around her, lifted her off her feet, and kissed the breath out of her.

CHAPTER TWENTY

Two months later

Gwen nodded along as the beautiful little girl talked around a mouthful of cake, swinging her arms.

Lounging in the chair beside Gwen's, Zander leaned in and whispered, "Did you understand what she just said?"

"Not a word of it." But Gwen figured it was probably another creepy line from a movie—the Alphas' daughter had a habit of repeating them to freak people out. It worked.

Gwen was surprised the two pups were still awake. The barbecue had started at noon, and it was now the evening. The kids had spent the day cycling, arguing over toys, playing in the outdoor area, and chasing the dog that was currently lying on the grass.

Most of the adults were close to falling asleep too. In fact, Kathy had passed out on one of the lawn chairs. Ally was sprawled on top of Derren in the hammock that was strung up near the play area. Other people were settled on patio chairs or sharing blankets on the ground.

Although it was almost dark, the glow of the fairy lights that were strung on the trees enabled Gwen to see well enough. She figured the shifters didn't need any such light, given they had excellent night vision—she envied them that.

She sighed as the evening breeze brushed over her skin and ruffled her bangs. It had been one hell of a hot day, and she'd almost wilted from the glare of the sun. The chirping of birds and the lively partying had been replaced by the sounds of grasshoppers, crickets, soft laughter, quiet chatter, and the wood snapping in the fire pit.

The coolers that had earlier been brimming with drinks were now pretty much empty. Very little food was left, even though there had been a lot of it. Damn, shifters ate like horses. She wasn't sure how they were still eating. She'd stuffed herself on hamburgers, potato salad, lasagna, cake, and pecan pie, and there was no way she could manage anything else.

That hadn't stopped her from enjoying a few drinks, though. She wasn't gonna lie, she was a little tipsy. She hadn't touched any of the hard liquor; she only had a couple of beers. Well, she'd *intended* to only have a couple. But those *couple of beers* had soon become *four.* Or maybe it was five. Still, she could feel the effects beginning to wear off.

As Willow demolished the rest of her cake, Gwen handed her lemon Popsicle to Zander and said, "Hold that for me a sec, please." Gwen then used a wipe to clean the crumbs and sticky icing from Willow's fingers.

That was when the Alphas appeared with Cassidy, the other pup. Nick sighed at his daughter, who was still trying to talk around her food. When Gwen had first arrived, she'd braced herself for an awkward reception from Nick. But his welcome had been genuine, and the pack had actually thrown a really cool party for her.

"Thanks for cleaning her up," said Shaya, stabbing a plastic fork into the piece of pie on her paper plate. "Missy, you should be tired by now." Willow just shrugged.

Grinning, Cassidy uncurled her hand. "I found a worm."

Gwen smiled, taking her Popsicle back from Zander. "A worm, huh?"

"Let me see!" said Willow, hopping off the chair. But Cassidy sprinted away, laughing, and Willow gave chase.

Shaya shook her head as she watched them. "I really don't know where they get all their energy, but I want some."

"The motel will be ready in a few months," Nick said to Gwen. "I appreciate you agreeing to help us run it. After working at a B&B for years, it will be a breeze for you."

Zander barely resisted the urge to grunt. He wasn't so happy about Gwen working at the motel. He'd prefer for her to permanently remain deep in their territory where she'd be safest, which of course would never happen but was a pretty dream. He knew his mate, knew she wouldn't cope if she didn't have *something* to do. He also knew she liked that she'd have a role, of sorts.

The motel would be well protected at all times, he assured himself. And she was good with that Glock she'd insisted on bringing with her—along with a switchblade, knuckle stun gun, and a bunch of other stuff. The other females of the pack now wanted their own "collection of violent treasures," as Harley called it.

Even the Phoenix Pack females wanted their own, especially after watching Gwen give "a basic demonstration" of how to use the stun gun on Dominic—who had idiotically volunteered out of sheer curiosity—at her welcome party. The little shit had also flirted with Gwen, which wasn't a surprise and meant he got whacked a few times across the head. How the guy didn't have special needs after years of that shit, Zander didn't know.

"Speaking of the B&B," said Shaya, "the sale went through on it today. Some couple fascinated by paranormal stuff bought it. Ally said the place was spooky."

Gwen snorted softly. "Not half as spooky as your kid."

"A kid you adore," Shaya insisted with a smile.

Gwen shrugged. "She brings me flowers." Both pups were great. And they knew they were loved, knew the people around them would keep them safe and be there for them. That was a special thing, in Gwen's opinion.

Nick quietly swore. "The dog's lying on our blanket!" He stormed off, reprimanding Bruce. Rolling her eyes, Shaya followed him.

Glad to be alone with Gwen again, Zander inhaled deeply, taking in their combined scent. Even among the scents of wood smoke, charred meat, and the leftover food, it was damn strong and potent. He cupped her nape. "Do you miss it?"

She blinked. "What?"

"The marsh. Oregon."

"Not in the way that you're thinking. I loved the marsh; I'll always miss it. But I don't regret coming here. I don't wish I was there. I'm happy where I am."

He lightly squeezed her nape. "Good."

Gwen smiled. She'd expected to find it hard to adjust to living within a pack. It had been odd at first, considering how often they socialized and just appeared at each other's lodges without invitation. But she'd quickly gotten used to it—probably because she'd lived most of her life at a B&B, always sharing her private space.

Some of their ways had taken a little getting used to, though. Like eating pretty much every meal together, answering to Alphas, and adhering to all kinds of security measures. Despite being human, she'd gone along on their pack runs, which had been *awesome*. Watching them all play and interact in their animal forms was supercool.

The mating ceremony . . . well, that had been weird. It had taken place a week after she moved there. Basically, she'd gotten all dolled up in a dress that Ally had chosen before Shaya applied her makeup. Then Nick had escorted Gwen through the forest to the center of a huge circle of people that consisted of her other pack mates, the

Phoenix Pack, her family, Zander's sister—who Gwen thought was great—and a few others.

Inside the circle, Zander had waited, looking absolutely edible in a suit and staring at her with eyes that said she'd be getting ruthlessly fucked if they were alone. Nick had then asked them to make their vows, spouting the ceremonial words that had no power. According to Kathy, it was all a big excuse for a party. Still, it had been fun.

Yvonne and Donnie, who'd moved into the house near the lake that Yvonne had once spoken of, had attended the ceremony. Marlon and Dylan had also been there; they were now living together and were ridiculously happy. They'd brought along the unexpected news that Colt had retired from his position as sheriff. Gwen figured it was a good thing for Oregon in general.

They'd also told her that Aidan had not only closed his practice, he'd been dealt a thorough beating by someone. When Gwen had mentioned it to Zander, he'd looked at her with such innocence that she knew he was behind it.

Her family melded with the pack just fine. Donnie had loved Mercury territory, and he got along with Shaya's ex-military human father like a house on fire. Yvonne and Kathy had become fast friends, probably because they both knew what it was like to lose the man they loved. Marlon and Dylan had gravitated toward Caleb and Kent, a mated couple whom Gwen found hilarious.

To her surprise, Kenny hadn't disowned her on hearing from Geena that she'd mated into a pack. He'd actually passed on a congratulatory message through Geena, who said he wasn't being sarcastic about it and truly seemed happy for her. Gwen wasn't sure what to think of that, so she'd decided not to think of it at all. It was probably dumb to expect a normal response from someone like him anyway.

"Roni!" shouted Eli from a deck chair. *"Why do you have to be such a goddamn bitch?!"*

Lifting his head up from the blanket, Marcus chuckled. "What did she do?" Lying beside him, Roni didn't even stir.

Face red, Eli ground his teeth. "She changed my Facebook profile picture!"

"To what?" asked Marcus.

"To a picture of a guy in a black rubber bondage suit! She then put on my status, 'Do I look cute in this or what?' Roni, you are *dead*! Do you hear me?"

Roni lifted her head to glare at her brother. "Well, next time you're thinking about fucking with me, *you won't put laxatives in my coffee machine*!"

Marcus arched a brow at Eli. "Did it not bother you that *I* could have used the coffee machine before her?"

"Nope." Eli barely ducked the spoon that Marcus flung at his head.

Cassidy wrinkled her nose as she looked at Eli. "What's a bondage suit?"

Snorting a laugh, Gwen turned to Zander. "Don't know about you, but I'm tired. Ready to hit the sack yet?"

Zander took her hand, twining his fingers through hers. "Baby, I've been hard as a rock watching you suck on a Popsicle for the last fifteen minutes. I'm more than ready to go."

She chuckled. "Then let's go."

They said their good nights and then headed through the trees to their lodge. He liked that it was *their* lodge. Liked that their combined scent was all over the place and all over their things. Liked that she'd put her own personal touches here and there, making the space *theirs* and marking her territory.

Inside the lodge, they kicked off their shoes. Zander smiled at Gwen's sparkly, painted toenails. He never thought he could have described feet as *pretty*, but hers were.

As they walked into the den, he pulled her to him and kissed her. Savored her. Indulged in a long, deep taste. She melted against him, moaning. He nipped her lip. "I like drunk sex with my baby. And make-up sex. And kinky sex. And just about any sex."

"You're easy that way."

He kissed his way down her neck and licked at the claiming mark there. His wolf rumbled in contentment at the sight of it. Nothing had ever truly belonged to Zander before—not in the way that she did. Gwen had given herself fully to him, held nothing back, and was his with no strings attached. He treasured that. Treasured her.

He yanked out her hair tie and unraveled her braid. He fucking loved her hair. Loved how soft and glossy it was. Loved how it always smelled of vanilla and coconut. Loved the feel of it when it was wrapped around his fist as he fucked her mouth. Zander thrust his hands into the silky curls left by the braid. "So pretty and soft."

"If you're finished playing with my hair, can we get down to business?" Gwen's knees went a little weak as Zander began sucking on her claiming bite. She was in the mood to fuck. Hard and fast. But it was clear that he had no plans to rush, that he was in the mood to *savor*. She wasn't sure she had the patience for that. There were ways to eat at that control he kept so carefully over himself.

Slipping her hands under his shirt, she smoothed them up his back. The muscles beneath that sleek skin bunched slightly, and she could almost feel the contained power there. Gwen lightly dragged her nails down to his lower back and then followed the waistline of his jeans around to his stomach. His abdomen reflexively contracted, and he growled.

As Gwen snapped open the top button of his jeans, Zander placed his hands over hers. "Not yet." Instead of protesting as he'd expected, she smiled, pulled her hands free, and stepped back. Before he could close the distance, she snapped open her own fly. The sound of her zipper lowering made his cock twitch.

Zander shot her a reprimanding look. "I'm not ready for you to get undre—" The little minx let her shorts puddle at her feet. While he was busy admiring her black lacy panties, she peeled off her tank top. *No bra.* With a smirk, she turned toward the stairs. Apparently his mate thought she was in control.

Gwen wasn't sure exactly what had happened. She'd been heading for the stairs, quite pleased with herself. Then big hands had grabbed her, and she suddenly found herself flat on her back on the soft rug in front of the fireplace. She smiled at the male standing over her. "Smoothly done, Devlin."

"Tonight . . . there will be some rules."

"Rules? I don't like rules. I vote we scrap the rules."

"You can't vote—it's against the rules." He pinned her gaze. "Tonight, *I* say what goes. You don't argue. You don't defy me for the hell of it. You don't try to take control. You do what I tell you to do."

Gwen pursed her lips. "Yeah, I'm not sure that's gonna work for me."

"No point in lying, Gwen. I can sense how much you like that idea."

Yeah, okay, she did. Damn that fucking bond. Was it weird that she just wanted him to use her? Probably. She'd worry about it tomorrow, when she was sober. When he wasn't using his sex-tone—it was almost hypnotic, and it seemed to make her entire body melt for him.

Zander whipped off his shirt. "You don't have to worry, Gwen. I'd never hurt you. I take care of what I own." He arched a brow. "And I do own you."

Gwen opened her mouth to speak, but he chose that moment to tear open the rest of his fly, and *bam*, she was officially distracted. His cock sprang out, so long and thick that her pussy fluttered. She wanted him inside her badly, but he still seemed in no rush.

She let her thighs fall open, inviting him. "You own me, huh? Then what's stopping you from taking what's yours?" Oh yeah, *that* made his eyes blaze with heat. Not just heat, but possessiveness and determination. Still, he remained standing. *Awkward fucker.*

Drinking in the delectable sight of her from head to toe, Zander felt his mouth water. His wolf released a territorial growl. "There are so many things I want to do to you." And there was one thing he needed to do. Snatching her gaze, he said, "I'm going to claim your ass tonight."

Gwen shook her head. "I'm not curious about what it's like to have my ass split open."

Mouth curving, Zander shoved his jeans to the floor and kicked them aside. He knew through their bond that she wanted this, that she was using humor to get past her nerves. "We've been working up to it. You're ready. I told you before, you were made to take me." He fisted his cock. "And you will, because you're not in control tonight. I am."

Watching him unashamedly pump his cock, Gwen bit her lip. She loved seeing him do that. It made her think of that night he'd told her to finger herself while he watched, jerking himself off. He'd come all over her pussy and stomach, *marking* her, he'd said.

"You don't just want what's going to happen, Gwen. You need it. You need me. Like I need you." Zander dropped to his knees between her legs and skimmed his hands up the velvety skin of her thighs as he spread them wider. Eyes locked with hers, he slipped his thumbs under her panties and stroked the plump folds of her pussy. He could scent how wet she was; the smell made his wolf crazy. He needed a taste.

With a low growl, Zander tore off her panties, liking her little gasp. He cupped her ass, curled her hips, and stabbed his tongue inside her. God, her taste . . . it was like an electric shock to his senses. It shot straight to his cock, making it throb painfully. "I could spend hours right here, tasting you."

Gwen frowned. "No, I don't want to wait hours to come."

"It's not about what you want."

She gaped. "Oh, you bastard."

He chuckled. “I told you. Tonight, you do what I tell you.”

“See, you’re an utter bastard.” But the words came out kind of breathy because he was fluttering his tongue between her folds. “You need to—”

“I don’t have time to talk. My priority right now is making my baby come.” He set about making that happen, teasing her pussy with long, sensual licks before driving his tongue inside her. He feasted. Gorged. Fucked her with his tongue just like he intended to fuck her with his cock.

Needing more, Zander sat back on his heels, lifted her, and dropped her right on his cock. Her eyes snapped to his, shocked and a little dazed. He groaned as her walls contracted around him. “My baby’s pussy is so hot and tight.” Cinching her hips, he slowly raised her until only the head of his cock was inside her. Then he impaled her in one smooth, fast move. “Fuck yourself on me.”

Gwen rode him hard. The feel of his cock slicing through her again and again was exactly what she needed. One of his hands alternated between pinching and tugging her nipples to cupping and squeezing her breasts. It was so much sensation, and she could feel her orgasm coming toward her. Stilling her with his hands, he began punching his hips, fucking her hard. He dug his teeth into her neck. Didn’t bite. Just held her skin between his teeth. And that was all it took to throw her over.

Zander battled the urge to come as her back bowed, her pussy clamped down on his dick, and she groaned his name. He brushed her bangs out of her face. “That’s my girl. I love watching you come.” Carefully, he lay her back down on the rug.

She blinked up at him. “You didn’t come.”

“No, because I’m not done with you yet.” Feeling a little nervousness hum along their bond, he said, “Shh. Just lie back, let me have you.”

Using her cream to lubricate his finger, Zander gently worked it into her ass. He thrust it in and out, and he quickly got caught up in the rhythm of it. They'd played with her ass enough times for him to add another finger pretty soon. But only when she was moaning, squirming, and trying to counter his thrusts did he slip a third inside her. She didn't even flinch. At that point, the tension in her muscles was gone, and her body was begging for more.

Satisfied that she was ready, Zander used his free hand to angle her hips just right. "I'm going to take your ass like this so I can look in those big blue eyes." In one quick movement, he replaced his fingers with the head of his cock. "Now, push out as I push in." It was so damn hard not to just thrust fast and deep, but he held on to his control and slowly sank inside.

His eyes fell closed for a second. She was tighter than anything he'd ever felt, and he just wanted more. When he was finally fully sheathed, he groaned. "My baby is fucking amazing. And such a good girl." He squeezed her hip. "You okay?"

Okay? Gwen was a lot of things—full from his dick, totally turned on, and surprised by just how much she liked it. Although she'd enjoyed their past anal play, she'd expected this to be less fun and more painful. But as he'd assured her it would, her body had accommodated him. "Zander . . . I really won't last long."

"You never do."

She couldn't help smiling at that. He was totally right. "Get moving, Devlin." He kept his thrusts slow and deep, hitting all kinds of virginal nerve endings that were making her wind tighter and tighter. It was the *slow* part that she had a problem with. "Faster, Zander. In fact, make it faster *and* harder."

"Such a slutty little girl at times," Zander teased. She gasped, and he chuckled. "*My* slutty little girl."

She couldn't even dispute that. "Would you just fuck me already?"

Zander upped his pace, pumping his hips again and again. She looked so fucking amazing right then. Eyes languid. Mouth swollen. Cheeks flushed. Nipples hard. Pussy glistening. And then there was the sight of his cock repeatedly sinking into her ass . . . For once, he was sure he'd come before she did.

"Harder, Zander."

He shook his head. "I'll fuck you hard whenever you want, but not so hard it hurts you." Right now, she was enjoying it. He didn't want that to change, even if it was *so* tempting to give his wolf what he wanted and slam his cock deep.

"I don't mind when it hurts. I like it."

He groaned. "Don't say shit like that, Gwen."

Gwen was torn between hitting him and crying in frustration. Her orgasm was just out of her reach. *"Please."*

She'd never begged him before . . . and that just smashed Zander's resolve to pieces. He plunged hard and fast, giving her what they both wanted. He felt no pain through their bond. Only need and hunger and pleasure. "Come, Gwen." He felt it as she came, *felt* her almost violent release vibrate up their bond as it swept her under and she imploded with a silent scream.

Zander buried himself deep and came, claiming her ass just as he'd claimed every other part of her. Now he had it all. The satisfaction of that went bone deep and fed his soul. Settled something in his wolf.

Withdrawing his softening cock, Zander lay on his back and heaved her pliant, quivering body on top of him. She buried her face in the crook of his neck, and Zander smoothed a hand down her back. "You okay?"

"Yowza."

He chuckled, running his fingers up and down her spine as the aftershocks eased away. Feeling her body go slack, he squeezed her nape. "Don't fall sleep. We need to shower."

"Not sleeping. Just relaxing." Gwen propped her chin up on his chest. "You know, it's kind of a shame that a shifter bite can't change a human into a shifter. I'd be so at the front of the line."

He tilted his head slightly. "You'd really turn into a shifter if you could?"

"Having an inner wolf would be awesome. And it would mean I had a wolf for yours."

Zander framed her face with his hands. "I've told you, he adores you exactly as you are."

"I know. I adore him right back."

"Good. I mean it, Gwen, you don't have to feel bad." But he knew she stupidly did. "He's not disappointed—he only needs you. And so do I."

"You both have me."

He skimmed his hands down her back. "Of course we do. We wouldn't have settled for anything else."

She chuckled. "Lying here all relaxed, I was just thinking . . ."

"What?" he pushed.

"Nothing. Doesn't matter."

He growled. "Gwen, what were you going to say?"

Stifling a smile because she knew it drove him insane and, well, that would *always* be fun, she said, "Nothing, forget it."

Honestly, Zander wanted to throttle her. *"Tell me."*

"It doesn't matter."

"I hate it when you do that."

"Yeah? Take a guess at how many fucks I give."

He rolled her onto her back. "You're lucky I love you."

She smiled. "Yeah, well, you're lucky I love you. Although . . ."

"What?"

"Nothing. Doesn't matter."

"Gwen." Growling, he dropped his forehead to hers. "You're trying to drive me out of my mind."

"Now what makes you say that?"

ACKNOWLEDGMENTS

Okay, I have a list—my awesome family (I love you all); my hyperactive yet nocturnal muse (can we work on the nocturnal thing?); the voices chatting in my head (you guys are the best); my superefficient assistant, Melissa (I salute you); Melody Guy (I'm impatient to read your book); and absolutely everyone at Montlake Romance (couldn't do it without you). Last but not least, a humongous thanks to all my readers (you all rock, and you all know it).

If you wish to contact me, you can reach me by e-mail at suzanne_e_wright@live.co.uk or via social media.

Website: www.suzannewright.co.uk

Blog: www.suzannewrightsblog.blogspot.co.uk

Twitter: www.twitter.com/suz_wright

Facebook: www.facebook.com/suzannewrightfanpage

ABOUT THE AUTHOR

Photo © 2012 Steven Wright

Suzanne Wright can't remember a time when she wasn't creating characters and telling their tales. Even as a child in England, she loved writing poems, plays, and stories. As an adult, Wright is the author of the novel *From Rags*, the Deep in Your Veins novels, the Dark in You series, and the Phoenix Pack series. *Lure of Oblivion* is the third novel in her Mercury Pack series. Wright, who lives in Liverpool with her husband and two children, freely admits that she hates housecleaning and can't cook . . . but always shares chocolate. Visit her online at www.suzannewright.co.uk.

Printed in Great Britain
by Amazon

48930745R00201